"Now then," Jordan explained, smiling reassuringly into Alexandra's enormous blue-green eyes as he matched his actions to his words, "a kiss is a thing to be shared. I'll put my hands on your arms, thus, and draw you close."

Alexandra looked at his strong fingers gently imprisoning her upper arms, then finally dragged her embarrassed gaze to his. "Where do my hands go?"

Jordan squelched his shout of laughter, as well as the suggestive reply that automatically sprang to his lips. "Where would you like to put them?" he asked instead.

"In my pockets?" Alexandra suggested hopefully.

"The point I was trying to make," he continued mildly, "is that it's perfectly all right for you to touch me."

I don't want to, Alexandra thought frantically.

You will, he silently promised with an inner smile, correctly interpreting her mutinous expression. Before she could react, he took her lips in a slow, deliberately seductive kiss, while his hand curved around her nape, his fingers stroking her sensitive skin. Lost in a sea of pure sensation, Alexandra slid her hands up his hard chest, innocently molding herself to his length. Desire exploded in Jordan's body, and the girl in his arms became an enticing woman. Automatically, he deepened the kiss . . .

Books by Judith McNaught

Double Standards
A Kingdom of Dreams
Once and Always
Something Wonderful
Tender Triumph
Whitney, My Love

Published by POCKET BOOKS

Judith McNaught

Something Wonderful

POCKET BOOKS

New York   London   Toronto   Sydney   Tokyo

An *Original* Publication of POCKET BOOKS

POCKET BOOKS, a division of Simon & Schuster Inc.
1230 Avenue of the Americas, New York, NY 10020

ISBN: 0-671-68132-X

First Pocket Books printing April 1988

10 9 8 7 6 5

POCKET and colophon are trademarks of Simon & Schuster Inc.

Printed in the U.S.A.

For Jeffrey Clark, who had the superb
intelligence and foresight to
ask the loveliest young woman I've ever known
to be his wife
and
For my daughter, Whitney, who was wise
enough to say "Yes."

My special thanks
To Melinda Helfer for her support
and encouragement throughout the
creation of this novel

And to Robert A. Wulff, whose competence
and kindness enabled me to concentrate
on my work and leave other matters to him.

Something Wonderful

Chapter One

THE VOLUPTUOUS BLOND WOMAN lifted up on an elbow and pulled a sheet to her breasts. Frowning slightly, she studied the darkly handsome youth of eighteen who was standing at the window of his bedchamber, his shoulder propped against the window frame, looking out across the back lawns, where a party in honor of his mother's birthday was in progress. "What do you see that interests you more than I?" Lady Catherine Harrington asked as she wrapped the sheet around herself and walked over to the window.

Jordan Addison Matthew Townsende, the future Duke of Hawthorne, seemed not to hear her as he looked out across the grounds of the palatial estate that would, upon his father's death, become his. As he gazed at the hedge maze below, he saw his mother emerge from the shrubbery. Casting a brief, furtive look about her, she straightened the bodice of her dress and smoothed her heavy dark hair into some semblance of order. A moment later Lord Harrington emerged, retying his neckcloth. Their laughter drifted up through Jordan's open window as they linked arms.

Mild cynicism marred the youthful handsomeness of his lean features as Jordan watched his mother and her newest lover cross the lawns and saunter into the arbor. A few moments later, his father emerged from the same hedge maze, looked about him, then retrieved Lady Milborne, *his* current paramour, from the bushes.

"Evidently my mother has acquired a new lover," Jordan drawled sarcastically.

"Really?" Lady Harrington asked, peering out the window. "Who?"

"Your husband." Turning fully toward her, Jordan studied her lovely face, searching for some sign of surprise. When he saw none, his own features hardened into an ironic mask. "You knew they were in the maze together, and that accounts for your sudden, unprecedented interest in *my* bed, is that it?"

She nodded, uneasy under the relentless gaze of those cool grey eyes. "I thought," she said, running her hand up his hard chest, "it would be amusing if *we* were also to . . . ah . . . get together. But my interest in your bed isn't sudden, Jordan, I've wanted you for a long time. Now that your mother and my husband are enjoying each other, I saw no reason not to take what I wanted. Where's the harm in that?"

He said nothing and her eyes searched his inscrutable features, her smile coy. "Are you shocked?"

"Hardly," he replied. "I've known about my mother's affairs since I was eight years old, and I doubt I could be shocked by what any woman does. If anything, I'm surprised you didn't contrive for all six of us to meet in the maze for a little 'family' get-together," he finished with deliberate insolence.

She made a muffled sound, part laughter, part horror. "Now you've shocked *me.*"

Lazily he reached out and tipped her chin up, studying her face with eyes too hard, too knowledgeable for his years. "Somehow I find that impossible to believe."

Suddenly embarrassed, Catherine pulled her hand from his chest and wrapped the sheet more securely around her nakedness. "Really, Jordan, I don't see why you're looking at me as if I'm beneath contempt," she said, her face reflecting honest bewilderment and a little pique. "You aren't married, so you don't realize how insufferably dull life is for all of us. Without dalliance to take one's mind off the tedium, we would all go quite mad."

At the tragic note in her voice, humor softened his features and his firm, sensual lips quirked in a derisive smile. "Poor little Catherine," he said dryly, reaching out and brushing his knuckles against her cheek. "What a miserable lot you women have. From the day you're born, anything you want is yours for the asking, and so you have nothing to work for—and even if you did, you'd never be permitted to work for it. We don't allow you to study and you're forbidden sports, so you cannot exercise your mind or your body. You don't even have honor to cling to, for although a man's honor is his for as long as he wishes, yours is between your legs, and you lose it to the first man who has you. How unjust life is to you!" he finished. "No wonder you're all so bored, amoral, and frivolous."

Catherine hesitated, struck by his words, not certain whether he was ridiculing her, then shrugged. "You're absolutely right."

He looked at her curiously. "Did it ever occur to you to try to change all that?"

"No," she admitted bluntly.

"I applaud your honesty. It's a rare virtue in your sex."

Although he was only eighteen, Jordan Townsende's potent attraction for women was already a topic of much scintillating feminine gossip, and as Catherine gazed into those cynical grey eyes, she suddenly felt herself drawn to him as if by some overwhelming magnetic force. Understanding was in his eyes, along with a touch of humor and hard knowledge far beyond his years. It was these things, even more than his dark good looks and blatant virility, that impelled women toward him. Jordan understood women; he understood *her,* and although it was obvious he didn't admire or approve of her, he accepted her for what she was, with all her weaknesses.

"Are you coming to bed, my lord?"

"No," he said mildly.

"Why?"

"Because I find I'm not quite bored enough to want to sleep with the wife of my mother's lover."

"You don't—you don't have a very high opinion of women, do you?" Catherine asked, because she couldn't stop herself.

"Is there any reason I should?"

"I—" She bit her lip and then reluctantly shook her head. "No. I suppose not. But someday you'll have to marry in order to have children."

His eyes suddenly glinted with amusement, and he leaned back against the window frame, crossing his arms over his

3

chest. "Marry? Really? Is that how one gets children? And all this time, I thought—"

"Jordan, really!" she said, laughing, more than a little enthralled by this relaxed, teasing side of him. "You'll need a legitimate heir."

"When I'm forced to pledge my hand in order to produce an heir," he replied with grim humor, "I'll choose a naive chit right out of the schoolroom who'll leap to do my merest bidding."

"And when she becomes bored and seeks other diversion, what will you do?"

"Will she become bored?" he inquired in a steely voice.

Catherine studied his broad, muscular shoulders, deep chest, and narrow waist, then her gaze lifted to his ruggedly hewn features. In a linen shirt and tight-fitting riding breeches, every inch of Jordan Townsende's tall frame positively radiated raw power and leashed sensuality. Her brows lifted over knowing green eyes. "Perhaps not."

While she dressed, Jordan turned back to the windows and gazed dispassionately at the elegant guests who had gathered on the lawns at Hawthorne to celebrate his mother's birthday. To an outsider on that day, Hawthorne doubtless looked like a fascinating, lush paradise populated by beautiful, carefree, tropical birds parading in all their gorgeous finery. To eighteen-year-old Jordan Townsende, the scene held little interest and no beauty; he knew too well what went on within the walls of this house when the guests were gone.

At eighteen, he did not believe in the inherent goodness of anyone, including himself. He had breeding, looks, and wealth; he was also world-weary, restrained, and guarded.

With her small chin propped upon her fists, Miss Alexandra Lawrence watched the yellow butterfly perched upon the windowsill of her grandfather's cottage, then she turned her attention back to the beloved white-haired man seated across the desk from her. "What did you say, Grandfather? I didn't hear you."

"I asked why that butterfly is more interesting than Socrates today," the kindly old man said, smiling his gentle scholar's smile at the petite thirteen-year-old who possessed her mother's glossy chestnut curls and his own blue-green

4

eyes. Amused, he tapped the volume of Socrates' works from which he had been instructing her.

Alexandra sent him a melting, apologetic smile, but she didn't deny that she was distracted, for as her gentle, scholarly grandfather oft said, "A lie is an affront to the soul, as well as an insult to the intelligence of the person to whom one lies." And Alexandra would have done anything rather than insult this gentle man who had instilled her with his own philosophy of life, as well as educating her in mathematics, philosophy, history, and Latin.

"I was wondering," she admitted with a wistful sigh, "if there's the slightest chance that I'm only in the 'caterpillar stage' just now, and someday soon I'll change into a butterfly and be beautiful?"

"What's wrong with being a caterpillar? After all," he quoted, teasing, " 'Nothing is beautiful from every point of view.' " His eyes twinkled as he waited to see if she could recognize the quotation's source.

"Horace," Alexandra provided promptly, smiling back at him.

He nodded, pleased, then he said, "You needn't worry about your appearance, my dear, because true beauty springs from the heart and dwells in the eyes."

Alexandra tipped her head to the side, thinking, but she could not recall any philosopher, ancient or modern, who had said such a thing. "Who said that?"

Her grandfather chuckled. "*I* did."

Her answering laughter tinkled like bells, filling the sunny room with her musical gaiety, then she abruptly sobered. "Papa is disappointed I'm not pretty, I can see it whenever he comes to visit. He has every reason to expect me to turn out better, for Mama is beautiful and, besides being handsome, Papa is also fourth cousin to an earl, by marriage."

Barely able to conceal distaste for his son-in-law and for his dubious claim to an obscure connection to an obscure earl, Mr. Gimble quoted meaningfully, "Birth is nothing where virtue is not."

"Molière." Alexandra automatically named the source of the quotation. "But," she continued glumly, reverting to her original concern, "you must admit it is excessively unkind of fate to give him a daughter who is so very common-looking. Why," she went on morosely, "could I not be tall

5

and blond? That would be so much nicer than looking like a little gypsy, which Papa says I do."

She turned her head to contemplate the butterfly again, and Mr. Gimble's eyes shone with fondness and delight, for his granddaughter was anything but common. When she was a child of four, he had begun instructing Alexandra in the fundamentals of reading and writing, exactly as he'd instructed the village children entrusted to his tutelage, but Alex's mind was more fertile than theirs, quicker and more able to grasp concepts. The children of the peasants were indifferent students who came to him for only a few years and then went out into the fields of their fathers to labor, to wed, to reproduce, and begin the life cycle all over again. But Alex had been born with his own fascination for learning.

The elderly man smiled at his granddaughter; the "cycle" was not such a bad thing, he thought.

Had he followed his own youthful inclinations and remained a bachelor, devoting all his life to study, rather than marrying, Alexandra Lawrence would never have existed. And Alex was a gift to the world. His gift. The thought uplifted and then embarrassed him because it reeked of pride. Still, he couldn't stem the rush of pleasure that flowed through him as he looked at the curly-haired child seated across from him. She was everything he hoped she'd be, and more. She was gentleness and laughter, intelligence and indomitable spirit. Too much spirit, perhaps, and too much sensitivity as well—for she repeatedly turned herself inside out, trying to please her shallow father during his occasional visits.

He wondered what sort of man she would marry—not such a one as his own daughter had wed, he devoutly hoped. His own daughter lacked Alexandra's depth of character; he had spoiled her, Mr. Gimble thought sadly. Alexandra's mother was weak and selfish. She had married a man exactly like herself, but Alex would need, and deserve, a far better man.

With her usual sensitivity, Alexandra noticed the sudden darkening of her grandfather's mood and strove immediately to lighten it. "Are you feeling unwell, Grandpapa? The headache again? Shall I rub your neck?"

"I do have a bit of the headache," Mr. Gimble said, and

as he dipped his quill in the inkpot, forming the words that would someday become "A Complete Dissertation on the Life of Voltaire," she came around behind him and began with her child's hands to soothe away the tension in his shoulders and neck.

No sooner had her hands stilled than he felt the tickle of something brush against his cheek. Absorbed in his work, he reached up and absently rubbed his cheek where it tickled. A moment later, his neck tickled and he rubbed it there. The tickle switched to his right ear and he bit back an exasperated smile as he finally realized his granddaughter was brushing a feather quill against his skin. "Alex, my dear," he said, "I fear there's a mischievous little bird in here, diverting me from my labors."

"Because you work too hard," she said, but she pressed a kiss against his parchment cheek and returned to her seat to study Socrates. A few moments later, her lagging attention was diverted by a worm inching its way past the open door of the thatched cottage. "If everything in the universe serves God's special purpose, why do you suppose He created snakes? They're ever so ugly. Quite gruesome, actually."

Sighing at her interruption, Mr. Gimble laid down his quill, but he was not proof against her sunny smile. "I shall make it a point to ask God about that when I see Him."

The idea of her grandfather dying made Alexandra instantly somber, but the sound of a carriage drawing up before the cottage caused her to leap to her feet, running to the open window. "It's Papa!" she burst out joyously. "Papa has come from London at last!"

"And about time it is, too," Mr. Gimble grumbled, but Alex didn't hear. Clad in her favorite garb of breeches and peasant shirt, she was racing through the doorway and hurtling herself into her father's reluctant arms.

"How are you, little gypsy?" he said without much interest.

Mr. Gimble arose and went to the window, watching with a frown as the handsome Londoner helped his daughter up into his fancy new carriage. Fancy carriage, fancy clothes, but his morals were not fancy at all, thought Mr. Gimble angrily, recalling how his daughter, Felicia, had been blinded by the man's looks and suavity from the moment he had arrived at their cottage one afternoon, his carriage

7

broken down in the road in front of it. Mr. Gimble had offered to let the man spend the night and, late in the afternoon, against his better judgment, he had yielded to Felicia's pleading and allowed her to walk out with him so she might "show him the pretty view from the hill above the stream."

When darkness fell and they had not returned, Mr. Gimble struck out after them, finding his way easily by the light of the full moon. He discovered them at the foot of the hill, beside the stream, naked in each other's arms. It had taken George Lawrence less than four hours to convince Felicia to abandon the precepts of a lifetime and to seduce her.

Rage beyond anything he had ever known had boiled up inside Mr. Gimble and, without a sound, he had left the scene. When he returned to the cottage two hours later, he was accompanied by his good friend the local vicar. The vicar was carrying the book from which he would read the marriage ceremony.

Mr. Gimble was carrying a rifle to make certain his daughter's seducer participated in the ceremony.

It was the first time in his life he had ever held a weapon.

And what had his righteous fury gotten for Felicia? The question darkened Mr. Gimble's features. George Lawrence had bought her a large, run-down house that had been vacant for a decade, provided her with servants, and for nine months following their marriage, he had reluctantly lived with her here in the remote little shire where she had been born. At the end of that time Alexandra arrived, and soon afterward George Lawrence went back to London, where he stayed, returning to Morsham only twice each year for two or three weeks.

"He is earning a living in the best way he knows how," Felicia had explained to Mr. Gimble, obviously repeating what her husband had told her. "He's a gentleman and therefore cannot be expected to work for a living like ordinary men. In London, his breeding and connections enable him to mingle with all the right people, and from them he picks up hints now and then about good investments on the 'Change, and which horses to bet on at the races. It's the only way he can support us. Naturally, he would like to have us with him in London, but it is dreadfully expensive in the city, and he would not dream of subjecting us to the sort of cramped, dingy lodgings he must live in there. He comes to us as often as he can."

Mr. Gimble was dubious about George Lawrence's explanation for preferring to remain in London, but he had no doubt why the man returned to Morsham twice each year. He did so because Mr. Gimble had promised to seek him out in London—with his borrowed rifle—if he did not return at least that often to see his wife and daughter. Nevertheless, there was no point in wounding Felicia with the truth, for she was happy. Unlike the other women in the tiny shire—Felicia was married to "a true gentleman" and that was all that counted in her foolish estimation. It gave her status, and she walked among her neighbors with a queenly air of superiority.

Like Felicia, Alexandra worshiped George Lawrence, and he basked in their unquestioning adoration during his brief visits. Felicia fussed over him, and Alex tried valiantly to be both son and daughter to him—worrying about her lack of feminine beauty at the same time she wore breeches and practiced fencing so she could fence with him whenever he came.

Standing in the window, Mr. Gimble glowered at the shiny conveyance drawn by four sleek, prancing horses. For a man who could spare little money for his wife and daughter, George Lawrence drove a very expensive carriage and team.

"How long can you stay this time, Papa?" Alexandra said, already beginning to dread the inevitable time when he would leave again.

"Only a week. I'm off to the Landsdowne's place in Kent."

"Why must you be gone so much?" Alexandra asked, unable to hide her disappointment even though she knew he, too, hated to be away from her and her mother.

"Because I must," he said, and when she started to protest, he shook his head and reached into his pocket, extracting a small box. "Here, I've brought you a little present for your birthday, Alex."

Alexandra gazed at him with adoration and pleasure, despite the fact that her birthday had come and gone months before, without so much as a letter from him. Her

9

aquamarine eyes were shining as she opened the box and removed a small, silver-colored locket shaped like a heart. Although it was made of tin and not particularly pretty, she held it in her palm as if it were infinitely precious. "I shall wear it every single day of my life, Papa," she whispered, then she put her arms around him in a fierce hug. "I love you so much!"

As they passed through the tiny sleepy village, the horses sent puffs of dust up into the air, and Alexandra waved at the people who saw her, eager for them to know that her wonderful, handsome papa had returned.

She needn't have bothered to call their attention to him. By evening, everyone in the village would be discussing not only his return, but the color of his coat, and a dozen other details, for the Village of Morsham was as it had been for hundreds of years—sleepy, undisturbed, forgotten in its remote valley. Its inhabitants were simple, unimaginative, hard-working folk who took immeasurable pleasure in recounting any tiny event that occurred to alleviate the endless sameness of their existence. They were still talking about the day, three months ago, when a carriage came through with a city fellow wearing a coat of not just one cape but *eight*. Now they would have George Lawrence's wondrous carriage and team to discuss for the next six months.

To an outsider, Morsham might seem a dull place populated by gossipy peasants, but to thirteen-year-old Alexandra, the village and its inhabitants were beautiful.

At thirteen she believed in the inherent goodness of each of God's children and she had no doubt that honesty, integrity, and cheerfulness were common to all mankind. She was gentle, gay, and incurably optimistic.

Chapter Two

THE DUKE OF HAWTHORNE slowly lowered his arm, the smoking pistol still in his hand, and gazed dispassionately at the crumpled figure of Lord Grangerfield lying motionless on the ground. Jealous husbands were a damned nuisance, Jordan thought—almost as troublesome as their vain and frivolous wives. Not only did they frequently leap to totally unwarranted conclusions, but they also insisted on discussing their delusions at dawn with pistols. His impassive gaze still resting on the elderly, wounded opponent, who was being tended by the physician and seconds, he cursed the beautiful, scheming young woman whose relentless pursuit of him had caused this duel.

At twenty-seven, Jordan had long ago decided that dallying with other men's wives often resulted in more complications than any sexual gratification was worth. As a result, he had long made it a practice to restrict his frequent sexual liaisons to only those women who were unencumbered by husbands. God knew there were more than enough of them, and most were willing and eager to warm his bed. Flirtations, however, were a normal part of life amongst the *ton*, and his recent involvement with Elizabeth Grangerfield, whom he had known since they were both children, had been little more than that—a harmless flirtation that sprang up when she returned to England from an extended trip of more than a year. The flirtation had begun as nothing more than a few bantering remarks—admittedly with sexual overtones—exchanged between two old friends. It would never have gone further, except that one night last week Elizabeth had slipped past Jordan's butler and, when Jordan came home, he found her in his bed—all lush, naked, inviting woman. Normally, he would have hauled her out of his bed and sent her home, but that night his mind was already dulled by the brandy he'd been imbibing with friends, and while he deliberated over what to do with her, his body had overruled his sluggish mind and insisted he accept her irresistible invitation.

Turning toward his horse, which was tethered to a nearby tree, Jordan glanced up at the feeble rays of sunlight that streaked the sky. There was still time to get a few hours of sleep before he began the long day of work and social engagements that would culminate late tonight at the Bildrups' ball.

Chandeliers dripping with hundreds of thousands of crystals blazed above the vast mirrored ballroom where dancers attired in satins, silks, and velvets whirled in time to a lilting waltz. Pairs of French doors leading out onto the balconies were thrown open, allowing cool breezes to enter —and couples, desiring a few moments' moonlit privacy, to exit.

Just beyond the furthest pair of doors, a couple stood on the balcony, their presence partially concealed by the shadows of the mansion itself, apparently unconcerned with the wild conjecture their absence from the ballroom was creating among the guests.

"It's disgraceful!" Miss Leticia Bildrup said to the group of elegant young men and women who composed her personal retinue. Casting a ferociously condemning look, liberally laced with envy, in the direction of the doors through which the couple had just exited, she added, "Elizabeth Grangerfield is behaving like a strumpet, chasing after Hawthorne, with her own husband lying wounded from his duel with Hawthorne this very morning!"

Sir Roderick Carstairs regarded the angry Miss Bildrup with an expression of acid amusement for which he was known—and feared—by all the *ton*. "You're right, of course, my beauty. Elizabeth ought to learn from your own example and pursue Hawthorne only in private, rather than in public."

Leticia regarded him in haughty silence, but a telltale flush turned her smooth cheeks a becoming pink. "Beware, Roddy, you are losing the ability to separate what is amusing from what is offensive."

"Not at all, my dear, I *strive* to be offensive."

"Do not liken me to Elizabeth Grangerfield," Leticia snapped in a furious underbreath. "We have nothing in common."

"Ah, but you do. You both want Hawthorne. Which gives you something in common with six dozen other women I could name, particularly"—he nodded toward the beautiful red-haired ballerina who was waltzing with a Russian prince on the dance floor—"Elise Grandeaux. Although Miss Grandeaux seems to have gotten the best of all of you, for she is Hawthorne's new mistress."

"I don't believe you!" Letty burst out, her blue eyes riveted on the graceful redhead who had reportedly bewitched the Spanish king and a Russian prince. "Hawthorne is unattached!"

"What are we discussing, Letty?" one of the young ladies asked, turning aside from her suitors.

"We are discussing the fact that *he* has gone out on the balcony with Elizabeth Grangerfield," Letty snapped. No explanation of the word "he" was necessary. Amongst the *ton*, everyone who mattered knew "he" was Jordan Addison Matthew Townsende—Marquess of Landsdowne, Viscount Leeds, Viscount Reynolds, Earl Townsende of Marlow, Baron Townsende of Stroleigh, Richfield, and Monmart— and 12th Duke of Hawthorne.

"He" was the stuff of which young ladies' dreams were made—tall, dark, and fatally handsome, with the devil's own charm. Amongst the younger females of the *ton*, it was the consensus of opinion that his shuttered grey eyes could seduce a nun or freeze an enemy in his tracks. Older females were inclined to credit the former and discard the latter, since it was well-known that Jordan Townsende had dispatched hundreds of the French enemy, not with his eyes, but with his deadly skill with pistols and sabers. But regardless of their ages, all the ladies of the *ton* were in

13

complete agreement on one issue: A person had only to look at the Duke of Hawthorne to know that he was a man of breeding, elegance, and style; a man who was as polished as a diamond. And, frequently, just as hard.

"Roddy says Elise Grandeaux has become his mistress," Letty said, nodding toward the stunning, titian-haired beauty who appeared to be oblivious to the Duke of Hawthorne's departure with Lady Elizabeth Grangerfield.

"Nonsense," said a seventeen-year-old debutante who was a stickler for propriety. "If she was, he certainly wouldn't bring her here. He couldn't."

"He could and he would," another young lady announced, her gaze glued to the French doors through which the duke and Lady Grangerfield had just departed, as she waited eagerly for another glimpse of the legendary duke. "My mama says Hawthorne does whatever he pleases and the devil fly with public opinion!"

At that moment, the object of this and dozens of similar conversations throughout the ballroom was lounging against the stone railing of the balcony, gazing down into Elizabeth's glistening blue eyes with an expression of unconcealed annoyance. "Your reputation is being shredded to pieces in there, Elizabeth. If you have any sense, you'll retire to the country with your 'ailing' husband for a few weeks until the gossip over the duel dies down."

With a brittle attempt at gaiety, Elizabeth shrugged. "Gossip can't hurt me, Jordan. I'm a countess now." Bitterness crept into her voice, strangling it. "Never mind that my husband is thirty years older than I. My parents have another title in the family now, which is all they wanted."

"There's no point in regretting the past," Jordan said, restraining his impatience with an effort. "What's done is done."

"Why didn't you offer for me before you went off to fight that stupid war in Spain?" she asked in a suffocated voice.

"Because," he answered brutally, "I didn't want to marry you."

Five years ago, Jordan had casually considered offering for her in the distant, obscure future, but he hadn't wanted a wife then any more than he did now, and nothing had been settled between them before he left for Spain. A year after his departure, Elizabeth's father, intent on adding another title to the family tree, had insisted she marry Grangerfield. When Jordan received her letter, telling him she'd been married off to Grangerfield, he'd felt no keen sense of loss. On the other hand, he'd known Elizabeth since they were in their teens, and he had harbored a certain fondness for her. Perhaps if he had been around at the time, he might have persuaded her to defy her parents and refuse old Grangerfield's suit. Or perhaps not. Like nearly all females of her social class, Elizabeth had been taught since childhood that her duty as a daughter was to marry in accordance with her parents' wishes.

In any case, Jordan had not been here. Two years after his father's death, despite the fact that he hadn't produced an heir to ensure the succession, Jordan had bought a commission in the army and gone to Spain to fight against Napoleon's troops. At first his daring and courage in the face of the enemy were simply the result of a reckless dissatisfaction with his own life. Later, as he matured, the skill and knowledge he acquired in countless bloody battles kept him alive and added to his reputation as a cunning strategist and invincible opponent.

Four years after departing for Spain, he resigned his commission and returned to England to resume the duties and responsibilities of a dukedom.

The Jordan Townsende who had returned to England the year before was very different from the young man who had left. The first time he walked into a ballroom after his return, many of those changes were startlingly evident: In contrast to the pale faces and bored languor of other gentlemen of his class, Jordan's skin was deeply tanned, his tall body rugged and muscular, his movements brisk and authoritative; and, although the legendary Hawthorne charm was still evident in his occasional lazy white smile, there was an aura about him now of a man who had confronted danger—and enjoyed it. It was an aura that women found infinitely exciting and which added tremendously to his attraction.

"Can *you* forget what we've meant to each other?" Elizabeth raised her head, and before Jordan could react, she leaned up on her toes and kissed him, her familiar body willing and pliant, pressing eagerly against his.

His hands caught her arms in a punishing grip and he moved her away. "Don't be a fool!" he snapped scathingly, his long fingers biting into her arms. "We were friends, nothing more. What happened between us last week was a mistake. It's over."

Elizabeth tried to move against him. "I can make you love me, Jordan. I know I can. You almost loved me a few years ago. And you wanted me last week—"

"I wanted your delectable body, my sweet," he mocked with deliberate viciousness, "nothing else. That's all I've ever wanted from you. I'm not going to kill your husband for you in a duel, so you can forget that scheme. You'll have to find some other fool who'll purchase your freedom for you at the point of a gun."

She blanched, blinking back her tears, but she didn't deny that she'd hoped he would kill her husband. "I don't want my freedom, Jordan, I want *you,*" she said in a tear-glogged voice. "You may have regarded me as little more than a friend, but I've been in love with you since we were fifteen years old."

The admission was made with such humble, hopeless misery that anyone but Jordan Townsende would have realized she was telling the truth, and perhaps been moved to pity her. But Jordan had long ago become a hardened skeptic where women were concerned. He responded to her painful admission of love by handing her a snowy white handkerchief. "Dry your eyes."

The hundreds of guests who surreptitiously watched their return to the ballroom a few moments later, noted that Lady Grangerfield seemed tense and left the ball at once.

However, the Duke of Hawthorne looked as smoothly unperturbed as ever as he returned to the beautiful ballerina who was the latest in his long string of mistresses. And when the couple stepped onto the dance floor a few moments later, there was a glow of energy, a powerful magnetism that emanated from the beautiful, charismatic pair. Elise Grandeaux's lithe, fragile, grace complemented his bold elegance; her vivid coloring was the perfect foil for his darkness, and when they moved together in a dance, they were two splendid creatures who seemed made for one another.

"But then that is always the way," Miss Bildrup said to

16

her friends as they studied the pair in fascinated admiration. "Hawthorne always makes the woman he is with look like his perfect *mate.*"

"Well, he won't marry a common stage performer no matter how excellent they look together," said Miss Morrison. "And my brother has promised to bring him to our house for a morning call this week," she added on a note of triumph.

Her joy was demolished by Miss Bildrup: "My mama said he plans to leave for Rosemeade tomorrow."

"Rosemeade?" the other echoed blankly, her shoulders drooping.

"His grandmother's estate," Miss Bildrup clarified. "It's to the north, beyond some godforsaken little village called Morsham."

Chapter Three

*I*T DEFIES THE IMAGINATION, Filbert, it truly does!" Alexandra announced to the old footman who shuffled into her bedchambers carrying a small armload of wood.

Filbert squinted nearsightedly at his seventeen-year-old mistress, who was sprawled across the bed on her stomach, her small chin cupped in her hands, her body clad in her usual ensemble of tight brown breeches and faded shirt.

"It positively boggles the mind," Alexandra repeated in a voice reeking with disapproval.

"What does, Miss Alex?" he inquired, approaching the bed. Spread out before his mistress upon the coverlet was something white and large, which the myopic footman deduced was either a towel or a newspaper. Squinting his eyes, he stared hard at the white object, upon which he perceived there appeared to be blurry black blotches, which in turn led him to correctly conclude that the object was a newspaper.

"It says here," Alexandra informed him, tapping the newspaper dated April 2, 1813, with her forefinger, "that Lady Weatherford-Heath gave a ball for eight hundred people, followed by a supper consisting of no less than forty-five different dishes! Forty-five dishes! Can you conceive of such extravagance? Furthermore," Alex continued, absently brushing her dark curls off her nape as she glared at the offending newspaper, "the article drones on and on about the people who attended the party and what they wore. Listen to this, Sarah," she said, looking up and smiling as Sarah Withers padded into the room carrying an armload of freshly laundered linens.

Until Alexandra's father died three years ago, Sarah had held the title of housekeeper, but as a result of the dire financial circumstances resulting from his death, she had been discharged along with all the other servants—excepting Filbert and Penrose, who were both too old and infirm to find new employment. Now Sarah returned only once a month, along with a peasant girl to help out with the laundering and heavy cleaning.

In a gushing falsetto voice, Alexandra quoted for Sarah's benefit, "Miss Emily Welford was escorted by the Earl of Marcham. Miss Welford's ivory silk gown was adorned with pearls and diamonds." Chuckling, Alex closed the paper and looked at Sarah. "Can you believe people actually want to read such tripe? Why would anyone care what gown somebody wore or that the Earl of Delton has lately returned from a sojourn in Scotland, or that 'Rumor has it he is showing a particular interest in a certain young lady of considerable beauty and consequence'?"

Sarah Withers lifted her brows and stared disapprovingly at Alex's attire. "There are *some* young ladies who care about making the *most* of their appearance," she pointedly replied.

Alexandra accepted that well-intentioned gibe with cheerful, philosophical indifference. "It would take more than a little powder and puce satin to make me look like a grand lady." Alex's long-ago hope to emerge from a "cocoon" as a classically beautiful blonde had not come to fruition at all. Instead, her short-cropped, curly hair was dark chestnut, her chin was still small and stubborn, her nose still pert, and her body was just as slim and agile as a lad's. In point of fact, her only truly remarkable feature was a pair of sooty-lashed, huge aqua eyes that completely dominated her face—a face that was now lightly tanned from working and riding in the sun. However, her looks no longer concerned Alex in the least; she had other, more important matters to occupy her mind.

Three years ago, after the death of her grandfather was followed almost immediately by the demise of her father, Alex had become technically, albeit inaccurately, the "man of the house." Into her youthful hands had fallen the job of looking after the two elderly servants, stretching the meager family budget, providing food for the table, and dealing with her mama's temper tantrums.

An ordinary girl, brought up in the ordinary way, would never have been able to rise to the challenge. But there was nothing ordinary about Alexandra's appearance *or* her abilities. As a young girl, she had learned to fish and shoot for sport to become a good companion to her father when he came to visit. Now, with calm determination, she simply used those same skills to feed her family.

The clatter of wood being dumped into the wood box banished from her mind all thoughts of ball gowns dusted with diamonds. Shivering from the chill that seeped through the thick walls of the house, making it damp and cold even in the summer, she wrapped her arms across her chest. "Don't waste that, Filbert," she said quickly, as the footman bent to add one of the small logs he'd brought up to the feeble little fire. "It's not really cold in here," she prevaricated, "it's merely a little brisk. Very healthy. Besides, I'm leaving in a few minutes for Mary Ellen's brother's party, and there's no point in wasting good wood."

Filbert glanced at her and nodded, but the log slipped out of his grasp and rolled across the scuffed wooden floor. He straightened and glanced about him, trying to distinguish the brown log from the sea of floorboards about him. Conscious of his failing eyesight, Alexandra said gently, "It's by the foot of my desk," then watched with sympathy as the old footman padded over to the desk and crouched down, feeling about him for the log. "Sarah?" she asked suddenly, as the same strange feeling of expectation she had occasionally experienced over the last three years gathered in her breast. "Did you ever have the feeling that something special was going to happen?"

Sarah briskly closed the drawers of the bureau and bustled over to the armoire. "Indeed I have."

"Did the feeling come true?"

"It did."

"Really?" Alexandra said, her aqua eyes bright, inquisitive. "What happened?"

"The chimney caved in, just as I warned your papa it was going to do, did he not see to having it repaired."

Musical laughter erupted from Alexandra and she shook

her head. "No, no, that's not the sort of feeling I mean." A little embarrassed, Alexandra confided, "I've had this feeling now and then since shortly after Grandfather died, but it's been ever so much stronger and constant this past week. I feel as if I'm standing on a precipice, waiting for something that's about to happen."

Taken aback by Alexandra's dreamy voice and prolonged languor when she was normally matter-of-fact and a whirlwind of busy activity, Sarah studied her. "What is it you think is going to happen?"

Alexandra shivered deliciously. "Something wonderful." She started to say more, but her thoughts were scattered by a loud feminine screech that came from Uncle Monty's bedroom across the hall, followed by the sound of a slamming door and a pair of running feet. Alexandra flipped upright and jumped off the bed in a graceful, energetic motion that was far more natural to her nature than her previous state of dreamy stillness, just as Mary, the young peasant girl whom Sarah brought with her to help with the laundering, charged angrily into the bedroom.

"'E swatted me, 'e did!" Mary burst out, rubbing her ample bottom. Raising her arm, she pointed an accusing finger toward Uncle Monty's room. "I don't 'ave to take that from the likes o' him, nor nobody! I'm a nice girl, I am, an'—"

"Then act like a nice girl and mind your tongue!" Sarah snapped.

Alexandra sighed as the full weight of her responsibility for this household settled around her again and drove away all thoughts of forty-five-course dinners. "I'll go and speak to Uncle Monty," she told Mary. "I'm sure he won't do it again," and then with smiling candor, she added, "At least, he won't do it if you don't bend over within his reach. Sir Montague is something of a . . . well . . . a *connoisseur* of the female anatomy, and when a female has a particularly well-rounded bottom, he tends to show his approval with a pat—rather like a horseman who pats the flank of a particularly fine thoroughbred."

This speech had the effect of flattering and subduing the peasant girl, since despite Montague Marsh's ungentlemanly behavior, he was nevertheless a knight of the realm.

When everyone had left, Sarah glowered gloomily at the

empty room with the *Gazette* left upon the bed. "Something wonderful," she snorted, thinking with bitter sorrow of the seventeen-year-old girl who was trying, without complaint, to carry the burden of a bizarre household whose only servants were a stooped, elderly butler who was too proud to admit he was going deaf and a hopelessly nearsighted footman. Alexandra's family was as much a burden to her as her servants, Sarah thought with disgust. Her great-uncle Montague Marsh, although good-natured, was rarely sober, while never drunk enough to overlook any opportunity to show his amorous attention to anyone wearing skirts. Mrs. Lawrence, Alexandra's mother, who should have taken charge after Mr. Lawrence died, had abdicated all responsibility for the running of Lawrence House to Alexandra, and was the greatest of Alex's burdens.

"Uncle Monty," Alexandra said in a mildly exasperated voice to her father's uncle, who'd come to live with them two years ago when none of his closer relatives would have him.

The portly gentleman was seated before the feeble fire, his gouty leg propped upon a footstool, his expression soulful. "I suppose you've come to ring a peal over me about that girl," he muttered, eyeing her with baleful, red-rimmed eyes.

He looked so much like a chastened, elderly child that Alexandra was unable to maintain a suitably stern demeanor. "Yes," she admitted with a reluctant little smile, "and also to discover where you've hidden that bottle of contraband Madeira your friend Mr. Watterly brought here yesterday."

Uncle Monty reacted with a poor imitation of righteous indignation. "And who, may I ask, dared to presume there is such a bottle present in these rooms?"

He watched askance as Alexandra ignored him and began methodically and efficiently searching his favorite hiding places—beneath the cushion of the settee, under his mattress, and up the chimney. After trying a half-dozen other places, she walked over to his chair and held out her hand good-naturedly. "Give it over, Uncle Monty."

"What?" he asked blankly, shifting uneasily as the bottle of Madeira beneath him poked him in one side of his ample rear end.

Alexandra saw him shift and chuckled. "The bottle of Madeira you're sitting upon, that's what."

"You mean my *medicine,*" he corrected. "As to that, Dr. Beetle told me I'm to use it for its curative benefits, whenever my old war wound kicks up."

Alexandra studied his bloodshot eyes and rosy cheeks, assessing the extent of his inebriation with the expertise that came from two years of dealing with her reckless, irresponsible, but lovable old uncle. Stretching her hand nearer to him, she insisted, "Give over, Uncle. Mama is expecting the squire and his wife to supper, and she wants you there, too. You'll need to be as sober as a—"

"I'll need to be *foxed* in order to endure that pompous pair. I tell you, Alex m'gel, the two o' them give me the shudders. Piety is for saints and saints aren't fit company for a flesh-and-blood man." When Alexandra continued to hold out her hand, the old man sighed resignedly, lifted his hip and withdrew the half-empty bottle of Madeira from beneath him.

"That's a good fellow," Alexandra praised, giving him a comradely pat on the shoulder. "If you're still up when I return, we'll have a cozy game of whist and—"

"When you return?" Sir Montague uttered in alarm. "You don't mean to go off and leave me alone with your mama and her insufferable guests!"

"I do indeed," Alexandra said gaily, already heading off. She blew him a kiss and closed the door on his mutterings about "expiring from boredom" and "being cast into eternal gloom."

She was passing her mother's bedchambers when Felicia Lawrence called out in a frail but imperious voice, "Alexandra! Alexandra, is that you?"

The angry note in her mother's plaintive voice made Alex pause and mentally brace herself for what was bound to be another unpleasant confrontation with her mother over Will Helmsley. Squaring her thin shoulders, she stepped into her mother's room. Mrs. Lawrence was seated before a dressing table, wearing an old mended wrapper, frowning at her reflection in the mirror. The three years since her husband's death had added decades to her mother's once-beautiful face, Alex thought sadly. The vivacious sparkle that had once lit her mother's eyes and enlivened her voice had faded, along with the rich mahogany color of her hair. Now it was dull brown, streaked with grey. It wasn't just grief that had ravaged her mother's face, Alex knew. It was also anger.

Three weeks after George Lawrence's death, a splendid carriage had drawn up at their house. In it was Alex's beloved father's "other family"—the wife and daughter he'd been living with in London for over twelve years. He had kept his legitimate family tucked away in near-poverty in Morsham, while he lived with his illegitimate one in grand style. Even now, Alex winced with pain as she recalled that devastating day when she'd unexpectedly come face to face with her half-sister in this very house. The girl's name was Rose, and she was excessively pretty. But that didn't hurt Alex nearly so much as the beautiful gold locket Rose was wearing around her slender white throat. George Lawrence had given it to her, just as he had given one to Alex. But Alex's was made of tin.

The tin locket, and the fact that he had chosen to live with the lovely little blond girl, made her father's opinion of Alex and her mother eloquently clear.

Only in one area had he treated both his families equally —and that was in the matter of estate: He had died without a shilling to his name, leaving both families equally penniless.

For her mother's sake, Alex had buried the pain of his betrayal in her heart and tried to behave normally, but her mother's grief had turned to rage. Mrs. Lawrence had retired permanently to her rooms to nurse her fury, leaving everything else to Alex to handle. For two and a half years, Mrs. Lawrence had taken no interest in her household or her grieving daughter. When she spoke, it was only to rail about the injustice of her fate and her husband's treachery.

But six months ago Mrs. Lawrence had realized that her situation might not be so hopeless as she'd thought. She had hit upon a means of escape from her plight—and Alexandra was to be that means. Alexandra, she had decided, was going to snare a husband who could rescue both of them from this impoverished life-style. To that end, Mrs. Lawrence had turned her acquisitive attention to the various families in the neighborhood. Only one of them, the

Helmsleys, had enough wealth to suit her, and so she decided upon their son Will—despite the fact that he was a dull, henpecked youth, greatly under the influence of his overpowering parents, who were nearly puritanical in their religious leanings.

"I've asked the squire and his wife to supper," Mrs. Lawrence said to Alex in the mirror. "And Penrose has promised to prepare an excellent meal."

"Penrose is a butler, Mama, he can't be expected to cook for company."

"I am well aware of Penrose's original position in the household, Alexandra. However, he does cook better than Filbert or you, so we will have to make do with his skills this evening. And with fish, of course," she said, and a delicate shudder shook her thin shoulders. "I do wish we didn't have to eat so much fish. I never cared overmuch for it."

Alexandra, who caught the fish and shot whatever game she could find for their table, flushed, as if she was somehow failing in her duty as head of the strange household. "I'm sorry, Mama, but game is scarce just now. Tomorrow, I'll ride out into the countryside and see if I can get something better. Just now, I'm leaving, and I won't be home until late."

"Late?" her mother gasped. "But you must be here tonight, and you must, must, *must* be on the most excellent behavior. You know what sticklers the squire and his wife are for modesty and decorum in a female, although it galls my soul that *that man* has left us so low in the world that we must now cater to the preferences of a mere squire."

Alexandra didn't need to ask who "that man" referred to. Her mother always referred to Alex's father either as "that man" or as "your father"—as if Alexandra herself were somehow to blame for choosing him and she, Mrs. Lawrence, were the mere innocent victim of that choice.

"Then you mustn't cater to the squire," Alexandra said with gentle, but unshakable firmness, "for I wouldn't marry Will Helmsley if it would save me from starving—which we are not in the least danger of doing."

"Oh yes, you will," her mother said in a low, angry voice that sprang from a mixture of desperation and terror. "And you must comport yourself like the wellborn young lady you

25

are. No more gallivanting about the countryside. The Helmsleys won't overlook a breath of scandal if it is attached to their future daughter-in-law."

"I am not their future anything!" Alexandra said, hanging on to her shaky composure with an effort. "I loathe Will Helmsley and for your information," she finished, pushed to the point of forgetting about her mother's fragile hold on sanity, "Mary Ellen says Will Helmsley prefers young boys to girls!"

The horror of that statement, which Alex only partially understood herself, sailed right over Mrs. Lawrence's greying head. "Well, of course—most young men prefer other young men as companions. Although," Mrs. Lawrence continued, getting up and beginning to pace with the fevered awkwardness of one who has been an invalid for a long time, "that may be exactly why he hasn't shown a strong reluctance to wed you, Alexandra." Her gaze was riveted up on Alexandra's thin frame clad in threadbare, tight brown breeches, a white, full-sleeved shirt opened at the throat, and brown boots that showed she'd attempted to shine them. She looked much like a once-prosperous young lad whose family had fallen on hard times and who was forced to wear clothes he'd outgrown. "You must begin wearing gowns, even though young Will doesn't seem to object to your breeches."

Hanging on to her temper with an effort, Alex said patiently, "Mama, I do not own a gown that is not inches above my knees."

"I told you to alter one of mine for you."

"But I'm not handy with a needle, and—"

Mrs. Lawrence stopped pacing and glared at her. "I must say you're putting every obstacle you can think of in the way of your betrothal, but I mean to end this mockery of a life we've been living, and Squire Helmsley's son is the only hope we have." She frowned darkly at the stubborn child-woman standing in the doorway, a shadow of bitter regret crossing her pale features. "I realize that we have never been truly close, Alexandra, but it is *that man's* fault you've grown into the wild, unruly hoyden you are today, gallivanting about the countryside, wearing pants, shooting that rifle, and doing all manner of things you ought not."

Helpless to keep the angry embarrassment from her

26

voice, Alexandra retorted stiffly, "If I were the demure, vapid, helpless creature you seem to want me to be, this household would have starved long ago."

Mrs. Lawrence had the grace to look slightly embarrassed. "What you say is true, but we cannot go on this way much longer. Despite your best efforts, we're in debt to everyone. I know I've not been a good mother these three years past, but I've come to my senses at last, and I must take steps to see you safely married."

"But I don't love Will Helmsley," Alexandra burst out desperately.

"Which is all to the good," Mrs. Lawrence said harshly. "Then he can't hurt you as your father hurt me. Will comes from a steady, solid family. You won't find him keeping an extra wife in London and gambling everything away." Alexandra winced at this cruel reminder of her father's perfidy, as her mother continued, "Actually, we're very lucky Squire Helmsley is so very pushing—otherwise, I daresay he wouldn't have you for a daughter."

"Just what *is* my attraction as a daughter-in-law?"

Mrs. Lawrence looked shocked. "Why, we are connected to an earl, Alexandra, and to a knight of the realm," she said as if that answered everything.

When Mrs. Lawrence fell into a pensive silence, Alexandra shrugged and said, "I'm off to Mary Ellen's. It's her brother's birthday today."

"Perhaps it's better if you aren't present at supper," Mrs. Lawrence said, absently picking up her hairbrush and running it haphazardly through her hair. "I believe the Helmsleys mean to broach the subject of the marriage tonight, and it wouldn't do to have you here frowning and looking mutinous."

"Mama," Alexandra said with a mixture of pity and alarm, "I would rather starve than marry Will."

Mrs. Lawrence's expression made it clear that she, for one, did not prefer starvation to her daughter's marriage. "These matters are best left for adults to decide. Go along to Mary Ellen's, but do wear a gown."

"I can't. In honor of John O'Toole's birthday, we're going to have a jousting tournament like in days of old—you know, the sort of tournament the O'Tooles always have on birthdays."

"You're entirely too old to go parading about in that rusty old suit of armor, Alexandra. Leave it in the hallway where it belongs."

"No harm will come to it," Alex assured. "I'm only taking a shield, the helmet, the lance, and the breastplate."

"Oh, very well," her mother said with a weary shrug.

Chapter Four

MOUNTED UPON OLD THUNDER, a swaybacked, evil-tempered gelding who was older than she was and who had belonged to her grandfather, Alexandra plodded down the rutted road toward the O'Tooles' sprawling cottage, her rifle in a scabbard beside her, her gaze sweeping the side of the road in hopes of spying some small game to shoot on the way to Mary Ellen's. Not that there was much chance of surprising any animal this afternoon, for the long lance tucked under her arm clanked noisily against the breastplate she wore and banged against the shield she carried.

Despite her unhappy confrontation with her mother, Alex's spirits rose, buoyed up by the glorious spring day and the same sense of excited expectation she'd tried to describe to Sarah.

Down in the valley on her left and in the woods on her right, spring flowers had burst into bloom, filling her eyes and nose with their rainbow colors and delicious scent. On the outskirts of the village there was a small inn, and Alexandra, who knew everyone within the eight-mile circle that encompassed her entire world, shoved the visor of her helmet up and waved gaily at Mr. Tilson, the proprietor. "Good day, Mr. Tilson," she called.

"Good day to you, Miss Alex," he called back.

Mary Ellen O'Toole and her six brothers were outside the O'Tooles' rambling cottage, a rollicking game of knights-of-yore already in full progress in their yard. "Come on,

Alexandra," fourteen-year-old Tom called from atop his father's ancient horse. "It's time for a joust."

"No, let's duel first," the thirteen-year-old argued, brandishing an old saber. "I'll best you this time, Alex. I've been practicing day and night."

Laughing, Alexandra awkwardly dismounted and hugged Mary Ellen, then both girls threw themselves into the games, which were a ritual reenacted on each of the seven O'Toole children's birthday.

The afternoon and evening passed in exuberant games, cheerful rivalry, and the convivial laughter of a large family gathered together—something that Alexandra, an only child, had always longed to be part of.

By the time she was on her way home, she was happily exhausted and nearly groaning from the quantity of hearty food she'd eaten at the insistence of kindly Mrs. O'Toole.

Lulled by the steady clip-clop of old Thunder's hooves on the dusty road, Alexandra let her body sway in rhythm with the horse's gentle motion, her heavy eyelids drooping with fatigue. Left with no other way to bring her suit of armor back home, Alexandra was wearing it, but it made her uncomfortably warm, which made her feel even drowsier.

As she passed the inn and turned old Thunder onto the wide path that led through the woods and intersected the main road again a mile away, she noticed that several horses were tied in the innyard and the lamp in the window was still lit. Masculine voices, raised in lusty song, drifted through the open window to her. Overhead the branches of the oak trees met, swaying in the spring night, casting eerie shadows on the path as they blotted out the moon.

It was late, Alexandra knew, but she didn't urge her mount to quicken its walking pace. In the first place, Thunder was past twenty, and in the second, she wanted to be sure that Squire and Mrs. Helmsley had departed by the time she arrived.

The visor of her helmet abruptly clanked down across her face again, and Alexandra sighed with irritation, longing to take the heavy helmet off and carry it. Deciding that Thunder was unlikely to feel either the energy or the inclination to try to run off with her, particularly after his exhausting day at the "lists," Alexandra pulled him to a stop, then let go of his reins and transferred the heavy shield she was carrying to her left hand. Intending to take off the helmet and carry it in the crook of her right arm, she reached up to pull the helmet off, then halted, her attention suddenly drawn to the muffled, unidentifiable sounds coming from the perimeter of the woods, a quarter of a mile ahead near the road.

Frowning slightly, wondering if she was about to encounter a wild boar, or a less threatening—perhaps edible—species of game, she withdrew her rifle from its scabbard as quietly as her armor would allow.

Suddenly the serenity of the night was shattered by the explosion of a gunshot, and then another. Before Alexandra had time to react, old Thunder bolted in wild-eyed confusion through the thinning woods—galloping blindly, straight toward the source of the shots, his bridle reins flicking the ground beside his flying hooves, with Alexandra's legs clamped in a death grip against his sides.

The bandit's head jerked toward the eruption of clanking metal from the woods beside them, and Jordan Townsende tore his gaze from the deadly hole at the end of the pistol that the second bandit was aiming straight at his chest. The sight that greeted him made him doubt his eyesight. Charging out of the woods to his rescue atop a swaybacked nag was a knight in armor with his visor pulled down, a shield at the ready in one hand and a rifle in his other.

Alexandra stifled a scream as she crashed out of the woods and catapulted straight into the midst of a moonlit scene more sinister than any of her worst nightmares: A coachman was lying wounded in the road beside a coach, and two bandits with red handkerchiefs concealing their faces were holding a tall man at gunpoint. The second bandit turned as Alexandra clattered down on them—and pointed his gun straight at her.

There was no time to think, only to react. Tightening her grip on her rifle and unconsciously counting on the protection of her shield and breastplate against the inevitable bullet, Alexandra leaned to the right, intending to launch herself at the bandit and knock him to the ground, but at that moment his gun exploded.

In a frenzy of terror, Thunder stumbled and lost his balance, pitching Alexandra helplessly through the air to land in a heap of rusty metal atop the second bandit. The impact nearly dislodged her helmet, sent her rifle skidding uselessly into the road, and knocked her half-unconscious.

Unfortunately, the bandit recovered before Alexandra's head stopped reeling. "What the bloody hell—" he grunted and, with a mighty shove, pushed her limp body off him and delivered a vicious kick to her side before running over to help his accomplice, who was now engaged in a physical struggle with their tall victim for possession of the pistol.

In a blur of panic and pain, Alexandra saw both bandits pounce on the tall man, and she heaved herself forward with a strength born of sheer terror—crawling, scrambling, and clanking toward the dark gleaming shaft of her rifle lying on the rutted road. Just as her hand closed around the stock of her rifle, she saw the tall man wrest the pistol from the thin bandit and shoot him, then crouch and whirl, pointing his pistol straight at the other one.

Mesmerized by the terrible deadly grace of the tall man's swift maneuver, Alexandra watched him coldly and calmly level the gun at the second assailant. Still sprawled on her stomach, she closed her eyes, waiting for the inevitable explosion. But there was only the loud click of an empty gun.

"You poor, stupid bastard," the bandit said with an evil laugh and lazily reached inside his shirt, pulling out his own pistol. "Do you think I'da let yer grab that second gun off the ground if'n I didn' know fer sure it was empty? You're going to die real slow for killing me brother. It takes a long time for a man to die when he's been shot in the stomach—"

Her mind screaming with fear, Alexandra rolled onto her side, rammed the bolt of her rifle into place and sighted down the barrel. When the bandit raised his pistol, she fired. The powerful recoil slammed her onto her back, knocking the air from her chest. When she turned her head in the dirt and opened her eyes, the bandit was lying in a shaft of moonlight, the side of his head blown off.

She hadn't merely wounded him as she'd hoped to do, she had *killed* him. A groan of terror and anguish rose in her throat and tore from her constricted chest, and then the world began to spin, slowly at first, than faster as she watched the tall man kick over the bandit she'd killed, then start toward her, his long-legged gait swift, menacing somehow. . . . The world spun faster, carrying her down through a black hole. For the first time in her life, Alexandra fainted.

Jordan crouched down beside the fallen knight, his hands rough in his urgent haste to tug off the helmet so he could assess the injuries to the inhabitant of the suit of armor. "Quick, Grimm!" he called over to his coachman, who was staggering to his feet, recovering from the bandit's blow which had knocked him unconscious. "Give me a hand with this damned armor."

"Is he hurt, your grace?" Grimm said, rushing over to his master's side and kneeling down.

"Obviously," Jordan said brusquely, wincing at the cut on the left side of the small face.

"He wasn't shot, was he?"

"I don't think so. Hold his head—gently, dammit!— while I pull this monstrosity off him." Tossing the helmet aside, Jordan pulled off the breastplate. "God, what an absurd costume," he uttered, but his voice was worried as he surveyed the limp body before him, looking for a bullet wound or a sign of blood in the moonlight. "It's too dark to tell where he's hurt. Turn the coach around and we'll take him to the inn we passed a few miles back. Someone there will be bound to know who his parents are, as well as the direction of the nearest doctor." Reaching down, Jordan gently grasped his young rescuer under the arms, shocked to discover how light in weight the lad beneath the armor was. "He's just a boy, no more than thirteen or fourteen," Jordan said, his voice gruff with guilt at the harm he had evidently caused the courageous youth who had charged to his rescue. Effortlessly scooping the child into his arms, he carried him to his coach.

Jordan's arrival at the inn with an unconscious Alexandra in his arms caused a furor of lewd comments and bawdy suggestions from the occupants of the common room who, because of the lateness of the hour, were deeply in their cups.

With the supreme indifference of the true aristocrat toward lesser mortals, Jordan ignored the raised voices and stalked toward the barmaid. "Show me to your best room and then send the innkeeper to me at once."

33

The barmaid glanced from the back of Alexandra's curly dark head to the tall, impeccably dressed gentleman and scurried off to carry out all his commands in the order they had been given, beginning with the inn's finest bedchamber.

Gently, Jordan laid the lad upon the bed and unfastened the laces at the neck of the boy's shirt. The boy groaned, his eyelids fluttered open, and Jordan found himself staring into an amazingly large pair of eyes the startling color of liquid aquamarines, fringed with absurdly long, curly lashes —eyes that were gazing back at him in disoriented bewilderment. Smiling reassuringly, Jordan said gently, "Welcome back to the world, Galahad."

"Where—" Alexandra wet her parched lips, her voice an unfamiliar croak. Clearing her throat, she tried again and managed little more than a hoarse, thready whisper. "Where am I?"

"You're at an inn near where you were hurt."

The gory details came flooding back, and Alexandra felt hot tears burn the backs of her eyes. "I killed him. I *killed* that man," she choked.

"And saved two lives by doing it—mine and my coachman's."

In her dazed state, Alexandra seized on that reassurance and clung to it for all the comfort it offered. Not able to focus perfectly yet, she watched as if from a distance as he began running his hands up and down her legs. No hands but her mother's had ever touched her person—and that not for years and years. Alexandra found the sensation both faintly pleasant and oddly disturbing, but when the man's hands began gently probing at her lower rib cage, she gasped and clutched his thick wrists. "Sir!" she croaked desperately. "What are you doing?"

Jordan's gaze flicked to the slender fingers gripping his wrists with a strength that seemed born of fear. "I'm looking for broken bones, stripling. I've sent for a doctor and the innkeeper. Although, since you're awake now, you can tell me yourself who you are and where to locate the nearest physician."

Alarmed and indignant at the exorbitant cost of a physician's services, Alex burst out desperately, "Do you have any idea how much a leech *charges* nowadays?"

Jordan stared down at the pale lad with the amazing eyes and felt a deep stirring of compassion mingled with admiration—a combination of emotions that was completely foreign to him. "You incurred these injuries on my behalf. Naturally, I'll stand good for the charges."

He smiled then, and Alexandra felt the last vestiges of haziness abruptly clear from her mind. Smiling down at her was the largest and unquestionably the most handsome male she had ever seen, ever imagined. His eyes were the silver-grey of satin and steel, his shoulders very wide, his baritone voice rich and compelling. In contrast to his tanned face, his teeth were startlingly white, and although rugged masculine strength was carved into the tough line of his jaw and chin, his touch was gentle, and there were tiny lines at the corners of his eyes to testify to his sense of humor.

Looking up at the giant who loomed above her, she felt very small and fragile. Oddly, she also felt safe. Safer than she had felt in three years. Loosening her grip on his hands, she raised her own hand and touched her fingers to a cut on his chin. "You've been hurt, too," she said, smiling shyly at him.

Jordan caught his breath at the unexpected glamour of the lad's glowing smile and froze in amazement when he felt an odd, inner tingle from the boy's touch. A boy's touch. Brusquely shaking off the small hand, he wondered grimly if his boredom with life's ordinary diversions was turning him into some sort of perverted dilettante. "You haven't yet told me your name," he said, his tone deliberately cool as he began exploring the boy's lower ribcage, watching his small face for any sign of pain.

Alexandra opened her mouth to give her name, but gave a shriek of outraged panic instead when he suddenly slid his hands onto her breasts.

Jordan jerked his hands away as if they'd been scorched. "You're a girl!"

"I can't help it!" Alexandra flung back, stung by the sharp accusation in his voice.

The absurdity of their exchanged words struck them both at the same time: Jordan's black scowl gave way to a sudden grin and Alexandra started to laugh. And that was how Mrs.

Tilson, the innkeeper's wife, found them—both on the bed, laughing, the man's hands arrested a few inches above Miss Alexandra Lawrence's gaping shirt and bosom.

"Alexandra Lawrence!" she exploded, barging into the room like a battleship under full sail, sparks shooting from her eyes as they leveled on the man's hands above Alexandra's open shirt. "What is the meaning of this!"

Alexandra was blessedly oblivious to the portent of what Mrs. Tilson was seeing and thinking, but Jordan was not, and he found it nauseating that this woman's evil mind could apparently accuse a young girl of no more than thirteen years of collaborating in her own moral demise. His features hardened and there was a distinct frost in his clipped, authoritative voice. "Miss Lawrence was hurt in an accident just south of here on the road. Send for a physician."

"No, do not, Mrs. Tilson," Alexandra said and lurched into a sitting position despite her swimming senses. "I'm perfectly well and wish to go home."

Jordan spoke to the suspicious woman in a curt, commanding voice. "In that case, I'll take her home, and you can direct the physician to the bend in the road a few miles south of here. There, he'll find two thugs who are beyond needing his skill, but he can ensure they're properly disposed of." Reaching into his pocket, Jordan withdrew a card with his name engraved on it beneath a small gold crest. "I'll return here to answer any questions he may have, once I've taken Miss Lawrence to her family."

Mrs. Tilson muttered something scathing under her breath about bandits and debauchery, snatched the card from his hand, glowered at Alexandra's unbuttoned shirt, and marched out.

"You seemed surprised—about my being a girl, I mean," Alexandra ventured uncertainly.

"Frankly, this has been a night of surprises," Jordan replied, dismissing Mrs. Tilson from his mind and turning his attention to Alexandra. "Would I be prying if I were to ask you what you were doing rigged out in that suit of armor?"

Alexandra slowly swung her legs over the side of the bed and tried to stand. The room swayed. "I can walk," she protested when the man reached out to lift her into his arms.

"But I'd prefer to carry you," Jordan said firmly and did exactly that. Alexandra smiled inwardly at the blithe way he stalked through the common room, serenely indifferent to the staring villagers, carrying in his arms a disheveled, dusty girl clad in breeches and shirtsleeves.

Once he had set her gently onto the deep, luxurious squabs of his coach and settled in across from her, however, her amusement vanished. Soon, she realized, they would pass by the gruesome scene she'd partially caused. "I took a man's life," she said in a tortured whisper as the coach headed toward the dreaded bend. "I will never forgive myself."

"I would never forgive you if you hadn't," Jordan said with a teasing smile in his voice. In the glow of the lighted coach lamps, huge aqua eyes brimming with tears lifted to his face, searching it, silently beseeching him for more comfort, and Jordan responded automatically. Reaching forward, he lifted her off the seat and onto his lap, cradling her in his arms like the distraught child she was. "It was a very brave thing you did," he murmured into the soft, dusky curls that brushed his cheek.

Alexandra drew in a shuddering breath and shook her head, unknowingly rubbing her cheek against his chest. "I wasn't brave, I was simply too frightened to run away like a sensible person."

Holding the trusting child in his arms, Jordan was startled by the unprecedented thought that he might like to have a child of his own to hold someday. There was something profoundly touching about the way this little girl was snuggled against him, trusting him. Remembering that fetching little girls inevitably become spoiled young women, he promptly discarded the notion. "Why were you wearing that old suit of armor?" he asked for the second time that night.

Alexandra explained about the jousts, which were a ritual whenever one of the O'Toole children had a birthday, then she made him repeatedly laugh aloud by describing some of her foibles and triumphs during today's lists.

"Don't people outside of Morsham have jousts and such?

I always assumed people were the same everywhere, although I don't know it for certain, since I've never been beyond Morsham. I doubt if I ever will."

Jordan was shocked into momentary silence. In his own wide circle of acquaintances, everyone traveled everywhere, and often. It was hard to accept that this bright child would never see any place beyond this godforsaken tiny village on the edge of nowhere. He glanced down at her shadowy face and found her watching him with friendly interest, rather than the deferential awe he was accustomed to. Inwardly he grinned at the image of uninhibited peasant children throwing themselves into jousts. How different their childhood must be from that of the children of the nobility. Like himself, they were all raised by governesses, ruled by tutors, admonished to be clean and neat at all times, and constantly reminded to act like the superior beings they were born to be. Perhaps children who grew up in remote places like this were better and different—guileless and courageous and unaffected, as Alexandra was. Based on the life Alexandra described to him, he wondered if perhaps peasant children were the lucky ones, after all. Peasant children? It dawned on him that there was nothing of the rough peasant in this child's cultured speech.

"Why did your coachman call you 'your grace'?" she asked, smiling, and a dimple appeared in her cheek.

Jordan jerked his eyes away from the fetching little dent. "That is how dukes are generally addressed."

"Dukes?" Alexandra echoed, disappointed by the discovery that this handsome stranger obviously dwelled in a world far beyond her reach and would therefore vanish from her life forever. "Are you truly a duke?"

"I'm afraid so," he answered, noting her crestfallen reaction. "Are you disappointed?"

"A little," she floored him by replying. "What do people call you? Besides Duke, I mean?"

"At least a dozen names," he said, both amused and confused by her genuine, unguarded reactions. "Most people call me Hawthorne, or Hawk. My close friends call me by my given name, Jordan."

"Hawk suits you," she remarked, but her agile mind had already leapt ahead to an important conclusion. "Do you

38

suppose those bandits specifically chose you to rob because you're a duke? I mean they took a terrible risk in accosting you on the road not far from an inn."

"Greed is a powerful motivation for risk," Jordan replied.

Alexandra nodded her agreement and softly quoted, "'There is no fire like passion, no shark like hatred, no torrent like greed.'"

In blank amazement, Jordan stared at her. "What did you say?"

"*I* didn't say that, Buddha did," Alexandra explained.

"I'm familiar with the quotation," Jordan said, recovering his composure with an effort. "I'm merely surprised that *you* are familiar with it." He saw a faint light coming from a shadowy house directly ahead and assumed the home was hers. "Alexandra," he said quickly and sternly as they neared the house, "you must never feel guilty about what you did tonight. You have nothing whatever to feel guilty about."

She looked at him with a soft smile, but as the coach drew up in the rutted drive of a large, run-down house, Alexandra suddenly exclaimed, "Oh no!"

Her heart sank as she beheld the squire's shiny carriage and fancy mare, which were still tied near the front door. She had so hoped they'd be well gone by now.

The duke's coachman opened the door and let down the stairs, but when Alexandra attempted to follow the duke out of the coach, he reached in and scooped her into his arms. "I'm certain I can walk," she protested.

His lazy, intimate smile made her catch her breath as he said, "It's embarrassing in the extreme for a man of my dimensions to be rescued by a slip of a girl, even one wearing a suit of armor. For the sake of my wounded ego, you'll have to permit me to be gallant now."

"Very well," Alexandra agreed with a resigned chuckle. "Who am I to crush the ego of a noble duke?"

Jordan scarcely heard her; his sweeping glance was registering the overgrown lawns surrounding the house, the broken shutters hanging askew at the windows, and all the other signs of a house that was sadly in need of repair. It was not the humble cottage he'd expected to find; instead it was an old, eerie, neglected place, which the inhabitants could obviously not afford to keep up. Shifting Alexandra's weight against his left arm and leg, he raised his right hand and knocked upon the door, noting the peeling paint.

When no one answered, Alexandra volunteered, "I'm afraid you'll have to knock more loudly. Penrose is quite deaf, you see, although he's much too proud to admit it."

"Who," Jordan said, rapping more loudly upon the heavy door, "is Penrose?"

"Our butler. When Papa died, I had to discharge the staff, but Penrose and Filbert were too old and infirm to find new employment. They had nowhere to go, so they remained here and agreed to work in return for only lodging and food. Penrose does the cooking, too, and helps with the cleaning."

"How very odd," Jordan murmured the thought aloud, waiting for the door to be opened.

In the light of the lamp above the door, her piquant face was turned up to him in laughing curiosity. "What do you find 'odd'?"

"The idea of a deaf butler."

"Then you will surely find Filbert even more of an oddity."

"I doubt that," Jordan said dryly. "Who is Filbert?"

"Our footman."

"Dare I ask what his infirmity is?"

"He's shortsighted," she provided ingenuously. "So much so that only last week he mistook a wall for a door and walked into it."

To his horror, Jordan felt laughter welling up inside him. Trying to spare her pride, he said as solemnly as possible, "A deaf butler and a blind footman. . . . How very—ah—unconventional."

"Yes, it is, isn't it," she agreed almost proudly. "But then, I shouldn't like to be conventional." With a jaunty smile, she quoted, "'Conventionality is the refuge of a stagnant mind.'"

Jordan raised his fist and pounded so hard she could hear the sound thunder through the inside of the house, but his puzzled gaze was riveted on her laughing face. "Who said that about conventionality?" he asked blankly.

"I did," she admitted impenitently. "I made it up."

"What an impertinent little baggage you are," he said,

grinning, and before he realized what he was doing, he started to press an affectionate, paternal kiss on her forehead. He checked the impulse as the door was flung open by a white-haired Penrose, who glared indignantly at Jordan and said, "There is no need to hammer on the door like you're trying to waken the dead, sir! No one in this house is deaf!"

Stunned into momentary silence by this dressing-down from a mere butler and, moreover, one whose uniform was faded and threadbare, Jordan opened his mouth to give the servant the blistering setdown he richly deserved, but the old man had just realized that it was Alexandra whom Jordan held, and that there was a bruise on her jaw. "What have you done to Miss Alexandra?!" the servant demanded in a furious hiss, and reached out his feeble arms with the obvious intention of snatching Alexandra into them.

"Take me to Mrs. Lawrence," Jordan ordered curtly, ignoring the butler's gesture. "I said," Jordan enunciated more loudly when the servant seemed not to hear, "take us to Mrs. Lawrence at once."

Penrose glowered. "I heard you the first time," he declared irately, turning to do as he was bidden. "The dead could hear you . . ." he muttered as he walked off.

The faces that turned to stare at them in the drawing room were beyond Alexandra's worst imaginings. Her mother jumped up with a startled scream; the stout squire and his stouter wife both leaned forward in their chairs, intent, avidly curious—staring at Alexandra's shirt, which was gaping open nearly to her breasts.

"What happened?" Mrs. Lawrence burst out. "Alexandra, your face—dear God, what has happened?"

"Your daughter saved my life, Mrs. Lawrence, but in the process, she suffered a blow to her face. I assure you it looks much more serious than it really is."

"Please put me down," Alexandra said urgently, for her mother seemed about to swoon. When Jordan complied, she decided to belatedly make the introductions and thus restore some semblance of decorum to the atmosphere. "Mother," she said in a quiet, reassuring voice, "this is the Duke of Hawthorne." Despite her mother's gasp, Alexandra continued in a polite, matter-of-fact tone, "I came upon him when he and his coachman had been set upon by bandits and I—I shot one of them." Turning to Jordan, she said, "Your grace, this is my mother, Mrs. Lawrence."

Silence reigned complete. Mrs. Lawrence seemed to be struck dumb and the squire and his wife continued to gape, their mouths slack. Embarrassed by the total silence in the room, Alexandra turned with a bright relieved smile as Uncle Monty tottered into the room, swaying slightly, his glassy eyes testifying to an evening spent secretly imbibing his forbidden Madeira. "Uncle Monty," she said a little desperately, "I've brought home a guest. This is the Duke of Hawthorne."

Uncle Monty leaned heavily on his ivory-handled cane and blinked twice, trying to focus on the face of their guest. "Good God!" he exclaimed in sudden shock. "It *is* Hawthorne, by Jove! It truly is." Belatedly recalling his manners, he executed a clumsy bow and said in a hearty, ingratiating voice, "Sir Montague Marsh, your grace, at your service."

Alexandra, who was embarrassed only by the awkwardness of the prolonged silences and not by her shabby house, ancient servants, or peculiarly behaving relatives, smiled brightly at Jordan, then inclined her head toward Filbert who was shuffling into the room bearing a tea tray. Ignoring the fact that she was probably committing a grave social faux pas by introducing a nobleman to a mere footman, she said sweetly, "And this is Filbert, who takes care of everything which Penrose does not. Filbert, this is the Duke of Hawthorne."

Filbert glanced up in the act of putting the tea tray on a table and squinted nearsightedly over his shoulder at Uncle Monty. "How do," he said to the wrong man and Alexandra saw the duke's lips twitch.

"Would you care to stay for tea?" she asked the duke, studying the suspicious glimmer of laughter in his grey eyes.

He smiled, but shook his head without a trace of regret. "I cannot, moppet. I've a long journey ahead of me and before I can resume it, I will have to return to the inn and meet with the authorities. They will require some sort of explanation for tonight's debacle." Directing a brief nod of farewell at his watchful audience, Jordan looked down at the beguiling face turned up to his. "Would you see me out?" he invited.

Alexandra nodded and led him to the front door, ignoring the babble of voices that erupted behind them in the drawing room, where the squire's wife was saying in a shrill voice, "What did he mean 'back to the inn'? Surely, Mrs. Lawrence, he cannot possibly have meant Alexandra was there with—"

In the hallway, the duke paused and gazed down at Alexandra with a warmth in his grey eyes that made her entire body feel overheated. And when he lifted his hand and laid it tenderly against her bruised jaw, her pulse leapt in her throat. "Where—where do you go on your journey?" she asked, trying to delay his leavetaking.

"To Rosemeade."

"What is that?"

"My grandmother's small country estate. She prefers to spend most of her time there because she thinks the house 'cozy.'"

"Oh," Alexandra said, finding it quite difficult to speak or breathe because his fingertips were now deliciously sliding over her cheek, and he was looking at her in a way that struck her as being almost reverent.

"I'll never forget you, poppet," he said, his voice low and husky as he bent down and pressed his warm lips to her forehead. "Don't let anyone change you. Stay exactly the way you are."

When he left, Alexandra stood stock still, reeling from the kiss that seemed branded into her forehead.

It did not occur to her that she might have just fallen under the spell of a man who automatically used his voice and smile to charm and disarm. Practiced seducers were beyond the realm of her experience.

Dishonest rakes and practiced seducers were not, however, beyond the experience of Mrs. Lawrence, who had fallen victim to just such a treacherous charmer when she was scarcely older than Alexandra. Like the Duke of Hawthorne, her husband had been outrageously handsome, with suave manners, beautiful clothes, and absolutely no scruples.

Which was why, when Alexandra awakened the next morning, it was to see her mother storming into her room, her voice vibrating with fury. "Alexandra, wake up this instant!"

Alexandra wriggled into a sitting position and pushed her curly hair out of her eyes. "Is something wrong?"

"I'll tell you what's wrong," her mother said, and Alexandra was shocked at the virulent rage emanating from her mother. "We've had four visitors this morning, beginning with the innkeeper's wife, who informed me you shared a bedroom there with that low, conniving seducer of innocents last night. The next two visitors were curiosity seekers. The fourth visitor," she enunciated in a voice shaking with pent-up wrath and tears, "was the squire, who told me that, because of your scandalous behavior last night, your state of undress, and your general lack of modesty and sense, he now considers you beyond the bounds of a fit wife for his son or for any other self-respecting man."

When Alexandra merely stared at her in visible relief, Mrs. Lawrence lost control. She grabbed Alexandra by the shoulders and shook her. "Do you have any idea what you've done," she screamed. "Do you? Then I'll tell you— you've disgraced yourself beyond recall. Gossip has stretched everywhere, and people are talking about you as if you were a slut. You were seen being carried into an inn in a state of undress and you occupied a bedroom alone with a man. You were carried out of that same inn a half hour later by the same man. Do you know what everyone thinks?"

"That I was tired and needed to rest?" Alexandra suggested sensibly, more alarmed by her mother's pallor than her words.

"You fool! You're a bigger fool than I ever was. No decent man will have you now."

"Mama," Alexandra said with firm quiet, trying to reverse their roles as she had needed to do so often in the past three years, "calm yourself."

"Don't you dare use that condescending tone on me, miss!" her mother shouted, her face only inches from Alexandra's. "Did that man *touch* you?"

Growing increasingly alarmed by her mother's hysteria, Alexandra said matter-of-factly, "You know he did. You saw him carry me in here and—"

"Not that way!" Mrs. Lawrence cried, positively shaking with rage. "Did he put his hands on you? Did he *kiss* you? Answer me, Alexandra!"

Alexandra actually considered defying the principles her

grandfather had ingrained in her, but before she could open her mouth to lie, her mother had already spotted the telltale flush blooming brightly in her cheeks.

"He did, didn't he!" she screamed. "The answer is written all over your face." Mrs. Lawrence reared back and stood up, pacing frantically back and forth in front of Alexandra's bed. Alexandra had heard of women who became so overwrought that they tore at their own hair, and her mother looked on the verge of doing just that.

Swiftly climbing out of bed, she put her hand out to stop her mother's aimless pacing. "Mama, please don't upset yourself like this. Please don't. The duke and I did nothing wrong."

Her mother almost ground her teeth in rage. "You may not understand that what you did was wrong, but that low, conniving, corrupt degenerate knew it. *He* knew. He waltzed in here as bold as brass, knowing you were too naive to understand what he'd done. God, how I hate men!"

Without warning, she pulled Alexandra into her arms in a fierce hug. "I'm not the blind fool I used to be. I let your father use us for his own amusement and then discard us, but I'll not let Hawthorne do that to us. He ruined you, and I'll make him pay, you'll see. I'll force him to do what's right."

"Mama, please!" Alexandra burst out, pulling free of her mother's suffocating embrace. "He did nothing wrong, not really. He only touched my limbs, looking for broken bones, and bade me farewell by kissing my forehead! That can't be wrong."

"He destroyed your reputation by taking you to a public inn. He's ruined any chance of your making a decent marriage. No other man will have you now. From this day forward, wherever you go in the village, scandal will follow you. For that he must pay, and dearly. When he returned to the inn last night, he gave the doctor his direction. We shall go after him and demand justice."

"No!" Alexandra cried, but her mother was deaf to all but her own inner voice that had been screaming for vengeance these three long years.

"I've no doubt he'll be expecting us to call," she continued bitterly, ignoring Alexandra's pleas, "now that we've learned the whole truth of last night's debacle."

Chapter Five

THE DOWAGER DUCHESS of Hawthorne regarded her grandson with a stern smile on her lips and an attentive expression in her hazel eyes. At seventy, she was still a handsome woman with white hair, regal bearing, and the aloof, unshakable confidence and poise that comes from living a thoroughly privileged life.

Despite the stony dignity that characterized her every gesture, she was no stranger to grief, having already outlived her husband and her sons. Yet so rigid was her self-control that not even her closest acquaintances were certain she had loved them in life or that she was aware they were dead—and so enormous was her consequence among the *ton* that none of them ever dared to ask.

She betrayed no sign of alarm now as she serenely listened to her eldest grandson, who was sitting on one of the sofas in her drawing room, a booted foot propped upon the opposite knee, casually explaining that he was delayed because two highwaymen had tried to kill him last night.

Her other grandson, however, made no effort whatsoever to conceal his feelings about his cousin's explanation. Lifting his brandy glass to his lips, Anthony grinned and said drolly, "Jordan, admit it—the truth is you wanted another blissful evening with your beautiful ballerina. Er, your pardon, Grandmama," Anthony added belatedly when the dowager duchess sent him a withering look. "But the truth is, there were no highwaymen, and no twelve-year-old girl came to your rescue. Right?"

"Wrong," Jordan said imperturbably.

The duchess watched the by-play between the two cousins. They were as close as brothers and as different as night and day, she thought: Jordan was more like her, reserved, cool, detached, while Anthony was easy to know and incurably good-natured. Anthony had two doting parents who loved him; Jordan had never known real affection from either of his. She approved wholeheartedly of Jordan's demeanor; she disapproved of Anthony's easygoing ways. Disapproval—in varying degrees—was the only emotion the dowager duchess permitted herself to display.

"It happened exactly as I said, although it wounds my pride to admit it," Jordan continued wryly as he stood up and walked to the sideboard to replenish the port in his glass. "One moment I was staring down the barrel of a pistol and the next moment there she was—charging straight into our midst atop a swaybacked nag, with her visor down, brandishing a lance in one hand and a rifle in the other."

He poured more of the Portuguese port he especially preferred into his glass and returned to his chair. In a voice that was matter-of-fact rather than critical, he continued, "Her armor was rusty and her house is straight out of a bad gothic novel—complete with cobwebs on the beams, faded tapestries, creaking doors and damp walls. She has a butler who's deaf as a post, a blind footman who walks into walls, an old sot of an uncle who calls himself Sir Montague Marsh . . ."

"Interesting family," Anthony murmured. "No wonder she's so . . . ah . . . unconventional."

"'Conventionality,'" Jordan quoted dryly, "'is the refuge of a stagnant mind.'"

The dowager, whose entire life had been religiously and scrupulously dedicated to the precepts of convention, glowered. "Who said such a ridiculous thing?"

"Alexandra Lawrence."

"*Very* unconventional." Anthony chuckled, studying the almost fond smile upon his cousin's rugged face as he spoke of the girl. Jordan seldom smiled, Anthony knew—unless the smile was seductive or cynical—and he rarely laughed. He had been brought up by a father who believed sentimentality was "soft," and anything that was soft was abhorrent, forbidden. So was anything that made a man vulnerable.

Including love. "What does this extraordinary female look like?" Anthony asked, anxious to discover more about the girl who'd had such an unusual effect on his cousin.

"Small," Jordan said as a picture of Alexandra's laughing face danced across his mind. "And too thin. But she has a smile that could melt rock and a pair of the most extraordinary eyes. They're the color of aquamarines and, when you look at her, they're all you see. Her speech is as cultured as yours or mine, and despite that morbid house of hers, she's a cheerful little thing."

"And brave, apparently," Anthony added.

Nodding, Jordan said, "I'm going to send her a bank draft—a reward for saving my life. God knows they can use the money. Based on things she said—and things she was careful not to say—I gathered that the responsibility for the entire outlandish household rests on her shoulders. Alexandra will undoubtedly be offended by the money, which is why I didn't offer it last night, but it will ease her plight."

The duchess sniffed disdainfully, still irked by Miss Lawrence's definition of conventionality. "The lower classes are always eager for coin, Jordan, regardless of the reason it's given. I'm surprised she didn't try to wheedle some sort of monetary reward last night."

"You've become a cynic," Jordan teased blandly. "But you're wrong about this girl. She's without guile or greed."

Startled by this announcement from Jordan, whose opinion of the female character was notoriously low, Tony suggested helpfully, "In a few years, why don't you have another look at her and set her up as—"

"Anthony!" the duchess warned in tones of direst disapprobation. "Not in my presence, *if* you please!"

"I wouldn't dream of taking her from where she is," Jordan said, completely inured to his grandmother's ferocious scowl. "Alexandra is a rare jewel, but she wouldn't last a day in London. She's not hard enough or brittle enough or ambitious enough. She—" He broke off and looked inquiringly at the butler, who had coughed politely to obtain recognition. "Yes, Ramsey, what is it?"

Ramsey drew himself up ramrod straight, his face contorted with distaste, his eyebrows positively levitating with ire. Directing his remarks to Jordan, he said, "There are three persons here, your grace, who insist upon seeing you.

48

They arrived in a cart that defies description, drawn by a horse which is unworthy of the name, wearing clothing which no person of any merit would be seen in—"

"Who are they?" Jordan interrupted impatiently.

"The man claims to be Sir Montague Marsh, and the two ladies with him are his sister-in-law Mrs. Lawrence and his niece Miss Alexandra Lawrence. They say they've come to collect upon a debt owed by you."

The word "debt" caused Jordan's eyebrows to snap together into a frown. "Show them in," he said shortly.

In an uncharacteristic lapse from her normal hauteur, the duchess permitted herself a satisfied, I-told-you-so glance at Jordan. "Miss Lawrence is not only greedy, she's pushing and encroaching. Imagine, calling upon you here and claiming you owe a debt."

Without replying to his grandmother's undeniable assessment of the situation, Jordan walked over and sat down at the carved oaken desk at the far end of the room. "There's no reason for either of you to sit through this. I'll handle it."

"On the contrary," said the duchess in a glacial voice. "Anthony and I shall be present as witnesses in case these persons should resort to extortion."

Keeping her eyes focused on the back of the butler, Alexandra followed reluctantly in the wake of her mother and Uncle Monty, her entire being engulfed in mortification, her misery increased a thousandfold by the magnificence of Rosemeade.

She'd expected a duke's grandmother to occupy a grand home, but nothing in her imagination or experience had prepared her for the sight of this gigantic, brooding place set amid acres of gardens and lawns. Until they arrived here, she'd clung to the vision of the duke as he had seemed the other night—friendly and accessible. Rosemeade, however, had banished that absurd notion from her mind. He was from another world. To him, Rosemeade was "a small country home." Instead, it was a *palace,* she thought miserably, as her feet sank into thick Aubusson carpet, a palace that made her feel even smaller and more insignificant than she already felt.

The butler swept open a pair of carved oaken doors and stepped aside to admit them to a room lined with paintings in ornate frames. Repressing an urge to curtsy to the stiff-backed servant, Alexandra walked forward, dreading the moment when she would have to confront her newfound friend and see what she knew would surely be contempt written all over his features.

She was not wrong. The man seated behind the richly carved desk bore little resemblance to the laughing, gentle man she'd met only two days ago. Today, he was an aloof, icy stranger who was inspecting her family as if they were bugs crawling across his beautiful carpet. He did not even make a pretense at politeness by standing or by introducing them to the other two occupants of the room. Instead, he nodded curtly to Uncle Monty and her mother, indicating they should be seated in the chairs before his desk.

When his gaze finally shifted to Alexandra, however, his granite features softened and his eyes warmed, as if he understood how humiliated she felt. Coming around his desk, he drew up an additional chair especially for her. "Does the bruise cause you much pain, moppet?" he asked, studying the bluish mark upon her cheek.

Absurdly flattered by his courtesy and concern, Alexandra shook her head. "It's nothing, it doesn't hurt a bit," she said, immeasurably relieved because he didn't seem to hold *her* in aversion for invading his house in this brassy manner. Awkward in her mother's ill-fitting gown, Alexandra sat down on the edge of the chair. When she tried to wriggle demurely backward, the skirt of her gown caught on the velvet nap of the chair and the entire gown tightened until its neckline jerked at her throat and the high collar forced her chin up. Trapped like a rabbit in her own snare, Alexandra gazed helplessly up into the duke's inscrutable grey eyes. "Are you comfortable?" he asked, straight-faced.

"Quite comfortable, thank you," Alexandra lied, morbidly certain that he was aware of her predicament and was trying hard not to laugh.

"Perhaps if you stood up and sat down again?"

"I'm perfectly fine as I am."

The amusement she thought she'd glimpsed in his eyes vanished the moment he sat back down behind his desk. Looking from her mother to her Uncle Monty, he said without preamble, "You could have spared yourselves the embarrassment of this unnecessary visit. I had every intention of expressing my gratitude to Alexandra by means of a bank draft for £1,000, which would have been delivered to you next week."

Alexandra's mind reeled at the mention of such an enormous sum. Why, £1,000 would keep her entire household in relative luxury for at least two years. She'd have firewood to waste, if she wished, which of course she didn't . . .

"That won't be enough," Uncle Monty announced gruffly and Alexandra's head jerked around.

The duke's voice turned positively glacial. "How much do you want?" he demanded, his dagger gaze pinning poor Uncle Monty to his chair.

"We want what's fair," Uncle Monty said and cleared his throat. "Our Alexandra saved your life."

"For which I am prepared to pay handsomely. Now," he said, and each word had a bite, "how much do you want?"

Uncle Monty squirmed beneath the icy gaze leveled at him, but he persevered nonetheless. "Our Alexandra saved your life and, in return, you ruined hers."

The duke sounded ready to explode. "I did *what?*" he grated ominously.

"You took a young lady of good breeding to a public inn and cohabited in a bedroom with her."

"I took a child to a public inn," Jordan bit out. "An unconscious child who needed a doctor!"

"Now, see here, Hawthorne," Uncle Monty blustered in a surprisingly strong voice, "you took a *young lady* to that inn. You took her up to a bedroom with half the villagers looking on, and you carried her out thirty minutes later—fully conscious, her clothes in disarray, and without ever having summoned the leech. The villagers have a moral code, just like everybody else, and you publicly breached that code. Now, there's a huge scandalbroth over it."

"If the righteous citizens of your little backwater can make a scandal out of a child being carried into an inn, they need their minds laundered! Now, enough caviling over insignificant details, how much do you—"

"Insignificant details!" Mrs. Lawrence screeched furiously, leaning forward and clutching the edge of his desk so tightly her knuckles whitened. "Why, you—you vile, unprincipled lecher! Alexandra is seventeen and you've ruined her. Her fiancé's parents were there in the salon when you

51

carried her into our home, and they've already broken off marriage negotiations. You ought to be hanged! Hanging is too good for you—"

The duke seemed not to have heard the last of that; his head turned sharply to Alexandra and he studied her face as if he'd never seen her before. "How old are you?" he demanded as if her mother's word was not good enough.

Somehow Alexandra managed to drag her voice through the strangling mortification in her chest. This was all worse, much worse, than she'd dreamed it could be. "Seventeen. I—I will be eighteen next week," she said in a weak, apologetic voice, then she flushed as his gaze swept over her from the tip of her head to her small bosom, obviously unable to believe her dress concealed a woman fully grown. Driven to apologizing for her deceptively boyish shape, she added miserably, "Grandfather told me that all the women in our family bloom late, and I—" Realizing that what she was saying was inexcusably crude, not to mention irrelevant, Alexandra broke off, blushed furiously, and shot an anguished glance at the two unknown occupants of the room, hoping for some sort of understanding or forgiveness. She saw none. The man was watching her with a mixture of shock and amusement. The lady looked as if she were chiseled out of marble.

Alexandra's glance skidded from them back to the duke, and she saw that his expression had become positively savage. "Assuming that I made such a mistake," he said to Alexandra's mother, "what is it you want of me?"

"Since no decent man will marry Alexandra after what you've done, we expect *you* to marry her. Her birth is unexceptionable and we are connected with an earl and a knight. You can have no objection to her suitability."

Fury ignited in the duke's eyes. "No objection—" he thundered, then he bit back the rest of his words, clenching his jaw so tightly a muscle jerked in the side of his cheek. "And if I refuse?" he bit out.

"Then I shall bring you up on charges before the magistrates in London. Don't think I won't," Mrs. Lawrence cried.

"You won't do anything of the sort," he said with scathing certainty. "To bring me up on charges would only broadcast throughout London the very scandal you apparently find so damaging to Alexandra."

Pushed past the bounds of reason by his arrogant calm and the recollection of her own ill-use at her husband's hands, Mrs. Lawrence sprang from her chair, shaking with wrath. "Now you listen to me—I'll do exactly what I said I'd do. Alexandra is either going to have the respectability of your name, or she's going to be able to buy respectability with your money—every cent of it, if I have my way. Either way, we have nothing to lose. Do you understand me?" she nearly screamed. "I'll not let you take advantage of us and cast us off the way my husband did. You're a monster, just as he was. All men are monsters—selfish, unspeakable monsters . . ."

Jordan stared icily at the nearly demented woman standing before him, her eyes feverishly bright, her hands clenched into fists so tightly that blue veins stood out beneath her skin. She meant it, he realized. She was evidently so consumed with loathing for her husband that she would actually subject Alexandra to a public scandal, simply to get even with another man—himself.

"You kissed her," Mrs. Lawrence rasped in furious accusation. "You put your hands on her, she admitted it—"

"Mama, don't!" Alexandra cried, wrapping her arms around her middle and doubling over with shame or pain, Jordan wasn't certain which. "Don't, please don't do this," she whispered brokenly. "Don't do this to me."

Jordan looked at the child-woman who was huddled into a pitiful ball and could scarcely believe she was the same brave, laughing girl who had charged to his rescue two days ago.

"God knows what else you let him do—"

Jordan's palm crashed down on the desk with a force that exploded throughout the oak-paneled room. "Enough! he thundered in a murderous voice. "Sit down!" he commanded Mrs. Lawrence, and when she'd rigidly obeyed, Jordan got out of his chair. Stalking around his desk, he took Alexandra's arm in a none-too-gentle grasp and drew her out of her chair. "You come with me," he clipped. "I want to speak privately with you."

Mrs. Lawrence opened her mouth to object, but the old

duchess spoke at last, and when she did her voice dripped icicles. "Silence, Mrs. Lawrence! We have heard enough from you!"

Alexandra nearly had to run to keep up with the duke as he marched her across the drawing room, through the doorway, and down the hall to a small salon decorated in shades of lavender. Once inside, he let go of her arm, strode across the room to the windows, and shoved his hands into his pockets. The silence scraped against her raw nerves as he stared rigidly out across the lawns, his profile harsh, forbidding. She knew he was thinking hard for some way out of marrying her, and she also knew that beneath that tautly controlled facade of his there was a terrible, volcanic rage—a rage that was undoubtedly going to erupt against her at any moment. Shamed to the depths of her being, Alexandra waited helplessly, watching as he lifted one hand and massaged the taut muscles in his neck, his expression becoming darker and more ominous as each second ticked by.

He turned so abruptly that Alexandra took an automatic step backward. "Stop behaving like a frightened rabbit," he snapped. "I'm the one who's caught in a trap, not you."

A deadly calm settled over Alexandra, banishing everything but her shame. Her small chin lifted, her spine stiffened, and before his eyes Jordan saw her put up a valiant fight for control—a fight she won. She stood before him now, looking incongruously like a proud, boyish queen in refurbished rags, her eyes sparking like twin jewels. "I could not speak in the other room," she said with only a slight tremor in her voice, "because my mother would never have let me, but had you not asked to speak privately to me, I intended to ask to speak to you."

"Say what you have to say and have done with it."

Alexandra's chin lifted even higher at his chilling tone. Somehow she had let herself hope he would not treat her with the same brutal contempt he'd treated her family. "The idea of our marrying is ludicrous," she began.

"You're absolutely right," he snapped rudely.

"We're from two different worlds."

"Right again."

"You don't want to marry me."

54

"Another bull's-eye, Miss Lawrence," he announced in an insulting drawl.

"I don't want to marry you either," she retorted, humiliated to the core by every unkind word he said.

"That's very wise of you," he agreed caustically. "I'd make an exceedingly bad husband."

"Moreover, I do not wish to be anyone's wife. I wish to be a teacher, as my grandfather was, and to support myself."

"How extraordinary," he mocked sarcastically. "And all this while, I've been harboring the delusion that all girls yearn to snare wealthy husbands."

"I am not like other girls."

"I sensed that from the moment I met you."

Alexandra heard the insult in his smoothly worded agreement, and she almost choked on her chagrin. "Then it's settled. We won't wed."

"On the contrary," he said, and each word rang with bitter fury. "We have no choice, Miss Lawrence. That mother of yours will do exactly as she's threatened. She'll bring me up on public charges before the Court. In order to punish me, she'll destroy you."

"No, no!" Alexandra burst out. "She won't do it. You don't understand about my mother. She's—ill—she's never recovered from my papa's death." Unconsciously, she caught at the sleeve of his immaculately tailored grey jacket, her eyes imploring, her voice urgent. "You mustn't let them force you to marry me—you'll hate me forever for it, I know you will. The villagers will forget the scandal, you'll see. They'll forgive me and forget. It was all my fault for stupidly fainting so you had to take me to the inn. I never faint, you see, but I'd just killed a man and—"

"That's enough!" Jordan said harshly, and felt the noose of matrimony tighten inexorably around his neck. Until Alexandra began to speak, he had been searching madly for some means of escape from this dilemma—he had even been ready to seize on her assurance that her mother was likely bluffing. He had, in fact, been preparing to start listing all the reasons why she would hate being married to him—only he had not counted on her selflessly pleading with him not to sacrifice himself on the altar of matrimony for her sake. He had also managed, temporarily, to forget that she had killed a man to save his own life.

He stared down at the proud, pathetic child before him in her shabby gown. She had saved his life at the risk of her own, and in return he had effectively destroyed all her chances of getting a husband. With no husband to lighten her cares, she would be carrying the burden of that bizarre household on her thin shoulders for as long as she lived. He *had* inadvertently, but effectively, destroyed her future.

Impatiently, he pulled her hand away from his sleeve. "There's no way out of it for either of us," he clipped. "I'll arrange for a special license and we'll be married here within the week. Your mother and your uncle," he said with blistering contempt, "can stay at the local inn. I'll not shelter either of them under my roof."

That last comment caused Alexandra more shamed anguish than anything else he had said to her.

"I'll pay for their lodgings," he said shortly, misunderstanding the reason for her stricken expression.

"It isn't the expense!" she denied.

"Then what's bothering you?" he demanded impatiently.

"It's—" Alexandra turned her head, her gaze traveling desperately over the stultifying formality of the room. "It's *everything!* It's all wrong. This isn't the way I imagined being married." In her anxiety, she seized on the least of her worries. "I always thought I'd be married in a church in the village, with my best friend—Mary Ellen—to attend me, and all the—"

"Fine," he interrupted shortly. "Invite your friend here, if it will make you easier in the days before the wedding. Give her direction to the butler and I'll send a servant after her. You'll find writing materials in the drawer of that desk over there. You do know how to write, I presume?"

Alex's head jerked as if he had slapped her, and for one brief instant Jordan glimpsed the proud, spirited woman she would someday become. Her blue-green eyes snapped with disdain as she replied, "Yes, my lord, I know how to write."

Jordan stared at the scornful child who was regarding him down the length of her pert nose and felt a glimmer of amused respect that she would dare to look at him thus. "Good," he said curtly.

"—in three languages," she added with regal hauteur.

Jordan almost smiled.

When he left, Alexandra walked rigidly over to the small desk in the corner and sat down behind it. She pulled out a drawer and removed a writing sheet, quill, and inkpot. Too overwrought to concentrate on explaining her predicament, she wrote simply,

Dearest Mary Ellen, please accompany the bearer of this letter and come to me as soon as you may. Disaster has struck and I'm quite horribly desolate! My mother is here and so is Uncle Monty, so your mama needn't worry about your safety. Hurry, please. There isn't much time before I have to leave you—

Two tears welled in Alex's eyes, trembling on sooty black lashes, then they trickled down her cheeks. One by one, they fell in damp splotches onto the letter until she gave up the hopeless struggle and laid her head on her arms, her shoulders shaking with wrenching sobs.

"Something wonderful?" she whispered brokenly to God. "Is this Your idea of wonderful?"

Three-quarters of an hour later, Ramsey ushered a satisfied, if very subdued, Mrs. Lawrence and Sir Montague out of the house, leaving the dowager duchess alone with her two grandsons. The duchess arose slowly, her shoulders stiff as she turned to Jordan. "You cannot *seriously* mean to go through with this!" she announced.

"I intend to do exactly that."

Her face whitened at his words. "Why?" she demanded. "You can't expect me to believe you feel the slightest desire to marry that provincial little mouse."

"I don't."

"Then why in heaven's name are you going to do it?"

"Pity," he said with brutal frankness. "I pity her. And, like it or not, I'm also responsible for what happens to her. It's as simple as that."

"Then pay her off!"

Leaning back in his chair, Jordan wearily closed his eyes and shoved his hands in the pockets of his pants. " 'Pay her off,' " he repeated bitterly. "I wish to God I could, but I can't. She saved my life and, in return, I ruined her chances of having any sort of respectable life of her own. You heard what her mother said—her fiancé has already cried off because she's 'ruined.' As soon as she returns to the village, she'll be fair game for every lusting male. She'll have no respectability, no husband, no children. In a year or two, she'll be reduced to selling her favors at the same inn where I took her."

"Nonsense!" the dowager said stoutly. "If you pay her off, she can go somewhere else to live. Somewhere like London where the gossip won't follow her."

"In London, the most she could hope to be is some man's mistress, and that's assuming she could attract some wealthy old fool or foolish young fop to keep her. You saw her—she's hardly the sort of female to incite a man's lust."

"There is no need to be vulgar," the duchess said stiffly.

Jordan opened his eyes, his expression sardonic. "Frankly, I find it rather 'vulgar' to consider rewarding the chit for saving my life by consigning her to a life of glorified prostitution, which is what *you're* suggesting."

They regarded each other across the room, two fiercely indomitable wills clashing in silence. The duchess finally conceded defeat with an imperceptible inclination of her immaculately coiffed head. "As you wish, Hawthorne," she said, reluctantly yielding to his authority as the head of the family. Then another thought struck her and she sank into her chair, her face turning a grim, deathly white. "For seven hundred years, the bloodlines of this family have been unsullied. We are descendants of kings and emperors. Yet you mean for that utter nobody to produce the next heir." In supreme frustration, her grace turned her ire on her other grandson. "Don't just sit there, Anthony, say something!"

Lord Anthony Townsende leaned back in his chair, his expression wry. "Very well," he said amiably, accepting Jordan's decision with a fatalistic grin, "when am I going to be presented to my future cousin? Or do you intend to leave her in the salon until the wedding?"

The duchess shot him a killing glance, but she said nothing more. She sat quite still, her back ramrod straight, her white head high, but the bitter disappointment of the last hour had added a decade to her face.

Anthony glanced at Jordan and raised his glass in a gesture of a toast. "To your future wedded bliss, Hawk." He grinned.

Jordan shot him an ironic glance, but other than that, his features were perfectly composed. Anthony was not surprised at this lack of visible emotion. Like his grandmother, Jordan nearly always kept his emotions under rigid control, but unlike the duchess, Hawk did it effortlessly—so effortlessly that Tony and many others often wondered if he *felt* any really deep emotion other than anger.

In this instance, Tony was correct. Jordan was feeling nothing stronger than a certain grim, angry resignation toward his marriage. As he lifted his glass to his lips, Jordan contemplated with bitter amusement this unexpected twist of fate. After years of unrestrained wenching among England's most experienced, most sophisticated—and least virtuous—females, fortune had perversely saddled him for life with a child-bride who was the supreme, eternal ingénue. Every instinct he possessed warned him that Alexandra's lack of sophistication sprang not from mere inexperience, but rather from an ingenuous nobility of spirit and gentleness of heart.

At his hands, she would lose her physical innocence, but he doubted if she would ever lose her wide-eyed naiveté, nor would she acquire the smooth veneer of bored sophistication and droll wit that was as much a requirement for admission into the *ton* as were the right family connections.

It bothered him slightly that she would never be able to fit into his world, his life. It bothered him—but not much, for in truth he had no intention of spending much time with her in the years to come, nor did he intend to greatly alter his life-style. He would install her at his house in Devon and visit her there, he decided.

With a sigh, he realized that his mistress would have to be informed that she wasn't going to accompany him to Devon next week as planned. Thank God Elise was as sophisticated as she was beautiful and sensual; he would not have to endure a scene from her when he explained about the trip to Devon and his marriage.

"Well, when are we going to be properly presented to her?" Anthony repeated.

Reaching behind him, Jordan tugged on the bell cord. "Ramsey," he said, when the butler materialized in the doorway, "retrieve Miss Lawrence from the yellow salon and bring her here."

"Where are my mother and my Uncle Monty?" Alexandra asked a little frantically as soon as she entered the drawing room.

Jordan arose and came forward. "They have repaired to the local inn where they will remain in happy expectation of our forthcoming nuptials," he replied with unconcealed irony. "You, however, will remain here."

Before Alexandra could finish digesting all that, she was being introduced to the dowager duchess, who inspected her through a lorgnette. Humiliated past all endurance by the duchess' contemptuous appraisal, Alexandra lifted her chin and stared right back at the old woman.

"Do not stare at me in that rude, disrespectful fashion," the duchess snapped when she caught Alexandra's expression.

"Oh, was I being rude, ma'am?" Alexandra inquired with deceptive meekness. "I apologize, then. You see, I know it is rude to stare at someone. However, I am woefully ignorant of the etiquette involved when one is the *recipient* of the stare."

The duchess' lorgnette slid from her fingers and her eyes narrowed to slits. "How *dare* you lecture me! You are a nobody, a person without bloodlines or breeding or ancestry."

" 'It is certainly desirable to be well-descended,' " Alexandra quoted angrily, " 'but the glory belongs to our ancestors, not to us.' "

Anthony emitted a strangled, laughing sound and hastily interposed himself between his infuriated grandmother and the unwise child who had chosen to enter into verbal combat with her. "Plato, wasn't it?" he asked with a smile and extended his hand.

Alexandra shook her head, smiling timidly in the hope she'd found an ally in this den of unfriendly strangers. "Plutarch."

"I was close, anyway," he chuckled. "Since Jordan seems to be struck dumb, permit me to introduce myself. I'm Jordan's cousin, Tony."

Alexandra put her hand into his extended palm. "How do you do."

"Curtsy," the duchess ordered icily.

"Pardon?"

"A young lady curtsies when she is introduced to a person of superior age or rank."

Chapter Six

At DUSK the following evening, Alexandra was standing at the windows of her bedchamber, looking out across the drive, when she saw a stately coach drawing up, its lanterns twinkling in the dusky light. "Mary Ellen!" she breathed and ran from her room, hurrying down the long hall on the third floor.

Ramsey opened the door just as Mary Ellen erupted from the coach and ran up the front steps of the huge house, her long red hair streaming out behind her, her arms laden with oddly shaped parcels, the brim of her bonnet clutched in a fist. Skidding to a halt in the foyer, Mary Ellen curtsied to the astonished butler, whom she judged from his haughty demeanor to be An Important Personage, and then demanded in an agonized voice, "Please, milord, where is Alexandra? Is she still alive?"

When the butler merely gaped at her, Mary Ellen whirled around and confronted a footman, executed another curtsy, and then implored, "Where is Alexandra, sir? *Please* tell me!"

Alexandra plummeted down the staircase and into the foyer, throwing her arms around Mary Ellen, packages, bonnet, and all. "Mary Ellen!" she burst out joyously. "I'm so happy you've come—"

In the normal tomblike silence of the duchess' stately home, this noisy greeting ranked as an uproar and therefore drew not only three more servants into the foyer, but the dowager duchess and her eldest grandson as well.

In Morsham, Mary Ellen came from a simple, straightforward farm family which neither knew nor cared about refined manners, genteel behavior, or the opinions of their betters, whom they never came into contact with anyway. And so Mary Ellen was blessedly unaware of, and supremely unconcerned with, the fact that she was being judged on sight and found wanting by the inhabitants of Rosemeade, including the butler and footmen.

She cared naught for their opinions; all that mattered to her loyal heart was that Alexandra was apparently in some sort of trouble. "Oh, Alex!" Mary Ellen exclaimed in an agitated, disjointed rush. "I thought you were dying! And here you are looking almost as well as ever, except a little pale, which probably comes from inhabiting this *gloomy* house with these *gloomy* people." Scarcely pausing for breath, she continued anxiously, "Your note sounded so grim, and Mama was going to come too, but she couldn't, because my papa's not well again. And that dreadful coachman wouldn't tell me a *thing* about what was wrong with you, although I *pleaded* with him to do so. All he would do was look down his huge nose at me and say, 'I'm sure it isn't my place to know.' Now tell me at once before I burst! Why are you 'desolate' and what is the 'horrible disaster' you wrote about and—and whoever are these people!"

Behind them the duchess' voice snapped like a whip, "I believe Miss Lawrence is 'desolate' because she is about to be married to the owner of this 'gloomy' house, who happens to be my grandson."

Mary Ellen's mouth dropped open and she whirled on Alexandra. "Oh, no!" she wailed, her horrified gaze flying to Ramsey, whom she erroneously deduced from his fine black suit to be the owner of the house. "Alex, you aren't going to marry that man! I won't let you! Alex, he's *fat!*"

Seeing the electrified wrath which was beginning to emanate from his grandmother, Jordan cleared his throat from the doorway across the hall, where he had been observing the scene with mingled irritation and amusement. "Alexandra, perhaps your friend would like to be relieved of her parcels and then properly introduced?"

Alexandra jumped at the unexpected sound of his deep voice. "Yes. Yes, of course," she said hastily as Ramsey stepped forward and took a bundle from each of Mary

Ellen's arms. "Whatever is in that large one?" Alexandra asked in an underbreath as Ramsey turned and started down the hall.

"Remedies made from entrails and mold," Mary Ellen lied loudly, "which Mama made for whatever might have ailed you."

Ramsey's arm shot straight out, and both girls choked back their laughter, but Alexandra's amusement vanished as quickly as it had come. Grasping Mary Ellen's elbow and giving it a warning squeeze, she turned her friend around so they faced Jordan and his grandmother. Mary Ellen took one look at the duchess' granite features and took an alarmed step back, while Alexandra stumbled nervously through the introductions.

Ignoring Mary Ellen's stammered greeting, the duchess snapped a question at the girl: "Irish?" she demanded in an awful voice.

More confused than intimidated, Mary Ellen nodded.

"I should have expected that," her grace replied bitterly. "And Catholic, too, no doubt?"

Mary Ellen nodded again.

"Naturally." With a long-suffering look at Jordan, the duchess turned on her heel and marched into the salon—a queen unable to endure the offensive presence of such lowly, repulsive mortals.

Mary Ellen watched her leave, a perplexed expression on her pretty face as she peered after her, then she turned while Alex introduced the tall man as the Duke of Hawthorne.

Too thunderstruck to say a word to the man, Mary Ellen looked to Alex, her eyes wide. "A *duke?*" she whispered, ignoring the holder of that title, who was waiting for her curtsy.

Alexandra nodded, already realizing that having Mary Ellen come here had been impossibly unfair to the simple country girl.

"A real, genuine, honest-to-goodness *duke?*" Mary Ellen persisted in an underbreath, so intimidated she could not bear to look upon his face.

"The real thing," Jordan drawled dryly. "A real, genuine, honest-to-goodness duke. Now that we've all decided who I am, why don't we guess who you are?"

Flushing to the roots of her flaming red hair, Mary Ellen

curtsied, cleared her throat, and said, "Mary Ellen O'Toole, sir. My lord. Your highness." She curtsied again. "At your service, sir. Er—my lor—"

" 'Your grace' will do," Jordan interrupted.

"What?" Mary Ellen echoed blankly, her flush deepening.

"I'll explain upstairs," Alexandra whispered. Regathering her wits, she looked uncertainly at Jordan, who was looming in the doorway like a dark, giant god. Larger than life. Forbidding. Yet strangely compelling. "If you'll excuse us, your grace, I will take Mary Ellen upstairs."

"By all means," Jordan drawled, and Alexandra had the humiliating feeling that he found the pair of them as absurdly amusing as a pair of clumsy mongrel puppies tumbling about in a stableyard.

As they passed the salon, the duchess' voice rolled out like a muted clap of thunder: "Curtsy!" she snapped.

Both girls lurched around and curtsied in unison to the doorway of the salon.

"Is she demented?" Mary Ellen burst out the moment they had gained the privacy of Alexandra's bedchamber. Her eyes wide with fright and affront, she looked around the luxurious room as if she expected the duchess to materialize like an evil specter. "Does she always go about snapping single words at people—'Irish'? 'Catholic'? 'Curtsy'?" Mary Ellen mimicked.

"This is bedlam," Alexandra agreed, her spontaneous laugh choked off as her dire predicament reclaimed her thoughts. "And I'm marrying into it."

"But why?" Mary Ellen breathed, her open features a mask of alarm. "Alex, what has *happened* to you? Only four days ago, we were jousting and laughing together, and then you vanished, and now the whole village is talking about you. Mama says I mustn't pay any mind to anything I hear until we talk to you ourselves, but the squire's wife told Honor, who told me, that we mustn't ever speak to you again. We must cross the street if we see you coming and avoid you because you are soiled now."

Alexandra did not know it was possible to feel more alone and wretched than she already did, but this piece of news made her heart cry out in anguished protest. Everyone had believed the worst of her, after all. The people she had known since babyhood were willing to make her an outcast, without ever hearing her side of the story. Only Mary Ellen and her family believed in her enough to wait for explanations.

Sinking down on the gold coverlet, Alexandra raised her stricken eyes to her only friend. "I'll tell you what happened . . ."

For several long minutes after Alexandra finished explaining everything, Mary Ellen could only stare at her in amazed silence. Slowly though, Mary Ellen's blank expression faded and became more thoughtful, then it became positively luminous. "Alex!" Mary Ellen breathed, breaking into a broad smile as her mind conjured up a fresh vision of the tall man Alexandra was about to marry. "Your betrothed husband is not only a duke, he's positively gorgeous! He is—don't deny it. I thought so the moment I clapped eyes on him downstairs, only I was very distressed over you, and so I didn't really think about it."

Well aware of Mary Ellen's fascination with and for the opposite sex, Alexandra said a little self-consciously, "His appearance is—not entirely displeasing."

"Not displeasing?" Mary Ellen hooted in disbelief and plunked her hands on her hips, her eyes turning dreamy. "Why, I vow he's even better-looking than Henry Beechley, and Henry is the handsomest boy I know. Why, Henry quite takes away my breath!"

"Six months ago, you thought George Larson was the handsomest boy you knew," Alexandra pointed out, smiling. "And George took away your breath."

"Only because I hadn't really *looked* at Henry," replied Mary Ellen defensively.

"And six months before that, you thought Jack Sanders was the handsomest boy in the world and *he* took your breath away," Alexandra continued, her brows raised in amusement.

"But only because I hadn't really looked at George and Henry," replied Mary Ellen, genuinely bewildered by Alexandra's obvious amusement.

"I think," Alexandra teased, "your difficulty with breathing is the result of spending too much time sitting in one place, bent over romantic novels. I think they're ruining your eyesight and making every young man you see seem like a handsome, romantic hero."

Mary Ellen opened her mouth to vehemently protest this slur against her abiding love for dear Henry Beechley, then she changed her mind and smiled mischievously at Alexandra. "No doubt you are quite right," she said, sauntering over to the opposite side of the bed and sitting down. Sadly, she admitted, "Your duke is a man of barely passable looks."

"Barely passable!" Alexandra exclaimed defensively. "Why, his features are noble and manly and—and very nice!"

"Really?" Mary Ellen asked, hiding her laughter and pretending to study the tips of her short fingernails. "You don't find his hair too dark, or his face too tanned, or his eyes a very odd color?"

"They're grey! A beautiful, rare shade of grey!"

Looking directly into Alexandra's irate eyes, Mary Ellen said with sham innocence, "But surely, neither of us would go so far as to pretend he looks in any way like a Greek god?"

"Greek god, indeed," scoffed Alexandra. "I should say not."

"Then how *would* you describe him?" Mary Ellen said pointedly, unable to hide her amusement at her friend's obvious state of high infatuation any longer.

Alexandra's shoulders drooped as she admitted the truth: "Oh, Mary Ellen," she breathed in an awed, unhappy whisper, "he looks *exactly* like Michelangelo's David!"

Mary Ellen nodded sagely. "You're in love with him. Don't deny it. It's written all over your face when you speak of him. Now tell me," she said eagerly, scooting forward and peering at Alexandra closely, "what does it feel like to you—loving a man, I mean?"

"Well," Alexandra said, warming to her subject despite her strongest wish to be sensible, "it's the queerest sort of feeling, but exciting too. When I see him in the hall, I feel rather like I used to feel when I saw my papa's carriage draw up in the drive—you know, happy, but worried that I look a fright, and sad too, because I'm afraid he'll leave if I'm not amusing and just right, and then I'll lose him."

So eager was she to hear more about being in love that Mary Ellen spoke without thinking. "Don't be silly. How can he possible leave you if you are married to him?"

"Exactly like my papa left my mama."

Sympathy flickered in Mary Ellen's green eyes, but she brightened almost immediately. "Never mind about that. It is all in the past after all, and besides, in four more days you'll be eighteen and that definitely makes you a woman—"

"I don't feel like a woman!" Alexandra said miserably, finally putting into words all that had been worrying her since she first met the man who had stolen her heart within an hour after he first looked at her. "Mary Ellen, I don't know what to *say* to him. I was never the least bit interested in boys and now, when he's near, I haven't a clue what to say or do. Either I blurt out the first thing that comes to mind—and make a complete cake of myself—or else I lose my wits entirely and stand there like a piece of mutton. What should I do?" she implored.

Mary Ellen's eyes shone with pride. Alexandra was the acknowledged scholar of the village, but no one thought she was pretty. Mary Ellen, on the other hand, was the acknowledged village beauty, but no one thought she housed a brain between her ears. In fact, her own dear papa consistently called her his "lovely little corkbrain."

"What do you discuss with the boys who come calling on you at home?" Alexandra begged earnestly.

Mary Ellen furrowed her brow, valiantly trying to use the fine mind Alexandra was finally giving her credit for having. "Well," she said slowly, "I observed long ago that boys love to talk about themselves and the things that interest them." She brightened as the matter resolved itself completely. "All you have to do is ask a boy the right question and he'll talk you into distraction. There, it's as simple as that."

Alexandra threw up her hands in frustrated panic. "How could I *possibly* know what interests him and, besides, he isn't a boy at all, he's a man of twenty-seven."

"True," Mary Ellen admitted, "but my mama has often remarked that men, even my papa, are all just boys at heart. Therefore, my scheme will still work. To engage him in conversation, merely ask him about something that interests him."

"But I don't *know* what interests him!" Alexandra sighed.

Mary Ellen lapsed into silence, thinking heavily on the

problem. "I have it! He will be interested in much the same manly things as my papa speaks of. Ask him about—"

"About what?" Alexandra prodded, leaning forward in her eagerness when Mary Ellen seemed lost in thought.

Suddenly Mary Ellen snapped her fingers and beamed. "About bugs! Ask him how the crops on his estate are faring and if he's had problems with bugs! Bugs," she added informatively, "are an all-consuming interest of men who raise crops!"

Doubt wrinkled Alexandra's forehead into a thoughtful knot. "Insects don't seem a very pleasant topic."

"Oh, males don't enjoy pleasant or truly interesting topics at all. I mean if you try to tell them about a beautiful bonnet you saw in a shop window they positively wilt. And if you dare to discuss, at any length, the sort of gown you are longing to make someday, they are perfectly likely to doze off in the middle of your description of it!"

Alexandra stored this vital piece of information away, along with the advice about bugs.

"And do not, under any conditions," Mary Ellen warned severely, "discuss your fusty old Socrates and dull old Plato with him. Men despise a woman who is *too* smart. And another thing, Alex," Mary Ellen said, warming more and more to her subject. "You'll have to learn how to flirt."

Alexandra winced, but she knew better than to argue. Boys of all ages hung about Mary Ellen's skirts and cluttered up the family parlor, hoping for a moment with her; therefore, Mary Ellen's advice on the subject was definitely not to be taken lightly. "Very well," she said reluctantly, "how do I go about flirting?"

"Well, use your eyes, for one thing. You have excellent eyes."

"Use them to do what?"

"To look steadily into the eyes of the duke. And flutter your lashes a little to show how long they are—"

Alexandra experimentally "fluttered" her lashes, then collapsed onto the pillows, laughing. "I would look a perfect fool."

"Not to a man. They like that sort of thing."

Alexandra sobered and turned her head on the pillow to gaze thoughtfully at Mary Ellen. "You're quite certain?"

"Absolutely positive. And another thing—men like to know you like them. I mean, when you tell them they're oh so strong or brave or clever, they like that. It makes them feel special. Have you told the duke you love him?"

Silence.

"Have you?"

"Certainly not!"

"You should. Then he'll tell you he loves you!"

"Are you certain?"

"Of course."

Chapter Seven

I WON'T DO IT, I tell you," Alexandra burst out, her cheeks flushed with angry color. She glowered at the seamstresses who for three days and nights had been measuring, pinning, sighing, and cutting on the rainbow of fabrics which were now strewn about the room in various stages of becoming day dresses, riding habits, walking costumes, and dressing gowns. She felt like a stuffed mannikin who was permitted no feelings and no rest, whose only purpose was to stand still and be pinned, prodded, and poked, while the duchess looked on, criticizing Alexandra's every mannerism and movement.

For three entire days she had repeatedly asked to speak with her future husband, but the duke had been "otherwise occupied" or so Ramsey, the stony-faced butler, had continually informed her. Occasionally she had glimpsed him in the library talking with gentlemen until late in the afternoon. She and Mary Ellen were served their meals in Alexandra's room, while he apparently preferred the more interesting company of his grandmother. "Otherwise occupied," she had now concluded, obviously meant that he didn't wish to be bothered with her.

After three days of this, Alexandra was tense, irritable, and—much to her horror—very frightened. Her mother and Uncle Monty were as good as lost to her. Even though they were supposedly staying at an inn a few miles away, they were not permitted to call at Rosemeade. Life yawned before her, a lonely, gaping hole where she would be denied the companionship of her family and Mary Ellen and even the old servants who had been her friends since babyhood.

"This is a complete farce!" Alexandra said to Mary Ellen, stamping her foot in frustrated outrage and glaring at the seamstress who had just finished pinning the hem of the lemon-yellow muslin gown Alexandra was wearing.

"Stand still, young lady, and cease your theatrics," her grace snapped frigidly, walking into the room.

For three days the duchess hadn't spoken a single personal word to her, except to criticize, lecture, instruct, or command. "Theatrics—" Alexandra burst out, as rage swept through her, hot and satisfying. "If you think *that* was a theatric, wait until you hear the rest of what I have to say!" The duchess turned as if she intended to leave and, for Alexandra, that was the last straw. "I suggest you wait a moment and let me finish, ma'am."

The duchess turned then, lifting her aristocratic brows, waiting.

The sheer arrogance of her pose made Alexandra so angry that her voice shook. "Kindly tell your invisible grandson that the wedding is off, or, if he chooses to materialize, you may send him to me and *I'll* tell him so." Afraid she would burst into tears, which she knew the old woman would only mock, she ran from the room, along the balcony and down the staircase.

"What," asked the butler as he opened the front door for her, "shall I tell his grace—should he inquire as to your whereabouts?"

Pausing in her headlong flight, Alexandra looked Ramsey right in the eye and mimicked, "Tell him I'm 'otherwise occupied.'"

An hour later, as she wandered through the rose garden, her hysteria had cooled to a steely determination. Irritably, she bent and plucked a lovely pink rose and raised it to her nose, inhaling its scent, then she began absently snapping the petals off, one by one, her thoughts in a turmoil. Pink rose petals floated down about her skirts, joining those of the red roses, the white, and the yellow which she had also unconsciously shredded.

"Based on the message you left for me with Ramsey," said a deep, unperturbed voice behind her, "I gather you're displeased about something?"

Alexandra whirled in surprise, her relief at finally being able to speak to him eclipsed by the growing panic she'd been trying unsuccessfully to stifle for days. "I'm displeased about *everything.*"

His amused glance slid to the rose petals strewn about her skirts. "Including the roses, evidently," he observed, feeling slightly guilty for ignoring her these last several days.

Alexandra followed the direction of his gaze, flushed with embarrassment, and said with a mixture of distress and frustration, "The roses are beautiful, but—"

"—But you were bored with the way they looked when they had their petals on, is that it?"

Realizing that she was being drawn into a discussion about flowers when her entire life was in chaos, Alexandra drew herself up and said with quiet, implacable firmness, "Your grace, I am not going to marry you."

He shoved his hands into his pockets and regarded her with mild curiosity. "Really? Why not?"

Trying to think of the best way to explain, Alexandra ran a shaky hand through her dark curls and Jordan's gaze lifted, watching the unconscious grace of her gesture— really studying her for the first time. Sunlight glinted in her hair, gilding it with a golden sheen, and turned her magnificent eyes a luminous, turquoise green. The yellow of her gown flattered her creamy complexion and the peach tint glowing at her cheeks.

"Would you please," Alexandra said in a long-suffering voice, "stop looking at me in that peculiar, appraising way, as if you're trying to dissect my features and discover all my flaws?"

"Was I doing that?" Jordan asked absently, noting for the first time her high cheekbones and the soft fullness of her lips. As he gazed at that arresting, delicately carved face with its winged brows and long, sooty eyelashes, he couldn't imagine how he'd ever mistaken her for a lad.

"You're playing Pygmalion with my life, and I don't like it."

"I'm what?" Jordan demanded, his attention abruptly diverted from her fascinating face.

"In mythology, Pygmalion was—"

"I'm familiar with the myth, I'm merely surprised that a female would be familiar with the classics."

73

"You must have a very limited experience with my sex," Alexandra said, surprised. "My grandfather said most women are every bit as intelligent as men."

She saw his eyes take on the sudden gleam of suppressed laughter and assumed, mistakenly, that he was amused by her assessment of female intelligence rather than her remark about his inexperience with women. "Please stop treating me as if I haven't a wit in my head! Everyone in your house does that—even your servants are haughty and behave oddly to me."

"I'll instruct the butler to put wool in his ears and pretend to be deaf," Jordan teased, "and I'll order the footmen to wear blinders. Will that make you feel more at home?"

"Will you kindly take me seriously!"

Jordan sobered instantly at her imperious tone. "I'm going to marry you," he said coolly. "That's serious enough."

Now that she had decided not to marry him, and had told him so, the sharp pain of her decision was lessened a little by the discovery that she no longer felt intimidated and uncomfortable with him. "Do you realize," she said with a winsome smile as she tilted her head to the side, "that you become positively *grim* when you say the word 'marry'?" When he said nothing, Alexandra laid her hand on his sleeve, as if he was her friend, and gazed into his unfathomable grey eyes, seeing the cynicism lurking in their depths. "I don't mean to pry, your grace, but are you happy with life—with your life, I mean?"

He looked irritated by her question, but he answered it. "Not particularly."

"There you see! We would never suit. You're disenchanted with life, but I'm not." The quiet inner joy, the courage and indomitable spirit Jordan had sensed in her the night they met, was in her voice now as she lifted her face to the blue sky, her entire being radiant with optimism, innocence, and hope. "I love life, even when bad things happen to me. I can't stop loving it."

Transfixed, Jordan stared at her as she stood against a backdrop of vibrant roses and distant green hills—a pagan maiden addressing the heavens in a sweet, soft voice: "Every season of the year comes with a promise that something wonderful is going to happen to me someday.

I've had that feeling ever since my grandfather died. It's as if he's telling me to wait for it. In winter, the promise comes with the smell of snow in the air. In summer, I hear it in the boom of thunder and the lightning that streaks across the sky in blue flashes. Most of all, I feel it now, in springtime, when everything is green and black—"

Her voice trailed off and Jordan repeated blankly, "Black?"

"Yes, black—you know, like tree trunks when they're wet, and freshly tilled fields that smell like—" She inhaled, trying to recall the exact scent.

"Dirt," Jordan provided unromantically.

She dropped her gaze from the heavens and looked at him. "You think me foolish," she sighed. Stiffening her spine and ignoring the sharp stab of longing she felt for him, she said with calm dignity, "We cannot possibly wed."

Jordan's dark eyebrows drew together over incredulous grey eyes. "You've decided that, merely because I don't happen to think wet dirt smells like perfume?"

"You haven't understood a word I've said," Alexandra said desperately. "The fact of the matter is that if I marry you, you'll make me as unhappy as you are—and if you make me unhappy, I'll undoubtedly retaliate by making you unhappy, and in a few years, we'll both be as sour as your grandmother. Don't you dare laugh," she warned when his lips twitched.

Taking her arm, Jordan walked with her along the flagstone path that separated the rose beds and led to an arbor filled with trees decked out in spring blossoms. "You've failed to take one vital fact into consideration: From the moment I carried you into the inn, nothing in your life could ever be the same again. Even if your mother was only bluffing about putting us both through a public trial, your reputation is already destroyed." Stopping at the entrance to the arbor, he leaned against the trunk of an oak tree and said in a detached, impersonal voice, "I'm afraid you have no choice except to do me the honor of becoming my wife."

Alexandra chuckled, diverted by his ever-present, courteous formality, even now when she was bluntly refusing his hand in marriage. "Marrying an ordinary girl from Morsham is hardly an 'honor' for a duke," she reminded him with cheerful, artless candor, "and despite what you so

75

glibly said when we last parted, you are not my 'servant.' Why do you say those things to me?"

He grinned at her infectious merriment. "Habit," he admitted.

She tipped her head to the side, an enchanting, spirited girl with the wit and courage to spar with him. "Do you never say what you *really* mean?"

"Rarely."

Alex nodded sagely. "Apparently, speaking one's mind is a privilege reserved for what your grandmother disdainfully refers to as 'the lower classes.' Why do you always seem to be on the verge of laughing at me?"

"For some unfathomable reason," he replied in an amused drawl, "I like you."

"That's nice, but it isn't enough to base a marriage on," Alexandra persisted, returning to her original concern. "There are other, essential things like—" Her voice trailed off in horrified silence. *Like love,* she thought. Love was the only essential.

"Like what?"

Unable to choke out the word, Alexandra hastily looked away and shrugged noncommittally.

Love, Jordan silently filled in with a resigned sigh, longing to return to his interrupted meeting with his grandmother's bailiff. Alexandra wanted love and romance. He'd forgotten that even innocent, sheltered girls of her tender years would undoubtedly expect a little ardor from their affianced husbands. Adamantly unwilling to stand out here like a besotted fool and try to persuade her to marry him with tender words he didn't mean, he decided a kiss would be the quickest, most effective, and most expedient way to fulfill his duty and neutralize her misgivings, so that he could resume his meeting.

Alex jumped nervously when his hand suddenly lifted and cupped her cheek, forcing her to give up her embarrassed study of the entrance to the arbor.

"Look at me," he said in a low, velvety, unfamiliar voice that sent tingles of apprehensive excitement darting up her spine.

Alexandra dragged her eyes to his tanned face. Although no one had ever attempted to seduce or kiss her before, she took one look at the slumberous expression in his heavy-lidded eyes and *knew* something was in the wind. Instantly wary, she demanded without preamble: "What are you thinking?"

His fingers splayed sensuously across her cheek, and he smiled—a slow, lazy smile that made her heart leap into her throat. "I'm thinking about kissing you."

Alexandra's fevered imagination promptly ran away with itself as she recalled the novels she'd read. When kissed by the man they secretly loved, the heroines invariably swooned, or abandoned their virtue, or blurted out professions of undying love. Terrified that she would make just such a cake of herself, Alexandra gave her head an emphatic shake. "No, really," she croaked. "I—I don't think you should. Not just now. It's very nice of you to offer, but not just now. Perhaps another time when I—"

Ignoring her protests, and struggling to hide his amusement, Jordan put his fingertips beneath her chin and tilted her face up for his kiss.

He closed his eyes. Alexandra's opened wide. He lowered his head. She braced herself to be overcome with ardor. He touched his lips lightly to hers. And then it was over.

Jordan opened his eyes and looked at her to assess her reaction. It was *not* the naively rapturous one he expected to see. Alexandra's eyes were wide with bewilderment and—yes—*disappointment!*

Relieved that she hadn't made a fool of herself like the heroines of the novels, Alexandra wrinkled her small nose. "Is *that* all there is to kissing?" she asked the nobleman whose fiery kisses purportedly made maidens despise their virginity and married women forget their vows.

For a moment, Jordan didn't move; he studied her with heavy-lidded, speculative grey eyes. Suddenly Alexandra saw something exciting and alarming kindle in those silvery eyes. "No," he murmured, "there's more," and his hands encircled her arms, drawing her so close that her breasts almost touched his chest.

His conscience, which Jordan had assumed was long dead, chose that unlikely moment to suddenly assert itself after years of silence. *You are seducing a child, Hawthorne!* it warned in acid disgust. Jordan hesitated, more from surprise at the unexpected presence of that long-forgotten inner voice than from guilt at his actions. *You are deliberate-*

*ly seducing a gullible child into doing your bidding because
you don't want to bother taking the time to reason with her.*

"What are you thinking now?" Alexandra asked warily.

Several evasions occurred to him, but recalling that she'd
scorned polite platitudes, he decided to be truthful. "I'm
thinking that I'm committing the unforgivable act of seducing a child."

Alexandra, who was relieved rather than disappointed
that his kiss had not affected her, felt laughter bubble up
inside of her. "Seducing me?" she repeated with a merry
chuckle and shook her head, sending her curly hair into
fetching disarray. "Oh, no, you may put your mind at ease
on that score. I think I must be made of sterner stuff than
most females who swoon from a kiss and abandon their
virtue. I," she finished candidly, "was not at all affected by
our kiss. Not," she added charitably, "that I thought it was
gruesome, for it wasn't, I assure you. It was . . . quite nice."

"Thank you," Jordan said, straight-faced. "You're very
kind." Tucking her hand firmly into the crook of his arm, he
turned and led her a few steps into the arbor.

"Where are we going?" she inquired conversationally.

"Out of sight of the house," he replied dryly, stopping
beneath the branches of an apple tree covered with blossoms. "Chaste pecks are permissible between an engaged
couple in the rose garden; however, more passionate kissing
must be done with more discretion, in the arbor."

Alexandra, who was misled by the matter-of-fact tone of
this lecture, failed to instantly absorb the import of his
words. "It's amazing!" she said, laughing up at him. "There
are rules for absolutely everything amongst the nobility. Are
there books with all this written down?" But before he could
answer, she gasped, "K-kiss me passionately? Why?"

Jordan glanced toward the entrance of the arbor to make
certain they were private, then he turned the full seductive
force of his silver gaze and lazy smile on the girl standing
before him. "It's my vanity," he teased in a low voice. "It
chafes at the idea that you nearly dozed off in the middle of
my last kiss. Now, let's see if I can wake you up."

For the second time in minutes, Jordan's heretofore silent
conscience was outraged. It roared at him: *You bastard,
what do you think you're doing?*

But this time, Jason didn't hesitate for even a moment.

He already knew *exactly* what he was doing. "Now then," he said, smiling reassuringly into her enormous blue-green eyes as he matched his actions to his words, "a kiss is a thing to be shared. I'll put my hands on your arms, thus, and draw you close."

Puzzled by so much fuss over a kiss, Alexandra glanced down at the strong, long fingers gently imprisoning her upper arms, then at the front of his fine white shirt, before she finally raised her embarrassed gaze to his. "Where do my hands go?"

Jordan squelched his shout of laughter, as well as the suggestive reply that automatically sprang to his lips. "Where would you like to put them?" he asked instead.

"In my pockets?" Alexandra suggested hopefully.

Jordan, who suddenly felt more in the mood for a hearty laugh than a seduction, was nevertheless determined to continue. "The point I was trying to make," he explained mildly, "is that it's perfectly all right for you to touch me."

I don't want to, she thought frantically.

You will, he silently promised with an inner smile, correctly interpreting her mutinous expression. Tipping her chin up, he gazed into those wide, luminous eyes of hers, and tenderness began to unfold within him—a sensation that had been as foreign to him as the voice of his conscience until he met this unspoiled, unpredictable, artless child-woman. He felt, for the moment, as if he was gazing into the eyes of an angel, and he touched her smooth cheek with unconscious reverence. "Have you any idea," he murmured softly, "how enchanting you are—and how rare?"

The words he spoke, combined with the touch of his fingertips against her cheek, and the deep, compelling timbre of his voice, had the seductive impact Alexandra had dreaded his kiss would have. She felt as if she were beginning to melt and float inside. She couldn't pull her gaze from his hypnotic grey eyes; she didn't want to try. Without realizing what she was doing, she raised her shaking fingertips to his hard jaw, touching his cheek as he was touching hers. "I think," she whispered achingly, "that you are beautiful."

"Alexandra—" The softly spoken word contained a poignant tenderness she hadn't heard in his voice before, and it made her want to tell him everything in her heart. Unaware of the stimulating effect of her caressing fingers and candid turquoise eyes, she continued in the same aching voice, "I think you are as beautiful as Michelangelo's David—"

"Don't—" he whispered achingly, and his lips took hers in a kiss that was nothing at all like the first one. His mouth slanted over hers with fierce tenderness, while his hand curved around her nape, his fingers stroking her sensitive skin, and as his other arm encircled her waist, moving her tightly to him. Lost in a sea of pure sensation as his lips tasted and courted hers, Alexandra slid her hands up his hard chest and wrapped her arms around his neck, clinging to him for support, innocently and unconsciously molding her body to his length. The moment she did, the seducer became the seduced: Desire exploded in Jordan's body, and the girl in his arms became an enticing woman. Automatically, he deepened the kiss, his mouth moving with hungry, persuasive insistence on hers, while Alexandra clung tighter to him, sliding her fingers into the crisp hair above his collar, her entire body racked with jolt after jolt of wild pleasure. He kissed her long and lingeringly, then he touched his tongue to her trembling lips, coaxing them to part, insisting, and when they did, his tongue slid between them, filling her mouth. His hand shifted from her back to her midriff, sliding upward toward her breasts.

Whether from fear or desire, Alexandra moaned softly, and the sound somehow penetrated his aroused senses, dousing his desire and dragging him reluctantly back to reality.

Jordan dropped his hands to her narrow waist and raised his head, staring down into her intoxicating young face, unable to believe the passion she had unexpectedly evoked in him.

Dizzy with love and desire, Alexandra felt the heavy thudding of his heart beneath her hand. Gazing up at the firm sensual mouth which had gently, and then fiercely, explored hers, she raised her eyes to his smoldering grey ones.

And she knew.

Something Wonderful had happened. This magnificent,

handsome, complicated, sophisticated man was her promised gift from fate. He was hers to love.

Bravely ignoring the painful memories of her equally complicated, handsome, sophisticated father's treatment, Alexandra accepted fate's gift with all the humble gratitude in her bursting heart. Unaware that sanity had returned to Jordan and the expression in his eyes had changed from desire to irritation, Alexandra raised her shining eyes to his. Quietly, without emphasis or shame, she softly said, "I love you."

Jordan had been expecting something like that the moment she raised her eyes to his. "Thank you," he said, trying to pass her statement off as a casual compliment rather than an avowal he did not want to hear. Mentally he shook his head at how incredibly, disarmingly romantic she was. And how naive. What she felt, he knew, was desire. Nothing more. There was no such thing as love—there were only varying degrees of desire, which romantic women and foolish men called "love."

He knew he ought to end her infatuation with him right now by telling her bluntly that his own feelings did not match hers and, moreover, that he did not want her to feel as she did about him. That was what he *wanted* to do. However, his conscience, which was suddenly making a damned nuisance of itself after a silence of decades, would not let him wound her. Even he, callous and cynical and impatient with this nonsense as he now felt, was not callous enough, or cynical enough to deliberately hurt a child who was looking at him with the adoration of a puppy.

So much did she remind him of a puppy that he reacted automatically and, reaching out, he rumpled her thick, silky hair. With smiling gravity, he said, "You will spoil me with so much flattery," then he glanced toward the house, impatient to return to his work. "I have to finish going over my grandmother's accounts this afternoon and tonight," he said abruptly. "I'll see you in the morning."

Alexandra nodded and watched him walk out of the arbor. In the morning, she would be his wife. He had not reacted at all as she'd hoped he would, when she told him she loved him, but it didn't matter. Not then. Then she had enough love bursting into bloom in her heart to sustain her.

"Alex?" Mary Ellen rushed into the arbor, her face alive with eager curiosity. "I watched from the windows. You were in here ever so long. Did he kiss you?"

Alexandra sank down on a white, ornamental iron bench beneath a plum tree and chuckled at her friend's avid expression. "Yes."

Mary Ellen eagerly sat down beside her. "And did you tell him you love him?"

"Yes."

"What did he do?" she demanded gleefully. "What did he say?"

Alexandra shot her a rueful smile. "He said, 'thank you.'"

Firelight danced gaily in the hearth, banishing the chill of a spring night and casting shadows that cavorted and bobbed on the walls like sprites at an autumn festival. Propped against a pile of pillows in her huge bed, Alexandra watched the entertainment, her expression pensive. Tomorrow was her wedding day.

Drawing her knees up, she wrapped her arms around her legs, staring into the fire. Despite her thrilling discovery that she had fallen in love with her husband-to-be, she was not foolish enough to think she understood him, nor was she naive enough to believe she knew how to make him happy.

She was certain of only two things: She wanted to make him happy and somehow, some way, she would discover the means to do it. The awesome weight of that responsibility was heavy on her mind, and she wished devoutly she had a better notion of what being the wife of a nobleman entailed.

Her knowledge of marriage was limited and not very helpful. Her own father had been like a charming, elegant, eagerly awaited stranger who, when he deigned to visit them, was greeted with eager adoration by his wife and daughter.

Propping her chin on her knees, Alexandra remembered with a pang of pain how she and her mother had fussed over him for as long as he remained, hanging on to his words and following him around, as eager to please him as if he were a god and they his willing worshipers. Humiliation shot through her when she imagined how dull and provincial and gullible she and her mother must have seemed to him. How he must have laughed at their eager adoration!

With brave determination, Alexandra shifted her thoughts to her own marriage. She was quite certain the duke wouldn't like being treated by his wife with the extreme deference her own mother had shown her father. His grace seemed to enjoy it when she spoke her mind, even if she said something outrageous. Sometimes, she could make him laugh out loud. But how to go on for the next forty years with him?

The only other marriages she had witnessed firsthand were peasant marriages, and in those marriages the wife cooked and cleaned and sewed for her husband. The idea of doing those things for the duke filled her with quiet longing, even while she knew the notion was sheer foolish sentimentality. This house was crawling with servants who anticipated the occupants' needs in advance and took steps to make certain their every wish was carried out almost before they thought of it.

With an audible sigh, Alexandra accepted the fact that the Duke of Hawthorne didn't need her to look after his needs in the way ordinary country-bred wives looked after their husbands'. Even so, she couldn't help conjuring up a wonderful vision of herself, seated across from him in a chair before the fire, her fingers nimbly adding stitches to one of his snowy white shirts. Wistfully, she imagined the look of gratitude and pleasure on his ruggedly handsome face as he watched her mend his shirt. How grateful he would be . . .

A smothered laugh escaped her as she reconsidered her utter lack of talent with a needle. If she didn't prick her finger and bleed all over his shirt, she would surely sew the armhole closed or something equally disastrous. The picture of cozy marital bliss faded and her expression became determined.

Every instinct she possessed told her that the duke was a highly complex man, and she hated her youthful inexperience. On the other hand, she was not a featherbrain, despite the fact that his grace seemed to regard her as an amusing child. When necessary, she could draw on a wealth of common sense and practicality. Hadn't she managed to

hold her household together from the time she was fourteen?

Now she had a new challenge ahead of her. She needed to
make herself fit to be the Duke of Hawthorne's wife. His
grandmother had already, in the last several days, made a
hundred critical remarks about Alexandra's manners and
mannerisms, and although Alex had bridled over what
seemed to her be an excessive emphasis on superficial
matters of conduct and convention, she secretly intended to
learn everything she needed to know. She would make
certain her husband never had reason to be ashamed of her.

My husband, Alexandra thought as she snuggled down
into the pillows. That huge, handsome, elegant aristocrat
was going to be her husband . . .

Chapter Eight

*L*OUNGING IN A big wingback chair the next morning, Anthony studied his cousin with a combination of admiration and disbelief. "Hawk," he chuckled, "I swear to God, what everyone says about you is true—you *don't* have a nerve in your entire body. This is your wedding day, and *I'm* more nervous about it than you are."

Partially dressed in a frilled white shirt, black trousers, and a silver-brocade waistcoat, Jordan was simultaneously carrying on a last-minute meeting with his grandmother's estate manager and pacing slowly back and forth across his bedchamber, glancing over a report on one of his business ventures. One step behind him, his beleaguered valet followed doggedly in his wake, smoothing a tiny wrinkle from his finely tailored shirt and brushing microscopic specks of lint from the legs of his trousers.

"Hold still, Jordan," Tony said, laughing with sympathy for the valet. "Poor Mathison is going to drop dead in his tracks from exhaustion."

"Hmm?" Jordan paused to glance inquiringly at Tony, and the stalwart valet seized his chance, snatched up a splendidly tailored black jacket, and held it up so Jordan had little choice but to slide his arms into the sleeves.

"Do you mind telling me how you can be so damned nonchalant about your own marriage? You *are* aware that you're getting married in fifteen minutes, aren't you?"

Dismissing the estate manager with a nod, Jordan laid aside the report he was reading, and finally shrugged into the jacket Mathison was still holding out to him, then he turned to the mirror and ran a hand over his jaw to verify the closeness of his shave. "I don't think of it as getting married," he said dryly. "I think of it as adopting a child."

Anthony smiled at the joke and Jordan continued more seriously, "Alexandra will make no demands on my life, nor will my marriage to her require any real changes. After stopping in London to see Elise, I'll take Alexandra down to Portsmouth and we'll sail along the coast so that I can see how the new passenger ship we've designed handles, then I'll drop her off at my house in Devon. She'll like Devon. The house there isn't so large as to completely overwhelm her. Naturally, I'll return there to see her from time to time."

"Naturally," Anthony said wryly.

Without bothering to answer that, Jordan picked up the report he'd been reading and continued scanning it.

"Your beauteous ballerina is not going to like this, Hawk," Tony put in after a few minutes.

"She'll be reasonable," Jordan said absently.

"So!" the duchess said tautly, sweeping into the room wearing an elegant brown satin gown trimmed in cream lace. "You truly mean to go through with this mockery of a marriage. You actually intend to try to pass that countrified chit off on Society as a young lady of breeding and culture."

"On the contrary," Jordan said blandly. "I mean to install her in Devon and leave the last part of that to *you*. There's no rush, however. Take a year or two to teach her what she needs to know in order to take her place as my duchess."

"I couldn't accomplish that feat in a *decade*," his grandmother snapped.

Until then, he had tolerated her objections without rancor, but that remark seemed to push him too far, and his voice took on the cutting edge that intimidated servants and socialites alike. "How difficult can it be to teach an intelligent girl to act like a vapid, vain henwit!"

The indomitable old woman maintained her stony dignity, but she studied her grandson's steely features with something akin to surprise. "That is how you see females of your own class, then? Vapid and vain?"

"No," Jordan said curtly. "That is how I see them when

they are Alexandra's age. Later, most of them become much less appealing."

Like your mother, she thought.

Like my mother, he thought.

"That is not true of all females."

"No," Jordan agreed without conviction or interest. "Possibly not."

The grooming and dressing preparations for her wedding had taken Alexandra and two maids three hours. The wedding took less than ten minutes.

An hour later, self-consciously holding a crystal glass of bubbling golden champagne in her hand, Alexandra stood alone with her groom in the center of the huge blue and gold salon, as Jordan poured champagne for himself.

Despite her determination to ignore it, her wedding had a distinct aura of unreality, of strain. Her mother and Uncle Monty had attended and been barely tolerated by the duke and his grandmother, even though Uncle Monty was on his very best behavior and had scrupulously refrained from eyeing the derrière of any female in the room, even the duchess'. Lord Anthony Townsende and Mary Ellen had also been here, but now everyone was already on the way home.

Surrounded by the stifling elegance of the gilt salon and garbed in Jordan's mother's fabulous wedding gown of ivory satin encrusted with pearls, Alex felt more like an interloper than she had at any time since coming to Rosemeade. The feeling that she was a trespasser, who had invaded a world where she was no more welcome than her relatives, was nearly choking her.

It was odd that she felt so insecure and uneasy now, Alexandra mused, for she was wearing a gown more glorious than any she had ever imagined, and she looked far prettier than she had ever believed she could. Craddock, the duchess' dresser, had personally supervised Alexandra's toilette this morning. Under her exacting ministrations, Alexandra's riotous curls had been brushed until they gleamed, then swept into a mass at the crown and held in place at the sides with a beautiful pair of pearl combs that matched the pearls at her small ears.

Alexandra had looked at her reflection in the full-length

mirror in her room and been privately overjoyed. Even Craddock had stood back and announced that she looked "very well indeed, considering—" But Jordan had said nothing about her appearance. He had smiled reassuringly at her when Uncle Monty placed her hand in his, and that had been enough to sustain her during the hour since the ceremony had taken place. Now, however, they were alone together as husband and wife for the first time, and the only sound was that of servants carrying their heavy trunks down the stairs and out to the traveling chaise, where they were being loaded for the wedding journey.

Uncertain of what to do with the champagne, Alexandra chose the path of least resistance and drank some of it, then she put it down on an elaborately carved gilt table.

When she turned, Jordan was studying her as if seeing her for the first time. Not once all morning had he commented on her appearance, but now, as his gaze drifted from the top of her shining hair to the hem of her gleaming satin gown, she sensed that he was finally going to comment, and she held her breath expectantly.

"You're taller than I originally thought."

The unexpected observation, added to his genuinely puzzled expression, wrung a startled laugh from Alexandra. "I don't think I've grown more than a few inches in the last week."

He smiled absently at her quip and then continued thoughtfully, "In the beginning, I mistook you for a boy, and you would be small for a boy."

Determined to inject gaiety into their relationship at every possible opportunity from this day forward, Alexandra said teasingly, "I am not, however, a boy."

Despite his intention to treat her impersonally after yesterday's kiss, Jordan was not proof against her sunny, entrancing smile. It even dispelled the gloom of his marriage ceremony from his heart. "You are not a boy," he agreed, smiling back at her. "Nor are you a young girl exactly. But then, neither are you a woman."

"I seem to be at an awkward age, don't I?" she agreed, her eyes aglow with gentle mockery of his fixation with her age.

"Evidently," he chuckled. "How do you describe a young lady who is not quite eighteen?"

"I am already eighteen," Alexandra said seriously. "Today is my birthday."

"I had no idea today was your birthday," he said, truly apologetic. "I'll buy you a present on our trip. What do girls your age like?"

"We like not to be constantly reminded of our extreme youth," Alexandra said lightly, but with a meaningful look.

Jordan's sharp bark of laughter echoed throughout the salon. "God, you have a quick wit. Amazing in one so youn—so pretty," he corrected swiftly. "I apologize once again—for teasing you about your age *and* for forgetting the matter of a present."

"I greatly fear that, like it or not, *you* were my birthday present."

"What a way to phrase it," he chuckled.

Alexandra glanced at the clock; it was less than a half hour before Jordan had said he wished to be off for their ship. "I'd better go upstairs and change my gown," she said.

"Where has my grandmother gone?" he asked as she started to leave.

"I believe she has taken to her bed, prostrate with grief over your unfortunate marriage," Alexandra said with a lame attempt at humor. More seriously, she added, "Will she be all right, do you think?"

"It would take more than our marriage to send her to her couch calling for her hartshorn," Jordan said with what sounded very much like fondness and admiration. "My grandmother could take on Napoleon himself and emerge victorious from the encounter. When she was through with him, he'd be plumping up her pillows and begging her pardon for his bad manners in making war on us. A little thing like my 'unfortunate marriage' won't send her into a decline, believe me. And now that you bear my name, she will flay anyone alive who dares to cast aspersions on you."

A half hour later, clad in the cherry traveling costume the dressmakers had designed for her, Alexandra climbed into a shiny black-lacquered coach with Jordan's ducal seal emblazoned in silver upon the door, and settled back against incredibly luxurious grey velvet squabs. The coachman put up the stairs and closed the door, and with scarcely any sensation of motion, the well-sprung traveling chaise glided down the long drive behind four prancing bays, escorted by six liveried outriders.

Alexandra glanced about her, admiring the heavy silver handles at the doors and the crystal-and-silver lamps. Luxuriating in the unexpected comfort of the spacious conveyance, she tried to believe she was really married, really leaving on her wedding trip. Across from her, Jordan stretched his legs out, crossed them at the ankles, and stared out the window, lapsing into a comfortable silence.

He had changed for the trip, and Alex quietly admired the way his tight-fitting biscuit breeches and shiny brown boots emphasized his long, muscular legs. His cream shirt was open at the neck, displaying a glimpse of tanned throat, and his coffee-colored jacket set off his powerful shoulders to wonderful advantage. She uttered a silent prayer that some-day he might find her as pleasing to look at as she found him, then she decided that some form of pleasant conversation might be in order.

"Your mother's wedding gown was very beautiful," she ventured softly. "I was worried that some harm might come to it, but nothing happened."

He flicked a glance in her direction. "You needn't have worried," he said dryly. "I'm certain you are far more worthy of that symbol of chaste purity than my mother was when she wore it."

"Oh," Alexandra said, aware that she had just been complimented, though in the context the compliment was given, "thank you" seemed highly inappropriate.

When he made no attempt to converse further with her, Alexandra sensed that he was grappling with some sort of weighty problem, and she let the silence continue, content to watch the lush, rolling landscape pass the windows.

At three o'clock in the afternoon, they finally stopped for dinner at a large, rambling inn with ivy covering its mel-lowed brick exterior and a neat, white fence enclosing its huge yard.

One of the outriders had obviously been sent ahead, because both the innkeeper and his wife greeted them and then promptly ushered them through the common rooms, into a cozy private dining parlor where a sumptuous meal in covered trays was already laid out.

"You were hungry," her husband remarked later, as she laid her knife and fork down and sighed with relief.

"Starved," Alexandra agreed. "My stomach is not yet accustomed to the town hours you keep at Rosemeade. When you are eating your supper at ten o'clock, I am normally in bed."

"We'll be stopping for the night about eight o'clock, so you won't have to wait as long as that for your next meal," he volunteered politely.

When he seemed to want to linger over his wine, Alexandra asked, "Would you mind very much if I waited for you outside? I'd love to walk around a bit before we get into the coach again."

"Fine. I'll join you in a few minutes."

Alexandra strolled outside, enjoying the sunshine beneath the steady, watchful eye of Jordan's coachman. Two more coaches pulled into the innyard, both of them handsome and shiny, but not nearly so magnificent as her husband's wonderful traveling chaise with its silver seal and shiny silver harnesses on the horses. Hostlers ran forward to take charge of the horses, and for a few moments Alexandra simply watched, savoring each sight.

Jordan's horses were being put to when Alexandra noticed a young boy crouched on his haunches near the corner of the fence, apparently speaking to the ground. Curious, she wandered over, then smiled when she saw that he was talking to a litter of frolicking, long-haired puppies.

"How cute they are!" she exclaimed. The puppies' heads and front legs were white, their hindquarters brown.

"Would yer like t'buy one?" the boy said eagerly. "I could let yer have th' pick o' the litter fer a good price. They be pure bred."

"What kind are they?" Alexandra asked, laughing delightedly when the smallest of the balls of white and brown fluff detached itself from the others, scampered over to her, and clamped its tiny teeth onto the hem of her skirt, tugging playfully at it.

"Fine English sheepdogs," the boy provided, as Alexandra bent down to separate the puppy from her hem. "Very smart, they be."

The moment her hands touched the thick, silky fur, Alexandra was enchanted. Long ago she'd had a collie, but

91

after her father died, food had been too precious to waste on any animal that didn't earn its keep, and she'd given her collie to Mary Ellen's brother. Scooping the puppy up, she held it at eye level while its tiny legs flailed the air and a small pink tongue eagerly licked her hand. She was still holding the puppy, discussing its merits with its enthusiastic owner when her husband came up behind her and said, "It's time to leave."

Alexandra never considered asking her new husband to let her have the puppy, but the unconscious appeal was there in the large eyes and soft smile she turned up to him. "I had a collie once, a long time ago."

"Did you?" he asked noncommittally.

Alexandra nodded, put the puppy on the ground, patted it, and smiled at the boy. "Good luck finding homes for them," she said.

She had not taken three steps before she felt a tug on the back hem of her skirt. She turned, and the puppy she'd been holding let go of her skirt and sat down, its pink tongue lolling, its expression comically worshipful.

"She likes me," Alexandra explained helplessly, laughing. Bending down, she turned the puppy back toward the litter and patted its backside, urging it to go back to the boy. The puppy stubbornly refused to budge. Left with no other choice, Alexandra cast an affectionate, apologetic smile at the small ball of fur, then she turned her back on it, and let Jordan escort her to the coach.

After pausing to issue instructions to his driver, he climbed in and sat down beside her. A few minutes later they were off.

"This stretch of road must be much less smooth than it was to the north," she remarked a little nervously an hour later as the heavy traveling chaise again swayed sharply, pitched to the left, then righted itself and continued on.

Sitting across from her with his arms folded imperturbably across his chest and his legs stretched out, Jordan said, "It isn't."

"Then why is the coach lurching and swaying like this?" she asked a few minutes later when it happened again. Before Jordan could answer, she heard their coachman shout "Whoa" to the team and pull over to the side of the road.

Alexandra peered out the window into the woods alongside the road. A moment later the door of the coach was pulled open and a harassed, apologetic coachman's face appeared. "Your grace," he said contritely, "I can't handle the horses and keep control of this perpetual-motion machine at the same time. I nearly put us into a ditch back there."

The "perpetual-motion machine," which he was holding in the crook of his right arm, was a squirming ball of brown-and-white fur.

Jordan sighed and nodded. "Very well, Grimm, put the animal in here. No, take it for a walk first."

"I'll do it," Alexandra volunteered, and Jordan climbed out of the coach, too, walking with her into a little clearing in the woods beside the road. Turning, Alexandra lifted her shining eyes to her husband's amused grey ones. "I think you must be the very kindest of men," she whispered.

"Happy birthday," he said with a resigned sigh.

"Thank you—so much," she said, her heart swelling with gratitude because it was perfectly obvious he had a low opinion of the gift she'd wanted so much. "The puppy won't be a bit of trouble, you'll see."

Jordan directed a dubious look at the puppy, who was now sniffing every inch of ground it could put its nose to, its stubby tail wagging excitedly. Abruptly it seized a twig and began tearing at it.

"The boy told me she's very smart."

"Mongrels frequently are."

"Oh, but she isn't a mongrel," Alexandra said, bending down to pluck some of the pink wildflowers blooming at her feet. "She's an English sheepdog."

"A what!" Jordan demanded, thunderstruck.

"An English sheepdog," Alexandra explained, thinking his surprise sprang from a lack of knowledge about the breed. "They're very smart and they don't grow very large." When he stared at her as if she'd taken complete leave of her senses, Alexandra added, "That nice young boy told me all that about her."

"That nice, young *honest* boy?" Jordan asked sardonically. "The same one who told you this is a pureblood?"

"Yes, of course," Alexandra said, tipping her head to the side and wondering about his tone. "The very same."

"Then let's hope he also lied about its pedigree."

"Did he lie to me?"

"Through his teeth," Jordan averred grimly. "If that dog *is* an English sheepdog, it will be the size of a large pony with paws the size of saucers. Let's hope its father was actually a small terrier."

He looked so disgusted that Alexandra turned quickly away to hide a smile and knelt to pick up the puppy.

The skirt of her cherry traveling dress created a bright circular splash of color against a carpet of mossy-green grass as she knelt down, scooping the wriggling puppy into her arms, holding the pink wildflowers she'd picked in her free hand. Jordan looked at the child-woman he had married, watching the breeze tease her hair, blowing mahogany curls against her alabaster cheek as she knelt in the clearing, holding a puppy in her arms and flowers in her hand. Dappled sunlight filtered through the trees above, surrounding her in a halo of light. "You look like a Gainsborough portrait," he said softly.

Mesmerized by the husky sound of his voice and the strange, almost reverent intensity in his grey eyes, Alexandra slowly stood up. "I'm not very pretty."

"Aren't you?" There was a smile in his voice.

"I wish I were, but I fear I'm going to be very ordinary."

A slow, reluctant smile tugged at his sensual lips and he slowly shook his head. "There is nothing 'ordinary' about you, Alexandra," Jordan replied. His decision to stay away from her, until she was a few years older and able to play the game of romance by his rules, was suddenly overpowered by a compelling need to feel those soft lips beneath his. Just one more time.

As he walked slowly, purposefully toward her, Alexandra's heart began to hammer in expectation of the kiss she sensed he was going to give her. Already, she was learning what it meant when his eyes turned sultry and his voice became low and husky.

Cradling her face between his palms, Jordan threaded his fingers through her dark curls. Her cheeks felt like satin, and her hair was crushed silk in his hands as he tipped her head up. With infinite tenderness, he took her lips, telling himself he was a thousand kinds of madman for what he was doing, but when her lips softened and responded to his, he ignored the warning. Intending to deepen the kiss, he started to put his arms around her, but the puppy she was holding let out a sharp, indignant bark of protest and he abruptly pulled back.

Alexandra was still trying to suppress her disappointment over his abbreviated kiss when she climbed into the coach.

Jordan, however, was vastly relieved that one kiss hadn't led to another, which in turn would have undoubtedly led to another declaration of love from the romantic girl he'd married. He didn't think "thank you" would satisfy her as a reply the second time, and he didn't want to crush her with silence or shatter her with a lecture. He would wait a year or two to take her to bed, he decided firmly—wait until she'd been out in Society and would be more realistic in her expectations for their marriage.

The decision made and reinforced by his experience in the woods, his mood lightened tremendously. "Have you thought of a name for it?" he asked when the coach was again moving smoothly ahead.

He was eyeing the puppy, who was busily sniffing about the floor, happily exploring its new surroundings.

Alexandra looked fondly at the soft white ball of fur. "What do you think of Buttercup?"

He rolled his eyes in masculine disgust.

"Daisy?"

"You must be joking."

"Petunia?"

His eyes gleamed with laughter. "He won't be able to hold up his head among the other dogs."

Alexandra stared blankly at him. "The boy told me it's a 'she.'"

"He most definitely is not."

Unwilling to believe she'd been so completely duped by a mere child, Alexandra longed to lift the puppy up and see for herself, but she was not bold enough to do it. "You're quite certain?"

"Positive."

"No!" she said sharply when the puppy clamped small teeth on the hem of her skirt and began to tug. Its only response was to tug more violently.

"Cease!" commanded the duke in a low, booming voice. Instantly sensing The Voice of Authority, the puppy let go,

95

wagged his tail, and promptly curled up at Jordan's feet, laying his head on one brightly polished brown boot. This unwelcome show of affection earned from Jordan a glare of such excruciating distaste that Alexandra gave in to a helpless fit of laughter. "Don't you like animals, my lord?" she asked, swallowing a fresh onslaught of giggles.

"Not untrained, undisciplined ones," he said, but even he was not proof against the infectious gaiety of her musical laughter.

"I shall call him Henry," Alexandra decreed suddenly.

"Why?"

"Because if he's going to be a great hairy beast, he'll resemble Henry VIII."

"True," Jordan said, chuckling, his mood improving with each moment in her cheerful company.

They spent the rest of the journey talking about anything and everything. Alexandra discovered to her pleasure that her new husband was extremely well-read, intelligent, and deeply involved in the management of his vast estates, as well as a myriad of business interests which were completely beyond her ken. From that, she gathered that he was a man who shouldered responsibility quite effortlessly, and well. She was, in fact, well on her way to developing an extreme case of hero worship.

For his part, Jordan confirmed what he had already guessed about Alexandra—she was sensitive, intelligent, and witty. He also discovered that she was even more hopelessly naive about lovemaking than he would have imagined possible. The proof of this came later, when they had finished a highly satisfying meal in the inn where they were to spend the night. The longer Jordan lingered over his port, the more nervous and preoccupied Alexandra seemed to become. Finally, she leapt up and began carefully smoothing the wrinkles from her gown, then she made a great show of turning around and examining a perfectly common little oak table. "Excellent workmanship, is it not?"

"Not particularly."

Almost desperately, Alexandra continued. "When I look at a piece of furniture, I always wonder about the man who labored to make it—you know, whether he was short or tall, grim or pleasant . . . things like that."

96

"Do you?" he asked blandly.

"Yes, of course. Don't you?"

"No."

With her back still turned to him, Alexandra said with great care, "I think I'll go get Henry and take him for a walk."

"Alexandra." The word, spoken in a calm, no-nonsense tone, stopped her in her tracks, and she turned.

"Yes?"

"You needn't work yourself into a fever of anguished terror. I've no intention of sleeping with you tonight."

Alexandra, whose only concern had been a need to use the inn's facilities, looked at him in surprise and unconcern. "I never imagined you would. Why ever should you want to sleep in my room when this inn is so very large, and you can afford a room of your own?"

This time it was Jordan's turn to look blank. "I beg your pardon?" he uttered, unable to believe his ears.

"It isn't that you aren't *welcome* to share my room," she amended cordially, "but why you would *wish* to do so, I can't imagine. Sarah—our old housekeeper—always said I flail about like a fish out of water at night, and I'm sure I'd make you very uncomfortable. Would you mind terribly if I went upstairs now?"

For a moment Jordan simply stared at her, his wineglass arrested partway to his mouth, then he shook his head as if trying to clear it. "Of course not," he said in an odd, choked voice. "Go ahead."

Chapter Nine

J ORDAN CALLED TO his coachman to pull up at the next clearing beside the road, and Alexandra sighed with relief. They'd been traveling at a fast pace since lunch, and she longed to walk about and work the kinks from her body. Her husband, however, seemed perfectly comfortable and relaxed in the confines of the coach—probably, she decided, because his clothing was far more sensible than hers.

Clad in buff-colored breeches, shiny brown boots, and a wide-sleeved, peasant-style shirt that was open at the throat, Jordan was more suitably attired for a long coach journey than she was. She, on the other hand, was wearing three petticoats beneath the wide skirt of her bright yellow traveling costume and a white silk shirt beneath the tight-fitting yellow pelisse that was trimmed in dark-blue braid. A scarf of yellow, white, and blue stripes was tied at her throat, her hands were encased in yellow gloves, and a pert straw bonnet trimmed with yellow ribbons and silk roses was perched upon her mahogany curls and tied beneath her ear. She felt hot, confined, and rather resentful that fashionable young ladies were evidently required to dress so foolishly, while fashionable *gentlemen*, like her husband, could apparently dress as they wished.

As soon as the coach came to a complete stop at a wide place in the road and the steps were let down, Alexandra scooped up Henry and bumped into Jordan in her haste to escape. Instead of preceding her, as he would normally have done, Jordan shot her an understanding look and relaxed against the squabs. Allowing her a decent interval in which to take care of personal needs, which he assumed was the reason for her haste, he then climbed down and strolled through the bushes at the side of the road into the pretty little clearing.

"Doesn't this feel marvelous, Henry?" She was standing in the center of the clearing, stretching, her hands linked high over her head, her puppy sitting at her feet. For the second time, Jordan wished an artist could capture her on canvas. In her bright yellow finery, surrounded by sloping hills covered with yellow and white wildflowers, she was youth and grace and suppressed energy—a gay wood nymph dressed in the latest fashion.

He grinned at the poetic bent of his thoughts and stepped into the clearing.

"Oh, it's you!" she said, dropping her arms hastily to her sides, but looking relieved.

"Who else were you expecting?"

Stalling for time before she had to return to the coach, Alexandra bent down and snapped off a long, slender branch from a dead sapling. "No one, but when one is traveling with two coachmen, two postilions, and six outriders, it's hard to guess who will appear. What an army!" she laughed, and then, lightning-quick, she excuted a saber salute with the branch and thrust it at Jordan's chest. *"En garde!"* she said teasingly, then pointed the wooden saber at the ground, put her palm atop it, and jauntily crossed one ankle in front of the opposite leg, looking like a remarkably pretty, youthful swordsman.

The thrusting motion with the wooden "saber" had been executed with such flawless technique that Jordan couldn't believe she was merely mimicking something she'd seen. On the other hand, he couldn't believe she possessed any real knowledge or skill, either. "Do you fence?" he asked, his dark brows furrowed in disbelief.

She nodded slowly, her smile widening. "Care to try me?"

Jordan hesitated, aware that daylight was slipping past, but his fascination rapidly won out over his common sense. Besides, he too was tired of being confined in the coach. "I might consider it," he replied, deliberately baiting her. "Are you good enough?"

"There's only one way to find out."

Accepting her challenge with a gleam of amusement, he turned and looked around for a suitable branch. By the time he'd found one the right length and width, Alexandra had already removed her bonnet and pelisse. Arrested, he watched her unknot the scarf from around her neck, pull it off, then unbutton the top buttons of her silk shirt. At the sound of his approach, she whirled around in a swirl of yellow skirts, her color gloriously high, her aquamarine eyes sparkling with anticipation. "I wish I could remove my petticoats and slippers," she announced. As she spoke, she lifted her skirts, exposing slim, surprisingly shapely calves to Jordan's view, while she wriggled her dainty foot and ruefully considered the offending yellow slippers on her small feet. "I suppose I'd ruin my stockings if I took my slippers off. Wouldn't I?"

She glanced at him for advice, but Jordan's mind was momentarily preoccupied with how adorable she looked in that particular pose, and another, less welcome awareness: Desire. Without warning, he felt hot desire pulsing to life within him—unexpected, unwelcome, but undeniable.

"My lord?"

His gaze shot to hers.

"Why are you glowering at me in that ferocious fashion?"

With an effort, Jordan shifted his thoughts to her predicament, but somewhere in the back of his mind, he knew he was going to have her before their journey ended. "If you're worried about your stockings, take them off," he said, then he mentally shook his head at her naiveté when she ingenuously turned her back to him and peeled them off, allowing him glimpses of smooth, bare calves and ankles.

Finished, she picked up her makeshift saber and touched it to her forehead in a jaunty formal salute. Jordan returned the salute, though his mind was occupied with the bewitching sparkle in her mesmerizing blue-green eyes and the exquisite rosy color at her smoothly carved cheeks.

She had scored two points on him before he finally managed to concentrate on the swordplay, and even then she proved to be a worthy opponent. What she lacked in strength, she made up in lightning-quick moves and flashy footwork. But in the end it was her footwork that finally cost her the match. She had stalked him halfway around the clearing, advancing quickly, holding her ground, never retreating unless he physically overpowered her. With only one point left to decide the outcome, Alexandra suddenly saw an opening and lunged at him. Unfortunately, as she lunged forward, she stepped on the hem of her gown, which sent her sprawling off balance, straight into Jordan.

"You lost," he chuckled as he caught her in his arms.

"Yes, but it was my long skirt, and not your swordsmanship, which gave you the match," she retorted, laughing. Pulling out of his arms, she stepped back, her chest rising and falling as she strove to catch her breath. But the heightened color on her cheeks owed far more to his touch than her exertion. "You should have spotted me some points at the outset," she reminded him. "After all, you're twice as strong as I am."

"True," he admitted, smiling impenitently, "but I didn't take advantage of my strength. Moreover, I'm a great deal more advanced in years than you."

Laughing, she plunked her hands on her slim hips. "You're a veritable antique, your grace. Next year or the year after, you'll be at your last prayers, with a shawl round your shoulders and Henry dozing at your feet."

"And where will you be?" he demanded with mock solemnity, his hands itching to pull her into his arms.

She stepped back with an arch smile. "In the nursery, playing with my dolls—as befits my tender years."

Jordan gave a shout of laughter, wondering what the *ton* would say if they could see him being treated with such total lack of respect by a country-bred chit of eighteen.

"Where else should I be," she teased, "if not in the nursery?"

On my lap, he thought. *Or in my bed.*

The laughter vanished from her face and she pressed her hands to her cheeks, staring over his shoulder. "Good heavens!"

Jordan turned sharply to see the cause of her chagrin and saw six outriders, two coachmen, and two postilions standing shoulder-to-shoulder, their abashed expressions testifying to the fact that they had witnessed the earlier swordplay and now the wordplay between the duke and his duchess.

His jaw tightened, his steady, icy gaze slicing across them, dispersing them as effectively as any words could have done.

"That's very impressive," Alexandra teased, reaching

101

down and plucking up her discarded garments. "That thing you do with your eyes," she clarified, looking around for Sir Henry. "You slay with a glance. You don't need a sword. Is that a natural talent that the nobility is born with, or is it a skill you acquire later, as befits your station?" She found Henry sniffing about beneath a bush and scooped him up. "Your grandmother can do it too. She quite terrifies me. Would you hold these for me?" Before Jordan realized what she was about, she dumped bonnet, pelisse, and hairy puppy into his arms. "Would you turn your back, please, while I put my stockings on?"

Obediently, Jordan did as bidden, but in his mind, he visualized the *ton* staring in collective, comical shock at Jordan Townsende—12th Duke of Hawthorne, holder of the most magnificent lands and fortune in Europe—who was now standing in a clearing with an armload of discarded clothing and one unwanted puppy who was determined to lick his face.

"Who taught you to fence?" he asked as they strolled back to the coach.

"My father. We used to practice together for hours at a time whenever he came home. When he left, I'd practice with Mary Ellen's brothers—with anyone else who was willing—so that when my father came home again, he'd admire my skill. I suppose, since I didn't show much promise of feminine beauty, he thought it was amusing to turn me into a son. On the other hand, it's possible he simply liked to fence, and he used our matches as a way of passing time." She had no idea that the pain and scorn she felt for her sire was obvious in her voice.

"Alexandra?"

Alexandra pulled her gaze from the countryside that was sliding past the coach windows. Ever since their mock duel two hours before, the duke had been watching her in an odd, speculative way that was making her increasingly uncomfortable. "Yes?"

"You said your father didn't come home very often. Where did he spend his time?"

A dark shadow dimmed the brilliance of her eyes, then it vanished behind a deliberately offhand smile. "He came two or three times a year and stayed a fortnight or so. He

102

spent the rest of his time in London. He was rather like a visitor."

"I'm sorry," Jordan replied, apologizing because he had made her talk about someone he could see had caused her some sort of hurt.

"You needn't be sorry, but if you could find it in your heart to think more kindly of my mother, I would appreciate that very much. My mother used to be charming and gay, but after my father died, she just sort of—went all to pieces."

"And left the burden of the household and the servants on the shoulders of a fourteen-year-old child," Jordan finished dampingly. "I saw that place, and I've met your mother and uncle. I can imagine exactly what it was like for you."

She heard the angry compassion in his voice and her love for him grew because he cared about her, but she shook her head, refusing his pity. "It wasn't as bad as you seem to think."

It felt so good, so safe and secure to have someone worry about her, that Alexandra scarcely knew how to contain the tenderness and gratitude she felt for him. Unable to tell him how she felt, she did the next best thing: Reaching into the bright yellow reticule that matched her skirt and pelisse, she lovingly extracted a heavy watch and chain. To Alexandra it was sacred—the most valuable possession of the man she had adored. She held it out to Jordan and when he took it with a quizzical expression, she explained, "It belonged to my grandfather. It was given him by a Scottish earl who admired his knowledge of the philosophers." Just looking at it in Jordan's wide palm made her eyes mist. Her voice aching with poignant memories, she said, "He would have wanted you to have it. He'd have approved of you."

"I doubt that," Jordan said with certainty.

"Oh, but he would! He said I should love a noble man."

"He *told* you to love a nobleman?" Jordan repeated in disbelief.

"No, no. A *noble* man. Which you are."

Unaware that he already owned several, far more beautiful gold watches, Alexandra said, "I sent one of your footmen to my house and Penrose fetched the watch for him. Your grandmother said it was all right."

Jordan's hand closed over the watch. "Thank you" was all he said.

She had given him the two most precious things she had, Alexandra realized, her love and the gold watch. And all he had said each time was an uncomfortable "Thank you." Obviously, her gifts made him feel uneasy.

The awkward silence that occurs whenever someone realizes they've revealed too much about themselves fell over the coach.

Eventually the gentle rocking motion of the chaise, combined with the large hot meal she'd eaten earlier, made Alexandra drowsy. Despite the luxurious interior of the vehicle, however, she could find no comfortable way to sleep. She tried leaning her head against the side, but every time the coach gave a small lurch, her head banged against it and woke her up. Sitting up straight, she crossed her arms over her chest and tried leaning her head back against the squabs. The wheels hit a rut and her entire upper body slid sharply to the right. Bracing her hand on the seat, Alexandra levered herself upright.

Across from her, Jordan chuckled and patted the seat beside him. "I will be happy to offer my shoulder as a pillow, my lady."

Alexandra accepted the invitation with sleepy gratitude and shifted onto the seat beside him, but instead of merely offering his shoulder, Jordan lifted his arm and put it around her so that her head was cradled snugly in the curve of his arm and chest. *My lady*, Alex thought sleepily. How lovely that sounded when he said it. She was asleep almost instantly.

Twilight had fallen when she awoke to the horrifying realization that she was lying almost completely atop him. Sometime during her nap, Jordan had shifted their positions so that his back was against the side of the coach with his legs stretched diagonally across the seat. Alexandra was lying on her side, wrapped in his arms, her legs tangled with his, her own arm curved around his waist.

Horrified that he might awaken and find her sprawled across him in this undignified fashion, Alexandra carefully lifted her cheek from his hard chest. Trying to think of some way to extricate herself without awakening him, she peered at him beneath her lashes. Sleep smoothed the harsh planes of his tanned face and softened the contours of his square jaw, she thought fondly. Seen like this, he looked much less forbidding, almost boyish, and . . . awake!

His eyes opened and he tipped his chin down, looking at her. Puzzlement registered on his features for a split second, as if he didn't quite recognize her, then he smiled—a deliciously warm, languid smile. "Did you sleep well?"

Alexandra, who had been too stricken to move, nodded and tried to lever herself up. His arms tightened, holding her. "Don't go," he whispered, and his heavy-lidded gaze dropped to her soft lips, lingering on her mouth for a long moment before he slowly lifted his eyes to her widened blue ones. "Stay here with me."

He wanted her to kiss him, Alexandra realized with mingled joy and apprehension—the invitation was there in those warm, compelling grey eyes. Shyly, Alexandra put her lips on his and felt his hand settle on the small of her back, stroking slowly upward, comforting her and encouraging her. His lips moved against hers, lightly exploring, inviting her to do the same, and when she began to follow his lead, his free hand cupped the back of her head, his fingers sliding tantalizingly against her nape while the other hand continued sensually stroking her back.

He kissed her endlessly, long drugging kisses that shook her to the core of her being and made her want more and more. His tongue traced the line between her lips, coaxing them to part for him, then it slipped between them, lightly exploring her mouth, then gently plunging and retreating, teasing and tormenting her, until Alexandra, feverish with the need to make *him* feel as *she* felt, touched her own tongue to his lips. The instant she did, the kiss exploded. He crushed her to him, drawing her tongue into his mouth and caressing it with his own. His other hand suddenly shifted, curving round her bottom, pulling her tightly to his hardened body, while his tongue began thrusting into her mouth and retreating again and again in some wildly exciting, forbidden rhythm that sent jolts of fierce pleasure rocketing through Alexandra's body.

Not until she felt his hand cupping her breast, then sliding inside her silk shirt, did she jerk free of the whirlpool of mindless pleasure where she was willingly drowning. And then it was surprise and guilt, rather than revulsion, that made her rear back.

Bracing her forearms against his chest, she tried to catch her breath, and then she raised her head, dragging her embarrassed gaze to his smoldering grey eyes.

"I've shocked you," he murmured huskily.

It was true, but Alexandra saw the amusement in his sultry eyes and stubbornly refused to admit it. Accepting his unspoken challenge, she put her lips against his again, and this time when his tongue slid between them, her body automatically fitted itself closer to his. A muffled sound that was part groan, part laugh, escaped him, but when she would have pulled away, his arms tightened around her and his mouth became more insistent. Alexandra surrendered to the heated demands of his mouth and hands, kissing him back with all the awakening desire flooding through her.

When he finally let her go, his breathing was almost as labored as hers. Lifting his hand, he rubbed his knuckles along her heated cheek. "So soft," he whispered. "So incredibly innocent."

Alexandra interpreted "innocent" to mean "naive" and jerked away from him in angry hurt. "I must be a dreadful bore for a man of your obvious sophistication."

His hands clamped her arms and hauled her right back. "That was a compliment," he retorted, his face only inches from hers, and the taut sound of his voice made her wonder a little wildly what he must be like when truly angry. Giving her a little shake, he clarified shortly. "'Unspoiled—unsullied—without artifice or pretense,' do you understand?"

"Perfectly!" Alexandra flung back, reacting to his tone and not his words, and then the absurdity of it all made her burst out laughing. "Are we having a quarrel over how *nice* I am?"

Her irresistible smile doused his momentary exasperation and brought a reluctant answering smile to his eyes. "So it would seem," he softly replied and, with inner resignation, Jordan finally faced the fact that he could no longer pretend the insistent, throbbing desire he felt for her didn't exist. She laid her cheek back on his chest and he stared fixedly over her head, mentally reminding himself of all the logical reasons why he would be making a mistake if he took her to bed tonight:

> She was young and naive and idealistic.
> He was none of those things.

> She wanted to give him her love.
> All he wanted was her body.

> She wanted to be loved by him.
> The only "love" he believed in was the kind made in bed.

> She was infatuated with him.
> He did not want to be burdened with an infatuated child.

On the other hand,

> She wanted him.
> He wanted her.

His decision made, he tipped his chin down. "Alexandra?" When she lifted her face inquiringly, he said in a calm, matter-of-fact voice, "Do you know how babies are made?"

The unexpected question jolted a stunned, embarrassed laugh from her at the same time hot color washed over her cheeks. "Do—do we have to discuss this?"

His lips quirked with self-mockery. "Yesterday, I would have said there was no need. An hour ago, I would have said it. Now, I'm afraid we do."

"What made you change your mind?"

It was Jordan's turn to look blank. "Our kissing," he said bluntly, after a pause.

"What has that to do with babies?"

Jordan leaned his head back, closed his eyes, and sighed with exasperated amusement. "Somehow, I *knew* you were going to say that."

After studying his odd expression, Alexandra sat up and self-consciously straightened her clothing. Mary Ellen had tried to convince her two years ago that babies were made the same way puppies were made, but Alexandra's intelligent mind had rejected that piece of appalling nonsense. Human beings would never behave in such a way, she knew, and only someone as corkbrained as Mary Ellen would believe such an absurd thing. But then Mary Ellen also believed that if you turned your back on a rainbow, you'd have bad luck, and that fairies cavorted under mushrooms in the forest. Which was why Mary Ellen walked backward whenever it rained and refused to eat mushrooms.

Alexandra stole a sidewise look at her husband and decided to ask him a simple question about something which young girls were kept in ignorance of, but which she felt she was entitled to know. Her grandfather had oft said that ignorance was a disease for which questions were the only cure, and so, with bright, candid interest, she inquired, "How *are* babies made?" Visibly startled, Jordan turned and opened his mouth, as if he intended to speak, but for some reason no words came out. At first Alexandra was puzzled by his involuntary silence, but then understanding dawned. She shook her head and sighed with sympathy for their mutual plight. "*You* don't know either, do you?"

Jordan's sharp crack of laughter exploded like a pistol shot, and he threw his head back, laughing with uncontrollable mirth until he finally managed to drag enough air into his lungs to choke, "Yes, Alexandra . . . I do know." He had laughed more in the week he'd known her, Jordan realized, than he had laughed in an entire year.

A little wounded by his reaction, Alexandra said, "Well then, how is it done?"

The remnants of mirth gleaming in his eyes slowly dissolved as he laid his hand against her cheek, running it back to tenderly smooth her hair. Finally he said in an odd, husky voice, "I'll show you how it's done tonight."

He had scarcely spoken the words when their coach turned off the road and pulled into the yard of an inn with lamps burning brightly in all the windows.

Chapter Ten

C ANDLES FLICKERED CHEERFULLY on the mantel and on the low table between them, left there by the maid who'd come to clear away their dinner plates. Curled up in a pretty chintz-covered settee, her stockinged feet tucked beneath her and Jordan's arm around her shoulders, holding her nestled into the curve of his arm, Alexandra had never felt so luxuriously, sublimely cozy.

Lifting her wineglass to her lips, she sipped the wine Jordan had seemed determined to press upon her for the last hour, wondering when he planned to retire to his own room. She wasn't entirely certain he even had a room of his own tonight. While she'd bathed in her room before dinner, he'd bathed in the small room adjoining hers, but there was only a narrow cot in there, obviously intended for use by a valet or lady's maid. Alexandra had no maid and was perfectly able to fend for herself; Jordan had said he preferred to leave his valet behind when he was only going on a short trip. Since neither of them had servants, she wondered if the inn was full and he therefore was forced to sleep in the adjoining room.

Firelight danced in the grate, dispelling the slight chill of the spring night, adding to the cozy atmosphere of the room, and her thoughts drifted lazily from their sleeping accommodations to babies. Jordan had promised to show her how babies were made tonight. She couldn't imagine why married people persisted in keeping the method cloaked in so much mystery. However it was done, it couldn't be a dreadful thing, because English couples obviously did it often enough to keep the country's population growing.

Perhaps it was kept secret because Society didn't want girls like herself, who would have liked a baby with or without a husband, to go around getting babies on their own.

That, evidently, was it, she deduced logically. Since the beginning of time, men had made the rules and men had obviously been the ones to decree that a girl was "ruined" if she had a baby without marrying one of them first. That made sense. Still . . . the theory had certain holes . . .

A baby, she thought wistfully. A baby.

As an only child, the thought of having a dark-haired baby boy to cuddle and nurse and play with filled her with delight. Moreover, she'd read enough history to know how important a male heir was to men with titles—particularly titles as illustrious as Jordan's. The sudden realization that she would be the one to give Jordan his heir filled her with a poignant pride and joy that was almost past bearing.

She stole a glance at him through her lashes, and her heart skipped a beat. He was lounging back against the cushions, his white shirt open partway down his muscled chest, his tanned skin a golden bronze in the firelight. With his dark, slightly curly hair, ruggedly chiseled features, and wonderful physique, Alexandra thought he looked like a god.

She wondered a little if she was behaving with a shocking lack of propriety, cuddling up to him like this, welcoming his kisses, but in truth she thought he was irresistibly wonderful. Besides, he was her husband before God and man, so she saw no reason to pretend she found his attentions unpleasant. Her grandfather, obviously worried about the impression of married life she was receiving from her parents' marriage, had lectured her gently but often on what marriage was supposed to be like. "There are two mistakes people make when it comes to marriage," he had repeatedly said. "The first mistake is marrying the wrong person. Once you are married to the right person, the second mistake is denying any part of yourself or your love to him. When you give your husband your unconditional love, he then has it to return to you."

Jordan's thoughts were less aimless and far more practical. He was, at that moment, trying to think of the easiest way to get her out of her clothes without scaring the hell out of her.

Above her, Alexandra felt Jordan's lips brush across the top of her head and she smiled with inner pleasure, but she was not surprised, because her husband had been kissing her like that rather frequently tonight. She was a little shocked a moment later, however, when he took her wineglass from her hand and abruptly pulled her onto his lap to kiss her long and passionately. And she was thoroughly flabbergasted when he lifted his lips from hers many minutes later and quietly but firmly suggested she use the screen in the corner of the room to change into her dressing gown.

Mentally searching through her trunks for the least indecent of the dressing gowns the French seamstress had made for her wedding trip, she stood up and inquired uneasily, "Where are you going to sleep?"

"With you," he blandly replied.

Alexandra's eyes narrowed suspiciously. For some reason, she sensed instinctively that this unprecedented decision to sleep beside her had something to do with the mystery of making a baby, and, without knowing exactly why, she suddenly wasn't completely certain she wanted to learn the secret after all. Not yet. "Wouldn't you rather have a nice, comfortable bed of your very own?" she suggested hopefully.

"Making a baby involves using one bed," he explained with calm patience, "not two."

Alexandra's eyes narrowed apprehensively. "Why?"

"I'll show you why in a few minutes."

"Couldn't you just *tell* me?" she implored persistently.

An odd, muffled sound escaped him, but he kept his face straight. "I'm afraid not."

Jordan watched her walk reluctantly toward the screen, and the grin he'd been fighting to hide flashed across his face as he admired her straight shoulders and gently swaying hips. She was already beginning to panic, he realized sympathetically, and he hadn't even touched her yet. Evidently a female was born with some sixth sense that warned her a male was dangerous and untrustworthy the moment she was without the protective barrier of her cumbersome

111

clothing. Alexandra was full of surprises, he mused, as he gazed thoughtfully at the dressing screen. She had the mind of a scholar, the heart of an innocent, and the wit of a sage. One minute she was bold and daring enough to aim a rifle and kill a man who was trying to kill him—the next minute she was unconscious from shock because she had done it. She had broached the topic of sex with the impartial curiosity of a scientist; now that the time was at hand to experience it, she was shaking with trepidation and stalling for time.

Her fear bothered Jordan, but not enough to dissuade him from satisfying his body's unexplainable, but undeniable, craving for her. Although Alexandra was extremely young in comparison to the sophisticated, worldly women he had taken to bed in the past, she was certainly old enough to be wed and even to bear his child. Moreover, he had paid dearly for the privilege of enjoying her body—paid for it by giving her his name and his hand.

Regardless of that, as each moment ticked past, his enthusiasm for making love to her tonight was severely diminished by two things: First, Alexandra was completely unaware of what he was about to do to her, and when she figured it out, Jordan expected her to be not only fearful but very likely resistant. Second, even if she weren't frightened and resistant, he did not especially relish the prospect of bedding an inexperienced girl who was completely untutored in the fine art of lovemaking.

Unlike other men who turned their eye toward innocent maidens, Jordan had always preferred the women he bedded to be knowledgeable in the ways of love—sensual, willing partners who knew how to please him and who accepted the pleasure he gave them without shyness or reserve.

The fact that the women who sought his attention frequently did so because they wanted something—either his title or the reflected glow of his fame and popularity—didn't particularly bother Jordan. After all, he wanted something from them, too, and self-gratification was the very axis on which their entire glamorous world revolved. But whatever their reasons for inviting his attentions, when his ardor was spent, Jordan always preferred to sleep alone.

The sounds behind the screen had ceased and Jordan

knew Alexandra was finished changing, just as he knew she was remaining behind the screen because she was afraid to show herself in her nightclothes.

Deciding that the most soothing thing he could do for her just now would be to treat the subject of clothing—or lack of it—in a calm, matter-of-fact way, Jordan got up and walked across the room, intending to pour himself another glass of wine. "Alexandra," he said in a firm, no-nonsense tone, "do you need any help undressing?"

"No!" came the horrified reply. "I—I've just finished."

"Then come out from behind that screen."

"I can't! Your grandmother's French seamstress is a *mad*woman—there are *holes* in everything she made for me."

"Holes?" Jordan repeated, nonplussed. Reaching for the bottle of wine, he glanced toward the screen. "What sort of 'holes'?"

She stepped from behind it, and Jordan stared at the indignant expression on her flushed face, then his gaze dropped to the daringly low oval bodice of her shimmering satin nightdress. "This nightdress," she announced, pointing an accusing finger at her exposed bodice, "has a hole cut out of the chest. The blue one has a square hole cut out of the back. The yellow one," she finished bitterly, "is the worst! It has a hole in the back, another in the front, and the side of the skirt is slashed up to my knees! That Frenchwoman," she finished darkly, "should not be *allowed* to hold a pair of scissors!"

Jordan gave a shout of laughter, snatched her into his arms, and buried his face in her fragrant hair, his shoulders rocking.

And in that moment, all the jaded cynicism of his past began to crumble.

"Oh, Alex," he gasped, "I can't believe you're real!"

Since she wasn't responsible for the design of these absurd clothes, Alex took no personal offense at his laughter but she warned him in a dire voice: "You won't be laughing when you see the rest of what you paid that woman good money for!"

With a superhuman effort, Jordan managed to subdue his mirth long enough to lift his head and gaze tenderly into her upturned, indignant face. "Why is that?"

113

"Because," she informed him darkly, "the gowns that don't have *holes* cut out of them are so sheer they're as transparent as *windows!*"

"Windo-?" For the second time, Jordan lost control. His shoulders shaking violently, he swung her up into his arms, captivated again by the sheer joy of her artlessness and unexpected wit.

He carried her to the bed, but when he took his arm from beneath her knees and her legs slid down his thighs, past his rigid erection, she tensed instantly. Uncertain, frightened suddenly—as if she sensed the meaning of his hardened body—her eyes searched his face. "What are you going to do to me?" she whispered shakily.

"I'm going to make love to you," he answered gently, deliberately vague.

Her entire body trembled. "How?"

Jordan smiled reassuringly, as touched by her fear as he was by the innocence in her huge liquid eyes. "I'll tell you as we go along," he promised, but when it was obvious that answer didn't satisfy her, he added, "To put it as simply as possible, the seeds of a baby are inside of me, and in a little while, I'll put them into you. But there's no way of knowing whether a baby will result from it this time. Alexandra," he added with gentle firmness, anticipating that some of the things he was going to do might seem "sinful" to her, "I give you my word that nothing we're going to do is 'wrong.' People do this whether they want a baby or not."

"They do?" she asked with heart-wrenching trust. "Why?"

Jordan bit back a smile, his fingers untying the satin bow at her breasts. "Because it feels good," he answered simply. He put his hands on her shoulders and, before Alexandra realized what he was about, her gown slid down her naked body, landing in a pool of shimmering satin at her feet. Jordan caught his breath at the unexpected beauty of her body. She was thin, but her breasts were surprisingly full, her waist tiny, and her legs long and shapely.

Her head bent, frozen with terror and embarrassment by her husband's gaze, Alexandra stood staring at her gown, relieved beyond words when Jordan reached down and lifted her onto the bed. Glad for the flimsy shelter offered by

114

the sheet, she pulled it up to her chin and swiftly averted her gaze as Jordan began undressing beside the bed.

Sternly she tried to remind herself that human beings had been making babies since time began, and so there could be nothing bizarre or ugly about what Jordan was going to do to her. Furthermore, it was her duty to give him an heir, she knew, and she adamantly refused to begin their marriage by shirking her duty. Despite those sensible conclusions, when he slid in beside her and leaned over her, bracing his forearm on her opposite side, her heart began to race like a maddened thing. "W-what are you going to do?" she asked fearfully, unable to drag her gaze above the tanned muscular chest looming above her.

Jordan gently tipped her chin up, forcing her to meet his gaze. "I'm going to kiss you and hold you close to me," he said in a voice as soft and caressing as velvet. "And I'm going to touch you. Later, something I do to you will hurt for a moment—only a moment," he promised. "I'll tell you when it's going to happen," he added, lest she begin dreading the pain long before it would come.

Her eyes widened with alarm at the mention of pain, but when she spoke it was with heartbreaking concern for him, rather than herself. "Will it hurt you, too?"

"No."

The girl who Jordan had feared would struggle and fight against him smiled tremulously and shyly laid her fingers against his cheek. "I'm glad," she said softly. "I wouldn't want you to be hurt."

A huge constricting knot of tenderness and desire tightened Jordan's throat and he bent his head, taking her lips in a fierce, stirring kiss, shaping and fitting the contours of her soft mouth to his. Forcing himself to go slower, Jordan deliberately lightened the pressure of his mouth, smoothing his lips tantalizingly back and forth over hers, his hand curving around her nape, stroking it sensually. His tongue traced the trembling line between her lips, coaxing them to part, and when they did, it slid between them, tangling with hers while his hand on her nape tightened possessively.

Driven by pure instinct and the pleasure coursing through her veins, Alexandra turned into his arms, and the moment she did, his strong arms went around her, molding her hips to the hardened contours of his. When she stiffened in alarm at the bold pressure of his hardened manhood and tried to draw back, his hand shifted comfortingly up and down her spine, holding her gently but firmly against him.

She quieted in his arms, but when his hand slid from her back to her breast, she gave a leap of alarm, recoiling from his touch, and this time Jordan reluctantly pulled his mouth from hers. Raising his head, he gazed into her apprehensive blue eyes, his thumb gently tracing the elegant curve of her jaw. "Don't be afraid of me, sweetheart."

Alexandra hesitated, her magnificent eyes searching deeply into his, and Jordan had the uncanny feeling she was looking into the depths of his black soul. What she saw, however, made her say softly, "You would never do anything to harm me, I know that. Although you seem hard on the outside, on the inside you are beautiful."

Her words struck some strange chord of intense feeling deep within Jordan. With a silent groan he bent his head, his mouth opening on hers with sudden, urgent hunger. This time she answered his passion with her own, her lips parting beneath his without urging, welcoming his tongue into her mouth and then giving him hers, her hands clasping him to her.

Without taking his mouth from hers, Jordan stroked his hand down her arm to her rib cage, then upward, cupping her breasts, circling her nipples with his thumb, feeling them rise up proudly against his palm. He kissed her temple, her eyes, and her cheek, then he nuzzled her neck, chuckling with throaty delight and desire as he touched his tongue to her sensitive ear and felt her press her body closer to his. His tongue plunged into it and she moaned with sweet desire, her nails biting into his arms.

Sliding his lips along the curve of her neck, Jordan moved lower, then he put his mouth where his hands had been, kissing her breasts, slowly drawing her hardened nipple into his mouth, flicking his tongue against it, teasing her with his mouth and hands. Her hands tangled in the hair at his nape, holding him closer to her breast, and when he sucked on her nipple, she gasped with pleasure, her whole body twisting against his. He trailed kisses along her flat stomach, his hands gliding ceaselessly up and down her sides and breasts and hips, and then he finally lifted his head.

Dazed with pleasure and wonder, Alexandra gazed into his scorching eyes, sensing instinctively the care he was taking with her, unaware of the practiced expertise he was using to make her body feel as if it were on fire beneath his hands and mouth.

All she knew was that she was bursting with love, and that she wanted—needed—to make him feel all the wondrous pleasure he was making her feel. And when Jordan slowly lowered his sensual lips to hers and whispered, "Kiss me, darling," it was all the invitation Alexandra needed.

Driven by pure instinct and the belief that what felt wonderful to her would surely feel wonderful to him also, Alexandra unknowingly turned the full force of his seductive skill on *him*. She kissed him with unrestrained ardor, curving her hand around his nape, kissing him exactly as he had kissed her, her tongue sliding along the crease between his lips, urging them to part and then driving inside in a kiss that made him gasp against her mouth.

The pressure of her mouth urged him back against the pillows as Alexandra leaned up on an elbow and then followed him down, brushing sweet, arousing kisses across his temple, eyes, and cheek while her hand slid downward to the mat of dark hair on his chest. She splayed her fingers wide, her fingertips sliding back and forth, grazing his nipples as she trailed her lips across his cheek and daringly traced the folds of his ear with her tongue. Beneath her palm, she felt the wild increase in the rapid pounding of his heart; encouraged, she slid her lips downward, following the path her hand had taken, raining kisses over the rippling muscles of his powerful chest until she finally reached his nipple. When she took it in her mouth, she heard the rasp of his sharply indrawn breath and felt his muscles leap reflexively.

His skin was like rough satin and Alexandra reveled in the taste and texture of it, loving the way his hands plunged into her hair as she continued to kiss and tease him with her mouth. But when she moved downward, sliding her lips along the hollow planes of his stomach, Jordan made a sound that was part laugh and part groan and abruptly hauled her upward, rolling her onto her back, leaning over her.

With passion raging through every pore of his body,

Jordan had no specific idea how he had become the seduced, rather than the seducer. All he knew was that the enchanting girl he had taken to bed had suddenly become a gloriously exciting woman who was deliberately driving him half mad with desire.

Hungrily, he opened her mouth with his own while his hand glided down her hips and thighs, then shifted, covering the curly triangle between her legs. She stiffened at his intimate touch and clamped her legs together, wildly shaking her head.

With an effort that nearly sapped his strength, Jordan made his hand still and slowly lifted his head, gazing down at her. "Don't be afraid of me, darling," he said in a throbbing whisper, as his hand began to move, gently but relentlessly caressing her most sensitive place, his fingers probing her moist warmth, seeking entrance. "Trust me."

After a moment's hesitation, the rigidity went out of her limbs and Alexandra's thighs parted sweetly. From the moment he had begun, Jordan had expected, *known,* she would struggle and fight him when his caresses became this intimate. Instead, she was giving herself to him without reservation, holding nothing bac , fighting down her own fears and trusting him not to harm her.

The surge of tenderness he felt for the innocent temptress with the melting eyes at that moment was almost more than he could contain. He stared down at her, feeling humbled by her sweet, selfless giving, and she closed her eyes, burying her heated face against his chest while his fingers toyed with her, probing gently to prepare her for him, her hands clasping the muscles of his upper arms.

With a combination of blazing desire and genuine dread at the knowledge he was going to have to hurt her, Jordan shifted on top of her. Bracing his weight on his forearms, he cradled her face between his hands, his throbbing shaft poised at the entrance to her body. "Alex," he said in an aching voice that sounded strangely shattered to his own ears.

Her long eyelashes fluttered open, and he could tell she already knew.

Her breath was coming in frightened, shallow little pants, but instead of closing her eyes, she kept them riveted to his as if seeking reassurance and comfort from the very man

118

who was about to hurt her. Moving his hips slowly, Jordan penetrated her a fraction with each stroke, pushing slightly deeper into her tight warmth until he found the barrier that blocked further entrance, but no amount of gentle, normal pressure would break it.

His last hope that this would be painless and easy died in his breast. Lifting her hips to receive him, he withdrew almost all the way and covered her trembling lips with his own. "I'm sorry, darling," he whispered hoarsely against her mouth. Holding her imprisoned, he drove swiftly into her. Her body arched and her soft cry of pain slashed across his heart, but she never once tried to push him away. Instead she let him hold her in his arms, whispering soothing endearments to her.

Swallowing convulsively, Alexandra opened her tear-brightened eyes, amazed and relieved as the brief pain began to subside. Her husband's handsome face was dark with passion and harsh with regret, and she put her arms around him. "It wasn't as bad as that," she whispered.

The fact that *she* was trying to console *him* was more than Jordan could withstand. The cynicism and cold reserve that had surrounded him like an impenetrable wall for most of his twenty-seven years began to disintegrate completely, washed away in a tidal wave of selfless passion that raged through every pore of his body. With painstaking slowness, Jordan began to move within her, plunging gently, then retreating to plunge again, watching her lovely flushed face, as she began instinctively to move with him.

With her nails biting into the bunched muscles of his back, Alexandra strained toward him in trembling need, pressing herself willingly to the demanding, rhythmic thrusts of his hard body, while within her an uncontrollable inner excitement began to build, jarring her body with quick, piercing stabs of desire.

"Don't fight it, darling," Jordan whispered thickly, his shoulders and arms taut with the strain of holding back, his chest heaving with the force of each labored breath. Steadily, he began to increase the tempo of his driving, rhythmic strokes. "Let it happen."

Ecstasy exploded in Alexandra, spilling through her veins while spasms racked her body, making her cry out. The moment she did, Jordan tightened his arms around her and drove fiercely into her. His body erupted like a volcano, pouring his seed into her welcoming warmth with a force that made his entire body jerk again and again. Convulsions of pleasure were still racking him as he gently lifted his weight from her and moved onto his side, taking Alexandra with him, his body still joined with hers.

Alexandra surfaced slowly from the sweet, hot oblivion to which he had sent her, eventually becoming aware of where she was. As she lay in his protective embrace, her head nestled beneath his chin, she did not know it was possible to feel so loved. Even now, she could still feel the warmth of his intimate caresses and wildly exciting kisses.

Almost from the moment he had joined her in bed, she had realized instinctively that her husband had desired and needed her, but she hadn't quite understood *what* it was he was seeking from her. Now she knew. He had wanted that explosion of pure pleasure—and he had wanted her to feel it, too. Pride and joy seeped through her at the knowledge that she had been able to give him that. She had been able to make his powerful body tremble as he had made hers tremble, she had made him gasp with delight.

It did not occur to her to feel embarrassment over the wanton way she had returned his passion. Love meant giving everything and holding nothing back, as her grandfather had said. It meant entrusting your happiness to another, and, in return taking full responsibility for that person's happiness. She had done both tonight.

Her mind drifted to babies. She had never understood why couples sometimes got babies they didn't seem to want. No doubt they got them because they couldn't help going to bed and doing this glorious thing Jordan called "making love."

Jordan moved slightly, tipping his head down to tenderly gaze at his wife. In the candle glow, the purity of her face was striking. With her unbelievably long eyelashes resting like curly fans against her smooth, high cheeks, she looked fragile and innocent and incredibly pretty. He had intended to introduce her to passion; instead she had taught him selfless, uninhibited giving. She was innocence and ardor; devoid of guile; trusting and candid and sweet. A natural temptress.

A faint smile curved his lips as he finally recognized the

fact that she had adroitly used his own technique at love-making to make love to him, but she had added something to it—something elusive and profoundly touching. Something that made him feel both proud and strangely humble; possessive and yet unworthy. And suddenly, very uneasy.

Wondering if she was already asleep, he touched his lips to her forehead and whispered her name, then he raised his hand, intending to brush her tousled curls off her forehead.

Her eyes opened, and what he saw in their glowing blue depths stilled his hand and made it tremble—he saw the same thing that had made his body tremble when she kissed and touched him:

All the love in the universe was shining in her eyes.

"Oh my God," he whispered hoarsely.

Hours later when he had made love to her for the second time, Jordan held her cradled in his arms, staring fixedly at the dying candles on the mantel, unable to banish the possessive jealousy he felt stirring to life within him. "Alexandra," he said more gruffly than he intended, "never believe a man who says 'trust me'—*especially* if you don't happen to have any clothes on at the time."

She opened her eyes and her smile was filled with amusement. "How many men do you expect to be talking to me while I have no clothes on, my lord?"

"None," he said sternly. "I was merely joking about that part." Unable to tell her bluntly not to trust him or any other man, Jordan said evasively, "It's foolish to trust people too much. You'll be hurt if you do."

Her smile sobered. "I would be hurting myself if I didn't. Don't *you* trust people?"

"Not very many and not completely."

Alexandra lifted her hand and brushed her fingertip against his warm, sensual lips. "If you don't trust," she told him with that combination of wisdom and naiveté that Jordan found so disarming, "you'll never be disappointed by someone. But you will also cheat yourself of the chance to ever be completely happy." Unable to stop touching him, Alexandra traced the curve of his hard jaw, unaware of the desire kindling in his eyes and sparking to life within her. "You are beautiful and gentle and wise and strong," she whispered, watching his eyes darken as her hand drifted down his throat to his chest. "But you need to learn to trust people, especially me. Without complete trust, love can't survive, and I love y—"

Jordan captured her lips in a devouring kiss that silenced her words and sent her spinning off into a warm sweet world, where nothing existed except the wild beauty of his lovemaking.

Chapter Eleven

THEY MADE A brief stop in London early the next evening,. and while Jordan attended to some sort of business he had there, their coachman gave Alexandra a two-hour tour of what she was convinced must be the most exciting city in the world.

The sun was sinking into the sea on the horizon when they arrived at their ship the following day. Alexandra drank in the sights and sounds of the seaport with greedy delight, watching stevedores walking up and down planks with huge crates slung effortlessly over their shoulders, while giant cranes lifted cargo nets off the docks and lowered them onto the vessels. Mighty warships with towering masts were being loaded with provisions and made ready to join their sister ships in the blockade of the American colonies, or to continue the battle with the French on the sea. Burly seamen strolled down the docks with their arms around women whose faces were rouged and whose gowns made Alexandra's peignoirs seem demure.

The captain of the *Fair Winds* greeted them personally as they came on board and invited them to join him for "a simple supper" in his cabin. The "simple" meal consisted of fourteen courses, each served with a different wine, and a great deal of animated conversation about the wars Britain was fighting with the French and Americans. In Morsham, when Alexandra had read about bloody land battles with Napoleon's forces and the clashes taking place on the sea, it had all seemed so far away and unreal. Now, with warships lying at anchor all around her, war was a tangible, frightening thing.

By the time Jordan escorted her down to their cabin, however, she had drunk so much wine at the captain's urging that she was feeling a little giddy and extremely sleepy. Jordan's trunks had been put in their cabin, and Alexandra smiled with rosy contentment, wondering if he intended to make love to her tonight. He'd seemed a little distant after he finally returned from his meeting in London last night, and he hadn't made love to her when they finally stopped in an inn south of the city. He had kissed her goodnight, though, and held her in his arms until she slept.

"Shall I play lady's maid?" Jordan asked. Without waiting for her to answer, he turned her around and began unfastening the long row of rose-silk-covered buttons down her back.

"Is this boat swaying?" Alexandra asked, grabbing for the small oaken table beside her.

Jordan's chuckle was rich and deep. "This is a ship, not a 'boat' and *you* are doing the swaying, my sweet—the result, I fear, of a shocking overindulgence in wine at supper."

"The captain was so determined I try each one," she protested. "He's very nice," she added, rather pleased with the world in general.

"You won't think so when you wake up in the morning," Jordan teased.

He obligingly turned his back while she changed, then he tucked her into their bed, drawing up the sheets to her chin.

"My lord," she asked, "aren't you coming to bed?" Alexandra wished devoutly that she wasn't required to address him always as "your grace" or "my lord," but the dowager duchess had lectured her very sternly that she must address him thus, unless and until her husband gave her permission to do otherwise. Which he hadn't.

"I'm going up on deck for a little while to get some air," he said, stopping to take his pistol out of his other jacket and tuck it in the waistband of his dark-blue trousers.

Alexandra was fast asleep before Jordan had finished walking down the narrow passageway toward the steps that led to the upper deck.

At the railing, Jordan reached into his pocket and took out one of the slender cheroots he usually enjoyed after supper. Cupping his hands around the tip, he lit it, then he stood looking out across the Channel, contemplating the highly complex problem of Alexandra. After years of associating with sophisticated, mercenary, shallow women—and of condemning the entire sex on the basis of those women—he had married a girl who was artless, candid, intelligent, and generous.

And he didn't know what to do with her.

Alexandra had some foolish, quixotic notion that he was noble and gentle and "beautiful." When, as he well knew, he was jaded, disillusioned, and morally corrupt. In his brief life, he'd already killed too many men to count and bedded more women than he could possibly recall.

Alexandra believed in openness, trust, and love—and she fully intended to try to make *him* participate in her beliefs. He wanted nothing to do with openness, trust, or love.

She was a gentle dreamer; he was a hard realist.

She was, in fact, such a dreamer that she actually believed "something wonderful" was going to happen—which wasn't that surprising, since she also believed wet dirt in the springtime smelled like perfume . . .

Alexandra wanted to make him see the world as she saw it—fresh and alive and unspoiled, but it was too late for that. All he could do was to try to keep the world that way for her for as long as possible. But he would not share her imaginary world with her. He didn't want to. He didn't belong there. At Devon she would be safe from the corrosive effects of Society, safe from the dissipations and brittle sophistication of his world—the world where he was comfortable—where he was not expected to *feel* things like love; where he wasn't expected to trust, or to reveal his inner thoughts and feelings . . .

He dreaded the hurt he knew he'd see on her face when she realized he did not intend to stay in Devon with her, but that he would not do. Could not do.

In front of him, the Channel stretched for as far as he could see, its inky surface swept by a giant yellow moonbeam. Irritably, Jordan flicked his cheroot over the side, then he remembered it was his only one. He'd left the flat gold case with the others in it at Elise's house in London the night before last.

Restless from days of enforced confinement in the coach

125

and from trying unsuccessfully to find a better solution to the problem of Alexandra, he turned from the rail and glanced along the wharf, where light spilled out from taverns and inebriated sailors staggered along, their arms flung over the shoulders of the whores who walked at their sides.

Less than four yards away, two men darted swiftly into the shadows of the ship and crouched down among the coiled ropes out of his sight.

Hoping to buy a few cigars in the tavern across the wharf, Jordan strolled across the deck and headed for the gangplank. Two shadows emerged from the ropes and followed him, hanging back, watching.

Jordan was aware that the wharf was a dangerous place to be at night, particularly with impressment gangs ranging about, pouncing upon the unwary and loading their unconscious victims onto His Majesty's warships, where they woke up to discover they had the "honor" of becoming seamen for months or years—until such time as the ship returned to port. On the other hand, Jordan was armed, all he saw on the wharf were drunken seamen, and, after surviving years of bloody battles all over Spain, he saw little to fear from the few yards of wharf that separated him from the tavern.

"Stay back, yer fool—let 'im get to th' wharf," one of the shadows whispered to the other as they moved silently down the gangplank in Jordan's wake.

"What the bloody hell are we waitin' for," the second shadow demanded of his cohort as they waited in the darkness under the eaves of the tavern, where their prey had disappeared. "We was supposed ter hit him over the head and dump him into the water, which we coulda done better while he was on the ship."

The first man smiled sardonically. "I got a better idea—it ain't more work, and it'll get us more blunt."

Jordan emerged from the tavern with three fat, unappealing cigars stuck in the inside pocket of his coat. Now that he had them, he doubted he'd want to light them. Behind him, shadows shifted suddenly, a board creaked, and Jordan tensed. Without changing his pace, he reached inside his coat for the pistol, but before his hand ever touched it, his skull had already exploded into shards of agonizing pain, sending him sliding into a black tunnel of oblivion. And then he was floating, drifting, moving toward a welcoming light at the end of the tunnel that seemed to beckon him.

Alexandra awoke at dawn to the shouts of seamen moving above her, getting the ship ready to put out to sea. Despite the fact that her head felt as if it was stuffed with wool, she was still eager to be up on deck when the lines were cast off and the ship set sail. Her husband must have had a similar idea in mind, she thought as she pulled on a fresh gown and wrapped herself in a matching cloak of soft lavender wool. He had already arisen and left the cabin.

A band of grey and pink was streaking the horizon when Alexandra arrived on deck. Seamen hurried about their tasks, sidestepping her as they uncoiled ropes and scrambled up the rigging. In front of her, the first mate stood with his feet braced wide apart, his back to her, calling out orders to the men climbing the masts. She looked about for her husband, but she seemed to be the only passenger on deck. At supper last night, she'd heard Jordan tell Captain Farraday that he always enjoyed being on deck when the lines were cast off and the ship set sail. Picking up her skirts, Alexandra walked over to the captain as he came on deck. "Captain Farraday, by any chance have you seen my husband?"

Seeing the impatience on his face, she quickly explained her reason for detaining him. "He isn't in our cabin and he's not on deck. Is there anywhere else on this ship he might be?"

"It's not likely, your grace," he said absently, his gaze on the lightening sky, assessing the amount of time before it was fully dawn. "Now, if you'll excuse me—"

Puzzled, trying to ignore the tingles of alarm dancing up and down her spine, Alexandra went down to their cabin and stood in the center of it, looking uncertainly about. Deciding Jordan had probably gone for a stroll on the docks, she walked over and picked up the tan coat he'd tossed over the back of the chair after they boarded the ship last night. Carrying it over to the wardrobe to hang it inside, she rubbed her cheek against the soft superfine fabric, inhaling the faint scent of Jordan's spicy cologne, then she put it away. He was accustomed to having a valet picking up after him, she realized with a fond smile, as she reached for his tan trousers and took them to the wardrobe. Turning, she looked for the dark blue coat he'd been wearing when he went up on deck late last night. The blue coat was nowhere in the cabin; neither was the rest of the clothing he'd had on last night when she last saw him.

Captain Farraday sympathized with her concern, but he did not intend to let the tide go out without his ship, and he said so. A terrible premonition of calamity was raging through Alexandra, making her tremble, but she knew instinctively that pleading would have no effect on the man in front of her. "Captain Farraday," she said, drawing herself up and speaking in what she hoped was a good imitation of Jordan's grandmother's imperious voice, "if my husband is lying injured somewhere on this ship, the blame will be on your head, not only for his injury, but for putting out to sea instead of getting him off this ship and into the hands of a proper doctor. Furthermore," she said, struggling to keep her voice from shaking, "unless I misunderstood what my husband told me yesterday, he *owns* part of the company that owns this ship."

Chapter Twelve

IN FULL-DRESS UNIFORM, Captain Farraday and his first mate stood at military attention on the deserted deck of the impounded *Fair Winds,* watching the black traveling chaise draw to a stop directly in front of their gangplank. *"That's her?"* the first mate said in disbelief, staring at the slender, ramrod-straight figure who was walking slowly up the gangplank, her hand on the arm of Sir George Bradburn, one of the most influential men in the Admiralty. "You mean to tell me that white-haired old woman has enough influence to make the Minister impound our ship and have both of us quarantined on it? Just so she can get here and listen to what we have to say?"

Alexandra jumped up at the sound of the knock upon her cabin door, her heart hammering with fear and hope as it had for the last five days, whenever there was a sound outside, but it was not the duke who stood in her doorway; it was his grandmother whom she hadn't seen since her wedding day. "Has there been any word?" Alexandra whispered desperately, too distraught to greet the woman.

"The captain and first mate know nothing," her grace said shortly. "Come with me."

"No!" Teetering on the brink of hysteria, where she had hovered for more than two days and nights, Alexandra shook her head wildly and backed away. "He'd want me to stay—"

The duchess drew herself up and regarded the pale, stricken girl down the full length of her aristocratic nose.

"My grandson," she said in her coldest voice, "would expect you to behave with the dignity and self-control that befits his wife, the Duchess of Hawthorne."

The words hit Alexandra like a slap in the face—and with the same result—bringing her back to her senses. Her husband *would* expect that of her. Fighting for control of her wild panic, Alexandra picked up the puppy, straightened her spine, and walked woodenly beside the duchess and Sir George Bradburn to the coach, but when the coachman took her elbow to help her inside, Alexandra drew back sharply, her eyes making one last, frantic search of the fronts of the taverns and warehouses lining the bustling wharf. Her husband was here somewhere. Sick or hurt. He had to be . . . Her mind refused to consider any possibility beyond that.

Hours later, the coach slowed, making its decorous way through the London streets, and Alexandra shifted her bleak gaze from the window to the duchess, who was seated across from, her back rigidly erect, her face so cold and emotionless that Alexandra wondered if the woman was capable of feeling anything. In the tomblike silence of the coach, Alexandra's hoarse whisper sounded like a shout. "Where are we going?"

After a deliberate, prolonged pause that made it eloquently clear the dowager resented having to explain her intentions to Alexandra, she said coldly, "To my town house. Ramsey will have already arrived there with a small staff who will keep the shades drawn and inform any callers that we are at Rosemeade. News of my grandson's disappearance is all over the papers, and I have no wish to be badgered by callers and curiosity seekers."

The duchess' brusque tone evidently evoked a pang of sympathy in the Minister, Bradburn, because he broke his own silence for the first time and tried to reassure her: "We are moving heaven and earth to discover what has happened to Hawthorne," he said gently. "Bow Street has a hundred men scouring the wharves, making official inquiries, and the Hawthorne family solicitors have employed another hundred investigators with instructions to use any means whatsoever to obtain information on their own. No demand for ransom has been received, so we do not think he was abducted for that purpose."

Stifling the tears that she knew the old duchess would despise, Alexandra made herself ask a question she feared to have answered: "What are the chances of finding him—?" Her voice trailed off. She could not say the word "alive."

"I—" He hesitated. "I don't know."

His tone implied the chances were not extremely good, and Alexandra's eyes blurred with scalding tears that she concealed by laying her cheek against Henry's soft fur while she swallowed against the painful knot of misery congealing in her throat.

For four endless days, Alexandra existed in the same house with the duchess, who persistently treated her as if she were invisible, neither speaking to her nor looking at her. On the fifth day, Alexandra was standing at the window of her bedchamber when she saw Sir George leaving the house. Too agitated to wait for a summons, she raced downstairs to the salon and burst in on the duchess. "I saw the Minister leaving. What did he say?"

The duchess glared her displeasure at Alexandra's peremptory entrance into the room. "Sir George's visits are of no concern to you," she coldly replied and turned her head away in rude dismissal.

Her words snapped the slender thread of control Alexandra had managed to keep on her emotions. Clenching her hands at her sides, she said in a voice shaking with frustration and fury, "Despite what you think, I am not a witless child, ma'am, and my husband is the most important person in the world to me now. You cannot, *must not,* keep information from me!"

When the duchess merely continued to regard her in stony silence, Alexandra switched to pleading. "It is so much kinder to tell me the truth than to hide it from me. I cannot bear not knowing—please don't do this to me. I won't embarrass you with hysterics. . . . When my father died and my mother could not resume her life, I took over the running of our household at the age of fourteen. And when my grandfather died, I—"

"There is no news!" her grace snapped. "When news comes, I will see that you hear it."

"But it's been so long!" Alexandra burst out.

The dowager's gaze raked over her, blazing with contempt. "You're quite a little actress, aren't you? However, you can stop worrying about your welfare. A marriage settlement was made between that mother of yours and my grandson, providing her with enough money to live in splendor for the rest of her days. She has more than enough to share with you."

Alexandra's mouth dropped open as she realized the duchess actually believed her concern was for her own future, instead of for her husband, who might even now be lying at the bottom of the English Channel.

Speechless with fury, Alexandra listened as the dowager scathingly finished: "Get out of my sight. I cannot abide your feigned concern over my grandson's well-being, not for another moment. You scarcely knew him, he was nothing to you."

"How *dare* you!" Alexandra cried. "How dare you sit there and say those things to me. You—you wouldn't understand how I feel about him, because *you* don't have any feelings! Even if you did, you're too—too *old* to remember what love is like!"

The duchess slowly arose, seeming to tower over Alexandra, but Alexandra was too hysterical, too enraged, to stop her mindless tirade: "You can't imagine what it was like for me to see him smile at me or to have him laugh with me. You can't know how it felt to look into his eyes—" A sob rose in Alexandra's throat and tears began pouring down her pale cheeks. "I don't want his money—I just want to be able to look into his eyes and to see him smile." To her horror, Alexandra's knees buckled and she sank to the floor, at the duchess' feet weeping. "I just want to see his beautiful eyes," she sobbed brokenly.

The duchess seemed to hesitate, then she turned on her heel and left the room, leaving Alexandra to weep out her grief and misery in lonely solitude. Ten minutes later, Ramsey entered the room bearing an ornate silver tea service. "Her grace said you were 'weak from hunger' and wishful of refreshment," he said.

Still on the floor with her arms on the settee and her face buried in them, Alexandra slowly raised her head and self-consciously brushed her tears away. "Please—take that away. I can't bear the sight of food."

Following the duchess' orders and ignoring Alexandra's request, Ramsey placed the unwanted tray on the table, then he straightened and, for the first time since Alexandra had met him, the servant looked uncertain and uneasy. "It is not my intent to gossip," he began stiffly after a pause, "but I am informed by Craddock, her grace's dresser, that her grace has scarcely eaten a meal in five days. A tray has just been brought to her in the small drawing room. Perhaps if you were to offer to dine with her, you could persuade her to eat."

"That woman doesn't need food," Alexandra gulped, listlessly getting up. "She isn't like mortal people."

Ramsey's chilly demeanor became positively glacial at the indirect criticism of his employer. "I have been with the Duchess of Hawthorne for forty years. My deep concern for her led me to presume incorrectly that you might also feel some concern for her, since you are now part of the family. I apologize for my error in judgment."

He bowed stiffly out of the room, leaving Alexandra feeling thoroughly obnoxious and completely bewildered. Ramsey was apparently devoted to the duchess, yet Alexandra well knew the duchess' attitude toward her servants: Twice at Rosemeade, she had sternly reprimanded Alexandra for "gossiping with the servants," when all Alexandra had done was ask Ramsey if he was married and a parlormaid if she had children. From the duchess' lofty view, talking to a servant consistituted gossiping with them, which in turn constituted treating them as equals—and that, Alexandra remembered from the duchess' blistering remarks, was *not done.* Despite all that, Ramsey was apparently devoted to her. Which meant there had to be more to the elderly woman than pride and hauteur, Alexandra decided.

That possibility led to another, and Alexandra gazed at the tea tray in blank confusion, wondering if the duchess could possibly have meant it as a "peace offering." Until five minutes ago, the duchess had never shown the slightest interest in whether Alexandra ate or not. On the other hand, the tray could just as easily have been intended as a sharp reminder to Alexandra to get control of herself.

Alexandra bit her lip as Ramsey's words rang ominously through her mind: Five days . . . the duchess had not eaten in five days. Alexandra had scarcely done so either, but she was young and healthy and strong. Alexandra's attitude softened yet more as it occurred to her that if the duchess had been unable to eat, she must be a great deal more distressed over her grandson's disappearance than she was letting on.

With a sigh of determination, Alexandra raked her hair back off her forehead and decided the tea tray had been intended as a peace offering. She did so because she could not endure the thought of a seventy-year-old woman wasting away.

Through the partially open door of the blue salon, Alexandra saw the duchess sitting in a high-backed chair, staring into the fire. Even in repose, the old woman presented a forbidding figure, yet there was something about her stiff, withdrawn features that reminded Alexandra poignantly of her own mother during the early days after her father's death, before the arrival of his other wife turned Mrs. Lawrence's grief to hatred.

She stepped softly into the room, throwing a shadow across the duchess' line of vision, and the old woman's head snapped up. Just as swiftly, she looked away—but not before Alexandra had glimpsed the suspicious sheen of tears in the duchess' pale eyes.

"Your grace?" Alexandra said softly as she stepped forward.

"I did not give you leave to interrupt me here," the woman snapped, but for once Alexandra was unfooled by that harsh voice.

In the same soothing tone she'd used with her mother, Alexandra said, "No, ma'am, you did not."

"Go away."

Deflated but determined, Alexandra said, "I shan't stay long, but I must apologize for the things I said to you a few minutes ago. They were unforgivable."

"I accept your apology. Now go away."

Ignoring the duchess' scathing glower, Alexandra walked forward. "I thought, since we both have to eat, it might be more tolerable if we shared a meal together. We—we could bear each other company."

Anger flared in the woman whose wishes were being ignored. "If you want company, you should go home to your mother, as I suggested to you not fifteen minutes past!"

"I can't."

"Why not?" the old woman snapped.

"Because," Alexandra said in a suffocated whisper, "I need to be near someone else who loves him."

Naked, uncontrollable pain slashed across the old duchess' features before she brought herself under control, but in that instant, Alexandra saw the torment that lay beneath her facade of stiff dignity.

Aching with pity, yet careful not to show it, Alexandra hastily sat down in the chair across from the duchess and uncovered one of the trays. Her stomach churned at the sight of food, but she smiled brightly. "Would you like a slice of this nice chicken—or would you prefer the beef?"

The duchess hesitated, her eyes narrowed on Alexandra. "My grandson is still alive!" she stated, her expression daring Alexandra to deny it.

"Of course he is," Alexandra said fervently, aware she was being warned to get out if she doubted it. "I believe that with all my heart."

The duchess studied Alexandra's face, assessing her sincerity, then she gave a small, hesitant nod and said gruffly, "I suppose I could eat a bit of chicken."

They ate in complete silence broken only by the occasional crackle from the little fire burning in the grate. Not until Alexandra arose and bade her goodnight did the old woman speak, as for the first time she addressed Alexandra by her given name:

"Alexandra—" she whispered hoarsely.

Alexandra turned. "Yes, ma'am?"

"Do you . . ." The duchess drew a ragged, pain-edged breath. "Do you . . . pray?"

Tears swelled in Alexandra's throat and burned the backs of her eyes for, as she instantly realized, the proud old woman was not interested in her personal religious habits. She was *asking* Alexandra to pray.

Swallowing painfully, Alexandra nodded. "Very, very hard," she whispered.

For the next three days, Alexandra and the duchess kept a quiet vigil in the blue salon, their sentences desultory, their voices unnaturally hushed—two strangers with little in common except the unspeakable terror that bound them together.

On the afternoon of the third day, Alexandra asked the duchess if she had sent for Anthony, Lord Townsende.

"I sent word to him to join us here, but he was—" She broke off as Ramsey materialized in the doorway. "Yes, Ramsey?"

"Sir George Bradburn has arrived, your grace."

Alexandra leapt anxiously to her feet, scattering the embroidery the duchess had pressed on her, but when the distinguished, white-haired man walked into the room a moment later, she took one look at his carefully expressionless face, and her whole body began to vibrate with terror.

Beside her, the duchess evidently drew the same conclusion from his features, because her face became drained of color and she slowly arose, leaning heavily on the cane she'd been using since they came to Grosvenor Square. "You have news, George. What is it?"

"The investigators have ascertained that a man meeting Hawthorne's description was seen in a tavern on the wharf at approximately eleven on the night Hawthorne disappeared. With the assistance of a sizable bribe, the proprietor of the tavern also recalled that the man was unusually tall—well over six feet—and was dressed as a gentleman. The gentleman purchased several cigars and left. The tavern was located almost directly across the wharf from where the *Fair Winds* was docked and we are certain the man was Hawthorne."

Bradburn paused and said miserably, "Would you ladies not prefer to be seated while you hear this?"

His dire suggestion made Alexandra grasp the side of her chair for support, but she shook her head.

"Continue," the duchess ordered hoarsely.

"Two seamen aboard the *Falcon,* which was docked near the *Fair Winds,* witnessed a very tall, well-dressed man leaving the tavern, followed by two men who looked like ordinary rabble. The seamen aboard the *Falcon* were not paying particular attention, and they were already in their cups, but one of them thinks he saw the tall gentleman bludgeoned over the head by one of the rabble. The other seaman did not see that happen, but he did see the gentleman—whom he assumed had passed out from too much drink—being slung over one of the ruffians' shoulders and carried off down the wharf."

"And they didn't do anything to help him?" Alexandra cried.

"Neither seaman was in a condition to offer aid, nor were they of a mind to interfere in a scene that is, unfortunately, all too common on the docks."

"There's more, isn't there?" the duchess predicted, her eyes searching his grim face.

Sir George drew a long breath and slowly expelled it. "We've known all along that press gangs were very active on the night in question, and after further investigation, we discovered that one of the gangs purchased a man whose description was unmistakably that of Hawthorne. Believing he was passed out from drink, and finding no identification on him, they paid the rabble for Hawthorne and then delivered him on board one of His Majesty's warships—the *Lancaster*."

"Thank God!" Alexandra cried as joy exploded in her heart. Without thinking, she caught the duchess' icy hand in her own and squeezed it tightly. But Bradburn's next words sent Alexandra's spirit plummeting into the depths of hell. "Four days ago," he said grimly, "the *Lancaster* was engaged in battle by a French ship, the *Versailles*. Another of our ships, the *Carlisle*, was limping back to port under cover of the fog, crippled from an encounter with the Americans. Unable to go to the aid of his sister ship, the captain of the *Carlisle* witnessed the entire battle through his glass. When the battle was over, the *Versailles* was barely under sail . . ."

"And the *Lancaster?*" Alexandra burst out.

Sir George cleared his throat. "It is my sad duty to inform you that the *Lancaster* was sunk, and all on board were lost—including his grace, the Duke of Hawthorne."

The room whirled before Alexandra's vision; a scream rose in her chest and she pushed her hand against her mouth, her wild gaze flying to the duchess' tormented face. She saw the duchess sway, and Alexandra automatically wrapped her arms around the weeping woman, rocking her back and forth as if she were a child, stroking her shaking back, whispering mindless reassurances to her, while torrents of tears raced down her own cheeks.

As if from a great distance, she heard Sir George Bradburn say he had brought a doctor with him, and she was dimly aware of someone gently but firmly pulling Jordan's weeping grandmother from her embrace, while Ramsey took her arm and guided her upstairs.

Chapter Thirteen

Nightmares pursued Alexandra all the way into wakefulness as she rolled onto her back, trying to escape from a dream where she stood in a churchyard, surrounded by hundreds of headstones, each one bearing the name of her father, or her grandfather, or her husband.

Her eyelids felt as if they were weighed down with iron when she made an effort to force them open, and when she finally succeeded, she wished she hadn't. Her head felt as if someone had buried an ax in her skull, and the sunlight pouring in from the window made her eyes ache. Wincing, she turned away from the source of the sunlight, and her gaze riveted on a thin woman in a starched black uniform, white apron, and cap, who was dozing in an armchair beside her bed. The parlormaid, Alexandra realized dimly.

"Why are you here?" she whispered in a feeble, rasping voice she scarcely recognized as her own. The parlormaid slept on, snoring softly, and Alexandra tilted her throbbing head on the pillow. Her gaze settled blankly on the table beside her bed, where a spoon and glass lay beside a bottle.

"What is that?" she whispered, more loudly this time.

The exhausted servant jerked erect, saw that Alexandra's eyes were open, and leapt from her chair. "Laudanum, my lady, and the doctor said you was to eat the very minute you came round. I'll fix you a nice tray and be back in a trice."

Too sleepy to sort that all out, Alexandra let her heavy lids slide closed. When she opened them again, there was a tray

139

beside the bed, and the sun had angled much lower in the sky. It was afternoon, Alexandra realized, feeling disoriented and fuzzy, but rested.

The parlormaid was awake this time, peering anxiously at her. "Goodness, you've been sleeping like the dead!" she burst out, then clapped her hand over her mouth, her eyes wide with horror.

Alexandra peered curiously at her, and awkwardly struggled into a sitting position so the maid could place the tray on her lap. On the laden breakfast tray, as was the custom, there was a red rose and a copy of the *Times* folded in half. "Why, was I given laudanum?" Alexandra asked, annoyed with her slurred speech and inability to concentrate properly.

"Because the doctor said you should have it."

Alexandra frowned in confusion, then automatically asked the same question she had asked each morning since she'd come to this house. "Has Sir George come to—" Pain shrieked through her body and erupted in a tortured moan as her mind snapped into focus and she remembered Bradburn's last visit on Tuesday. She shook her pounding head, trying to blot out the images marching across her mind, the voices saying, ". . . *Sad duty to inform you that all hands on board were lost. . . . Quick, get the doctor. . . . Authorities duly notified. . . . Ramsey, get her to bed . . .*"

"No!" Alexandra cried and jerked her face away from the maid, but the *Times* was lying on her lap. She stared at the bold print on the front page.

"What's wrong, my lady? What do it say?" the horrified maid asked, staring uncomprehendingly at the words she'd never been taught to read.

Alexandra understood every agonizing one of them. They said that Jordan Addison Matthew Townsende—12th Duke of Hawthorne, Marquess of Landsdowne, Earl of Marlow, Baron of Richfield—was dead.

Alexandra's head fell back on the pillows, and she closed her eyes, oblivious to everything but the torment searing her mind.

"Oh, Miss—your grace—I never meant to give you cause to be upset," the maid whispered, wringing her hands. "I'll get the doctor. Her grace has taken to her bed, so ill she be that he said he daren't leave her—"

The last of that slowly penetrated Alexandra's desolation. "I'll go to her in a little bit," she told the distraught maid.

"Oh, no, your grace, you've been ill yerself, and it won't do no good anyway. Craddock told Mr. Ramsey that her grace don't talk. She *can't*. She don't recognize no one—she just stares . . ."

Alarm overcame Alexandra's grief and, ignoring the maid's protests, she swung her legs over the side of the bed, grasped the bedpost to steady her swaying senses, then pulled on her dressing robe.

In answer to Alexandra's knock, the physician opened the door to the duchess' bedchamber and stepped out into the hallway. "How is she?" Alexandra asked anxiously.

The physician shook his head. "She's not good, not good at all. She is not a young woman and she has sustained a terrible shock. She will not eat or speak. She merely lies there, staring into the distance."

Alexandra nodded, remembering her mother's behavior when, shortly after her father's death, his mistress had called upon them. Her mother had also retired to her bed, where she would neither eat nor speak, nor let anyone console her. When her mother had eventually emerged from her self-imposed confinement, she never was herself again. It was as if all the grief and bitterness were still bottled up inside of her, eating away at her mind.

"Has she cried?" Alexandra said, knowing that it was dangerous to keep grief bottled up inside.

"Certainly not! Women of her station and constitution do not indulge in weeping. As Craddock and I have repeatedly told her, she must be strong and look on the bright side. After all, she has another grandson, so it's not as if the title will pass out of the family."

Alexandra's opinion of leeches, which had never been high, plummeted to an irretrievable low as she stared at the insensitive, pompous man before her. "I would like to see her, if you please."

"Try to cheer her up," he said, oblivious to Alexandra's look of unwavering scorn. "Don't talk about Hawthorne."

Alexandra walked into the darkened room, and her heart leapt in pity and alarm to behold the formerly brisk, robust woman who was propped up against the pillows, looking like a ghost of her former self. Beneath her crown of white

141

hair, the dowager's face was chalky and her pale eyes were glazed with pain and sunken into deep, dark hollows. No sign of recognition registered in her eyes as Alexandra crossed in front of her bed, then sat down on the edge of it beside her.

Frightened, Alexandra reached out and grasped the duchess' blue-veined hand, which was lying limply upon the golden coverlet. "Oh, ma'am, you must not go on this way," she said in a shaky, compassionate whisper, her eyes pleading with the elderly duchess to listen to her. "You must not. Jordan would hate to see you like this." When she got no reaction at all, Alexandra's desperation grew and she squeezed the fragile hand tightly. "Have you any idea how proud he was of your strength and spirit? Have you? I know he was, because he *boasted* of those very things to me."

The faded blue eyes never wavered. Not certain whether the duchess hadn't heard her, hadn't believed her, or simply didn't care, Alexandra redoubled her efforts to convince her. "It's true. I remember the occasion very well. After our wedding we were about to leave Rosemeade, and he asked where you'd gone. I told him you were upstairs and that I greatly feared you'd never recover from our marriage. He smiled when I said that—you know, one of his special smiles that made you feel like smiling in return? Then do you know what he said?"

The duchess didn't move.

"He said," Alexandra plowed on urgently, "'It would take more than our marriage to send my grandmother into a decline. Why, my grandmother could take on Napoleon himself and when she was through with him, he'd be begging her pardon for his bad manners in making war on us.' That is exactly what he—"

The duchess' eyes closed and Alexandra's heart missed a beat, but a moment later two tears rolled slowly down her pale cheeks. Tears were a good sign, Alexandra knew, and she plunged fiercely ahead: "He knew you were courageous and strong and—and loyal, too. From something he said to me, I don't think he believed women were capable of loyalty, except for you."

The duchess' eyes opened and she looked at Alexandra with anguished pleading and doubt.

Laying her hand upon the heartbroken woman's cheek,

Alexandra tried harder to convince her she spoke the truth, but her own control was slipping so fast she could hardly speak. "It's true. He was so certain of your loyalty to him, he told me that even though you detested our marriage, you would still flay anyone alive who dared to criticize me— simply because I bear his name."

The faded blue eyes filled with tears that began to race down the duchess' cheeks and over Alexandra's fingers. Several silent minutes later, the duchess swallowed convulsively, and lifted her eyes to Alexandra's face. In a broken voice she pleaded, "Did Hawthorne truly say that—about Napoleon?"

Alexandra nodded and tried to smile, but the duchess' next words sent tears spilling from her eyes and dripping from her lashes: "I loved him better even than my sons, you know," she wept. Reaching up, the duchess put her arms around the weeping girl who was trying valiantly to comfort her, and drew Alexandra close. "Alexandra," she sobbed, "I—I never told him I loved him. And now it's too late."

For the rest of that day and all of the next, Alexandra remained with the duchess, who seemed to need to talk about Jordan almost constantly, now that the dam of grief had been broken.

At eight o'clock the following evening, Alex left her elderly charge resting peacefully and went down to the blue salon rather than return to the depressing isolation of her own room. Trying to keep her aching sense of loss at bay, she picked up a book.

In the doorway, Ramsey cleared his throat to announce the arrival of a caller: "His grace, the Duke of Hawthorne—"

A cry of joy escaped Alexandra's lips as she rose to her feet and rushed forward. Ramsey stepped aside, the Duke of Hawthorne appeared in the doorway, and Alexandra stopped dead. Anthony Townsende was coming toward her. Anthony Townsende was now the Duke of Hawthorne.

Fury, irrational and uncontrollable, flamed in her breast that this man should *dare* to call himself by Jordan's title after such an indecently short time. Anthony Townsende had *benefited* from this tragedy, she realized, and he was probably *glad* . . .

Anthony abruptly stopped walking and stared at the blazing anger on Alexandra's pale face. "You're wrong, Alexandra," he said quietly. "I would give anything to see him walk into this room right now. If I'd known Ramsey would announce me as he did, I'd have asked him not to do so."

Alexandra's anger abruptly dissolved at the unmistakable sincerity she heard in his quiet voice and the sadness she saw in his eyes. Too honest to deny what she had thought, she said contritely, "Please forgive me, your grace."

"Tony," he corrected, holding out his hand for hers in a gesture of greeting and friendship. "How is my grandmother?"

"Sleeping now, but she's been up a little more each day."

"Ramsey told me you've been a tremendous source of comfort and support to her. I thank you for that."

"She's been very brave, and she's taking care of herself."

"And you?" he asked, walking over to a side table and pouring some sherry into a glass. "Are *you* taking care of yourself? You look terrible."

A flash of her old humor briefly lit her eyes. "Your memory is short, your grace. I was never more than passable-looking."

"Tony," he insisted, sitting down across from her and gazing into the flickering fire.

"Your grandmother does not wish to remain in London and be forced to endure the strain of hundreds of condolence calls," Alexandra said after a few minutes. "She prefers to have a small memorial service and then to leave for Rosemeade immediately after."

Anthony shook his head at the mention of Rosemeade. "I don't think she ought to shut herself up alone at Rosemeade, and I cannot remain there with her for more than a sennight. Hawthorne—Jordan's seat—is an enormous estate, with a thousand servants and tenants who are all going to require direction and reassurance when they learn of his death. I have my work cut out for me trying to learn to manage his investments and familiarize myself with running all of his estates. I would vastly prefer that my grandmother accompany me to Hawthorne and remain there."

"That would be much better for her," Alexandra agreed.

To set his mind at rest about her own plans, Alexandra told him she intended to go home after the memorial service. "My mother meant to begin traveling and enjoying herself immediately after my wedding," she explained. "She promised to write and let me know her direction, so if you will have her letters sent on to me at home, I'll write to her wherever she is and tell her my husband is . . ." She tried to say "dead" and couldn't. She could not believe the handsome, vital man she had married was no longer alive.

With a determined scowl upon her face and Ramsey trailing solicitously upon her heels, the duchess walked slowly into the yellow salon the next morning, where Anthony was reading the newspaper and Alexandra was sitting at a desk, staring pensively into space.

As the duchess gazed at the pale, courageous girl with the hollow cheekbones who had pulled her through her grief, her expression softened, then underwent an immediate, radical change as her glance fell on Henry, who was alternately chasing his own tail and tugging at the hem of Alexandra's black mourning gown. "Be still!" she commanded the undisciplined beast.

Alexandra started, Anthony jumped, but Henry merely wagged his tail in greeting and renewed his gleeful play, undeterred. Caught off guard by this unprecedented case of flagrant defiance, the dowager attempted to stare the rambunctious puppy into submission and, when that had no effect, she rounded on the stately butler. "Ramsey," she commanded imperiously, "see that this deplorable creature is taken for a long, exhausting walk."

"Yes, your grace. At once," the stately butler said, bowing again, his expression deadpan. Bending down, he grasped the puppy by the scruff of his neck with his right hand, placed his left hand under the dog's furry rump, and held the squirming puppy as far away from his fastidious self as the length of his arms permitted.

"Now then," the duchess said briskly, and Alexandra hastily stifled her wayward smile. "Anthony informs me you intend to go home."

"Yes. I'd like to leave tomorrow, after the memorial service."

"You'll do nothing of the sort. You will accompany Anthony and me to Hawthorne."

Alexandra had been dreading having to return to her old life and trying to go on as if Jordan had never lived, but she had not considered going to Hawthorne. "Why should I do that?"

"Because you are the Duchess of Hawthorne, and your place is with your husband's family."

Alexandra hesitated, then she shook her head. "My place is at home."

"Rubbish!" the duchess declared stoutly, and Alexandra couldn't help smiling at the return of the elderly woman's familiar, autocratic manner; it was vastly preferable to the hollow shell that grief had made of her. "On the same morning you wed Hawthorne," the duchess continued determinedly, "he specifically entrusted me with the task of making you into all you should be, in order that you might ultimately take your rightful place in Society. Although my grandson is no longer here, I trust I have enough *loyalty,*" she emphasized, "to carry out his wishes."

The emphasis on the word "loyalty" made Alexandra recall—as the dowager meant her to do—that she herself had told the duchess her grandson had admired that trait in her. Alexandra hesitated, caught between guilt, responsibility, and concern for her own welfare should she try to live at Hawthorne, removed from everything and everyone she knew and loved. The duchess was valiantly struggling to cope with her own grief; she could not help Alexandra shoulder hers. On the other hand, Alexandra wasn't certain she could carry the terrible burden alone, as she had done when her grandfather and her father died. "You are kindness itself to suggest I live with you, ma'am, but I fear I cannot," Alexandra declined after a moment's further thought. "With my mother gone away, I have responsibilities to others, which must take first consideration."

"What responsibilities?" the duchess demanded.

"Penrose and Filbert. With my mother gone away, they will have no one to look after them. I had intended to ask my husband to make a place for them at his house, but—"

"Who" she interrupted imperiously, "are Filbert and Penrose?"

"Penrose is our butler and Filbert our footman."

"I have long been under the impression," said her grace with asperity, "that servants exist to care for their employers, and not the other way round. However," she unbent enough to say, "I applaud your sense of responsibility. You may bring them to Hawthorne," she magnanimously decreed. "I daresay we can always use another servant or two."

"They're quite old!" Alexandra hastily interjected. "They can't work hard, but they're both proud, and they need to believe they're desperately helpful. I've, well, fostered that delusion in them."

"I, too, have always felt it my Christian duty to ensure elderly servants are allowed to work so long as they wish to and are able," the duchess lied baldly, hurtling a killing glance at her incredulous grandson. Converting Alexandra into a polished young socialite was a project she was bent on accomplishing. It was a challenge—a duty—a goal. She was unwilling to admit that the courageous girl with the gypsy curls, who had pulled her through her shock and grief, might have stolen a permanent place in her heart, or that she was loath to bid her goodbye.

"I don't think—" Alexandra began.

Realizing Alexandra was about to refuse again, the duchess pulled out all the stops: "Alexandra, you are a Townsende now, and your place is with us. Moreover, it is your avowed duty to honor your husband's wishes, and he specifically wished for you to become a credit to his illustrious name."

Alexandra's resistance dissolved as the duchess' last words finally struck home. Her name was *Townsende* now, not Lawrence, she realized with a burst of pride and pleasure. She had not lost everything when she lost him; he had given her his name! In return, Alexandra recalled with a sharp pang of nostalgia, she had solemnly pledged her word to Jordan to honor him and to obey his wishes. Apparently, he had wished her to become a proper lady worthy of his name and to take a place in Society—whatever that meant. Tenderness swelled in her heart as she raised her eyes to the duchess and softly promised, "I will do as he wished."

"Excellent," said the duchess gruffly. When Alexandra left to see to her packing, Anthony leaned back in his chair and leveled his amused gaze upon his grandmother, who reacted by drawing herself up stiffly in her chair and trying to stare him out of countenance. The ploy failed. "Tell me," he drawled in a laughter-tinged voice, "when did you develop this violent desire to employ elderly servants?"

"When I realized it was the only way to keep Alexandra from leaving," she replied bluntly. "I will not permit that child to lock herself away in some godforsaken village and wear widow's weeds for the rest of her life. She is scarcely eighteen years old."

Chapter Fourteen

*H*AWTHORNE, THE ANCESTRAL ESTATE of twelve generations of Townsendes comprised 50,000 acres of woods, parkland, rolling hills, and fertile fields. Imposing black iron gates bearing the Hawthorne coat of arms blocked the entrance, and a liveried gatekeeper came out of a stone gatehouse to push open the heavy gates so the elegant traveling chaises could pass.

Sitting beside the duchess, Alexandra gazed out the windows as the coach swept down a smooth, curving drive that wound decorously through acres and acres of immaculately clipped green velvet lawns.

Huge trees marched along on either side of the smooth drive, stretching their stately branches like leafy umbrellas above the coaches. Although Hawthorne belonged to Anthony now, in her heart Alexandra thought of it as Jordan's. This was his home, the place where he was born, and where he'd grown to manhood. Here she would learn about him and come to know him as she had never had the chance to do in life. Simply by being here, she already felt closer to him. "Hawthorne is more beautiful than any place I've ever imagined," she breathed.

Anthony grinned at her awed enthusiasm. "Wait until you see the house itself," he said, and from his tone Alexandra knew it would be very grand indeed. Even forewarned, however, she drew in her breath sharply when the coach rounded a bend in the drive. A half mile ahead, spread out before her in all its majestic splendor, was a three-story stone and glass mansion of over two hundred rooms, set against a backdrop of rolling green hills, crystal blue streams, and terraced gardens. In the foreground, across the drive from the house, swans drifted on the tranquil surface of an enormous lake, and, off to the right, a beautiful white gazebo with graceful columns in the classic Greek style overlooked the lake and parkland.

"It's beyond beautiful," Alexandra whispered, "it's beyond anything." A half-dozen footmen were standing at attention upon the shallow, graceful steps that led from the drive to the front door. Stifling the feeling that she was being very rude, Alexandra followed the duchess' example when she alighted from the coach and walked past the servants as if they were invisible.

The front door was opened wide by a servant whose lofty bearing instantly proclaimed him head butler and ruler of the household staff. The duchess introduced him as Higgins, then walked into the hall with Alexandra at her side.

A wide, curving marble staircase swept upward in a graceful half circle from the foyer to the second story, then across a balcony and up to the third story. Alexandra and the duchess ascended the curving staircase together, and Alexandra was shown into a splendid suite of rooms decorated in shades of rose.

After the maid left them, the duchess turned to Alexandra. "Would you like to rest? Yesterday was an ordeal for us both."

Alexandra's memory of Jordan's memorial service yesterday was a blur of pain and unreality—a grim haze populated by hundreds of somber faces glancing speculatively at her as she stood quietly beside the duchess in the huge church. Anthony's widowed mother and his younger brother, who was lame, stood on her other side, their faces pale and strained. A half hour ago, their coach had turned in to the drive of Anthony's former home. Alexandra liked them both and was glad they'd be nearby.

"Instead of resting, would it be possible for me to see his room, ma'am? You see, I was married to Jordan, but I never had an opportunity to truly know him. He was a boy in this house, and he lived in it until the week before I met him." The familiar, aching lump of tears swelled in Alexandra's throat and she finished in an unsteady voice, "I want to find him, to learn about him, and I can do it here. That is one of the reasons I agreed to come with you."

Tenderness so overwhelmed the duchess that she started to raise her hand and lay it against Alexandra's pale cheek, then she checked herself and said a trifle brusquely, "I'll have Gibbons, the head footman, sent up to you."

Gibbons, a spry, elderly man, appeared a few moments later and escorted Alexandra to what he called "the Master Bedchambers"—a majestic suite of rooms on the second floor, with an entire wall of mullioned glass from floor to ceiling, which overlooked the grounds.

The instant Alexandra stepped inside, she noticed the faint, achingly familiar scent of Jordan's spicy cologne, the same scent that had clung to his smoothly shaven jaw and chin when she had fallen asleep in his arms at night. The pain of his death seeped into her very bones and lodged there like a dull, aching throb, and yet, she felt strangely comforted being here, because it banished the haunting feeling that her sudden, four-day marriage to a splendid stranger had been imaginary.

Turning, she let her gaze rove lovingly over every inch of the room, from the lavishly carved plasterwork at the ceiling to the magnificent Persian carpets of deep blue and gold beneath her feet. Two massive fireplaces of cream marble were at opposite ends of the enormous room, their hearths so cavernous she could easily have stood up inside them. An immense bed with a deep-blue satin coverlet heavily embroidered with gold stood on a raised dais on her far left, beneath a stately canopy of blue and gold attached to the high ceiling. On her right, a pair of gold-silk settees faced each other in front of one of the fireplaces.

"I would like to look around," she explained to the footman, her voice a reverent whisper, as if she were in some holy, sanctified place, which indeed she rather felt she was. Walking over to the rosewood bureau, she lovingly touched his onyx-backed brushes, still laid out as if they were only waiting for his hand to grasp them, then she stood on tiptoe, trying to see her reflection in the mirror above the bureau. Jordan's mirror. The mirror was hung at a height to suit its former owner and, even standing on tiptoe, Alexandra could see only her forehead and eyes. *How very tall he was,* she thought, smiling winsomely.

Three more rooms opened off the bedchamber—a dressing room, a study with book-lined walls and soft leather chairs, and another room that made Alexandra gasp. Spread out before her was a huge semicircular room of gold-veined black marble walls and floors with a huge, round sunken marble pit of some sort in the center. "What in the world is this?" Alexandra asked.

"A bathing room, your grace," the footman replied and bowed again.

"A bathing room?" Alexandra repeated, staring in wonder at the gold faucets and graceful marble pillars that stood at the perimeter of the bathing pool, then soared to the ceiling beneath a round skylight.

"Master Jordan believed in modern-i-zations, your grace," the footman put in and Alexandra turned at the sound of pride and fondness in the old servant's voice.

"I'd rather be called simply 'Miss Alexandra,'" she explained with a warm smile. He looked so appalled that she conceded, "'Lady Alexandra' then. Did you know my husband well?"

"Better'n any of the staff, 'cept Mr. Smarth, the head groom." Sensing that he had an avid audience in Lady Alexandra, Gibbons promptly volunteered to give her a tour of the house and grounds, which lasted all of three hours and included visits to Jordan's favorite boyhood haunts, as well as introductions to Smarth, the head groom, who offered to tell her "all about Master Jordan," whenever she came down to the stables.

Late in the afternoon, Gibbons finished the tour by taking Alexandra to two places, one of which instantly became her favorite. It was the long gallery where a double row of life-size portraits of the previous eleven dukes of Hawthorne were displayed in identical gilt frames upon the long walls, along with other portraits of their wives and children.

"My husband was the handsomest of them all," she declared after studying each portrait.

"Me and Mr. Higgins have said that very thing ourselves."

"But his portrait isn't here with the other dukes."

"I heard him tell Master Anthony that he had better things to do with his time than stand about looking important and dignified." He nodded toward two of the portraits on the upper row. "That's him, right there—as a young boy, and then when he was sixteen. His papa insisted he stand for that last one, and Master Jordan was mad as fire about it."

A smile dawned across Alexandra's pale features as she looked up at the little boy with the dark curly hair standing solemnly beside a beautiful blond lady with sultry grey eyes. Standing on the other side of her thronelike red velvet chair was a handsome, unsmiling man with broad shoulders and the proudest features Alexandra had ever seen.

The last place Gibbons took her was to a rather small room on the third floor that smelled as if it had been closed for a very long time. Three small desks faced a much larger desk at the front of the room, and an old globe stood on a brass stand.

"This here's the schoolroom," Gibbons said. "Young Master Jordan spent more time tryin' to git out o' it than he spent inside it. Then Master Jordan felt the side of Mr. Rigly's cane more than once for neglectin' his studyin'. Still, he learnt what-all he needed to know. Smart as a whip he was."

Alexandra's gaze scanned the austere little room, then came to an abrupt stop at the desk right beside her. Carved into the top of it were the initials *J-A-M-T*. Jordan's initials. She touched them tenderly while glancing around with a mixture of pleasure and uneasiness. How very unlike her grandfather's cheerful, disorderly study where she had eagerly learned her own lessons this gloomy, austere place seemed. How unthinkable it was to be caned by one's teacher, instead of fascinated by him.

When the footman finally bade her goodbye, Alexandra stopped once more at the gallery to gaze upon the likeness of her husband as a sixteen-year-old. Looking up at him, she whispered solemnly, "I'll make you proud of me, my love, I promise."

In the days that followed, Alexandra embarked on that task with all the determination and intelligence she possessed, memorizing entire pages of Debrett's *Peerage,* and poring over volumes on conduct, convention, and protocol which the duchess gave her. Her diligence quickly earned the duchess' approval, as did everything else Alexandra did—with two significant exceptions, both of which led the duchess to summon Anthony to her drawing room a week after the family had arrived at Hawthorne.

"Alexandra is fraternizing with Gibbons and Smarth," she declared in tones of bewilderment and grave concern. "She's already conversed more with them than I have in the last forty years."

Anthony lifted his brows and said blandly, "She regards servants as family. That was evident when she asked us if her butler and footman might come here. It's a harmless attitude."

"You won't think Filbert and Penrose are 'harmless' when you see them," the duchess shot back darkly. "They arrived this morning."

Anthony recalled Alexandra had described her two servants as elderly, and started to say it. "They're—"

"Deaf and blind!" the indignant dowager declared. "The butler can't hear a word that isn't roared into his ear and the footman walks into doors *and* into the butler! Regardless of Alexandra's tender feelings, we shall have to keep them out of sight when we are receiving callers. We can't allow guests to see them crashing into each other in the front hall and shouting the walls down.

When Anthony looked amused rather than alarmed, she glowered at him. "If you will not see that as objectionable, I've little hope of persuading you to discontinue your fencing matches with Alexandra each morning. It is an entirely unacceptable endeavor for any young lady, besides requiring the wearing of—of breeches!"

Anthony was no more inclined to see his grandmother's side on this matter than he'd been on the subject of fraternization with servants. "For my sake and for Alexandra's I hope you won't forbid her to fence with me. It's harmless enough and she enjoys it. She says it keeps her fit."

"And for your sake?" the duchess said irritably.

Anthony grinned. "She's a formidable opponent, and she keeps me in top form. Jordan and I were considered two of the best swordsmen in England, but I have to work to hold my own with Alexandra, and she still bests me about half the time."

When Tony left, the dowager gazed helplessly at the empty chair across from her, knowing full well why she had not been willing to speak to Alexandra about the issues she'd just discussed with Anthony: She simply could not bear to dampen Alexandra's spirits, not when she knew how valiantly Alexandra was trying to be cheerful. For nearly a week, Alexandra's heartwarming smile and musical laughter had brightened the entire atmosphere at Hawthorne. And as the duchess well knew, Alexandra was smiling, not because she felt like it, but because she was desperately trying to buoy up everyone's spirits—including her own. She was, the duchess thought, a unique combination of candor, gentleness, determination, and courage.

Unaware that she had done aught to distress the duchess, Alexandra adjusted herself to the rigid routine of formal living in a ducal mansion. As spring drifted into summer, she continued with her studies and spent her free time wandering about the beautiful grounds or visiting the vast Hawthorne stables where Smarth told her wonderful stories about Jordan as a boy and a young man. Like Gibbons the footman, Smarth was a great fan of Master Jordan, and, within a few weeks, Smarth was completely won over by the charming girl Master Jordan had married.

For Alexandra, the days were busy ones, but Jordan was never out of her mind. A month after his death, at Alexandra's request, a small marble plaque, bearing Jordan's name and dates of birth and death, had been placed—not in the family cemetery, as was usual, but at the far side of the lake at the edge of the woods near the pavilion.

Alexandra thought the setting near the pavilion pretty—particularly in contrast to the lonely cemetery beyond the crest of a hill behind the mansion. Yet when the plaque had been placed, she was not entirely satisfied. She visited the head gardener, who gave her a few bulbs that she planted just inside the woods. Every few days, she returned to obtain more flowers. But not until she was finished did Alexandra realize she had unconsciously duplicated the little glade where Jordan had once told her she looked like a Gainsborough portrait.

She loved the place more when she realized it, and spent hundreds of happy hours seated in the pavilion, gazing into the miniature glade and recalling every moment they had spent together.

Alone in the pavilion, she dwelled with tenderness upon

every kindness Jordan had shown her—from buying her a puppy he obviously hadn't liked, to marrying her to save her from ruin. But mostly she relived the heady sweetness and hungry insistence of Jordan's kisses, the torturous pleasure of his caressing, wandering hands. When she tired of recalling their real kisses, she imagined more of them in different settings—wonderful kisses that ended in Jordan dropping to his knee, with his hand over his heart, and pledging his undying love to her. The longer she thought of their time together, the more certain she became that he had begun to love her before he died.

Aided and encouraged by Gibbons' and Smarth's exaggerated versions of Jordan's most minor boyhood braveries and manly skills, Alexandra enshrined Jordan in her heart, endowing him with the virtues of a saint, the courage of a warrior, and the beauty of an archangel. In the rosy glow of her memory, every gentle word he'd spoken, every warm smile, each stirring kiss, was immortalized—and then improved upon.

It did not occur to her that Smarth and Gibbons might have been blind to his faults or that they would, by unspoken mutual consent, carefully censor from their conversation any activities of his which might have put him in a less saintly light in the eyes of his legal wife. Never once did they mention a certain lovely ballerina or her many predecessors, or the governess who had shared his bed in this very house.

Based on the glowing stories that Smarth and Gibbons told her, Alexandra naturally assumed her husband had been noted for his bravery, daring, and honor. She had no way of knowing that he was equally well known for his flagrant flirtations, amatory conquests, and scandalous liaisons with women who possessed only one significant social asset in common: Beauty.

And so, with all the fervor of her eighteen years, Alexandra spent each day practicing at the pianoforte, memorizing tomes on social protocol, rehearsing polite conversation with her tutor, and emulating the manners of the only duchess she had available to use as an example—Jordan's grandmother. She did it all so that when she went to London, Society would look upon her and find her worthy of Jordan Townsende's name and reputation.

And while Alexandra was diligently applying herself to mastering all manner of accomplishments that would have bored a living Jordan to distraction, Nature—as if amused by her needless efforts—casually showered upon her in lavish bounty the one required social asset that would guarantee Society would truly find her "worthy" of Jordan Townsende: Beauty.

Standing at the windows, watching Alexandra gallop down the drive in a bright-blue riding habit, Anthony glanced at his grandmother beside him. "It's astonishing," he said wryly. "In one year, she's blossomed into a beautiful young woman."

"It's not in the least astonishing," the duchess said with gruff loyalty. "She always had good bones and excellent features, she was simply much too thin and too young. She had not filled out yet—I myself was just such a late bloomer."

"Really?" Anthony said, grinning.

"Indeed," she primly replied, and then she became somber. "She still brings flowers to lay on Jordan's plaque every day. Last winter, I thought I'd cry when I saw her wading through the snow with flowers from the conservatory in her arms."

"I know," Tony said somberly. His gaze shifted back to the window as Alexandra waved at them and handed Satan over to a groom. Her glossy, wind-tossed hair was long now, tumbling in waves and curls partway down her back; her complexion was rosy, and her sooty-lashed eyes were glowing like enormous aquamarines.

Jordan had once mistaken her for a boy, but now her bright-blue riding habit revealed an alluring female form with ripened curves in all the right places. Anthony's eyes followed the gentle sway of her hips as she walked up the front steps, admiring the easy, long-legged grace of her stride. Everything about her drew a man's gaze and held it.

"In a few weeks, when she makes her bow," Tony thought aloud, "we're going to have to beat off her suitors with a club."

Chapter Fifteen
LONDON

*A*NTHONY," THE DUCHESS SAID, nervously pacing the length of the drawing room in her silver satin gown. "Do you suppose I made a mistake in not hiring a younger woman to teach Alexandra how to go about in Society?"

Turning from the mirror, where he had been needlessly rearranging the intricate folds of his pristine white neckcloth, Tony smiled sympathetically at his grandmother's last-minute panic over Alexandra's debut tonight. "It's too late to change that now."

"Well, who could possibly be better suited than I to teach her how to behave properly? I am," the dowager reminded him bluntly, reversing her earlier opinion, "regarded as a paragon of proper behavior by Society, am I not?"

"You are indeed," Tony said, refraining from reminding her that he'd told her at the outset Alexandra shouldn't be taught to emulate a woman of seventy-one years.

"I can't go through with it," the duchess remarked suddenly and sank into a chair, her expression positively dire.

Tony chuckled at her unprecedented display of doubt and uncertainty, and she sent him a glowering look. "You won't be laughing a few hours from now," she predicted darkly. "Tonight, I will attempt to persuade the crème de la crème of Society to accept a female without fortune, family connections, or ancestry to recommend her. The chances for disaster are mind-boggling! I'm bound to be found out and exposed for a trickster."

Anthony approached the stricken woman whose blighting eye, razor tongue, and cold demeanor had intimidated Society and her entire family, with the exception of Jordan, for five decades. For the first time in his life, he pressed a spontaneous kiss to her forehead. "No one would dare oppose you by ostracizing Alexandra, even if they suspected her origins. You'll carry this off without a hitch. A lesser woman might fail, but not you, Grandmama—not a woman of your enormous consequence."

The duchess digested that for a moment and then slowly inclined her white head in a regal nod. "You're entirely correct, of course."

"Of course," Anthony said, hiding a smile. "And you needn't worry that Alexandra will betray her background."

"I'm as concerned about her revealing her mind as I am her background. I can't think what her grandfather could have been about when he filled her head with bookish nonsense. You see," she admitted anxiously, "I so wish for her to have a wonderful Season, to be admired for herself, and then to make a splendid match. I wish Galverston hadn't offered for the Waverly chit last week. Galverston's the only unmarried marquess in England, which means Alexandra will have to settle for an earl or less."

"If those are your hopes, Grandmama, you're bound to be disappointed," Tony said with a sigh. "Alexandra has no interest whatsoever in the Season's amusements or in being admired by any of the town beaux."

"Don't be absurd—she's been working and studying and looking forward to this for months!"

"But not for the reasons you evidently think," Anthony said somberly. "She's here because you convinced her Jordan wanted her to take her rightful place in Society as his wife. She's been working all these months for one reason only—that she may be worthy of that honor. She has no intention of remarrying. She told me that last night. She's convinced herself that Jordan loved her, I think, and she fully intends to 'sacrifice herself' to his memory."

"Good God!" said the duchess, thunderstruck. "She's barely nineteen years old! Of course she must marry. What did you say to her?"

"Nothing," Anthony replied sardonically. "How could I tell her that, in order to fit in with Jordan's crowd, she should have studied flirtation and dalliance, rather than drawing-room conversation and Debrett's *Peerage.*"

"Go away, Anthony," her grace sighed. "You're depressing me. Go and see what's keeping Alexandra—it's time to leave."

In the hall outside her bedchamber, Alexandra stood before a small portrait of Jordan which she'd discovered in an unused room when they first came to London, and which she'd asked to have rehung here, where she could see it every time she passed. The painting was done the year before last, and in it Jordan was sitting with his back against a tree, one leg drawn up, his wrist resting casually atop his knee, looking at the artist. Alexandra loved the lifelike, unposed quality of the painting, but it was his expression that held her like a magnet and made her pulse quicken— because Jordan looked very much as he had often looked when he was about to kiss her. His grey eyes were slumberous, knowing; and a lazy, thoughtful smile was hovering about his mobile lips. Reaching up, Alexandra touched her trembling fingertips to his lips. "Tonight is our night, my love," she whispered. "You won't be ashamed of me—I promise."

From the corner of her eye, she saw Anthony coming toward her and hastily snatched her hand away. Without taking her eyes from Jordan's compelling features, she said, "The artist who painted this is wonderfully talented, but I can't quite make out his name. Who is he?"

"Allison Whitmore," Anthony said curtly.

Surprised by the notion of a female painter and by Anthony's abrupt tone, Alexandra hesitated, then she shrugged the matter aside and pirouetted slowly in front of Anthony. "Look at me, Anthony. Do you think he would be pleased with me if he could see me now?"

Stifling the urge to give Alexandra a taste of reality by telling her Lady Allison Whitmore painted that picture while Jordan was indulging in a torrid affair with her, Anthony took his eyes from the portrait and did as Alexandra asked. What he saw stole his breath away.

Standing serenely before him was a dark-haired beauty wrapped in an alluring, low-cut gown of shimmering aquamarine chiffon the exact shade of her magnificent eyes. It draped diagonally across her full breasts and clung to her tiny waist and gently rounded hips. Her gleaming mahogany hair was pulled back off her forehead, falling in waving swirls over her shoulders and partway down her back. Diamonds nestled in the burnished waves, twinkling like stars on gleaming satin; they lay at her slender throat and sparkled at her wrist. But it was that face of hers that made it hard for Anthony to breathe.

Although Alexandra Lawrence Townsende was not beautiful in the classic tradition of fair hair and pale skin, she was nevertheless one of the most alluring, provocative creatures he had ever beheld. Beneath her sooty lashes, eyes that could enchant or disarm gazed candidly into his, completely unaware of their mesmerizing effect. Her rosy, generous mouth invited a man's kiss, yet her poised smile warned one not to get too close. At one and the same time, Alexandra managed to look seductive yet untouchable, virginal yet sensual, and it was that very contrast that made her so alluring—that, and her obvious unawareness of allure.

Some of the color drained from Alexandra's high, delicately carved cheekbones as she waited for the silent man before her to tell her Jordan would have been pleased with her appearance tonight. "That bad?" she asked, joking to cover her dismay.

Grinning, Anthony took both her gloved hands in his and said truthfully, "Jordan would be as dazzled by the sight of you tonight as the rest of the *ton* is going to be when they clap eyes on you. Will you save me a dance tonight? A waltz?" he added, gazing into her huge eyes.

In the coach on the way to the ball, the duchess issued last-minute instructions to Alexandra: "You needn't worry about your waltzing, my dear, nor any of the other social amenities you'll be expected to perform tonight. However," she warned in a dire tone, "I must remind you again not to allow *Anthony's*"—she paused to cast him a severely disapproving look— "appreciation of your intellect to mislead you into saying anything tonight which could make you appear bookish and intelligent. If you do, you will not *take* at all, I assure you. As I have told you time out of mind, gentlemen do not like overeducated females."

Tony squeezed Alex's hand encouragingly as they alighted from the coach. "Don't forget to save me a dance tonight," he said, smiling into her bright eyes.

"You may have all of them, if you wish." She laughed and tucked her hand in the crook of his arm, as unselfconscious of her beauty as she was unaware of its effect on him.

"I'm going to have to stand in line," Anthony chuckled. "Even so, this is going to be the most enjoyable evening I've had in years!"

For the first half hour of Lord and Lady Wilmer's ball, Tony's prediction seemed to come true. Tony had deliberately preceded them into the ballroom so that he could watch his grandmother and Alexandra make their grand entrance. And it was worth watching. The Dowager Duchess of Hawthorne marched into the ballroom like a protective mother hen shepherding her chick—her bosom puffed out, her back ramrod straight, and her chin thrust forward in an aggressive stance that positively *dared* anyone to question her judgment in lending her enormous consequence to Alexandra or to *consider* ostracizing her.

The spectacle literally "stopped the show." For a full minute, five hundred of the *ton's* most illustrious, languid, and sophisticated personages stopped talking to gape at England's most respected, most dour, and most influential noblewoman, who seemed to be hovering solicitously over a young lady no one recognized. Whispers broke out among the guests and monocles were raised to eyes as attention shifted from the dowager to the ravishing young beauty at her elbow, who no longer bore any resemblance to the gaunt, pale girl who had appeared briefly at Jordan's memorial service.

Beside Anthony, Sir Roderick Carstairs lifted his arrogant brows and drawled, "Hawthorne, I trust you'll enlighten us about the identity of the dark-haired beauty with your grandmother?"

Anthony regarded Carstairs with a bland expression. "My late cousin's widow, the current Duchess of Hawthorne."

"You're joking!" Carstairs said with the closest thing to surprise that Anthony had ever seen displayed on Roddy's eternally bored face. "You can't mean this entrancing creature is the same plain, pathetic, bedraggled little sparrow I saw at Hawk's memorial service!"

Fighting to suppress his annoyance, Tony said, "She was in shock and still very young when you last saw her."

"She's improved with age," Roddy observed dryly, raising his quizzing glass to his eye and leveling it at Alexandra, "like wine. Your cousin was always a connoisseur of wine and women. She lives up to his reputation. Did you know," he continued in a bored drawl, his quizzing glass still aimed straight at Alexandra, "that Hawk's beauteous ballerina has not admitted any other man into her bed in all this time? It boggles the mind, does it not, to think that the day is here when a man's mistress is more faithful to him than his own wife."

"What is that supposed to imply?" Anthony demanded.

"Imply?" Roddy said, turning his sardonic gaze on Anthony. "Why, nothing. But if you don't wish Society to reach the same conclusion I'm drawing, I suggest you cease watching Jordan's widow with that possessive look in your eye. She does reside with you, does she not?"

"Shut up!" Anthony snapped.

In one of his typical mercurial changes of mood, Sir Roderick Carstairs grinned without rancor. "They're about to begin the dancing. Come introduce me to the girl. I claim the right of her first dance."

Anthony hesitated, mentally grinding his teeth. He had no justification to refuse the introduction; moreover, if he did demur, he knew perfectly well Carstairs could and would retaliate by cutting Alexandra dead or—worse—repeating the innuendo he'd just made. And Roddy was the most influential member of Tony's set.

Tony had inherited Jordan's title, but he was well aware he did not possess Jordan's bland arrogance and the unnerving self-assurance that had made Jordan the most influential member of the *haute ton*. The dowager, Anthony knew, could force the entire *ton* not to cut Alexandra, and she could guarantee Alexandra's acceptance by her own age group, but she could not force Tony's generation to fully accept her. Neither could Tony. But Roddy Carstairs could. The younger set lived in terror of Roddy's biting tongue, and not even Tony's own set had any wish to become the object of Carstairs' scorching ridicule. "Of course," Tony agreed finally.

With much foreboding, he introduced Carstairs to Alexandra, then stood back and watched as Roddy made her a gallant bow and requested the honor of a dance.

It took Alexandra most of the waltz before she began to relax and stop counting off the steps in her head. In fact, she had just decided that she was not likely to miss a step and tread on the well-shod feet of her elegant, bored-looking dancing partner when he said something that nearly made her do exactly that. "Tell me, my dear," he said in a sardonic drawl, "how have you managed to blossom as you have in the frigid company of the Dowager Duchess of Hawthorne?"

The music was building to a crescendo as the waltz neared its end, and Alexandra was certain she must have misunderstood him. "I—I beg your pardon?"

"I was expressing my admiration for your courage in having survived a full year with our most esteemed icicle—the dowager duchess. I daresay you have my sympathy for what you must have endured this past year."

Alexandra, who had no experience with this sort of sophisticated, brittle repartee, did not know it was considered fashionable, and so she reacted with shocked loyalty to the woman she had come to love. "Obviously you are not well-acquainted with her grace."

"Oh, but I am. And you have my deepest sympathy."

"I do not need your sympathy, my lord, and you cannot know her well and still speak of her thus."

Roddy Carstairs stared at her with cold displeasure. "I daresay I'm well enough acquainted with her to have suffered frostbite on several occasions. The old woman is a dragon."

"She is generous and kind!"

"You," he said with a jeering smile, "are either afraid to speak the truth, or you are the most naive chit alive."

"And you," Alexandra retorted with a look of glacial scorn that would have done credit to the dowager herself, "are either too blind to see the truth, or you are extremely vicious." At that moment the waltz came to an end, and Alexandra delivered the unforgivable—and unmistakable —insult of turning her back on him and walking away.

Unaware that anyone had been watching them, she returned to Tony and the duchess, but her actions had indeed been noted by many of the guests, several of whom lost no time in chiding the proud knight for his lack of success with the young duchess. In return, Sir Roderick retaliated by becoming her most vocal detractor that same night and expressing to his acquaintances his discovery, during their brief dance, that the Duchess of Hawthorne was a vapid, foolish, vain chit and a dead bore without conversation, polish, or wit.

Within one hour, Alexandra innocently verified to the guests that she was certainly excruciatingly foolish. She was standing amidst a huge group of elegantly attired people in their twenties and early thirties. Several of the guests were enthusiastically discussing the ballet they'd attended the night before and the dazzling performance given by a ballerina named Elise Grandeaux. Turning to Anthony, Alexandra raised her voice slightly in order to be heard over the din, and had innocently asked if Jordan had enjoyed the ballet. Two dozen people seemed to stop talking and gape at her with expressions that ranged from embarrassment to derision.

The second incident occurred shortly thereafter. Anthony had left her with a group of people, including two young dandies who were discussing the acceptable height of shirt-points, when Alexandra's gaze was drawn to two of the most beautiful women she had ever seen. They were standing close together, but with their backs to one another, and they were both minutely scrutinizing Alexandra's features over their shoulders. One was a coolly beautiful blonde in her late twenties, the other a lush brunette a few years younger.

Jordan had once remarked that Alexandra reminded him of a Gainsborough portrait, she remembered fondly, but these two women were worthy of no less a master than Rembrandt. Realizing that Mr. Warren had been speaking to her, Alexandra begged his pardon for her lack of attention, and inclined her head toward the two women who had distracted her. "Are they not the two loveliest females you've ever beheld?" she asked with a smile of sheer admiration and no jealousy.

The group surrounding her looked first at the two women, then at her. Brows shot up, eyes widened, and fans lifted to conceal amused smiles. By the end of the ball, four hundred people had heard that Hawk's widow had been admiring two of his former paramours, Lady Allison Whitmore and

Lady Elizabeth Grangerfield. So diverting was that tidbit that even Lady Grangerfield and Lady Whitmore—whose friendship had long ago been destroyed by their mutual desire for the same man—heard about it. And for the first time in years, they were seen laughing uproariously together, like the best of friends.

Alexandra was blissfully unaware of her latest gaffe, but she was acutely aware as the evening progressed that people seemed to be laughing at her behind their hands.

On the way home in the coach, she pleaded with Anthony to tell her if something had gone awry, but he merely patted her shoulder and soothingly told her she was "a great success," while the duchess remarked that she had given "an excellent account" of herself.

Despite that, Alexandra knew instinctively that something was very wrong. During the following week of balls, soirées, Venetian breakfasts, and musicales, the sardonic, sidelong glances directed at her became almost unendurable. Hurt and bewildered, she sought refuge among the dowager's acquaintances who, although decades older than she, did not seem to eye her as an amusing, peculiar, pathetic creature. Moreover, with them, she could repeat some of the wondrous stories of Jordan's skill and daring which she'd heard from Hawthorne's head footman and chief groom, such as the time he saved the head groom from drowning.

It did not dawn on Alexandra that the polite, older people who listened to her glowing accounts were concluding that she had been sadly and ludicrously besotted with Hawthorne—or that these same people might repeat this observation to their younger relatives, who in turn spread the word to all *their* friends.

On rare occasions, Alexandra was asked to dance, but only by men who were interested in the huge dowry Anthony and the duchess had settled on her—or by men who were mildly interested in sampling the body of the young woman who had been married to one of England's most notorious libertines. Alexandra sensed, without knowing why, that none of these gentlemen truly liked her and she did the only thing she could think of to hide her confusion and misery: She put her chin up and with cool politeness made it infinitely clear she preferred to remain with the dowager's set.

As a result, Alexandra was dubbed the Ice Duchess, and the unkind sobriquet stuck. Jokes circulated amongst the *ton* which implied that Jordan Townsende may have thought drowning was preferable to being frozen to death in his wife's bed. It was recalled with considerable relish that Jordan had been seen emerging from the lavish lodgings he provided for his lovely ballerina on the very afternoon the announcement of his marriage appeared in the *Times*.

Moreover, it was remarked upon at length and with much derision that Jordan's mistress had laughingly told a friend that very same evening that Jordan's marriage had been one of "*In*convenience" and that he had no intention of breaking off their relationship.

Within two weeks, Alexandra was painfully aware that she was a hopeless social outcast, but as she did not hear the talk, she had no way of discovering why. All she knew was that the *ton* treated her either with patronization, amusement, or occasionally, outright scorn—and that she had failed Jordan miserably. It was the latter that hurt her most. She spent hours standing in the hall in front of his likeness, trying not to cry, silently apologizing to him for her failure and begging him to forgive her.

"Can you hear me, Hawthorne? Wake up, man!"

With an effort that nearly sapped his strength, Jordan responded to the whispered command and slowly forced his lids open. Blinding white light poured in through tiny openings in the walls high above, searing his eyes, while pain again sent him plunging into the dark oblivion of unconsciousness.

It was night again when he came around and saw the grimy face of George Morgan, another captive from the *Lancaster* whom he hadn't seen since they were taken off the ship three months ago. "Where am I?" he asked and felt blood ooze from his cracked, parched lips.

"In hell," the American said grimly. "In a French dungeon, to be more exact."

Jordan tried to lift his arm and discovered heavy chains were holding it down. His gaze followed the chain to the iron ring attached in the stone wall and he studied it in foggy confusion, trying to think why he was chained, when George Morgan was not.

Understanding his bewilderment, his companion answered, "Don't you remember? The chain's part of your reward for swinging on a guard and breaking his nose, not to mention nearly slitting his throat with his own knife when they brought you in here this morning."

Jordan closed his eyes, but could not remember fighting with a guard. "What was the rest of my reward?" he asked, his voice hoarse, unfamiliar to his own ears.

"Three or four broken ribs, a battered face, and a back that looks like raw meat."

"Charming," Jordan gritted. "Any particular reason they didn't kill me rather than maim me?"

His coolly dispassionate tone wrung an admiring laugh from George. "Damn, but you British bluebloods don't blink an eye no matter what, do you? Cool as anything, just like everyone always says." Reaching behind him, George dipped a tin cup into a bucket of slimy water, poured off as much of the mold that floated on top as he could, then held the cup against Jordan's bloodied lips.

Jordan swallowed, then spat it out in furious revulsion.

Ignoring his reaction, George pressed the cup to the helpless man's lips again and said, "Now I know it don't have the delicate bouquet of your favorite Madeira, and it ain't in a clean, genteel crystal goblet, but if you don't drink it, you'll deprive our guards of the privilege of killing you themselves, and they'll take out their disappointment on me."

Jordan's brows snapped together, but he saw the other man was joking, and he took a few sips of the vile, dank liquid.

"That's better. You're sure a glutton for punishment, man," he continued lightly, but he was worriedly binding Jordan's chest with strips torn from his own shirt. "You could have spared yourself this beating if your ma had taught you to be polite when addressing two men who have guns and knives and nasty dispositions."

"What are you doing?"

"Trying to keep your ribs in one place. Now then, to answer your earlier question about why they didn't kill you, the Frenchies are trying to keep you alive in case the British capture one of theirs—I heard one of the officers say you was a trump card they intend to use in case they want a trade. 'Course you're not doin' your share, which is to stay alive—not when you go around insultin' a guard and then rudely tryin' to steal his weapon. From the looks of you, I didn't do you any favors when I hauled you out of the ocean with me and onto that French frigate that brought us here."

"How bad do I look?" Jordan asked without much interest.

"I'd say one more beating like this one and you'll not find your two ladies nearly as amorous as they were when you left."

Unconsciousness was wrapping its tentacles around him, trying to pull him back into the familiar black pit, and Jordan fought against it, preferring the pain to oblivion. "What 'two ladies'?"

"I reckon you ought to know better'n me. One's named Elise. Is that your wife?"

"Mistress."

"And Alexandra?"

Jordan blinked, trying to clear his fogged senses. Alexandra. Alexandra— "A child," he said as a dim vision of a dark-haired girl brandishing a pretend sword danced before his eyes. "No," he whispered in pained regret as his life passed swiftly before him—a wasted life of empty flirtations and debauchery, a meaningless life culminating in his whimsical, impulsive marriage to a bewitching girl with whom he had truly shared a bed only once. "My wife."

"Really?" George said, looking impressed. "Got a mistress and a wife and a child? One of everything."

"No—" Jordan corrected hazily. "No child. One wife. Several mistresses."

George grinned and rubbed his hand across his dirty beard. "I don't mean to sound censorious. I admire a man who knows how to live. But," he continued, thunderstruck despite himself, *"several* mistresses?"

"Not," Jordan corrected, gritting his teeth against the pain, "at the same time."

"Where've they been keepin' you all this time? I haven't seen you since the Frenchies took us off their ship three months ago."

"I've had private accommodations and personal attention," Jordan sardonically replied, referring to the dark pit beneath the dungeon that he had inhabited between periodic bouts of torture that had nearly driven him insane with pain.

His cellmate stared at Jordan's battered body with a worried frown, but he tried to keep his voice light. "What did you tell the Frenchies to make them dislike you so much more than me?"

Jordan coughed and gritted his teeth against the searing pain in his chest. "I told them my name."

"And?"

"And they remembered it"—he gasped, fighting to stay conscious—"from Spain."

George's brows drew together in bewilderment. "They've done this to you for something you did to them in Spain?"

The semiconscious man nodded slightly, his eyes closing. "And because . . . they think I still have . . . information. About military."

"Listen to me, Hawthorne," George said desperately. "You were muttering about an escape plan when you came to a while ago. Do you have a plan?"

Another feeble nod.

"I want to go with you. But Hawthorne—you won't live through another beating like this one. I mean it, man. Don't anger any more guards."

Jordan's head dropped sideways as he finally lost the battle against unconsciousness.

Sitting on his heels, George shook his head with despair. The *Versailles* had lost so many men in its bloody battle with the *Lancaster* that the French captain had fished three men out of the water and used them to supplement his badly diminished crew. One of them had died of his wounds within a day. George wondered if his cellmate was about to become a second casualty.

Chapter Sixteen

BY THE NIGHT of Lord and Lady Donleigh's ball, during the third week after her debut, Alexandra was so miserable, and so tense, that she was numb inside. She felt as if she would never again laugh with joy or find solace in tears. On that fateful night, she did both.

At the dowager duchess' whispered urging, Alexandra had politely, but reluctantly, agreed to dance with Lord Ponsonby, a ponderous, mincing middle-aged fop who affected a lisp, dressed like a peacock, and pompously informed her while they danced that he was regarded as a man of superior intelligence. Tonight he was attired in orange satin knee breeches that swelled over his protruding midsection, a plum satin waistcoat, and a long yellow brocade coat—a combination that made Alexandra think of a large pile of overripe fruit when she looked at him.

Instead of returning Alexandra to the dowager duchess when the dance ended, Lord Ponsonby (who Alexandra had heard was in need of a wealthy wife to offset his substantial gaming debts) drew her firmly in the opposite direction. "You must accompany me to that delightful alcove over there, your grace. The dowager duchess mentioned to me last evening that you have an interest in things philosophical, therefore I shall endeavor to enlighten you a little upon one of the greatest philosophers of ancient times—Horace." Alexandra instantly realized that the duchess must be desperately concerned about her lack of partners to resort to actually boasting to Ponsonby about Alexandra's intellect.

"Pray do not alarm yourself," Sir Ponsonby urged, mistaking the cause of Alexandra's dismay. "I shall not forget for a moment that you are a female and, as such, unable to understand the complexities and subtleties of logic. You may depend upon me to keep the discussion very, very simple."

Alexandra was too despondent to be annoyed by his insulting estimation of female intelligence and too defeated to feel anything more than mild dejection at being treated this way by a man with no more sense than to attire himself like a tray of fruit.

Wearing an expression of polite interest, she allowed him to guide her into the alcove, which was separated from the main ballroom by a pair of crimson velvet curtains drawn back and held in place with matching velvet cords. Once inside the alcove, Alexandra realized there was another occupant, a gorgeously gowned young woman with a patrician profile and lustrous hair the color of spun gold. She was standing at the open French door with her back partially to them—obviously trying to enjoy a moment of solitude and fresh air.

The young woman turned slightly as Alexandra entered with Lord Ponsonby, and Alexandra recognized her immediately. Lady Melanie Camden, the beautiful young wife of the Earl of Camden had just returned to London earlier in the week from the country, where she'd been visiting her sister. Alexandra had been present at the ball where Lady Camden put in her first appearance of the Season, and she had watched from afar as the crowd of illustrious guests rushed to Lady Camden, welcoming her back with delighted smiles and eager hugs. She was "one of their own," Alexandra thought rather wistfully.

Realizing they were invading Lady Camden's privacy, Alexandra smiled tentatively, silently apologizing for their intrusion. The countess acknowledged the smile with a polite nod of her head and serenely turned back to the French doors.

Lord Ponsonby either failed to notice the countess, or refused to be distracted by her presence. After helping himself to a glass of punch from the tray on the table beside him, he positioned himself beside one of the marble pillars that were situated in front of the curtains, and then launched into a pompous, grossly inaccurate dissertation on Horace's philosophical remarks about ambition, but all the while his gaze seemed to be on Alexandra's bosom.

Alexandra was so disconcerted at being subjected for the first time in her life to visual fondling by a male—even such a comically poor specimen of a male as this—that when he casually attributed a remark of Socrates' to Horace, she scarcely noticed either the error or the fact that the Countess of Camden had glanced swiftly over her shoulder at him, as if startled.

A minute later, Lord Ponsonby declared importantly, "I agree with Horace, who said, 'Ambition is so powerful a passion in the human breast that however high we reach we are never satisfied—'"

Utterly unnerved by his unswerving gaze and unaware that Lady Camden had turned fully around and was listening to Lord Ponsonby with a mixture of disbelief, fascination, and ill-concealed mirth, Alexandra shakily stammered "M-Machiavelli."

"Horace," Lord Ponsonby decreed, and to Alexandra's horror, the absurdly dressed creature lifted his quizzing glass to his eye, trained it upon the ripe flesh swelling above her bodice and boldly inspected her while he simultaneously sought to improve his appearance of languid nonchalance by propping his shoulder against the pillar behind him. Unfortunately, his obsession with Alexandra's breasts prevented him from glancing over his shoulder to ascertain the exact location of the pillar. "Now perhaps you can begin to understand," he proclaimed, leaning back and opening his arms wide in an all-encompassing gesture, "why Horace's remarks caused him to—aagh!" Arms outspread, he fell backward, overturning the table with the punch and dragging down the curtain, landing spreadeagled on his back at the feet of three male guests, like a colorful bowl of fruit beneath a waterfall of punch.

Unable to prevent her mad desire to laugh, Alexandra clapped her hand over her mouth, whirled around, and found herself staring at the Countess of Camden, who had covered her own mouth and was staring at Alexandra, her shoulders shaking with mirth, her wide green eyes swimming with it. In unison, both young women sped for the French doors, colliding in their haste to get through the doorway, and fled onto the balcony. Once there, they collapsed against the side of the house and exploded into gales of laughter.

Side by side, they stood, oblivious to the hard stone behind their shoulder blades, shrieking with mirth, gasping for breath, and wiping at the tears running down their cheeks.

When the storm of laughter had dwindled into fits of helpless giggles, the Countess of Camden turned her face toward Alexandra and said brokenly, "Ly-lying on his back, h-he looked exactly like a giant macaw that fell from a tree."

Alexandra was scarcely able to drag her voice through the mirth in her chest. "I—I thought a bowl of fruit—no, fruit *punch,*" she declared, and they dissolved with laughter again.

"P-poor Ponsonby," Lady Camden giggled, "s-struck down in his pompous prime by Machiavelli's ghost for attributing his own words to Horace."

"It was Machiavellian revenge!" Alexandra gasped.

And beneath a black velvet sky carpeted with stars, two elegantly garbed young women leaned against a cold stone wall and laughed with all the giddy, helpless delight of barefoot children racing across a meadow.

When their laughter was finally spent, Melanie Camden weakly slumped against the wall and turned her head to Alexandra, regarding her with smiling curiosity. "How did you know the odious Lord Ponsonby was confusing Machiavelli with Horace?"

"I've read them both," Alexandra admitted after a guilty pause.

"Shocking!" said the countess, feigning a look of horror. "So have I."

Alexandra's eyes widened. "I was under the impression that reading the classics branded a female as a bluestocking."

"It usually does," Melanie admitted airily, "but in my case, Society has chosen to overlook my—er—unfeminine interest in things beyond petitpoint and fashions."

Alexandra tipped her head to the side, regarding her in rapt fascination. "Why have they done so?"

Lady Camden's voice softened with affection. "Because my husband would flay anyone alive who dared intimate

174

that I am anything less than a perfect lady." Suddenly, she peered suspiciously at Alex and demanded, "Do you play a musical instrument? Because if you do, I warn you—friend or not—I shall *not* come and listen to you play. The mere mention of Bach or Beethoven sends me galloping after my hartshorn, and the sight of a harp puts me into a violent decline."

Alexandra had spent one year learning to play the pianoforte because the duchess had told her the ability to play at least one musical instrument was absolutely mandatory for young ladies of quality; she could hardly believe she was now hearing these derogatory comments from a lady who was reputed to be a veritable trend setter amongst the haughty elite. "I've had lessons at the pianoforte, but I don't play well enough to perform," she admitted uncertainly.

"Excellent," said Melanie with great satisfaction. "How interested are you in shopping for fashions?"

"Actually, I think it's tedious."

"Perfect," she declared, and then suspiciously, "You don't sing, do you?"

Alexandra, who had been somewhat reluctant to admit her inability to play a musical instrument, was now conversely reluctant to admit that she could sing well. "Yes, I'm afraid so."

"No one's perfect," the Countess of Camden cheerfully and magnanimously declared, pardoning Alexandra. "Besides, I've been waiting forever to meet a female who's read Horace and Machiavelli, and I shan't be deterred from befriending you merely because you can sing. Unless, of course, you do it very well?"

Alexandra's shoulders began to shake with mirth, for she sang very well indeed.

Melanie saw the answer in Alexandra's laughing eyes and grimaced with comical horror. "You don't sing *often*, do you?"

"No." Choking back a giggle, Alexandra added irreverently, "and if it will help raise me in your estimation, I can promise you that I generally run out of polite conversation in less than five minutes." Having thus cheerfully disposed of some of the most sacred of conventions, both girls burst out laughing again.

Within the mansion at No. 45 Regent Street, dancers

continued to dance and laughing guests continued to laugh, oblivious to the momentous event that was taking place outside the French doors. Only the twinkling stars noticed that on a deserted London balcony, two kindred spirits had found each other at last.

"In that case," Melanie grandly decreed when they had stopped chuckling, "I shall consider you a most suitable and enjoyable companion." Blithely setting aside any remaining pretense of formality, Lady Camden said quietly, "My close friends call me Melanie."

For an instant, happiness radiated through Alexandra's entire being, then harsh reality shattered it as she realized that Melanie Camden's friends wouldn't want her included in their circle. The entire *ton,* including Melanie's sophisticated friends, already regarded Alexandra as a complete antidote. She had been judged by all of them and found sadly lacking. Evidently Melanie Camden hadn't been back in London long enough to know that yet. Alexandra's stomach clenched at the thought of the derisive looks Lady Camden would receive were she to walk back into that ballroom with Alexandra.

"What do your friends call you?" Melanie prompted, watching her.

I don't have friends anymore, Alexandra thought and hastily bent to brush off her skirts, carefully hiding the tears that burned her eyes. "They called—*call* me Alex." Deciding it was best to end this association now, herself, rather than bear the humiliation of having Melanie Camden cut her dead when they next met, Alexandra drew a deep breath and said in a painfully awkward rush, "I appreciate your offer of friendship, Lady Camden, but you see, I'm very busy these days with balls and luncheons and . . . and all sorts of amusements. . . . And so I very much doubt that you . . . we . . . would be able to find time . . . and I'm certain you already have dozens and dozens of friends who—"

"—who think you are the veriest greenhead ever to appear at a London ball?" Melanie prompted gently.

Before Alexandra could react to that, Anthony walked out of the shadows onto the balcony, and she rushed to him in relief, talking swiftly so that he couldn't gainsay her. "Have

176

you been looking for me, your grace? It must be time to leave. Good evening, Lady Camden."

"Why did you decline Melanie Camden's offer of friendship?" Tony demanded angrily, as soon as they were ensconced in his coach on the way home.

"I . . . It would not have worked out," Alex prevaricated slightly, her mind on Melanie Camden's softly spoken parting remark. "We do not 'move in the same circles,' as you say here."

"I know that, and I also know why," Tony said tightly. "Roddy Carstairs is part of the reason."

Alexandra started at the realization that Tony was aware of her lack of popularity; she had thought—hoped—he was oblivious to her mortifying predicament.

"I've asked Carstairs to call upon me tomorrow morning," Tony continued bluntly. "We'll have to do something to change his opinion of you and pacify him for the slight you gave him when you left him on the dance floor that first night—"

"Pacify him!" Alexandra exclaimed. "Anthony, he said dreadful—wicked—things to me about your grandmother!"

"Carstairs says objectionable things to people all the time." Tony's reassuring smile was preoccupied. "He particularly enjoys trying to shock or fluster or intimidate females, and if he succeeds he despises his victim for her cowardice and stupidity. Carstairs is like a bird who flits from tree to tree, dropping seeds of dissension wherever he goes. Much of what he says is very amusing—so long as it isn't about oneself. In any case, you should have stared him right out of countenance or said something equally shocking to him."

"I'm terribly sorry. I didn't know that."

"There is a great deal you don't know," Tony said between his teeth, as they drew up before his house on Upper Brook Street. "But once we're in the house, I'm going to remedy that."

Alexandra felt a terrible, unexplainable premonition of dread that mounted as they walked into the salon. Tony motioned for her to sit down on the light-green brocade settee and then poured whisky into a glass for himself. When he turned toward her, he looked angry and unhappy.

"Alex," he said abruptly, "you should have been a tremendous success this Season. God knows, you have all the requisite attributes for it—and in sinful abundance. Instead, you've become the decade's most notorious failure."

Shame almost doubled Alexandra over, but Anthony hastily held up his hand, awkwardly explaining, "It's my fault, not yours. I've kept things from you, things I would have told you before, but my grandmother forbade it—she couldn't bear to disillusion you. Now, however, we both agree that you must be told, before you destroy what's left of your chances to find happiness here—if it isn't already too late."

Lifting his glass to his lips, Anthony swallowed the whisky straight down, as if he needed it to give him courage, then he said, "Since you've come to London, you've heard many of Jordan's friends and acquaintances refer to him as 'Hawk,' have you not?" When she nodded, he said, "Why do you think they call him that?"

"I assume it's some sort of shortened name—a nickname —derived from 'Hawthorne.'"

"Some people mean it in that way. but especially among the men it means something different. A hawk is a hunting bird with a faultless eye and the ability to snare its prey before its prey even knows it's in danger."

Alexandra gazed at him with polite interest and complete lack of understanding, and Anthony raked his hand through his hair in frustration. "Jordan got that name years ago, when he made a conquest of a particularly proud young beauty for whom half the bachelors in London had been hanging out for months. Hawk did it in one evening by asking her to dance."

Leaning down, Anthony braced his hands on the arms of her chair. "Alex," he said sharply, "you've convinced yourself you loved, and were loved by, a man who was practically a . . . a *saint*. The truth is, Hawk was much closer to a devil than a saint where women were concerned, and *everyone knows it*. Do you understand me?" he asked bitterly, his face inches from hers. "Every single person in London who's heard that you speak of him as if he were some damned knight in shining armor, *knows* you are just another one of his victims . . . just another one of the countless women to fall prey to Hawk's fatal attraction. He didn't try to seduce them—half the time, he was more irritated than pleased when women fell in love with him, but they did it anyway, just as you did. But unlike his other victims, *you* are too guileless to hide it from anyone."

Alexandra pinkened with embarrassment, but she didn't think Jordan should be blamed if women fell in love with him.

"I loved him like a brother, but that doesn't change the fact that he was a notorious rake with a well-deserved reputation for profligacy." Swearing under his breath at her loyalty and innocence, Tony straightened. "You don't believe me, do you? All right, here's the rest of it: On the night of your first ball, you publicly commented on the beauty of two women—Lady Allison Whitmore and Lady Elizabeth Grangerfield. Both of them were his paramours. Do you understand what that means? Do you?"

The color slowly drained from Alexandra's face. A paramour shared a man's bed while he did the intimate things to her that Jordan had done to Alexandra.

Anthony saw her color fade and forged ahead, determined to get it out in the open. "During that same ball, you asked if Jordan enjoyed the ballet, and everyone nearly laughed their sides off because everyone knew that Elise Grandeaux was his mistress *until the day he died.* Alex, he stopped in London and was with her here on the way to your ship— *after* you were married. People *saw* him leaving her house. And she's told everyone your marriage was one of *in*convenience to him."

Alexandra leapt to her feet and wildly shook her head, trying to deny it. "You're wrong. I don't believe you. He said he had 'business' with someone. He would never have—"

"He would and he did, dammit! Furthermore, he intended to take you to Devon and leave you there, then he meant to return to London and continue where he left off with his mistress. He told me so himself! Jordan married you because he felt obliged to, but he had neither the desire nor the intent to live with you as his wife. All he felt for you was pity."

Alexandra's head jerked sideways as if she had been

slapped. "He *pitied* me?" she cried brokenly, drowning in humiliation. Clutching the folds of her skirt, she twisted the fabric until her knuckles turned white. "He thought I was *pitiful?*" Another realization hit her, and she covered her mouth, thinking she was going to be sick: Jordan had meant to do the same thing to her that her father had done to her mother—marry, leave his wife in some obscure place far away, and then return to his wicked woman.

Reaching for her, Anthony tried to put his arms around her, but she flung them off and stepped back, staring at him as if she thought he was as evil as Hawk. "How could you!" she burst out, her voice shaking with bitterness and pain. "How could you let me go on grieving for him and making a fool of myself over him? How could you have been so unutterably cruel as to let me go on believing he had actually c-cared for me!"

"We believed it was a kindness at the time," the dowager duchess said gruffly from behind her, walking into the room with the slight limp that appeared whenever she was deeply troubled.

Alexandra was too battered to worry about the elderly woman. "I'm going home," she said, fighting to control the wrenching anguish that was strangling her breath in her chest.

"No, you're not!" Anthony snapped. "Your mother's spending a year sailing about the islands. You can't live alone."

"I do not require your permission to go home. Nor do I require your financial support. According to your grandmother, I have money of my own from *Hawk,*" she enunciated bitterly.

"Which I control as your guardian," Anthony reminded her.

"I don't want or need a guardian. I've been managing on my own since I was fourteen years old!"

"Alexandra, listen to me," he said tautly, grasping her by the shoulders and giving her a slight, angry shake. "I know you're angry and disillusioned, but you can't run away from us or slink away from London. If you do, what happened to you here will haunt you forever. You didn't love Jordan—"

"Oh, *didn't* I?" Alexandra interrupted furiously. "Then

180

tell me why I spent an entire year trying to make myself worthy of him."

"You loved an illusion, not Jordan—an illusion you created out of whole cloth because you were innocent and idealistic—"

"And gullible and blind and stupid!" Alexandra hissed. Humiliation and anguish made her turn away from the sympathy Anthony was trying to offer and, in a desperate voice, she excused herself and ran to her room.

Only when she had gained the privacy of her bedchamber did she succumb to tears. She cried for her stupidity, for her gullibility, and for the year she had worked, driving herself to become worthy of a man who did not deserve to be called a gentleman. She cried until the sound of her own weeping made her despise herself for wasting her tears on him.

Finally, forcing herself to sit up, she dried her eyes while her mind continued to torment her with images of her own folly: She saw herself in the garden the day before they were wed: *"Are you going to kiss me?"* she had asked, and when he did, she nearly swooned in his arms, then promptly told him she loved him.

Mary Ellen had told her that gentlemen liked to know they are admired and she had certainly taken her friend's advice to heart! *I think you are as beautiful as Michelangelo's David,* she had told Jordan after his kiss.

Shame surged through Alexandra and she moaned aloud, wrapping her arms around her stomach, but the mortifying recollections wouldn't cease. God! She had given him her grandfather's watch. She had given it to him and told him that her grandfather would have *liked* him because he was a *noble* man. Liked him! Why, her grandfather would have barred that treacherous, overbred blueblood from their door!

In the coach she had let Jordan kiss her again and again—she had lain atop him like a stupid, besotted wanton! In bed she had let him do every intimate thing he wanted to do to her, and when he was finished, he had done the same things with his mistress the very next night.

Instead of shooting Jordan's assailant the night she met him, she should have shot Jordan Townsende! How boring her inexperience must have seemed to him, and no wonder he hadn't wanted to hear her naive declarations of love!

"How much longer?" George Morgan whispered to Jordan in the darkness.

"An hour, and then we can make a run for it," he answered tightly as he flexed his cramped muscles, forcing blood into them to strengthen them for their impending flight.

"Are you sure you heard them say your troops are fighting fifty miles south of here? I'd hate for us to walk fifty miles in the wrong direction, me with a game leg and you with a hole in yours."

"It's only a nick," Jordan answered, referring to the wound he'd received from the guard they overpowered yesterday.

The cave they'd been hiding in since yesterday while the French searched the woods for them was so small that they were both nearly doubled in half. Pain shot through Jordan's cramped leg and he stopped moving, his breathing shallow and fast as he automatically called up Alexandra's image and focused on it with every fiber of his being. He tried to imagine how she looked now, but today all he saw was a girl in a wooded glade, looking up at him with a puppy in her arms and all the love in the world shining in her eyes. With his eyes clenched shut, Jordan slowly traced every curve of her face in his mind. The pain in his legs retreated until it was an ache on the perimeters of his mind, still present but bearable now. It was a technique he'd used hundreds of times in the past, and it was as successful now as it had been before.

In the beginning of his imprisonment, when weeks of torture and deprivation drove him to the brink of madness, it was Alexandra he focused on to escape the pain that racked his body and tried to devour his mind. In his imagination, he relived, slowly, every second he had spent with her, concentrating fiercely on each minute detail of their surroundings, recalling every word, every inflection. He made love to her in the inn, time after time, undressing her and holding her, clinging to the memory of her incredible sweetness and the way she felt in his arms.

But as weeks faded into months, his memories of their

brief time together were no longer enough to counteract the torment; he needed another weapon to silence the sweetly insidious voice that urged him gently to give up the fight to live, to let himself succumb to the pleasant anesthesia of death. And so Jordan began to invent scenes and build them around her, using them to reinforce his flagging will to survive because he knew from his experience with wounded men in Spain that when despair set in, death soon followed.

In his mind, he invented all sorts of scenes—pleasant ones in which Alexandra ran ahead of him, laughing her musical laugh, then she turned, holding out her arms to him—*waiting* for him to come to her; frightening scenes where he saw her cast out on the streets by Tony and living in a London slum—*waiting* for Jordan to come home and rescue her; tender scenes where she lay in naked splendor on satin sheets—*waiting* for him to make love to her.

He invented dozens of scenes, and the only feature each one had in common was that Alexandra was always waiting for him. Needing him. He knew the scenes were fantasy, but he concentrated on them anyway. Because they were his only weapon against the demons in his brain that shrieked for him to give up the struggle, to loosen his grip on sanity—and then on life.

And so, in the squalor of his vermin-infested cell, he had closed his eyes and planned his escape so that he could go home to her. Now, after a year of looking back on the bleakness of his former world, he was ready to let Alexandra show him *her* world, where everything was fresh and alive and unspoiled—where "something wonderful" was waiting just around the corner. He wanted to lose himself in her sweetness and surround himself with her laughter and *joie de vivre*. He wanted to cleanse himself of the filth of that prison and then rid himself of the tarnish of his misspent life.

Beyond that, he had only one other goal, and it was less noble, but equally important to him: He wanted to discover the identity of whoever had twice tried to end his life. And then he wanted vengeance. Tony had the most to gain from his death, Jordan knew, but he couldn't bear to think about that yet. Not here. Not without proof. Tony had been like a brother to him.

Chapter Seventeen

ALEXANDRA AWAKENED feeling oddly refreshed after her awful night of tearful self-recriminations. The discovery of Jordan's treachery had destroyed her illusions, but as she slowly went about her morning routine of bathing and dressing, she began to realize that what she had learned last night had released her from the bonds of loyalty and devotion that had kept her tied to his memory for over a year.

She was free of Jordan Townsende now. A faint, wry smile touched her lips as she sat down before the dressing table and began brushing her long, heavy hair. How funny it was that, in trying to become "worthy" of being Jordan's wife, she had turned herself into a rigidly prim and proper female who would have suited a cleric, but never, ever the wife of a scandalous, unprincipled rake. Which was really rather funny, she thought wryly, because her true nature was any thing but rigid and starched.

She had always done that, Alexandra realized suddenly; she had always tried to be what those she loved wanted her to be: For her father, she had been more like a son than a daughter; for her mother, she had become the parent, rather than the child; for Jordan, she had become . . . a complete antidote.

However, from this day forward, all that was going to change. For better or for worse, Alexandra Lawrence Townsende was going to enjoy herself.

In order to do that, however, she first needed to eradicate

the reputation for hauteur and boundless idiocy she had unwittingly earned amongst the *haute ton.* Since Sir Roderick Carstairs was her most vocal, and most influential, detractor, he was obviously the best place to start. Anthony intended to speak to him this morning, but perhaps she could say or do something to change his opinion of her while he was here.

While she was contemplating that problem, she suddenly remembered the last part of her conversation with Melanie Camden last night. Lady Camden had said her friends thought Alexandra was *"the veriest greenhead ever to appear at a London ball,"* so she had obviously known Alexandra was persona non grata amongst the *ton,* yet she had still wanted to befriend her. She had, in fact, been hinting at the same thing Tony had said later. The brush stilled in Alexandra's hand, and a surprised smile lit her face. Perhaps she was going to have a true friend in London, after all.

Feeling more lighthearted than she had in over a year, she pinned her heavy hair atop her head and hurriedly pulled on a pair of the tight breeches and one of the shirts she wore each morning when she and Tony practiced their fencing. Snatching her rapier from the closet and picking up her face mask, she walked from the room, humming a cheerful tune, her steps light and buoyantly carefree.

Tony was standing alone in the center of the deserted ballroom where they practiced each morning, idly tapping the tip of his rapier against the sole of his boot. He turned at the sound of her brisk footsteps upon the polished floor, his face mirroring his relief at her appearance. "I wasn't certain you'd feel up to this, after last night . . ."

Alexandra's flashing smile told him she harbored no grudge against him for his silence on the matter of Jordan's perfidy, but she said nothing about last night. She wanted to forget it *and* Jordan Townsende. Picking up the padded chestplate from the ballroom floor, she put it on, then she put on her face mask, adjusted it, and touched her rapier to her forehead in a jaunty salute to her worthy opponent. *"En garde—"* she said gaily.

"My word, Hawthorne," Roddy Carstairs' drawl stopped Alexandra and Anthony in the middle of a furious parry. "Isn't it rather early to be cavorting about in such an energetic fashion?" Shifting his lazy gaze to Anthony's unknown fencing partner, he said admiringly, "Whoever you are, you're a damned fine swordsman."

Waiting for her labored breathing to even out, Alexandra stood with hands on her hips while she quickly weighed the relative merits of showing herself to Carstairs as she now stood, or waiting to see him in the salon later, as she had intended. Recalling what Anthony had told her about him last night, she decided to be daring, rather than cowardly.

Reaching behind her head, Alexandra unfastened her face mask and simultaneously pulled out the pins that secured her heavy hair. In one quick motion, she pulled off her face mask and gave her head a hard shake that sent dark hair tumbling down over her shoulders in a gleaming chestnut waterfall.

"I don't believe it!" the unshakable Sir Roderick uttered, staring at the laughing young woman before him, his expression almost comical as he tried to absorb the fact that the prim, proper peagoose Hawk had married was one and the same with the young woman standing before him, wearing tight buff breeches that were more physically alluring than the lowest-cut ballgown he had ever seen. Moreover, her blue-green eyes were dancing with laughter as she watched his shock register. "I'll be damned—" he began, but Alexandra's low, throaty laughter, which he had never heard before, interrupted his exclamation.

"No doubt you will be," she said with sham sympathy, walking toward him with the easy natural grace of a young athlete. "And if you aren't, you ought to be," she added, and then graciously extended her hand to him as if she hadn't just wished him to perdition.

Feeling as if some sort of trick—twins, perhaps—were being played on him, Roddy automatically took her hand in his own. "Why ought I?" he demanded, angry with himself for his inability to control his facial expression.

"Because," Alexandra said lightly, "you have made me an object of considerable ridicule here, which I partially deserved. However, perhaps you could consider making amends, so that you could spend eternity in a more comfortable climate?" One delicately arched brow lifted as she waited for his reply, and in spite of himself, Roddy nearly grinned.

Anthony stood back in pleased silence, watching Carstairs react to this lovely duelist exactly as he'd hoped when he instructed Higgins to send him to the ballroom as soon as he arrived.

"I gather you are blaming me for your lack of . . . er . . . shall we say, popularity?" Roddy Carstairs put in, beginning to recover his composure.

"I am blaming myself," the young beauty replied, her smile sweet, yet unconsciously seductive. "I am asking *you* to help me change matters."

"Why should I?" he demanded bluntly.

Alexandra lifted her brows and her smile widened, "Why, to prove you can, of course."

The challenge was thrown down as lightly as a glove, and Roddy hesitated before taking it up. From sheer perversity and extreme boredom, he had unscrupulously flayed the reputations of dozens of pretentiously proud females, but he had never once attempted to rebuild one of those demolished reputations. To try would be to put his influence with the *ton* to the acid test. Ah, but to fail . . . Still, the challenge was intriguing. The dowager duchess had enough influence to force the old crones to accept Alexandra, but only Roddy could make her popular with the younger set who followed *his* lead.

Glancing down at her, he noted that she was watching him out of the corner of her eyes, a tiny, irresistible smile playing about her soft lips. With a jolt of surprise, he noticed how incredibly long and curly her lashes were as they lay like dark fans, casting shadows on her high delicate cheekbones. Almost against his will—and against his better judgment—Roddy Carstairs offered his arm to her. "Shall we discuss our strategy later—say, tonight, when I arrive to escort you to the Tinsleys' ball?"

"You'll help me then?"

Sir Roderick affected a bland smile and answered with a philosophical quotation: "'Nothing is too high for the daring of mortals— We storm heaven itself in our folly.' That is a quote from Homer, I believe," he added informatively.

The nineteen-year-old vixen at his side shook her head and sent him an impertinent, plucky smile. "Horace."

Carstairs stared at her, momentarily lost in thought. "You're right," he said slowly, and there was the beginning glimmer of admiration in his hooded eyes.

How easy it had been, Alexandra thought with an inward smile four weeks later as she stood, surrounded by a crowd of friends and admirers. At Melanie's advice, she had ordered a whole new wardrobe in bright pastels and rich primary colors—gowns that emphasized her figure to advantage and flattered her vivid coloring. Beyond that, she had only needed to ignore many of the duchess' strictures on appropriate demeanor and, instead, to say virtually whatever came to mind.

Roddy had done the rest, by appearing in public with her and putting his stamp of approval upon her, along with giving her some pithy advice that included instructing her to put herself on good terms with Jordan's former paramours, Lady Whitmore and Lady Grangerfield: "Given your excruciatingly naive remarks about your husband's imaginary virtues," he had informed her as he escorted her to the first ball, "and your absurd compliments to his former paramours' beauty, there is nothing for it but that you must be seen to be on friendly terms with those ladies. Society will then assume that, rather than being an utter nitwit—which you were—you are instead a young lady with a heretofore unappreciated, highly developed sense of humor."

Alexandra had followed that and all the rest of his advice, and in four short weeks she had become A Success.

Amidst young, blushing girls in their first Season, Alexandra's natural wit and innate intelligence made her seem more sophisticated and desirable; surrounded by truly sophisticated married women, her unaffected candor and gentle smile made her seem softer, more feminine, less brittle. Against a sea of blondes with milk-white complexions, Alexandra, with her vivid coloring and lush mahogany hair, glowed like a jewel against pale satin.

She was impulsive and witty and gay, but Alexandra's popularity wasn't due primarily to her beauty and wit, or the huge dowry Anthony had settled on her, or even the valuable connection to the Townsende family she would bring to her next husband.

She had become an exciting enigma, a mystery: She had been married to England's most desired, and most notorious, rake; therefore it was naturally assumed she had been expertly initiated into the act of love. Yet even when she was her gayest, there was a glow of freshness and innocence that made most men hesitate to take liberties with her; a distinct aura of quiet pride about her that warned a man not to come too near.

As one besotted swain, Lord Merriweather, described it, "She makes me want to know everything about her at the same time she makes me feel as if I never really could. I daresay no one truly knows the 'real' her, not really. Hawthorne's young widow is a mystery, I tell you. Everyone thinks so. It's damned intriguing."

When Roddy repeated Lord Merriweather's remarks to her, Alexandra's soft lips trembled as she valiantly fought back gales of laughter. She knew *exactly* why the elegant gentlemen of the *haute ton* found her "mysterious" and difficult to understand—it was because, beneath her carefully acquired veneer of sophistication, Alexandra Lawrence Townsende was a complete sham!

On the surface, she had partially adopted the attitude of languid nonchalance that was *de rigueur* among Select Society—and particularly Jordan's lofty friends—but neither the strictures of Society, nor Alexandra herself, could completely repress her natural ebullience or her innate common sense. She could not prevent her eyes from glowing with laughter when someone paid her outrageously flowery compliments, nor could she stop the animated glow that leapt to her cheeks when she was challenged to a race in Hyde Park; nor completely hide her fascination with the tales a noted explorer told of his recent jaunt through the wild jungles of a distant continent, where, he said, the natives carried spears that had been dipped in deadly poison.

The world, and the people who inhabited it, had again become as exciting and interesting to her as they had been when she was a girl sitting at her grandfather's knee.

Beside her, one of Alexandra's swains handed her a glass of sparkling champagne, and she accepted it with a soft smile, raising the glass to her lips as she watched the swirling dancers waltzing before her. Across the room, Roddy raised his glass to her in a silent toast, and she lifted hers in answer. Roddy Carstairs, in many ways, was still a puzzle to her, but she was oddly fond of him and extremely grateful.

Only once in all these weeks had Roddy given Alexandra cause to dislike him and that was when he repeated the story of her original meeting with Jordan, which she had told him in confidence after obtaining his word not to spread the story.

Within twenty-four hours, London was on fire with the gossip that Alexandra Townsende, as a seventeen-year-old girl, had saved Hawk's life.

Within forty-eight more hours, the "mystery" surrounding Alexandra multiplied tenfold. So did her popularity and the number of her suitors.

When Alexandra confronted Roddy with his perfidy, he had looked at her as if she were a complete fool. "My dear girl," he had drawled, "I gave my word not to tell anyone that you shot a man to save dear Jordan, and I have not done so. I did not, however, promise not to tell anyone you saved his life—*that* tasty morsel was entirely too delicious to keep to myself. Your deceased husband, you see," he had explained with a derisive smile, "was purported to be a rather dangerous man when crossed. He was a crack shot and an expert swordsman, as several husbands, including Lady Whitmore's and Lady Grangerfield's, ascertained for themselves."

Inwardly, Alexandra was disgusted by the husbands' hypocritical attitudes, but she tried not to judge them too harshly. She tried not to judge *anyone* too harshly, for that matter, because she remembered with painful clarity how it had felt to be ostracized.

As a result, shy young men flocked to her side because they knew the beautiful young Duchess of Hawthorne would never humiliate them with a disdainful glance or a joke at their expense. Older, intelligent men jostled one another for the right to take her down to dinner or dance with her, because she did not require them to mouth absurd, prescribed platitudes. Instead, they could speak to her on a variety of interesting subjects.

The Corinthian set admired not only her abundant beauty, but her famous skill with a rapier, and they flocked to the house on Upper Brook Street in hopes of seeing her fence, which they were rarely permitted to do—or, better yet, to fence with Hawthorne and thus impress her with their *own* skill, so they might win her undivided notice.

In that last regard, young Lord Sevely, who was too clumsy to fence and too shy to ask her to dance with him, outdid them all. After noting that Lady Melanie Camden and the elderly under-butler at the house on Brook Street (who seemed to be quite deaf) called Alexandra by a special nickname, he wrote a poem to her and had it published. He called it "Ode to Alex."

Not to be outdone by a mere "weanling" like Sevely, the elderly Sir Dilbeck, whose hobby was botany, named a new variety of rose he'd grafted in her honor, calling it "Glorious Alex."

The rest of Alexandra's suitors, annoyed by the implied liberties taken by the other two, followed suit. They, too, began calling her Alex.

Chapter Eighteen

IN ANSWER TO his grandmother's summons, Anthony strolled into the drawing room and found her standing at the window, gazing down at the fashionable carriages returning to Upper Brook Street from the ritual afternoon promenade in the park.

"Come here a moment, Anthony," she said in her most regal voice. "Look out at the street and tell me what you see."

Anthony peered out the window. "Carriages coming back from the park—the same thing I see every day."

"And what else do you see?"

"I see Alexandra arriving in one of them with John Holliday. The phaeton drawing up behind them is Peter Weslyn's—and Gordon Bradford is with him. The carriage in front of Holliday's belongs to Lord Tinsdale, who is already in the salon, cooling his heels with Jimmy Montfort. Poor Holliday," Anthony chuckled. "He sent word he wishes to speak privately with me this afternoon. So did Weslyn, Bradford, and Tinsdale. They mean to offer for her, of course."

"Of course," the duchess repeated grimly, "and that is exactly my point. Today is *exactly* like all the others for nearly a month—suitors arriving in pairs and trios, jamming up traffic in the streets and cluttering up the salons downstairs, but Alexandra has no wish to wed, and she's made that clear to the lot of them. Even so, they keep parading into this house with bouquets in their hands, and marching back out of it with murder in their eyes."

"Now, Grandmama," Anthony soothed.

"Don't 'Now, Grandmama' me," she said, startling Anthony with her vehemence. "I may be old, but I am not a fool. I can see that something very unpleasant, very dangerous, is happening before my own eyes! Alexandra has come to represent some sort of challenge to your foolish sex. Once Alexandra discovered how Jordan had felt about her, and Carstairs took her under his wing, she began to change and shine almost overnight. When that happened, her connections to this family, along with the huge dowry you and I decided she should have, created a uniquely desirable package to any bachelor needful or wishful of acquiring a wife."

The duchess paused, waiting for an argument from her grandson, but Tony merely regarded her in noncommittal silence. "Had Alexandra shown the slightest partiality for one man, or even a preference for one *type* of man at that point," the duchess continued, "the others might have given up and gone away, but she did not. And that is what has brought us to the untenable pass for which I blame your *entire* sex."

"My sex?" he echoed blankly. "What do you mean?"

"I mean that when a *man* sees something that seems to be just beyond the grasp of other men, then of course *he* must try to grasp it to prove *he* can take it." She paused to glower accusingly at an amazed Anthony. "That is a nasty trait which males possess from the time of birth. Walk into any nursery and witness a male babe with his siblings. Whether they are older or younger than he, a male babe will try to snatch whatever toy everyone else is quarreling over. Not, of course, that he wants the toy, he merely wants to prove he can get it."

"Thank you, Grandmama," Anthony said dryly, "for that sweeping condemnation of half of the world's population."

"I am merely stating fact. You do not see *my* sex lining up to enter the lists whenever some silly contest is announced."

"True."

"And that is exactly what has happened here. More and more contestants, drawn by the challenge, have entered the lists to try and win Alexandra. It was bad enough when she was merely that—a challenge—but now she has become something worse, much worse."

"Which is?" Anthony said, but he was frowning at his grandmother's astute assessment of what had already become a very complex, trying situation.

"Alexandra has become a *prize,*" she said darkly. "She is now a prize to be won—or else taken—by the first male bold enough *and* clever enough to carry it off." Anthony opened his mouth, but she raised a bejeweled hand and waved his protest aside. "Do not bother to tell me it won't happen, because I already know it has: As I understand it, three days ago, Marbly proposed a short jaunt to Cadbury and Alexandra agreed to accompany him.

"One of her rejected suitors heard that Marbly had boasted of his intention to take her to his country seat in Wilton instead, and keep her there overnight. He carried the tale to you. You, I understand, caught up with Marbly and Alexandra an hour from here, before the Wilton turnoff, and brought her back, telling Marbly that I had requested her company—which was wise indeed of you. Had you demanded satisfaction, the scandal of a duel would have blackened Alexandra's reputation and compounded our problems tenfold."

"In any case," Tony put in, "Alexandra knew nothing of Marbly's intentions that day, nor does she now. I saw no reason to distress her. I asked her not to see him again, and she agreed."

"And what about Ridgely? What was he about, taking her off to a fair! All London is talking about it."

"Alexandra went to fairs as a child. She had no way of knowing she shouldn't go."

"Ridgely is purportedly a gentleman," the duchess snapped. "He knew better. What possessed him to take an innocent young lady to such a place!"

"You've just hit upon the rest of our problem," Anthony said wearily, rubbing the back of his neck. "Alexandra is a widow, *not* a maid. What few scruples 'gentlemen' possess rarely apply to their behavior with experienced women—particularly if the woman happens to dazzle them witless, which Alexandra does."

"I would hardly describe Alexandra as an experienced woman! She's barely a woman at all."

Despite the grimness of the problem, Anthony grinned at his grandmother's patently inept description of the intoxicating young beauty with the dazzling smile and stunning figure. His grin faded, however, as the problem again came to the fore. "This whole thing is so damn complicated because she is so young and yet she's already been married. If she had a husband now, as does the Countess of Camden, no one would blink an eye at her little larks. If she were older, Society would not expect her to live by the same rules that govern younger girls. If she were plain, then those suitors she's rejected out of hand would not be nearly so inclined to try to blacken her reputation out of spite and jealousy.

"Have they been doing that?"

"Only two or three of them, but they've been busy whispering in the right ears. You know as well as I how easily gossip stimulates gossip, and when it catches fire it begins to spread in every direction. Eventually, everyone hears enough of it to start believing there must be some truth in it."

"How bad is it?"

"Not bad, not yet. At this point, all her rejected suitors have accomplished is to cast an unsavory light on some tiny, harmless misadventures of hers."

"For example?"

Anthony shrugged. "Alexandra spent last weekend at Southeby, attending a party there. She and a certain gentleman made an engagement for an early ride and left the stables at about eight. They did not return until after dusk, and when they did come back, it was seen that Alexandra's clothing was torn and in disarray."

"Dear God!" the duchess expostulated, clutching at her heart in agitation.

Anthony grinned. "The gentleman was seventy-five years old and the vicar at Southeby. He had intended to show Alexandra the location of an old cemetery he'd discovered by chance the week before, so that she might admire some fascinating grave markers he'd seen there. Unfortunately, he could not remember its exact location, and by the time they found it several hours later, Alexandra was completely lost and the old gentleman was so exhausted from the exertion of riding that he was afraid to get back on his horse. Naturally, Alexandra could not have returned without him, even had she wanted to, which of course she didn't."

"What about her gown?"

"The hem of her riding habit was torn."

"Then the whole episode was too trifling to mention."

"Exactly, but the tale has been repeated and exaggerated so many times it's now become an instance of questionable conduct. The obvious solution is for us to employ some old dragon to act as Alexandra's chaperone wherever she goes, but if we do that—particularly in light of the recent gossip —everyone will think we don't trust her. Besides, it would spoil all the fun of her first Season for her."

"Rubbish!" the duchess said stoutly. "Alexandra is not having fun, and that is *precisely* why I asked you to attend me here. She is jaunting about hither, thither, and yon, flirting and smiling and wrapping men around her little finger for one reason only, and that is to prove to Jordan she can do it—to show him posthumously that she is beating him at his own game. If all her suitors dropped off the face of the earth, she wouldn't notice and, if she did, she wouldn't care a pin."

Anthony stiffened. "I'd scarcely call an innocent jaunt to a fair, or racing Jordan's horse in Hyde Park, or any of her other harmless little peccadillos 'beating Jordan at his own game.'"

"Nevertheless," the duchess replied, refusing to be gainsaid, "that is what she is doing, though I doubt she realizes it. Do you disagree?"

Tony hesitated and then reluctantly shook his head. "No, I suppose you're exactly right."

"Of course I am," she said with force. "Will you also agree Alexandra's current situation is placing her reputation and her entire future in serious jeopardy and, moreover, that the situation seems destined to worsen?"

Faced with his grandmother's piercing stare and her astute assessment of all the facts, Anthony shoved his hands in his pockets and sighed. "I agree."

"Excellent," she said, looking surprisingly satisfied. "Then I know you will understand when I say I do not wish to live out the rest of my days in a London house that is under siege from Alexandra's suitors, waiting on tenterhooks for another one of them to succeed at what Marbly tried to do, or to do something even more unspeakable to her—to us as a family. I wish to spend what years I have left at Rosemeade. But I cannot do that because Alexandra would have to accompany me there, which would make her future nearly as bleak as it is here, but for the opposite reasons. The only remaining solution would be to leave her here with you, which is beyond the bounds of consideration. It would cause a scandal that is not to be thought of." She paused, watching him very closely, waiting for his answer as if it were of momentous importance.

"Neither solution is feasible," Tony agreed.

The duchess pounced on that with ill-suppressed glee. "I *knew* you would see the situation exactly as I do. You are a man of superior understanding and compassion, Anthony."

"Er—thank you, Grandmama," Anthony said, visibly taken aback by such effusive compliments from his normally taciturn grandmother.

"And now that we've discovered we are in complete accord," she continued, "I have a favor to ask of you."

"Anything."

"Marry Alexandra."

"Anything but that," Anthony swiftly corrected, frowning darkly at her.

In response, she pointedly lifted her brows and disdainfully gazed at him as if he had just shrunk drastically in her estimation. It was a look which she had effectively employed for fifty years—and with singular success—to intimidate her peers, awe servants, silence children, and depress the pretensions of anyone who dared oppose her, including her husband and sons. Only Jordan had been immune to its effect. Jordan and his mother.

Anthony, however, was no more immune to it now than he had been at twelve, when that same look had silenced his outcry at having to learn Latin and sent him upstairs to ashamedly devote himself to his studies. Now he sighed, looking desperately around the room as if searching for some means of escape. Which he was.

The dowager duchess waited in silence.

Silence was the next weapon in her arsenal, Tony knew.

At moments like this she *always* waited in silence. It was so much nicer—so much more dignified and refined—to wait in polite silence for one's prey to stop struggling, rather than to swoop in for the kill with a barrage of unnecessary verbal fire.

"You don't seem to realize what you're asking of me," he said angrily.

His refusal to yield gracefully and at once made her brows lift a fraction higher, as if she were not only disappointed in him, but annoyed because she was now compelled to fire a warning shot. But she fired it without hesitation, striking home, exactly as Anthony expected she would. In verbal combat, his grandmother's aim was faultless. "I sincerely hope," she drawled with just the right touch of disdain, "that you don't intend to say you aren't *attracted* to Alexandra?"

"And if I *did* say that?"

Her white eyebrows shot straight into her hairline, warning him she was prepared to open fire if he continued to be obstinate.

"There's no need to bring out the heavy guns," Anthony warned cryptically, holding up his hand in the gesture of a weary truce. Although he resented the fact that in any clash of wills she could still reduce him to the level of a child, he was also adult enough and wise enough to know that it was truly childish to argue with her when she was right. "I don't deny it. Moreover, the idea has occurred to me on more than one occasion."

Her eyebrows dropped to their normal position and she favored him with a slight, regal inclination of her white head—a gesture meant to convey that *perhaps* he stood a slight chance of regaining her favor. "You're being very sensible." She was always gracious to those she subdued.

"I'm not agreeing to what you suggest, but I'll agree to discuss it with Alex and leave the decision up to her."

"Alexandra has no more choice in the matter than you have, my dear," she said, so carried away with pleasure that she had inadvertently used an endearment without waiting the usual interval of weeks or even months to forgive him for his tardy capitulation to her will. "And there's no need to fret about when and where to discuss the matter with her, because I took the liberty of instructing Higgins to have her join us here"—she stopped at the sound of the knock upon the door—"now."

"Now!" he exploded. "I can't do it now. There are three men downstairs who've come to ask me for her hand."

She dismissed that problem with a regal flick of her fingers. "I'll tell Higgins to send them away." Before Anthony could utter a protest, she pulled open the door to admit Alexandra, and he watched in amazement as his grand-mother's personality underwent another distinct change. "Alexandra," she said sternly, but not without a hint of affection, "your conduct has been giving us a deal of worry. I know you do not wish to worry me because I am no longer a young woman—"

"Worry you, ma'am?" Alexandra repeated, alarmed. "My conduct? What have I done?"

"I'll tell you," she said, and then she ruthlessly launched into a dissertation deliberately intended to alarm, intimi-date, and coerce Alexandra into falling into Anthony's arms the minute the duchess closed the door: "This dreadful coil we are all in is not *entirely* your fault," she began, her words coming in quick, rapid-fire succession. "But the fact re-mains that had Anthony not learned of your proposed jaunt to Cadbury with Sir Marbly in time to waylay you, you'd have found yourself in Wilton, compromised beyond recall, and forced to wed that blackguard. This willy-nilly jaunting about, flitting from suitor to suitor, must cease at once. Everyone thinks you are having a wonderful time, but I know you better! You are behaving in this wild, indiscrimi-nate manner solely to spite Jordan—to show him you can match him, deed for deed. Well, you can't, my dear! Your little peccadillos are nothing compared to the sorts of things gentlemen do, particularly gentlemen like Jordan. Further-more," she announced in a rising tone that indicated she was about to reveal news of tremendous import, *"Jordan is dead."*

Alexandra gazed at her in blank confusion. "I know that."

"Excellent, then there is no reason for you to go on as you have been." In a rare gesture of affection she laid her hand on Alexandra's cheek. "Give over before you do irreparable damage to your pride and reputation, and to the family's as well. You must marry someone, my dear, and I, who truly care about you, desire that it be Anthony, as does Anthony himself."

Removing her hand, she fired off the rest of her ammunition: "You need something to occupy your mind besides amusement, Alexandra. A husband and children will do nicely for that. You've been dancing to the tune, my dear, and now I fear it is time to pay the piper. Gowns for a London Season cost a fortune, and we are not made of money. I'll leave you and Anthony to discuss the details." With a benign smile at Alexandra and a pointed one at Anthony, she swept grandly to the door. Turning back, she said to both of them, "Do plan a nice *large* wedding in church this time, but right away, of course."

"Of course," Anthony said dryly. Alexandra said nothing, but stood rooted to the spot.

His grandmother glowered at him and directed her last remark to Alexandra. "I've never admitted this before, but I am superstitious. It seems to me that things which do not begin well rarely end well, and your wedding to Jordan— well, it was such a sad, inauspicious little affair. A large church affair will be just the thing. Society will be all agog over it, but it will give them something better to remember than all the talk about you that preceded it. Three weeks from today should do very well, indeed." Without waiting for a reply, she closed the door, effectively cutting off any attempt by Tony or Alexandra to argue with her.

When she left, Alexandra clutched at the back of a chair for support and slowly turned to Anthony, who was grinning at the closed door. "She's actually more ruthless than I ever realized," he observed with a mixture of affection and exasperation as he turned to look at Alexandra. "Hawk was the only one she couldn't wring out with one of her looks. My father was terrified of her, so was Jordan's. And my grandfather—"

"Tony," Alexandra interrupted miserably, drowning in guilt and confusion. "What have I done? I had no idea I was bringing disgrace down on us. Why didn't you tell me I was spending too much on gowns?" Shame engulfed her as she suddenly saw herself with new clarity, leading a frivolous, expensive, aimless life.

"Alexandra!" She turned and stared blankly at his grinning face as he said, "You have just been subjected to the most massive dose of guilt, coercion, and emotional blackmail that I have ever seen anyone hand out. My grandmother didn't miss a trick." He held out his palm, smiling reassuringly, and Alexandra placed her hand in his reassuring grasp. "There is nothing wrong with her health, you are not sending us down the road to financial ruin, and you assuredly are not jeopardizing the Townsende name."

Alexandra was not much reassured. Too much of what the duchess had said had often occurred to Alex herself. For more than a year she had been living with people who treated her as part of their family and who kept her in a manner befitting a royal duchess, when she was neither. At first, she had silenced her conscience with the knowledge that the dowager duchess truly needed her companionship in the months after Jordan's death. But of late Alexandra had not been much of a companion to the elderly lady; there never seemed to be time to do more than wave to one another when their carriages passed on the street or they met one another on the stairway, leaving for their individual entertainments. "The part about Marbly was the truth though, wasn't it?" she asked miserably.

"Yes."

"Marbly doesn't fancy himself in love with me like some of the younger dandies do. I can't think *why* he'd have tried to abduct me."

"My grandmother has an interesting theory on that subject. It has to do with little boys and toys. Ask her about it sometime."

"Pray, don't talk to me in riddles!" she pleaded. "Only tell me why all this is happening."

Tony gave her an abbreviated version of the entire discussion he had just had with his grandmother. "The fact is," he concluded, "you're simply too desirable for your own good and our peace of mind."

"What a rapper!" she chuckled. "There has to be more to it than that."

"Exactly how much *are* you enjoying the Season?"

"It's everything you said it would be—exciting and elegant and the people are so—elegant—exciting, and I've never seen such, such *elegant* carriages and phaetons or such—"

Tony's shoulders shook with laughter. "You're impossibly poor at lying."

"I know," she admitted ruefully.

"Then suppose we stick to the truth, you and I."

Alexandra nodded, but still she hesitated. "How do I like the London Season?" she repeated, seriously considering the question. Like all the well-born young women in London during the Season, she slept until midmorning, breakfasted in bed, and changed her clothes at least five times each day for a round of morning calls, promenades in the park, parties, suppers, and balls. She had never been so frantically busy. Yet as she went about the occupation which was supposed to consume her every waking hour—that of enjoying herself—one question kept tolling relentlessly through her mind. *Is this all there is? . . . Is there nothing more?*

Unable to face him, Alexandra walked over to the windows and then said, "The Season is all very amusing, and there is diversion everywhere, but sometimes it seems as if everyone is working very hard at playing. I will miss London when I leave it, and I know I will look forward to returning, but there's something missing. I think I must need work to do. I feel restless here, even though I've never been so busy. Am I making any sense?"

"You have always made sense, Alexandra."

Reassured by his gentle tone, Alexandra turned around and faced him squarely. "Alexander Pope said that amusement is the happiness of those who cannot think. I don't entirely agree with that, but as a goal in and of itself, I find the pursuit of amusement, well, a little unsatisfying. Tony, do *you* never weary of this ceaseless round of aimless amusements?"

"This year, I've scarcely had time to go about." Shaking his head, he made a sweeping gesture with his hand and said wryly, "You know, I used to envy Jordan all this—his houses, his lands, all his other investments. Now that they're mine, they're like jewels that weigh a ton; they're too valuable to neglect, too huge to ignore, and too heavy to carry. You can't believe how diverse his investments are or the time it takes me to try to figure out when to do what with each one. When Jordan inherited the title at twenty, the

Townsende holdings were respectable but not vast by any means. He increased them tenfold in seven years. Jordan worked like a demon, but he had time for amusements, too. I can't seem to strike the proper balance."

"Is that why you've been neglecting the ladies, who plague me to distraction, trying to discover where you plan to go next so they can be there?"

Tony laughed. "No. I've been neglecting them for the same reason you neglect your beaux. I'm flattered, but not interested."

"Hasn't any young lady suited you in all these years?"

"One," he admitted, grinning.

"Who was she?" Alexandra promptly demanded.

"She was the daughter of an earl," he said, his expression sobering.

"What happened to her," Alexandra prodded, "or is it too personal to discuss?"

"Not at all. It isn't even a unique story. She seemed to want me as much as I wanted her. I offered for her, but her parents wanted her to wait until the end of the Season before accepting an unpromising catch like me—a man of respectable birth, good family, but no title and no real fortune. And so we agreed to keep our feeling for each other a secret until the end of the Season."

"And then what?" Alexandra asked, sensing instinctively that he wanted to talk about it.

"And then someone with a title and a fortune and a very elegant address paid her passing notice. He stood up with her at a few balls, called on her a time or two—Sally fell for him like a rock."

Alexandra's voice dropped to a sympathetic whisper. "And so she married him instead of you?"

Tony chuckled and shook his head. "To the nobleman, the interlude with Sally had been nothing but a stupid, empty, meaningless flirtation."

"It—it wasn't Jordan, was it?" Alex asked, feeling a little sick.

"I'm happy to say it was not."

"In any case, you're better off without her," Alexandra announced loyally. "She was obviously either very mercenary or very flighty." One of Alexandra's warm, entrancing

203

smiles touched her soft lips and she laughed with sudden delight: "Now that you are the most important duke in England, I'll bet she regrets turning you away."

"She may."

"Well, I hope she does!" she exclaimed, and then she looked guilty. "That is a very wicked way for me to feel."

"We're *both* wicked," Tony laughed. "Because I rather hope she does too."

For a moment they merely regarded one another in silence and the friendly accord they had always enjoyed. Finally Tony drew a careful breath and said, "The point I was trying to make earlier is that too much work is no more satisfying than too much amusement."

"You're right, of course. I hadn't considered that."

"There's something else you ought to consider," Tony said gently.

"What is that?"

"You ought to consider the possibility that the indefinable thing you said you felt was lacking from your life might be love."

Alexandra's unexpected mirthful reaction to that suggestion stilled his hand as he reached for a pinch of snuff. "Good heavens, I should hope it's lacking!" she said, and her musical laughter bubbled over, spilling through the room without a single note of anger to reassure Tony that her reaction was merely one of temporary bitterness over Jordan's treatment. "I *have* been in love, your grace, and I didn't enjoy it in the least!" she chuckled. "I'd sooner have a stomachache, thank you very much."

She meant every word of it, Tony realized as he gazed at the beautiful shining face turned up to his. She meant it—and the knowledge filled him with almost uncontrollable rage at Jordan. "You only had a small taste of it."

"Enough to know I don't like it."

"Next time you might like it more."

"It gave me a dreadful feeling inside. Like—like I'd eaten eels," she laughed. "I—"

The curse that exploded from him stopped her short. "Damn Jordan! If he were alive, I'd strangle him with my bare hands!"

"No, you misunderstand!" Alexandra said, hurrying to him, her luminous eyes searching his, trying to make him

204

understand. "Even when I foolishly thought he cared for me, I felt horridly queasy inside. I couldn't stop worrying about every little thing I said. I wanted to please him, and I was quite turning myself inside out to do it. I think it must be a hereditary defect: The women in my family always fall in love with the wrong men, and then we worship them with blind devotion, tearing ourselves apart to please them." She grinned. "It's quite nauseating, actually."

A shout of laughter erupted from Tony an instant before he snatched her into his arms and hugged her, laughing into her fragrant hair. When their mirth had subsided, Tony gazed down into her eyes and soberly said, "Alexandra, what is it you want out of life?"

His steady gaze locked onto hers, holding her immobilized. "I don't know," she whispered, standing stock still as the man she had regarded as an older brother cupped her face between his big hands. "Tell me how you feel inside, now that you are one of the Reigning Queens of Society."

Alexandra could not have moved if someone had screamed that the house was afire. "Empty," she admitted in a ragged whisper. "And cold."

"Marry me, Alexandra."

"I—I can't!"

"Of course you can," he said, smiling at her resistance, as if he expected it and understood. "I'll give you the things you truly need to make you happy. I know what they are, even if you don't."

"What things?" Alexandra murmured, her eyes moving over his face as if seeing it for the very first time.

"The same things I need—children, a family, someone to care for," Tony said huskily.

"Don't," Alexandra cried as she felt her resistance begin to weaken and crumble. "You don't know what you're saying. Tony, I'm not in love with you, and you're not in love with me."

"You're not in love with anyone else, are you?"

Alexandra shook her head emphatically and he grinned. "There, you see, that makes the decision much easier. I'm not in love with anyone else, either. You've already met the best of the crop of eligible husbands during this Season. The ones who aren't here aren't much better. You can take my word on it."

When Alexandra bit her lip and continued to hesitate, Tony gave her a light shake. "Alexandra, stop dreaming. This is life as it really is. You've seen it. All that's left is more of the same unless you have a family."

A family. A real family. Alexandra had never been part of one—not a family with a father and mother and children; with cousins and aunts and uncles. Of course, their children would have only Tony's younger brother for an uncle, but still—

What more could any woman possibly hope for than what Tony was offering her? It dawned on Alexandra for the first time that, although she had teased Mary Ellen forever about her romantic notions, she herself had been acting like a romantic schoolgirl. Tony cared for her. And she had it in her power to make him happy. The knowledge warmed her and made her feel good inside, good about herself in a way she hadn't felt in ages. She could devote herself to making him happy, to bearing his children.

Children . . . The thought of holding her baby in her arms was a powerful motivation to marry this kind, gentle, handsome man. Of all the men she'd met in London, Tony seemed to be the only one who felt as she did about life.

With great effort, Jordan helped his weary friend to stand and pulled his arm over his own shoulders, bracing his weight against his side as he half-carried, half-dragged George Morgan across the shallow creek. Grinning and exhausted, Jordan glanced up, trying to gauge the time by the sun, which was low in the sky, blocked from his view by the hills and trees. He wanted to know the time, it was important to him. Five o'clock in the afternoon, he decided.

At five o'clock in the afternoon, he had first seen the uniformed troops moving stealthily through the trees ahead of him. English troops. Freedom. Home.

With luck, he could be home in three or four weeks.

Chapter Nineteen

EVERYONE WAS BEAMING at her as Alexandra came downstairs in a swirl of heavy ice-blue satin encrusted with a wide border of pearls, diamonds, and blue zircons at the low, square neck and the bottom of the wide sleeves.

Penrose opened the door for her as he had done thousands of times in her life, but today, as she prepared to leave for the huge gothic church where she and Tony were to be married, his kindly old face was wreathed in smiles, and he bowed deeply from the waist.

Filbert's shortsighted eyes swam with tears as Alexandra turned and reached around his neck to give him a hug. "Take care now," he whispered to her, "and mind you don't soil your frock." He had been admonishing her thus forever, and Alexandra felt tears of affection blur her own eyes.

These two old men, and Uncle Monty, were the only family she had in all England. Her mother had sold their home in Morsham and left for a long sojourn in the islands, so she couldn't be here to see Alex marry; Mary Ellen and her husband were expecting their first baby to be born at any hour, so they couldn't come to London either. But at least Uncle Monty was here to give her away. And although Melanie had just discovered she was with child, her pregnancy wasn't yet apparent, so she was able to be Alex's matron of honor.

"Are you ready, my dear?" Uncle Monty beamed, offering her his arm.

"See that you don't step on Alexandra's train," the

dowager duchess admonished him sharply, casting a critical eye from the top of his white head to the tips of his highly polished black slippers. For the last three days, she'd been lecturing Sir Montague on his general conduct, his duty at the wedding, and the merits of sobriety so unmercifully that he was now cowed by her. Suddenly her eyes narrowed on the suspicious tint of his round cheeks. "Sir Montague," she demanded with snapping eyes, "have you been at the claret this morning?"

"Certainly not!" Uncle Monty boomed, appalled. "Can't abide claret. No bouquet, no body," he said, puffing up like an offended rooster, even though he'd been liberally imbibing Madeira all morning long.

"Never mind all that," the old duchess interrupted with brusque impatience. "Just remember what I said to do: After you escort Alexandra to the altar, you are to leave her there and return to our pew. You will take your seat there, beside me, and you *will not move a muscle* until I arise, after the ceremony is concluded. Do you understand? I will signal you when it is time for us to arise and step out into the aisle. Everyone else must remain seated until we do so. Is that clear?"

"I ain't an imbecile, you know, madam. I am a knight of the realm."

"You'll be a dead and dishonored one if you make a single mistake," the worthy lady promised as she pulled on the long silver-grey gloves that Penrose handed her. "I'll not countenance another odious display of irreverence such as the one you gave last Sunday." The diatribe continued all the way into the coach. "I could not believe my ears when you dozed off in the middle of the service and began to snore in that appallingly loud fashion."

Uncle Monty climbed into the coach and cast a long-suffering look at his niece, which clearly said, *I don't know how you've managed to reside with this old harpy, my girl.*

Alexandra smiled. She knew, and he knew, that the high color at his cheekbones testified to his having consumed the better part of a bottle of Madeira.

Settling back against the luxurious squabs of the crested coach bearing her toward her future husband, she looked out the windows at the sights and sounds of the London streets. Melanie was riding in the coach just ahead of this one, along with Roderick Carstairs, who was acting as Anthony's best man.

Behind and ahead of the two vehicles bearing the bridal party was a veritable sea of elegant equipages—all bound for the same church. They were, Alexandra realized with a wry smile, causing a huge tie-up in traffic several miles long.

How odd, she thought, that she had felt so nervous, so jittery and excited about her wedding to Jordan. Fifteen months ago, when she had walked into that silent drawing room to join her life with Jordan's, her legs had been shaking and her heart nearly bursting with each thunderous beat.

Yet here she was, about to be married to Tony in one hour before three thousand members of the *haute ton,* and she felt—totally, utterly calm. Serene. Unafraid. Unexcited . . .

Alexandra hastily cast the disloyal thought aside.

"What's slowing us down?" Jordan demanded of the driver of the carriage that the captain of the *Falcon* had put at his disposal, which was bearing him with infuriating slowness to his house on Upper Brook Street.

"I don't know, your grace. 'Pears to be somethin' happenin' at that church back there."

Jordan glanced at the sun again, trying to ascertain the time. He had not enjoyed the luxury of a timepiece in over a year, yet he owned at least six solid-gold ones that he had never fully appreciated. He had taken everything he had for granted. After a year and a quarter of deprivation, however, he doubted if he would ever take anything for granted again.

The sights and sounds of London, which had pleased him so much since entering the city an hour ago, began to fade from his consciousness as he considered the shocks he was about to cause to those who loved him.

His grandmother was still alive—that much Jordan had learned from the captain of the *Falcon,* who said he recalled reading in the *Gazette* a few months ago that she was planning to reside in London for the Season. With any luck she was staying at her own town house and not at his, Jordan thought, so that he could send word to her first, rather than walk in on her without warning. Tony, if he was in London, would naturally be staying at Jordan's house on Upper Brook Street, believing it to be his own.

More than once, it had occurred to Jordan that Tony might resent having him return and dispossess him of the ducal title and estates, but that possibility was nearly as repugnant as the idea that Tony was involved in a plot to have him murdered. Jordan refused to believe either, until he had reliable proof.

He refused to believe it—but unfortunately he could not banish the nagging suspicion from his mind any more than he could silence the memory of the thug's voice on the wharf the night he'd been knocked unconscious: "The bloke paid us t' kill 'im, Jamie, not t' send him off on no ship . . ."

Jordan pushed all that aside. It was perfectly possible that some enraged husband—like old Grangerfield—was responsible for the plot to have Jordan killed. There were ways to find out who his enemy was. For today, however, he wanted to revel in the joy of coming home.

He thought about his impending arrival in Upper Brook Street, and he wanted to do everything at once—to walk into the house and shake Higgins' hand, to pull his grandmother into his arms and soothe away the tears of relief and gratitude he knew she and the old butler would shed when they realized he was alive. He would clasp Tony's shoulders and thank him for doing his best to manage the Hawthorne holdings. No matter how badly Tony had bungled Jordan's complex business affairs—and Jordan was discouragingly certain he had—he would always be grateful.

After that, Jordan wanted a bath and his own clothes. And then—then he wanted Alexandra.

Of all the things that lay before him, his interview with his young "widow" was the only thing Jordan was truly worried about. No doubt her childlike devotion to him had caused her to suffer an extreme form of prolonged grief after she learned of his death. She had been thin as a reed when he last saw her; by now she was probably gaunt. God, what a miserable life she had lived from the day she encountered him.

He realized that she would have changed during his absence, but he hoped the changes had not been too many or too drastic. She would have matured into a woman now, one who was old enough to have the responsibilities of a husband and children. He would bring her to London and introduce her to Society himself.

They would not stay long in London, though. He had lost more than a year of his life, but he'd had plenty of time to decide how he wanted to spend the rest of it. He knew now what mattered and what didn't, and he knew what he wanted—what he had probably always wanted. He wanted a life that had meaning, and a real marriage, not the shallow, empty arrangement that passed for marriage in his set. He wanted more of the love Alexandra had tried to give him—the love that had given him a reason to fight to survive. In return, he wanted to pamper her and pleasure her and keep her with him, safe from the corrosive effects of the outside world. Perhaps love was immune to the outside world. Or was that where trust came in? Was a man supposed to trust his wife not to change and to remain loyal to him no matter where she was, or with whom? Obviously, that was the case, Jordan decided. He didn't know much about trust, and he knew even less about love, but Alexandra was the embodiment of both, and she had volunteered to teach him. He was willing to let her try now.

He tried to imagine how she would look, but all he could see was a laughing face, dominated by a pair of magnificent aquamarine eyes. A face that was almost, but not quite pretty. His "funny-face."

She would have spent one year in mourning, he knew, then another six months learning the ropes of Society with his grandmother. She would only now be preparing to make her entrance into Society during the Little Season in the fall, assuming his grandmother had posthumously carried out his wishes to see her "polished."

It was far more likely, and far more alarming, Jordan thought grimly, that Alexandra might have been so grief-stricken and desolate that she had returned to her run-down house in Morsham—or shied away completely from people —or, God, lost her mind after everything she'd been through!

The coach pulled up before No. 3 Upper Brook Street and Jordan got out, pausing on the front steps to look up at the elegant three-story stone mansion with its graceful ironwork and bow windows. It seemed so familiar, and yet so strange.

He lifted the heavy polished knocker and let it fall, bracing himself for Higgins to open the door and fall upon him in a frenzy of joy.

The door swung open. "Yes?" an unfamiliar face demanded, peering at him through wire-rimmed spectacles.

"Who are you?" Jordan demanded, perplexed.

"*I* might ask the same question of *you,* sir," Filbert haughtily replied, looking around for Penrose, who hadn't heard the knocker.

"I am Jordan Townsende," Jordan replied brusquely, knowing that he would only be wasting his time if he tried to convince this unknown servant that he, and not Tony, was the Duke of Hawthorne. Brushing past the footman, Jordan stalked into the marble foyer. "Send Higgins here to me."

"Mr. Higgins has gone out."

Jordan frowned, wishing Higgins or Ramsey were here to help prepare his grandmother for his sudden appearance. Walking quickly forward, he looked into the large salon to the right of the foyer and the smaller one on the left. They were filled with flowers and empty of people. The whole downstairs seemed to be filled with baskets of white roses and greenery. "Are we giving a party later?"

"Yes, sir."

"It's about to become a 'homecoming party,'" Jordan predicted with a chuckle, then he said briskly, "Where is your mistress?"

"At church," Filbert replied, squinting at the tall, deeply tanned gentleman.

"And your master?" Jordan asked, meaning Tony.

"Also at church, of course."

"Praying for my immortal soul, no doubt," Jordan joked. Knowing that Tony surely would have retained the services of Mathison, Jordan's superior valet, Jordan said, "Is Mathison about?"

"He is," Filbert averred, then he watched in amazement as this unknown member of the Townsende family began walking up the staircase, issuing orders over his shoulder as if he owned the place. "Send Mathison to me at once. I'll be in the gold suite. Tell him I want a bath and a shave immediately. And a change of clothes. Mine preferably, if they're still around. If not, I'll wear Tony's, or his, or anyone's he can steal."

Jordan walked swiftly past the master bedroom suite, which Tony would undoubtedly be occupying, and opened

212

the door to the gold guest suite. It was not quite so lavish, but at that moment seemed like the most beautiful room he'd ever beheld. Pulling off the ill-fitting jacket that the captain of the *Falcon* had lent him, he flung it on a chair and began unbuttoning his shirt.

He stripped it off and tossed it atop the jacket, and was in the process of unbuttoning his pants when Mathison bustled into the suite like an outraged penguin, his black coattails flapping behind him. "There seems to be some misunderstanding as to your name, sir, good God!" The valet stopped short and gaped. "Good God, *your grace! Good God!*"

Jordan grinned. This was somewhat more like the homecoming he'd envisioned. "I'm sure we're all very grateful to the Almighty for my return, Mathison. However, at the moment, I'd be nearly as grateful merely for a bath and a decent change of clothes."

"Certainly, your grace. At once, your grace. And may I say how extremely happy, how very delighted I am to— *GOOD GOD!*" Mathison exploded, this time in horror.

Jordan, who had never seen the indomitable manservant exhibit any sign of fluster even under the most trying circumstances, watched in some amazement as his valet sprinted across the hall, disappeared into the master bedroom suite, then came dashing out again with one of Tony's shirts floating from his fingers and a pair of Jordan's own riding breeches and boots. "I discovered these at the back of the wardrobe only last week," Mathison panted. "Quickly! You must make haste," he gasped. "The church!" he uttered wildly. "The wedding—!"

"A wedding. So that's why everyone's at church," Jordan said, about to toss the trousers Mathison had thrust at him aside and insist on a bath. "Who's getting married?"

"Lord Anthony," Mathison panted in a strangled voice, holding up the shirt and trying to physically force one of Jordan's arms into its sleeve.

Jordan grinned, ignoring the shirt that was now being flapped at him like a flag. "Who is he marrying?"

"Your wife!"

For a moment, Jordan was unable to absorb the full shock of that. His mind was grimly preoccupied with the fact that, if Tony were getting married, he would already have also

213

signed a betrothal agreement as the Duke of Hawthorne and made pledges to his fiancée and her family that he could not keep now.

"Bigamy!" Mathison gasped.

Jordan's head jerked around as the import of what he was hearing slammed into him. "Get out in the street and flag down anything that moves," Jordan commanded shortly, snatching the shirt and pulling it on. "What time are they doing it and where?"

"In twenty minutes at St. Paul's."

Jordan flung himself into a hired hack he snatched from beneath the nose of an outraged dowager in the middle of Upper Brook Street. "St. Paul's," he snapped at the driver. "And you can retire for life on what I'll give you if you get me there in fifteen minutes."

"Ain't likely, guv," said the driver. "There's a wedding goin' on there that's had traffic tied up all mornin'."

During the ensuing minutes, a dozen conflicting thoughts and emotions whirled through the chaotic turbulence of Jordan's mind, the foremost being the need for urgent haste. Left with no way to control the flow of traffic, he had no choice but to sit back and grimly contemplate this enormous debacle.

Occasionally, during his absence, he had considered the unlikely possibility that when the required one-year mourning period had passed, Tony might have met someone and decided to marry her, but somehow he hadn't really expected it. Tony had never been any more anxious than Jordan to bind himself to a woman, not even with the tenuous ties of modern matrimony that left both spouses free to do as they wished.

Jordan had also considered the possibility that Alexandra might meet someone someday and wish to marry him, but not this damned soon. Not while she had supposedly been in mourning! Not when she had supposedly been wildly in love with Jordan . . .

But the one thing he had never imagined—even in his worst nightmares about the possible complications associated with his return—was that some misguided sense of honor might cause Tony to feel duty-bound to marry Jordan's poor widow. *Dammit!* Jordan thought as the spires of St. Paul's finally came into view, what could have possessed Tony to do such an idiotic thing?

The answer came to Jordan almost instantly. Pity would have made him do it. The same pity Jordan had felt for the cheerful little waif who had saved his life and looked at him with huge, adoring eyes.

Pity had caused this entire near-catastrophe, and Jordan had no alternative but to stop the marriage at whatever stage it was in when he entered the church, otherwise Alexandra and Tony would be committing public bigamy. It dawned on him that poor Alexandra was about to have her groom snatched from her for a second time, and he felt a brief pang of regret for destroying her peace yet again.

Before the hack had come to a full stop at St. Paul's, Jordan was already bounding up the long flights of steps leading to the doors, praying he might still be here in time to stop the damned wedding before it began. That hope died the moment he yanked open the heavy oaken doors of the candlelit church and saw the bride and groom standing with their backs to the crowded church.

Jordan stopped short, a long string of colorful oaths running through his mind, and then left with no choice, he started walking up the aisle, his booted footsteps echoing like sharp cannon shots in the crowded church.

Near the front, he stopped walking—waiting for the approaching moment when he would have to speak out. Then and only then, as he stood between the rows of lavishly dressed guests who had been his family and friends and acquaintances, did it finally dawn on Jordan that he had not been much mourned and that, if he *had* been duly mourned, he would not be forced to play this absurd part in the dramatic comedy that was about to unfold in this damned church. The realization sent a sudden surge of cold fury through him, but his features were impassive as he stood in the aisle between the second row of pews, his arms crossed over his chest—waiting for the moment that was nearing.

On both sides of him, guests were beginning to recognize him, and loud whispers were already racing through the crowd, bursting out like a brushfire. Alexandra heard the growing disturbance behind her and glanced uncertainly at Anthony, who seemed to be concentrating on the archbishop, who was intoning: "If there be any man present who knows any reason why this man, and this woman, should not be joined in matrimony, let him speak now or forever hold his peace . . ."

For a split second there was total silence—the taut, tense quiet that always follows that ancient challenge—but this time the challenge was answered, and the silence was exploded by a deep, ironic baritone voice: "There is *one* reason—"

Tony spun around, the archbishop gaped, Alexandra froze, and three thousand guests whirled in their seats. An agitated babble of voices broke loose and swept through the church like a tidal wave. At the altar, Melanie Camden's bouquet of roses slid through her numb fingers, Roddy Carstairs grinned broadly, and Alexandra stood there, convinced this was not really happening to her, this was a dream, she thought wildly, or else she had gone mad.

"On what grounds do you protest this marriage?" the archbishop finally barked.

"On the grounds that the bride is already married," Jordan replied, sounding almost amused—"to me."

This time there was no denying the reality of that achingly familiar deep voice, and shock waves roared up and down Alexandra's spine, buffeting her entire body. Joy exploded in her heart, obliterating all memory of his treachery and deceit. Slowly she turned, afraid to look for fear this was some cruel trick of fate, and then she raised her gaze to his. It was Jordan! He was alive. The sight of his handsome, ruggedly chiseled face almost sent her to her knees. He was standing there, looking at her, a faint smile lingering on his firm lips.

Her entire being aglow, Alexandra mentally reached out to touch his beloved face and assure herself he was real. His smile warmed as if he felt her touch; his eyes shifted over her face, registering the changes in her appearance, and then, for no comprehensible reason, Jordan's entire expression froze, and he looked sharply, accusingly at Tony.

In the front pew, the dowager duchess was immobilized, staring at Jordan, her right hand pressed to her throat. In the cataclysmic silence that ensued, only Uncle Monty seemed capable of speech or action—undoubtedly because the full bottle of Madeira he had secretly imbibed had

216

impaired his ability to recognize Jordan's profile. He did, however, vividly recall the dowager's biting lectures about the necessity for decorum at this wedding, and so he took it as his duty to remonstrate with the newcomer. Leaning toward the intruder standing in the aisle, Sir Montague warned in a booming voice, *"Take a seat, man!* And don't move a muscle till the archbishop walks off—otherwise, there'll be hell to pay from the dowager!"

His voice seemed to break the spell holding everyone in thrall. The archbishop suddenly announced that the ceremony could not continue and walked off; Tony took Alexandra's trembling hand in his and started down the aisle; Jordan stepped aside to let them pass; the stately duchess slowly rose, her gaze clinging to Jordan. In his muddled state, Uncle Monty assumed the wedding was happily complete and, following his previous instructions to the letter, he offered his arm to the dowager and escorted her proudly down the aisle in the bride and groom's wake, beaming benignly upon the gaping spectators who had come to their feet and were staring in mummified amazement.

Outside the church, Uncle Monty kissed Alexandra soundly, took Tony's hand, and was pumping it energetically, when Jordan's harsh voice stopped him cold. "You damned fool, the wedding is off! Do something useful, and take my wife home." Taking his grandmother's arm, Jordan started toward the waiting coaches. Over his shoulder, he said curtly to Tony, "I suggest we get out of here, before that mob in there descends on us. The morning papers will carry the explanation of my miraculous return. They can learn about it there. We'll meet you at my—at the town house in Upper Brook Street."

"No way to flag down a hack, Hawthorne," Uncle Monty said to Tony, taking charge when neither Alexandra nor Anthony seemed capable of movement. "There ain't a hack in sight. You'll ride with us." Forcibly clutching Anthony by one arm and Alexandra by the other, he marched them forward toward Tony's coach.

Jordan ushered his grandmother into her stately coach, snapped orders to her mesmerized coachman, and climbed in beside her. "Jordan—?" she whispered finally, staring up at him with joyous, tear-brightened eyes as the coach lurched forward. "Is it really you?"

A sympathetic smile softened his grim features. Putting his arm around her shoulders, he tenderly kissed her forehead. "Yes, darling."

In a rare show of affection, she laid her hand against his tanned cheek, then suddenly jerked her hand away and demanded imperiously, "Hawthorne, where have you been! We thought you were dead! Poor Alexandra almost wasted away with grief, and Anthony—"

"Spare me the lies," Jordan interrupted coldly. "Tony looked anything but thrilled to see me just now, and my 'grieving' wife was a radiant bride."

In his mind Jordan saw the ravishing beauty who had turned to him on that altar. For one wonderful, mortifying moment he thought he'd barged in on the wrong wedding, or that Mathison had been mistaken about the identity of Tony's bride, because Jordan hadn't recognized her—not until she'd raised those unforgettable aqua eyes of hers to his. Then and only then had he known for certain who she was—just as certainly as he knew in that instant that Tony had not been marrying her out of pity or charity. The intoxicating beauty on that altar would arouse lust in any man, but not pity.

"I was under the impression," he remarked with biting sarcasm, "that a mourning period of one year is customary after a death in one's immediate family."

"Of course it is, and we did observe it!" the duchess said defensively. "The three of us did not go out into company until April, when Alexandra made her bow, and I don't—"

"And where was my grieving wife living during that somber period?" he bit out.

"At Hawthorne, with Anthony and me, of course."

"Of course," Jordan repeated caustically. "I find it amazing that Tony wasn't contented with owning my titles, my lands, and my money—he had to possess my wife, as well."

The dowager paled, suddenly aware of how all this must look to him right now and equally cognizant that in his present mood, it would be a grave mistake to explain that Alexandra's *popularity* had necessitated her marriage. "You're wrong, Hawthorne. Alexandra—"

"Alexandra," he interrupted, "apparently liked being the Duchess of Hawthorne and therefore did the only thing she

218

could do to secure the position permanently. She decided to marry the current Duke of Hawthorne."

"She's—"

"A scheming opportunist?" he suggested bitingly, as rage and disgust ate at him like acid. While he had been rotting away in prison, lying awake nights worrying that Alexandra was wasting away in seclusion, tormented with grief and despair, Tony and Alexandra had been enjoying all his worldly goods. And in time they decided to enjoy each other as well.

The dowager saw the harshness in his taut features and sighed with helpless understanding. "I know how dreadful all this must look to you, Jordan," she said with a trace of guilt in her gruff voice, "and I can see that you are not ready or able to listen to reason. However, I should very much like it if you would at least explain to me what *you* have been about all this time."

Jordan sketched in the details of his absence, leaving out the worst of them, but talking about it only made him more furiously aware of the sick irony of the entire situation: While he had been in chains, Tony had happily usurped his titles, his estates, his money, and then he had decided to help himself to Jordan's *wife*.

Behind them, in a coach bearing the gold crest of the Duke of Hawthorne—an insignia which Anthony no longer had the right to use—Alexandra sat perfectly still beside Uncle Monty and across from Anthony, who was staring out the window. Her mind was racing in wild circles, her thoughts tumbling over themselves. Jordan was alive and well—except that he was much thinner than she remembered. Had he deliberately vanished because he wanted to escape from the pathetic child he had married, returning only when he discovered his cousin was about to become a party to bigamy? Her joy that he was alive and well gave way to bewilderment. Surely he could not have been so revolted by her as that!

No sooner had that thought consoled her dazed spirits than sharper ones began to stab at her in rapid, relentless succession: The man whose return she had just been rejoicing was the very same man who had pitied and despised her. He had mocked her to his mistress. Jordan Townsende, as she now knew and must *never* forget, was unprincipled, unfaithful, heartless, and morally corrupt. And she was *married* to him!

In her mind Alexandra called him every terrible name she could think of, but as their coach neared Upper Brook Street, her fury was already abating. Anger required mental energy and concentration, and at the moment her dazed mind was still nearly paralyzed with shock.

Across from her, Tony shifted in his seat and the movement suddenly made her remember that she was not the only one whose future had just been drastically altered by Jordan's reappearance. "Tony," she said sympathetically, "I'm . . . sorry," she finished lamely. "It's just as well your mother felt she ought to stay home with your brother. The shock of Jordan's return would surely have brought on an attack."

To her amazement, Tony started to grin. "Being the Duke of Hawthorne was not quite so delightful as I once thought it would be. As I said a few weeks ago, there's little joy in possessing fabulous wealth if one can't find the time to enjoy it. However, it has just occurred to me that fate has handed *you* quite a boon."

"What is that?" she said, staring at him as if he'd taken leave of his senses.

"Only consider this," he continued, and to her disbelief he began to chuckle out loud. "Jordan is back and his wife is now one of the most desired women in England! Be honest —isn't this exactly what you used to dream would happen?"

With grim amusement, Alexandra contemplated the shock that was in store for Jordan when he discovered that his unwanted, pitiful little wife was now the toast of the *ton*. "I have no intention of remaining married to him," she said with great finality. "I shall tell him as soon as possible that I want a divorce."

Tony sobered instantly. "You can't be serious. Do you have any idea how much scandal a divorce will cause? Even if you can get one, which I doubt, you will be a total outcast in Society."

"I don't care."

He looked at her and his voice gentled. "I appreciate your concern for my feelings, Alex, but there's no need for you to

220

think of a divorce on my behalf. Even if we were desperately in love, which we aren't, it wouldn't matter. You are Jordan's wife. Nothing can change that."

"Hasn't it occurred to you that he might *want* to change that?"

"Nope," Tony declared cheerfully. "I'll wager that what he *wants* to do right now is call me out and demand satisfaction. Didn't you see the murderous look he gave me in church? But don't fret," he continued, chuckling at her look of terror, "if Hawk wants a duel, I'll choose rapiers and send *you* in as my stand-in. He can't very well spill your blood, and you stand a better chance of drawing *his* than I do."

Alexandra would have argued tempestuously that Jordan wasn't likely to care that Tony and she had been about to marry, but argument required clear, rational thinking and she could not quite shake off the blur of unreality still surrounding everything. "Let me be the one to tell him I wish a divorce, Tony. For the sake of future family tranquillity, he must understand that this is entirely my decision and has nothing to do with you."

Caught between amusement and alarm, Tony leaned across and took her by the shoulders, laughing as he shook her lightly. "Alex, listen to me. I know you're in shock, and I certainly don't think you ought to fall into Jordan's arms this week or even this month, but divorcing him is carrying vengeance too far!"

"He cannot object in the least," Alexandra replied with a flash of spirit. "He never cared a pin for me."

Tony shook his head, his lips twitching with the smile he was trying unsuccessfully to hide. "You don't really understand about men and their pride—and you don't know Jordan if you believe he'll just let you go. He . . ." Suddenly Tony's eyes gleamed with laughter and he fell back against the squabs, chuckling with mirth. "Jordan," he declared mirthfully, *"hated* sharing his toys, and he's *never* passed up a challenge!"

Uncle Monty looked from one to the other of them, then reached inside his coat and removed a small flask. "Circumstances such as these," he announced, helping himself to a swallow, "require a bit of restorative tonic."

There was no time for further conversation, because just then their coach drew up behind Jordan's at the house on Upper Brook Street.

Carefully averting her eyes from Jordan, who was already helping his grandmother down from the other coach, Alexandra put her hand in Tony's and stepped down. But as Jordan followed her up the steps with his grandmother on his arm, the shock that had blessedly anesthetized Alexandra up until now, abruptly began to dissipate. Less than two feet behind her, his booted heels struck the pavement with sharp, relentless clicks that sent shivers of apprehension dancing down her spine; his tall body and broad shoulders threw an ominous shadow across her path and blocked the sunlight. He was real and alive and here, she thought, and her body began to tremble uncontrollably. This was not a dream—or a nightmare—from which she might awaken.

The group seemed to turn in unison toward the drawing room. Her senses heightened sharply by her growing awareness of his menace to her future, as well as Tony's concern about a possible duel, Alexandra paused inside the drawing room and swiftly surveyed the seating, weighing the psychological advantages and disadvantages of each location. Looking for a neutral position, she decided against the sofa, seating herself instead in one of the two wing chairs facing each other in front of the fireplace, then concentrated all her will on trying to subdue the sudden, quickened pounding of her heart. The dowager duchess apparently opted for neutrality also, for she chose the other chair for herself.

That left the sofa, at right angles to the chairs and facing the fireplace. Tony, with no other choice, sat upon that and was joined by Uncle Monty, who had rushed into the drawing room in hopes of enjoying some libation while simultaneously lending Alexandra his emotional support. Jordan crossed to the fireplace, draped his arm across the mantel and turned, regarding the entire assemblage in cool, speculative silence.

While the elderly duchess gave an extremely brief, nervous account of Jordan's whereabouts for the last fifteen months, Filbert walked in, a beaming smile upon his lips, a tray of champagne in his hands. Unaware of the charged atmosphere or of Jordan's relationship to Alex, the loyal footman carried the tray straight to Alexandra and filled five glasses. As soon as the duchess finished speaking, Filbert handed the first glass to Alexandra, and said, "May you always be as happy as you are at this moment, Miss Alex."

Alexandra felt hysterical laughter well up inside her, combined with escalating panic, as Filbert returned to the table and poured more champagne into the remaining glasses, then passed them out to the silent inhabitants of the room, including Jordan.

Seconds ticked past, but no one, not even Uncle Monty, had nerve enough to be the first one to lift his glass and partake of the vintage champagne that had been brought up from the cellars in advance to celebrate a wedding that had not taken place. . . . No one, except Jordan.

Seemingly impervious to the throbbing strain in the drawing room, he turned the glass in his hand, studying the bubbles in the sparkling crystal glass, then he took a long swallow. When he lowered the glass, he regarded Tony with a sardonic expression. "It's good to know," he coldly remarked, "that you haven't let your grief over my alleged demise prevent you from enjoying my best wines."

The duchess flinched, Alexandra stiffened, but Tony accepted the biting gibe with a nonchalant smile. "Be assured that we toasted you whenever we opened a new bottle, Hawk."

Beneath lowered lashes, Alexandra stole a swift, apprehensive glance at the tall, dark figure at the fireplace, wondering a little hysterically what sort of man he actually was. He appeared to feel no antagonism over Tony's having "usurped" his title, his money, his estates, and his *wife*—and yet he was angry because his *wine cellar* had been raided.

Jordan's next words immediately disabused her of the erroneous notion that he was unconcerned about his estates. "How has Hawthorne fared in my absence?" he asked, and for the next hour he snapped rapid-fire questions at Tony, interrogating him in minute detail about the state of each of his eleven estates, his myriad business ventures, his personal holdings, and even the health of some of his retainers.

Whenever he spoke, his deep voice scraped against Alexandra's lacerated nerves and, on those rare occasions when she stole a glance at him, apprehension made her quickly

223

jerk her gaze away. Dressed in tight breeches that outlined his long, muscular legs and an open-necked white shirt that clung to his wide shoulders, Jordan Townsende looked completely relaxed, yet there was an undeniable aura of forcefulness, of power—restrained now, but gathering force —waiting to be unleashed on her. She remembered him as being handsome, but *not* so . . . so ruggedly virile, or so formidably large. He was too thin, but the tan he'd acquired after his escape and on board the ship made him look far healthier than the white-skinned gentlemen of the *ton*. Standing almost within arms' reach of her, he loomed like a sinister specter, a dangerous, malevolent giant of a man who had suddenly imposed himself in her life, again, with the power to blot all happiness from her future. She was not callous enough to be sorry he was alive, but she sorely wished she'd never laid eyes on him.

For what seemed an eternity, Alexandra sat perfectly still, existing in a state of jarring tension, fighting to appear completely calm, clinging to her composure as if it were a blanket she could use to insulate herself against Jordan. With a mixture of terrible dread and utter determination, she waited for the inevitable moment when Jordan would finally bring up the matter of *her*. When Jordan was finished discussing estate matters with Tony, however, he switched to the status of his other ventures, and Alexandra felt her anxiety begin to escalate. When that topic was exhausted, he inquired about local events, and Alexandra's panic was mixed with bewilderment. But when he switched from that to gossip and trivialities and asked about the outcome of the races at Fordham last spring, Alexandra's bewilderment gave way to annoyance.

Obviously, he considered her less important than Lord Wedgeley's two-year-old mare or Sir Markham's promising colt, she realized. Not that she should have been surprised by that, she reminded herself bitterly, for as she had discovered to her mortification a short time ago, Jordan Townsende had never considered her anything but an irksome responsibility.

When all matters, down to the most trivial, had finally been discussed, an uneasy silence fell over the room, and Alexandra naturally assumed her time was finally here. Just when she expected Jordan to ask to see her alone, he abruptly straightened from his lounging posture at the fireplace and announced his intention to leave!

Prudence warned her to keep silent, but Alexandra could not bear another hour, let alone another day, of this awful suspense. Striving to sound calm and impersonal, she said, "I think there is one more issue that needs to be discussed, your grace."

Without bothering to so much as glance in her direction, Jordan reached out and accepted Tony's outstretched hand. "That issue can wait," he said coldly. "When I've seen to some important matters, you and I will talk privately."

The implication that she was not an "important" matter was unmistakable, and Alexandra stiffened at the deliberate, unprovoked insult. She was a fully grown young woman now, not an easily manipulated, wildly infatuated child who would have done anything to please him. Putting a tight rein on her temper, she said with unarguable logic, "Surely a human being warrants the same amount of your time as Sir Markham's colt, and I would rather discuss it now, while we are all together."

Jordan's head jerked toward her, and Alexandra's breath froze at the hard anger flaring in his eyes. "I said 'privately'!" he snapped, leaving her with the staggering realization that beneath his cool, impassive facade Jordan Townsende was burningly angry. Before she could assimilate that or withdraw her request for his time—as she was on the verge of doing—the duchess swiftly arose and beckoned Uncle Monty and Tony to follow her out of the room.

The door to the salon closed behind them with an ominous thud, and for the first time in fifteen months, Alexandra was alone with the man who was her husband—alarmingly, nerve-rackingly alone.

From the corner of her eyes, she watched him walk to the table and pour himself another glass of champagne, and she took advantage of his preoccupation to really look at him. What she saw made her tremble with foreboding. Wildly, she wondered how she could have been naive enough, or infatuated enough, to imagine that Jordan Townsende was *gentle*.

Seen now, through the eyes of an adult, she could not find a trace of gentleness or kindness anywhere in his tough, ruggedly chiseled features. How, she wondered in amaze-

225

ment, could she ever have likened him to Michelangelo's beautiful David?

Instead of gentle beauty, there was ruthless nobility stamped on Jordan Townsende's tanned features, implacable authority in the tough jawline and straight nose, and cold determination in the thrust of his chin. Inwardly she shivered at the harsh cynicism she saw in his eyes, the biting mockery she heard in his drawl. Long ago, she had thought his grey eyes soft, like the sky after a summer rain, but now she could see they were cold and unwelcoming as glaciers; eyes without kindness or understanding. Oh, he was handsome enough, she conceded reluctantly—devastatingly so, in fact, but *only* if one were drawn to dark, blatantly aggressive, wickedly sensual men, which she assuredly was not.

Racking her brain for the best way to broach the matter on her mind, she approached the table and poured herself another glass of champagne, oblivious to the fact that her first glass was still full, then she looked around, trying to decide whether to sit or stand. She decided to stand so he would not seem so tall and intimidating.

At the fireplace Jordan raised his glass to his lips, watching her. She could have only two possible reasons for insisting on this meeting, he thought. The first possibility was that she honestly believed she was in love with Tony, and that was why she wished to marry him. If that was the case, she would begin by telling him so—simply and truthfully—as had been her habit. The second possibility was that she wanted to be married to whoever was the Duke of Hawthorne. If that was the case, she would now try to soothe Jordan with some form of tender, feminine theatrics. But first she would wait a bit for his temper to cool—exactly as she was doing now.

Jordan drained his glass and put it down on the mantel with a sharp thud. "I'm waiting," he snapped impatiently.

Alexandra jumped and whirled to face him, appalled by his biting tone. "I—I know," she said, determined at all costs to speak to him with calm maturity and to make it infinitely clear to him that she no longer wished to be his concern or responsibility. On the other hand, she did not want to do or say anything which might reveal to him how hurt and angry and disillusioned she had been when she discovered the truth about his feelings for her, or what a fool she had made of herself grieving for London's most infamous libertine. To add to her dilemma, it was rapidly becoming obvious that in his current mood, Jordan was not likely to react reasonably to the scandalous subject of a divorce. In fact, she instinctively knew he would react the opposite. "I'm not quite certain how to begin," she said hesitantly.

"In that case," he drawled sarcastically as his blistering gaze sliced over her glorious ice-blue satin bridal gown, "allow me to offer a few suggestions: If you're about to tell me very prettily how sorely you've missed me, I'm afraid that gown you are wearing is a little incongruous. You would have been wiser to change it. It's extravagantly lovely by the way." His drawl became clipped and abrupt. "Did I pay for it?"

"No—that is, I don't know exactly how—"

"Never mind about the gown," he interrupted scathingly. "Let's get on with your charade. Since you cannot very well fling yourself into my arms and weep tears of joy at my return, while you're dressed as another man's bride, you'll have to think of something else to soften my attitude toward you and win my forgiveness."

"Win *your what?*" Alexandra exploded as outrage conquered her fears.

"Why not begin by telling me how deeply grieved you were when you first learned of my 'untimely demise'?" he continued savagely, ignoring her outburst of righteous indignation. "That would have a nice ring to it. Then, if you could manage one tear, or even two, you could tell me how you mourned me, and wept, and said prayers for my—"

That was so close to the truth that Alexandra's voice shook with shamed anger. "Stop it! I have no intention of doing anything of the sort! Furthermore, you arrogant hypocrite, your forgiveness is the *last* thing I care about."

"That was very foolish of you, my sweet," he drawled silkily, shoving away from the fireplace. "Tenderness and dainty tears are called for at times such as these, not insults. Moreover, softening my attitude ought to be your *first* concern. Well-bred females who aspire to be duchesses must seek to make themselves agreeable to any eligible duke at all times. Now then, since you can't change your gown and you can't weep, why not try telling me how much you missed me," he insolently suggested. "You did miss me, did you not? Very much, I'll vow. So much so that you only decided to marry Tony because he—ah—resembled me. That's it, isn't it?" he mocked.

"Why are you behaving like this?" Alexandra cried.

Without bothering to answer, he moved closer, looming over her like a dark, ominous cloud. "In a day or two, I'll tell you what I've decided to do with you."

Anger and confusion were warring in Alexandra's mind, sending her thoughts into a complete tumult. Jordan Townsende had never cared about her and he had no right, no *reason* to act like a self-righteous, outraged husband! "I am not a mindless piece of chattel!" she burst out. "You can't just dispose of me like a—a piece of furniture!"

"Can't I? Try me!" he clipped.

Alexandra's mind groped wildly for some way to neutralize his irrational anger and soothe what could only be his wounded ego. Raking a hand through her heavy hair, she sought desperately for some guiding logic. *She* was the innocent and injured party in their relationship, but at the moment he was the powerful and potentially dangerous party, and so she tried to reason with him. "I can see that you're angry—"

"How very observant of you," he mocked nastily.

Ignoring his sarcasm, Alexandra persevered in what she hoped was a reasonable tone, "And I can see there is no point in trying to reason with you in this mood—"

"Go ahead and try it," he invited, but the look in his eyes said the opposite as he took a menacing step toward her.

Alexandra hastily retreated a step. "There's—there's no point. You won't listen to me. Anger blows out the lamp of the mind . . ."

The quote from Ingersoll caught Jordan entirely off guard, reminding him poignantly of the enchanting, curly-haired girl who could quote from Buddha or John the Baptist, depending upon the occasion. Unfortunately, it only made him angrier now, because she was no longer that girl. Instead, she had become a scheming little opportunist. If she truly wanted to marry Tony because she loved him, she would have said so by now, he knew. Since she hadn't, she obviously wanted to remain the Duchess of Hawthorne.

And therein lay her problem, Jordan thought cynically: She could not convincingly throw herself into his arms and weep for joy when he had just witnessed her near-marriage to another man, but neither could she risk letting him walk out of this house without taking the first of many predictable steps toward reconciliation—not if she wanted to continue moving in Society with the full prestige and honor of her rank. To maintain that, the *ton* would need to see that she was in the good graces of the current duke.

She had become ambitious in the last fifteen months, he realized with blazing contempt. And beautiful. Arrestingly so at close range, with her glossy mahogany hair spilling over her shoulders and back in masses of waves and curls, contrasting vividly with her glowing alabaster skin, brilliant aqua eyes, and soft, rosy lips. In comparison with the pale blondes he remembered, who were usually the Acclaimed Beauties, Alexandra was incredibly more alluring.

He stared hard at her, convinced she was a scheming opportunist, yet despite all the evidence, he could not find a trace of guile in those flashing eyes of hers or her angry, upturned face. Furious with his inner reluctance to see her for what she had become, he turned on his heel and walked toward the door.

Alexandra watched him leave, buffeted by a myriad of conflicting emotions, including fury, relief, and alarm. He paused in the doorway and she tensed automatically.

"I will move in here tomorrow. In the meantime, let me leave you with some instructions: You are not to accompany Tony anywhere."

His tone promised terrible consequences should she choose to ignore his order, and although she couldn't imagine what form those reprisals might take, or why she should want to walk out and face a furor of gossip, Alexandra was momentarily quelled by the threat in his voice. "You will, in fact, not leave this house. Have I made myself perfectly clear?"

With a magnificent gesture of unconcern that completely belied her alarm, she shrugged lightly and said, "I speak three languages fluently, your grace. One of them is English."

"Are you *patronizing* me?" he asked in a silken, threatening voice.

Alexandra's courage warred with common sense, but neither of them won. Afraid to advance and unwilling to retreat, she tried to hold her ground by daring to say in the tone of an adult addressing a cranky, unreasonable child: "I have no wish to discuss that or anything else with you when you are in such an unreasonable mood."

"Alexandra," he said in an *awful* voice, "if you're wondering how far you can push me, you've just reached your limit. In my present 'unreasonable mood,' nothing would give me greater satisfaction than to close this door and spend the next ten minutes making certain you can't sit down for a week. Do you take my meaning?"

The threat of being spanked like a child stripped away Alexandra's hard-won confidence and made her feel as gauche and helpless as she had a year ago in his presence. She put her chin up and said nothing, but bright flags of humiliated color stained her cheeks, and tears of frustration stung her eyes.

He stared at her in silence and then, satisfied that she was adequately chastened, Jordan defied all the rules of courtesy and walked off without so much as a nod to her.

Two years ago, she had been ignorant of the rules of etiquette to which polite ladies and gentlemen always conformed; she had not realized then that Jordan was insulting her when he never bothered to bow to her, or to kiss her hand, or treat her solicitously. For that matter, he had never deigned to permit her to call him by his given name. Now, as she stood alone in the middle of the drawing room, she was acutely, furiously aware of all those bygone slights, as well as the new ones he had heaped upon her today.

She waited until she heard the front door close, and then she walked woodenly out of the salon and up the stairs to her room. Anguish and disbelief poured through her as she dismissed her maid and mindlessly stripped off her wedding gown. He was back! And he was *worse* than she remembered, *worse* than she'd imagined—more arrogant, more dictatorial, completely heartless. And she was married to him. *Married!* her heart screamed.

This morning, everything had seemed so simple and predictable. She had arisen and dressed to be married; she had gone to the church. Now, three hours later, she was married to the wrong man.

230

Fiercely struggling against her tears, she sat down on the settee and wrapped her arms around her stomach, trying to block out the images, but it was no use. They paraded across her mind, tormenting her with vivid scenes of the mindlessly infatuated, besotted girl she had been. . . . She saw herself looking up at Jordan in the garden at Rosemeade. *"I think you are as beautiful as Michelangelo's David!"* she had blurted. *"I love you."* And when he had made love to her, she had nearly *swooned* in his arms, and babbled to him about how strong and wise and nauseatingly wonderful he was!

"Dear God," Alex moaned aloud as another forgotten memory pranced across her mind: she had actually told Jordan—London's most infamous libertine—that *he* obviously wasn't well-acquainted with many women. No wonder he had grinned!

Hot tears of humiliation dripped from her eyes, but she brushed them angrily aside, refusing to cry one more time for that—that monster. She had already wept *buckets* of tears over him, she thought furiously.

Tony's words of a few weeks ago came back to hack at her lacerated emotions: *"Jordan married you because he pitied you, but he had neither the DESIRE nor the INTENT to live with you as his wife. He intended to pack you off to Devon when you returned from your wedding trip, and then he meant to continue where he left off with his mistress. . . . He was with his mistress AFTER you were married to him. . . . He told her your marriage was one of INconvenience . . ."*

There was a soft knock at the door, but Alexandra was so immersed in misery she didn't hear anything until Melanie had walked into the bedchamber and closed the door. "Alex?"

Startled, Alexandra turned her head and looked round. Melanie took one look at her friend's anguished, tear-streaked face, and rushed to her side.

"Dear God!" Melanie whispered in horror, kneeling in front of Alexandra and pulling out her handkerchief, almost babbling in her agitated alarm. "Why are you crying? Has he done something to you? Did he rage at you or—or strike you?"

Alexandra swallowed and looked at her, but she could not

drag her voice past the lump of tears in her throat. Melanie's husband had been Jordan's closest friend, she knew, and now she wondered where Melanie's loyalties would lie. She shook her head and took the handkerchief from Melanie.

"Alex!" Melanie cried in mounting alarm. "Talk to me, please! I'm your friend, and I'll always be," she said, correctly interpreting the reason for Alexandra's wary expression. "You can't keep this bottled up inside you— you're as white as a ghost and you look ready to faint."

Alexandra had briefly confided to Melanie that she had been an utter blind fool about Jordan, but she had never mentioned his complete lack of feeling for her, and had also concealed her shame behind a facade of amused self-mockery. Now, however, it was there in all its naked, mute misery for Melanie to see, as Alexandra haltingly related all the humiliating details of her relationship with Hawk, leaving nothing out. Throughout the tale, Melanie frequently shook her head in sympathetic amusement at Alexandra's naive outpouring of her heart to Jordan, but she did not smile when Alexandra told her of Hawk's intention to pack her off to Devon.

Alexandra finished by relating Jordan's explanation for his disappearance, and when she was done Melanie patted her hand. "All that's in the past. What about the future—do you have any sort of plan?"

"Yes," Alexandra said with quiet force. "I want a divorce!"

"What?" Melanie gasped. "You can't be serious!"

Alexandra was deadly serious and said so.

"A divorce is unthinkable," Melanie said, dismissing that alternative in a few short sentences. "You would be an outcast, Alex. Even my husband, who gives me my head in nearly everything, would forbid me to be in your company. You'd be barred from decent society everywhere, shut off from everyone."

"That is still preferable to being married to him *and* shut away somewhere in Devon."

"Perhaps it seems so to you now, but in any case it doesn't matter how you feel. I'm quite certain your husband would have to agree to a divorce, and I can't imagine that he will.

Even so, they must be very difficult to obtain, and you'd need grounds, as well as Hawk's consent."

"I was thinking about that when you came in, and it seems to me I already have grounds, and I may not need his consent at all. In the first place, I was coerced into this marriage by—by circumstances. Secondly, at our wedding, he vowed to love and honor me, but he had no intention of ever doing either—that surely must be grounds enough to get either an annulment or a divorce, with or without his consent. However, I don't see why he'll refuse his consent," Alexandra added with a flash of anger. "He never wished to marry me in the first place."

"Well," Melanie shot back, "that doesn't mean he'll like having everyone know you don't want *him* anymore."

"When he has time to consider the plan, he'll be bound to feel relieved to have me off his hands."

Melanie shook her head. "I'm not so certain he wants you off his hands. I saw the way he looked at Lord Anthony in church today—he did not look relieved, he looked furious!"

"He is ill-tempered by nature," Alexandra said with disgust, recalling their interview downstairs. "He has no reason whatsoever to be angry with Anthony or me."

"No reason!" Melanie repeated in disbelief. "Why, you were about to marry another man!"

"I can't see what difference that should make. As I just said, he didn't want to marry me in the first place."

"But that doesn't mean he'll want anyone *else* to marry you," Melanie wisely replied. "In any case it doesn't matter. A divorce is simply out of the question. There has to be some other solution. My husband returned from Scotland today," she said enthusiastically. "I shall ask John for advice. He is very wise." Her face fell. "Unfortunately, he also considers Hawk his closest friend, so his advice will be somewhat colored by that. However," she said with absolute finality, "a divorce is positively beyond considering. There must be an alternative."

She fell silent for several long moments, lost in her own thoughts, her forehead furrowed. "It's little wonder you fell like a rock for him," she said with a small, compassionate smile. "Dozens of the most sophisticated flirts in England tumbled head over heels for him," she continued thoughtfully. "But except for indulging in an occasional fling with one of them, he never showed any sign of reciprocating their feelings. Naturally, now that he is back, everyone will expect you to tumble straight into his arms—particularly because Society is, at this very moment, recollecting how blindly infatuated with him you were when you first came to town."

The realization that Melanie was perfectly correct made Alexandra feel quite violently ill. Leaning her head against the back of the sofa, she swallowed and closed her eyes in sublime misery. "I hadn't thought of that, but you're absolutely right."

"Of course I am," Melanie absently agreed. "On the other hand," she declared, her eyes beginning to shine, "wouldn't it be delightful if the opposite happens!"

"What do you mean?"

"The ideal solution to the entire problem is for *him* to fall in love with *you*. That would enable you to keep your pride *and* your husband."

"Melanie," Alexandra said dampingly. "First of all, I don't think anyone could make that man fall in love, because he doesn't have a heart. Secondly, even if he does have one, it's certainly immune to me. Thirdly . . ."

Laughing, Melanie caught Alexandra's arm, hauled her off the sofa and pulled her to the mirror. "That was *before.* Look into the mirror, Alex. The female looking back at you right now has London at her feet! Men are quarreling over you—"

Alexandra sighed, looking at Melanie in the mirror rather than her own image. "Only because I've become a sort of absurd, fashionable rage—like damping one's skirts. It's fashionable for the moment for men to fancy themselves in love with me."

"How delightful," said Melanie, more pleased than before. "Hawthorne is in for the shock of his life when he realizes it."

A brief flare of amusement stirred in Alexandra's eyes, then abruptly dimmed. "It doesn't matter."

"Oh, yes, it does!" Melanie laughed. "Only consider this: For the first time in his life, Hawthorne has competition—and for his own wife! Think how Society will relish the spectacle of England's most practiced libertine, trying without early success to seduce and subdue his own wife."

"There's another reason why it won't work," Alexandra said firmly.

"What is that?"

"I won't do it. Even if I could accomplish it, which I can't, I don't want to try."

"But why?" Melanie burst out. "Why ever not?"

"Because," Alexandra declared hotly, "I don't *like* him! I do not want him to love me, I do not even want him near me." So saying, she walked over to the bellpull to ring for tea.

"Nevertheless, it is still the only and best solution to this coil." Snatching up her gloves and reticule, Melanie pressed a kiss to Alexandra's forehead. "You're shocked and exhausted, you aren't thinking clearly. Leave everything to me."

She was halfway across the room when Alexandra realized that Melanie seemed to have a specific destination in mind and that she was in some haste to get there. "Where are you going, Mel?" she asked suspiciously.

"To see Roddy," Melanie said, turning in the doorway. "He can be depended upon to make certain Hawthorne is informed at the earliest possible moment that you are no longer the naive, unsophisticated country mouse he may think you are. Roddy will adore doing it," Melanie predicted cheerfully. "It's exactly the sort of rabble-rousing he most enjoys."

"Melanie, wait!" Alexandra burst out tiredly, but she did not particularly object to this part of Melanie's plan—not at this moment when exhaustion was beginning to overwhelm her. "Promise me you won't do anything else without telling me."

"Very well," Melanie said gaily and vanished with a wave.

Alexandra leaned her head back and closed her eyes as drowsiness began to overcome her.

The clock chiming the hour of ten, combined with the incessant arrivals of callers in the main hall downstairs, finally brought her fully awake. Leaning on an elbow, Alexandra blinked her eyes in the candlelit gloom of her bedchamber, surprised that she had somehow fallen asleep on the settee at what was normally considered a very early hour of the evening. She listened to the commotion downstairs, the constant opening and closing of the front door, and she sat up, groggily wondering why the entire *haute ton* seemed to be arriving on their doorstep. . . . And then she remembered.

Hawk was back.

Evidently everyone thought he was here, and they were too eager to see him and speak to him to follow their own precepts of decorum, which would have required them at least to wait until tomorrow to call.

Hawk must have anticipated this, Alexandra decided irritably, as she got up and changed into a silk peignoir and climbed into bed. That was probably why he had chosen to spend the night at the duchess' house, leaving the rest of them here to try to deal with the furor of callers.

Her husband, she had no doubt, was blissfully in his bed, and enjoying a peaceful night.

Chapter Twenty

*A*LEXANDRA WAS WRONG on both counts. Jordan was not in bed and he was *not* enjoying his evening.

Seated in the baroque drawing room at his grandmother's town house, with his legs negligently stretched out in front of him and a bland expression upon his face, he was with three friends who'd come to welcome him home, as well as Roddy Carstairs, who'd apparently come to regale him with "amusing" stories about Alexandra's escapades.

After listening to Carstairs' tales for nearly an hour, Jordan was not mildly exasperated, nor somewhat irritated, nor very annoyed. He was livid. While *he* had been lying awake at night, worrying that his adoring young wife would be out of her mind with grief, *she* had been setting London on its ear. While he rotted in prison, Alexandra had been carrying on a dozen widely publicized flirtations. While *he* lay in chains, "Alex" had evidently pursued victory in a race at Gresham Green, and fought a mock duel with Lord Mayberry while wearing tight-fitting men's breeches that reportedly so distracted her opponent that the famous swordsman lost the match. She had gallivanted about at fairs and participated in some sort of havey-cavey assignation with a vicar at Southeby, who Jordan could have sworn was at least seventy years old. And that was not the half of it!

If Carstairs were to be believed, Tony had apparently received six dozen offers for her hand; and her rejected suitors had taken first to arguing over her, then quarreling, and finally one of them, Marbly, had actually tried to abduct her; some young fop named Sevely had published a poem in praise of her charms called "Ode to Alex"; and old Dilbeck had named his new rose "Glorious Alex" . . .

Leaning back in his chair, Jordan crossed his long legs at the ankles, raised a brandy to his lips, and listened to Carstairs' voice drone on, his features carefully showing only mild amusement at his wife's antics.

It was exactly the reaction his three friends expected of him, he knew, for amongst the Quality it was understood that husbands and wives were free to do as they wished—so long as they behaved with discretion. On the other hand, among the close-knit fraternity of gentlemen, it was also understood that a man was to be informed by his closest friends—in as delicate a fashion as possible—when his wife's antics threatened to cross the line of acceptability and cause him embarrassment. Which, Jordan suspected, was why his friends had not tried harder to silence Carstairs tonight.

If Carstairs hadn't chanced to arrive tonight simultaneously with Jordan's friends, he would never have been admitted to the house. To Jordan, he was nothing but a distant acquaintance and an irritating gossip, but the other three men in the room were Jordan's friends. And even though they had repeatedly tried to force Carstairs to talk of something else besides Alexandra's antics, it was obvious from their carefully neutral expressions that what Carstairs was saying was mostly true.

Jordan glanced speculatively at Carstairs, wondering why he had bothered to dash over here so quickly to regale Jordan with his stories. The entire *ton* knew that Jordan had never regarded women as anything other than amusing bedwarmers. He was the last man on earth they might have suspected of losing his senses over a pretty face or voluptuous body. They would have been amazed had they known he'd lost his head over an enchanting, dark-haired moppet, and long *before* she had shown much sign of becoming a real beauty.

The four men in the drawing room on Gloucester Street would have been equally dumbfounded to know that as

Jordan languidly listened to Carstairs, he was seething inside. He was furious with Tony for letting Alexandra get out of hand and angry with his grandmother for not exerting some sort of control over her. Obviously, the fact that she was the Duchess of Hawthorne had enabled her to do as she pleased with relative impunity. Jordan could not change the past; however, he could drastically alter her future. But it was not Alexandra's antics that actually made him the angriest, or even her flirtations.

Irrationally, the thing that infuriated him the most was that they called her "Alex."

Apparently *everyone* called her Alex. The entire population of the *ton* seemed to be on the most intimate terms of friendship with his wife—particularly the male population.

Jordan glanced at the footman hovering in the doorway and imperceptibly shook his head, indicating that his guests' glasses were not to be replenished. Waiting until Carstairs paused to draw a breath, Jordan lied curtly, "I know you'll excuse us, Carstairs. These gentlemen and I have business matters to discuss."

Roddy nodded amiably and stood up to leave, but not before he got in one more verbal thrust: "I'm happy to have you back among us, Hawk. A pity for poor Tony, though. He's as mad for Alex as Wilston, Gresham, Fites, Moresby, and a few dozen others . . ."

"Including you?" Jordan speculated coolly.

Roddy's brows lifted imperturbably. "Of course."

As Roddy strode off, two of Jordan's friends, Lords Hastings and Fairfax also arose to leave, looking apologetic and embarrassed. Lord Hastings, casting about for something to say to diffuse the tension, seized on the subject of the Queen's Race, a two-day steeplechase event, which all the nobility traditionally either participated in or attended. "Do you mean to ride that black stallion of yours in the Queen's Race in September, Hawk?" Lord Hastings asked.

"I'll ride one of my horses in it," Jordan said, simultaneously trying to control his raging ire at Carstairs and call to mind the reckless joy of riding in the most important steeplechase of the year.

"Knew you would. My money's on you, if you decide to ride Satan."

"Aren't you entering it?" Jordan asked without interest.

"Naturally. But if you ride that black brute, I'm betting on you, not me. He's the fastest devil I've ever seen."

Jordan's brows snapped together in confusion. Satan, the prize foal of Jordan's stables, had been an evil-tempered, unpredictable three-year-old when Jordan was impressed a year ago. "You've seen the black run?"

"Indeed! Saw your wife race him in—" Hastings broke off in horrified chagrin when Jordan's jaw hardened with granite displeasure.

"She . . . er . . . handled him quite well and didn't press him too hard, Hawk," Fairfax put in desperately when he saw Jordan's reaction.

"I'm sure your duchess is merely high-spirited, Hawk," Lord Hastings inserted in a bluff voice with more volume than conviction as he clapped Jordan on the shoulder.

Lord Fairfax nodded instantly. "High spirits, that's all it is. Tighten her rein just a bit, and she'll be docile as a lamb."

"Docile as a lamb!" Lord Hastings concurred promptly.

Outside, both men who were avid horse-breeders and inveterate gamblers, paused on the steps to exchange dubious, looks. *"Docile as a lamb?"* Lord Hastings' repeated his friend's words incredulously, *"If Hawk but tightens her rein?"*

Lord Fairfax grinned. "Of course—but *first* he'll have to get the bit between her teeth, and to do it he'll have to hobble her. She's going to fight him when Hawk tries to tame her to his hand, you mark my word. She has more spirit than the average female—and, I suspect, more pride."

Hastings closed his eyes in amused disagreement. "You're discounting Hawk's extraordinary effect on women. In a few weeks, she'll be doting on him. By the day of the Queen's Race, she'll be tying her ribbon on his sleeve and cheering for him. Young Wilson and his friend Fairchild have already placed bets on exactly that. The odds in the book at White's are already four to one in favor of Hawk wearing her ribbon."

"You're wrong, my friend. She's going to give Hawk a devil of a time."

"Not a chance. She was besotted with him when she came to town. Have you forgotten what a complete cake she made of herself over him a few weeks back? Since Hawk walked into church this morning, that's all everyone's talking about."

"I know, and I'll wager *she* hasn't forgotten it either," said Fairfax bluntly. "I'm acquainted with Hawk's duchess and the lady has pride—her pride will prevent her from falling easily into his arms, you mark my words."

With a challenging lift of his brows, Hastings declared, "I have £1,000 that says she'll give Hawk her ribbon to wear in the Queen's Race."

"You're on," Fairfax agreed without hesitation, and they headed off to White's to relax and gamble in that exclusive gentlemen's club—but not to record this particular bet. It would be kept private, out of respect for their friend.

When Fairfax and Hastings were gone, Jordan walked over to the side table and refilled his glass. The anger he had carefully concealed from the others was evident now in the tautness of his clenched jaw as he glanced at his closest friend, John Camden. "I sincerely hope," he drawled with biting irony, "that you haven't remained here because you, too, know of some further indiscretion of Alexandra's, which you perhaps feel compelled to repeat to me privately?"

Lord Camden gave a sharp bark of laughter. "Hardly. When Carstairs was speaking of your wife's race in Hyde Park and her duel with Mayberry, he distinctly mentioned the name 'Melanie.' I believe he indicated that Melanie was cheering your duchess on to victory in both cases."

Jordan took a swallow of his drink. "So?"

"Melanie," John declared, "is my wife."

The glass in Jordan's hand stopped en route to his mouth. "What?"

"I'm married."

"Really?" Jordan dourly replied. "Why?"

Lord Camden grinned. "I couldn't seem to help myself."

"In that case, permit me to offer my belated congratulations," Jordan said sardonically. He lifted his glass in a mockery of a toast, then checked himself as years of good breeding came to the surface. "I apologize for my rudeness, John. At the moment, marriage is not high on my list of reasons for celebration. Is your Melanie anyone I know? Have I met her?"

"I should hope not!" John declared with laughing exaggeration. "She made her bow just as you left town, which is all to the good. You'd have found her irresistible, and I'd have had to call you out now that you've returned."

"Your reputation was not a great deal better than mine."

"I was never even in your league," John joked, making an obvious attempt to lighten his friend's spirits. "If *I* cast an appraising eye over an appealing Miss, her mama summoned an additional chaperone. When *you* did it, every mama in sight fell into spasms of terror and violent hope. Of course, *I* didn't have a dukedom to offer, which accounts for part of their anxiety and eagerness."

"I can't recall that I ever dallied with virtuous innocents," Jordan said, sitting down and staring into his glass.

"You didn't. But if your wife and mine have enough in common to become friends, I can only assume they're much alike. In which case, you're in for a life of torment."

"Why?" Jordan asked politely.

"Because you won't know from one day to the next what she's going to take it into her head to do—and when you do find out, it will scare the hell out of you. Melanie told me this afternoon that she's with child, and I already have the liveliest fear she'll misplace the babe when he's born."

"She's forgetful?" Jordan asked, trying without success to appear to be interested in his best friend's new wife.

John raised his brows and shrugged. "She must be. How else could she have forgotten to mention, when I returned from Scotland late today, that she and my best friend's wife—whom I haven't yet met—have been involved in several imbroglios together?"

Realizing his attempt to make light of Jordan's predicament was less than successful, John hesitated and then he said gravely, "What do you intend to do about your wife?"

"I have several choices and right now they're all appealing," Jordan said curtly. "I can wring her neck, put her under guard, or send her to Devon tomorrow and keep her there, out of the public eye."

"Good God, Hawk, you can't do that. After what happened in church today, people will think—"

"I don't give a damn what people think," Jordan interrupted, but in this case it was not the truth and both men knew it. Jordan was becoming increasingly furious at the idea of being made to look like a public laughingstock who couldn't control his own wife.

"Perhaps she is merely high-spirited," Lord Camden ventured. "Melanie knows her and likes her very well." Standing up to leave, he said, "If you're in a mood for it, join us at White's tomorrow evening. We're convening there to drink a toast to my impending fatherhood."

"I'll be there," Jordan said with a forced smile.

When Camden left, Jordan stared unseeing at the landscape framed above the mantel, wondering how many lovers Alexandra had taken to her bed. He had seen the loss of innocence, the disillusionment, in her eyes when they were alone in the drawing room this afternoon. Once, her magnificent eyes had been candid and trusting and soft when she looked at him. Now their radiance was dimmed with cold animosity.

Anger raged through Jordan like wildfire as he contemplated the reason Alexandra had treated him with such wary hostility today: She was *sorry* he wasn't dead. The artless, adoring child he had married was angry now because he was *alive!* The bewitching young girl he had wed had turned into a cold, calculating, beautiful . . . bitch.

He considered a divorce for a few minutes, then discarded the idea. Aside from the scandal, a divorce could take years to obtain, and he wanted an heir. The Townsende men seemed to be cursed with short lifespans, and even if Alexandra proved to be as lacking in virtue and decorum as she now seemed, she could still bear his children for him—in seclusion if necessary, to make certain the children she gave him were his, not someone else's.

Leaning his head against the back of his chair, Jordan closed his eyes and drew a long, harsh breath trying to bring his temper under control. When he finally managed to do that, it occurred to him that he was condemning Alexandra and deciding her future on the basis of common gossip. He owed his life to the artless, unspoiled girl he believed he had married. Surely, he also owed her the right to defend herself.

Tomorrow, he decided, he would confront her openly with the things he had heard from Carstairs tonight and give her a chance to deny them. She was entitled to that, provided she was not fool enough to lie to him. But if it became clear that she was indeed a scheming opportunist or voluptuous little wanton, then he would tame her with the ruthlessness she deserved.

She would either bend to his will, or he would break her to it, but either way she would learn to behave herself like a good and dutiful wife, he decided with cold resolve.

Chapter Twenty-One

ALEXANDRA WAS AWAKENED by the sound of footsteps rushing ceaselessly up and down the hall outside her bedchamber and the muted, excited voices of servants hurrying about their duties. Sleepily, she rolled onto her back and looked at the clock in surprised confusion. It was not yet nine o'clock, much too early for the staff to be working on this floor, where during the Season the inhabitants often slept until eleven o'clock after staying out until dawn.

No doubt they were preparing for their illustrious master's arrival later on, she thought with disgust.

Without bothering to ring for her maid, Alexandra climbed out of bed and went about her normal morning routine, her ears attuned to the unprecedented activity that seemed to be taking place outside her bedchamber.

Dressed in a pretty lavender morning gown with short puffed sleeves, she opened her door, then had to jump back as four footmen marched past, bound for what had been the master bedchamber, their view obstructed by towering armloads of boxes bearing the names of London's best tailors and bootmakers.

From the foyer below came the sounds of the doorknocker being lifted and lowered, followed by repeated openings and closings of the front door and deep, cultured masculine voices. The commotion today was much, much worse than what she had heard last night. Callers were evidently arriving in incredible numbers—hoping to see

"Hawk," Alexandra had no doubt. In the past, Alexandra and the duchess normally received a gratifying number of callers every day, but nowhere near so many and never, ever at such an early hour.

Curious, she walked along the hall to the balcony and looked down into the foyer where Higgins, not Penrose, was opening the door to admit three men whom Alexandra knew only by title. Two more, who had evidently also just arrived, were waiting politely to be shown to an appropriate salon, while all around them servants in immaculate uniforms were performing their duties with suppressed excitement and energetic fervor.

As Higgins guided the last of the newly arrived guests down a hall that led to the library, Alexandra stopped one of the maids who were scurrying down the hall carrying stacks of fresh linen. "Lucy?"

The maid bobbed a quick curtsy. "Yes, my lady?"

"Why are the servants all about so early?"

The little maid squared her shoulders and proudly proclaimed, "The Duke of Hawthorne has come home at last!"

Alexandra clutched the banister for support, her shocked gaze flying to the foyer: "He's already *here?*"

"Yes, my lady. Indeed."

Alexandra's shocked gaze flew to the floor below just as Jordan himself emerged from a salon, his tall frame clad in impeccably tailored dark blue trousers and a white shirt, casually open at the throat. With him was the unmistakable figure of George, the Prince Regent himself, decked out in rich peacock-bright satins and velvet, beaming up at Jordan while proclaiming in the royal plural, "It was a dark day for Us when you disappeared, Hawthorne. We command you to take better care of yourself in future. Your family has been plagued with too many tragic accidents. We shall expect you to take every precaution in future. Moreover," he decreed, "We should like you to attend to the business of producing heirs to properly secure the succession."

Jordan responded to that royal edict with nothing more than an amused grin, and then said something inaudible that made the prince throw back his head and guffaw.

Clapping Jordan on the shoulder, the prince apologized for having arrived unannounced this morning, then stepped aside just as Higgins glided into the foyer in time to open the door with a flourish. It took a moment for Alexandra to recover from the shock of seeing Britain's regent in the very same house with her and to see Jordan treating said monarch in a manner so casual it verged on amused geniality.

When the foyer was empty of all but the butler, Alexandra gave herself a hard mental shake and walked slowly down the stairs, struggling to find some sort of mental equilibrium. Firmly setting aside the awesome spectacle of the regent, she turned her thoughts to an even more awesome event—her forthcoming confrontation with Jordan.

"Good morning, Higgins," she said politely as she stepped into the foyer. "Where are Penrose and Filbert this morning?" she inquired, looking up and down the hall.

"His grace sent them down to the kitchens when he arrived this morning. He did not think they . . . ah . . . belonged here where they would . . . or could . . . that is . . ."

"He wanted them out of sight, is that it?" Alexandra said tautly. "So he banished them to the kitchens?"

"Quite."

Alexandra froze. "Did you happen to tell his grace that Penrose and Filbert were my fr—" She checked the automatic impulse to describe them as friends and said instead "servants."

"I mentioned that, yes."

With a superhuman effort, Alexandra fought down a disproportionate surge of rage. Obviously the two gentle old men were not capable of dealing with the Prince Regent, or even this increased barrage of callers, and she had no quarrel with Hawk in that regard. But to humiliate them in front of the rest of the staff by banishing them to the kitchens—instead of sending them to another part of the house to help out—that was grossly unjust and unkind. It was also, Alexandra suspected, an act of petty vindictiveness on Hawk's part.

"Kindly tell his grace that I wish to see him today," Alexandra said, careful not to take her anger out on Higgins. "As *early* as possible."

"His grace also wishes to see you—at one-thirty in his study."

Alexandra glanced at the stately clock in the hall. Her

appointment with her husband was three hours and fifteen minutes from now. Three hours and fifteen minutes to wait until she could tell the man she had mistakenly married that she wished to remedy the mistake. In the meantime, she would see the duchess and Tony.

"Alex—" Tony called from the opposite end of the upper hall, just as Alexandra was lifting her hand to knock upon the duchess' door. "How are you feeling this morning?" he asked as he walked toward her.

Alexandra smiled at him with sisterly affection. "I'm fine. I slept away the afternoon and night. And you?"

"I scarcely closed my eyes," Tony admitted, chuckling. "Have you seen this yet?" he asked as he handed her the newspaper.

Alexandra shook her head, her gaze scanning the page which was covered with news of Jordan's abduction and his escape, including a glowing report of his bravery contributed by a fellow prisoner, the American whom Jordan had rescued—at the repeated risk of his own life, according to the articles.

The door to the duchess' bedchamber swung open, and two footmen came out carrying a pair of heavy trunks on their shoulders. The duchess was standing in the middle of the room, directing three maids who were packing all her belongings into trunks and portmanteaux. Good morning, my dears," she called to Tony and Alexandra, motioning them inside. Dismissing her maids, she sank down into a chair and beamed her general approval at the disorderly room and the two young people who sat down across from her.

"Why are you packing?" Alexandra asked anxiously.

"Anthony and I are repairing to my town house," she said as if Alexandra should have expected that. "After all, you've no need of me to chaperone you with your own husband."

The words "your husband" made Alexandra's heart shriek in protest and her stomach twist into knots.

"You poor child," said the duchess, astutely observing Alexandra's sudden tension. "What a series of shocks you have suffered in your short life, culminating in the one yesterday. The house is under siege by every gossip in London. Still, the furor will soon die down. In a day or two, we shall resume our activities and engagements as if nothing has happened that is of concern to *anyone*—except to us. Society will naturally assume Anthony had intended to marry you out of a sense of duty to his 'deceased' cousin, and now that his cousin has returned, everything has worked out to our complete satisfaction."

Alexandra could not believe Society would think any such thing and she said so.

"They will, my dear," said the duchess with an expression of amused hauteur, "because *I* said exactly that to certain of my friends who came trotting over here while you were resting yesterday. Moreover, Anthony was quite desperately in love with Sally Farnsworth last year, which lends credibility to the idea that he was marrying you out of duty. My friends will whisper all that into the right ears, and word will spread as it always does."

"How can you be so certain?" Alexandra asked.

The duchess lifted her brows and smiled. "Because my friends have much to lose if they fail to direct the gossip as I asked them to do. You see, my dear, the old adage which says that it is 'whom you know that counts' is far off the mark. It is *what* you know about *whom* you know that truly makes the difference. And I know enough to make things very uncomfortable for most of my friends."

Tony laughed. "You are utterly unscrupulous, Grandmama."

"True," she admitted baldly. "Alexandra, why do you still look doubtful?"

"For one thing, because your plan seems to hinge on all of us going out in public right away. Your other grandson," Alexandra said, referring to Jordan in deliberately impersonal terms that clearly indicated she did not wish to acknowledge him by name, title, or temporary legal relationship to herself, "ordered me yesterday to remain in this house. An order, by the by, which I have no intention of following," she finished rebelliously.

The duchess' forehead furrowed into a brief frown. "He wasn't thinking clearly," she said after a moment's thought. "Doing so would indicate to everyone that you are ashamed of your attempted marriage to Tony. Moreover, it would imply an estrangement between your husband and yourself. No, my dear," she finished, brightening. "Jordan could not have thought the matter through when he ordered you thus.

We shall all go out into society in another day or two. He cannot object to that. I will speak to him in your behalf."

"No, Grandmama," Alexandra said gently, "please don't. I'm a grown woman now, and I don't need anyone to speak for me. Moreover, I have no intention of letting him order me about. He has no right."

The duchess started at this undutiful, unwifely statement. "What fustian! A husband has the legal right to govern his wife's activities. And while we're on the subject, my dear, will you let me give you some advice about dealing with your husband in the future?"

Each time the dowager referred to Jordan as Alexandra's husband, Alex mentally ground her teeth, but all she said was a polite "Yes, of course."

"Good. You were understandably upset yesterday when you insisted he speak with you at once, but you provoked him, and that is most unwise. You do not know him as I do. Jordan can be a harsh man when angered, and it was obvious he was already annoyed with you yesterday about your attempted marriage to Anthony."

Alexandra was indignant and hurt that the elderly duchess, whom she had come to love, apparently was wholly biased in Jordan's favor. "He was inexcusably rude yesterday," she said tightly. "And I'm sorry if it makes you despise me, ma'am, but I can't pretend to be happy I'm married to him. You have obviously forgotten how he felt about me and our marriage. Moreover, he has done things I cannot abide, and his character is—is flawed!" she finished lamely.

Unexpectedly, the old duchess grinned. "I cannot possibly hate you, my child. You are the granddaughter I never had." Putting her arm around Alexandra's shoulders, she smilingly added, "I would be the last to pretend that Jordan's dealings with women have been anything to boast about. I shall leave it up to you, however, to change all that. And remember this, my dear: Reformed rakes often make the best husbands."

"When and if they *do* reform," Alexandra said bitterly, "and I don't *want* to be married to him."

"Of course you don't. At least not at present. But you have no choice, you know, because you're already married to him. I'll confess that I am looking forward, with considerable glee, to watching you bring him to heel."

Alexandra's mouth dropped open at that announcement, which paralleled Tony's and Melanie's feelings exactly. "I can't, and even if I—"

"You can and you will," the duchess declared in a flat no-nonsense tone, and then her eyes softened as she pointedly said, "You'll do it, Alexandra, if only to even the score with him. You have pride and spirit and courage." Alexandra opened her mouth to argue, but the duchess had already turned to Tony.

"Anthony, I've no doubt Hawthorne will expect some sort of explanation from you about why you decided to marry Alexandra, and we ought to consider carefully what you say."

"You're too late, my dear. Hawk had me on the carpet in his library at the uncivilized hour of eight o'clock this morning, and that was the first thing he wanted to know."

The duchess looked slightly alarmed for the first time. "I hope you told him it was an—an 'expedient' measure. That explanation has a nice ring to it. Or you could have told him it was nothing more than a whim, or—"

"I told him no such thing," Tony grinned devilishly. "I told him I had to marry her because London's most eligibles were making damned nuisances of themselves offering for her hand, quarreling over her, and hatching schemes to abduct her."

The duchess' hand flew to her throat. "You didn't!"

"I did."

"Why, for heaven's sake?"

"Because it's the truth," Anthony said with a chuckle, "And because he'd have found out in a matter of days anyway."

"Some future time would have been far more propitious!"

"But not nearly so satisfying," Anthony joked (and Alexandra thought he was the dearest, kindest man alive), "because he'd have heard it from someone else, and I wouldn't have been there to see his reaction."

"How *did* he react?" Alexandra asked, because she couldn't stop herself.

"He didn't," Anthony said and shrugged. "But that's Hawk for you. He never shows how he feels. He's better known for his composure than his flir—"

"That will be enough, Anthony," said the duchess, going over to tug on the bellrope and summon her maids.

Alexandra and Tony also arose. "Do you feel up to some fencing this morning?" he asked.

Alexandra nodded. Fencing would be the perfect thing to help the time before her interview with Jordan pass more quickly.

Shortly before twelve-thirty, Higgins appeared in Jordan's study to deliver a note from a gentleman with offices in Bow Street, which explained that the sender was unwell and wished to postpone their confidential meeting until tomorrow.

Jordan glanced at the butler, deciding to move up his meeting with Alexandra. "Where is your mistress, Higgins?"

"In the ballroom, your grace, fencing with Lord Anthony."

Jordan opened the doors of the huge ballroom on the third floor and walked inside, unnoticed by the pair of skilled duelists moving ceaselessly about the floor, their rapiers clashing, then breaking free as they parried and thrust with grace and expertise.

Propping his shoulder against the wall, Jordan watched them, his unswerving gaze on the lithesome female figure clad in revealing men's breeches that clung to the graceful lines of her slim hips and long legs. She was, Jordan realized, not merely talented with the rapier as he had long ago supposed; she was, in fact, a brilliant swordsman with faultless timing, lightning-quick reflexes, and stunningly executed moves.

Still unaware of his presence, Alexandra suddenly called out that it was time to stop. Breathless and laughing, she reached behind her head, pulled off her face mask and gave her head a hard shake that sent her long, heavy hair falling over her shoulders in a riotous tumble of rich mahogany waves threaded with gold. "Tony, you're getting slow," she teased, her laughing face beguilingly flushed as she removed the protective padded chestplate and knelt on one knee to

252

put it against the wall. Anthony said something to her and she looked over her shoulder at him, smiling. . . . Suddenly Jordan felt himself catapulted backward through time while the image of the lush beauty before him abruptly blended into another image—that of an enchanting, curly-haired girl who had brandished a makeshift saber at him in a woodland glade and knelt down among the flowers, looking up at him with a puppy squirming in her arms and unconcealed love glowing in her eyes.

Within him, Jordan felt a pang of nostalgia, mingled with a sharp sense of loss because the girl in the glade was gone now.

Tony finally saw him standing there. "Hawk," he jokingly asked, "do you think I'm slowing down, because I'm getting old?" On the opposite side of the room, Alexandra lurched around and her face froze.

"I hope not," Jordan replied dryly. "I'm older than you are." Turning to Alexandra, he said, "Since I'm free earlier than I expected to be, I thought we could have our meeting now, rather than later."

In place of the cold animosity that had marked his mood yesterday, his tone today was impeccably polite, impersonal, and businesslike. Relieved but wary, Alexandra glanced down at her snug-fitting pants, erroneously thinking that she would be at a distinct disadvantage if she met with him dressed like this, with her face flushed and her hair in disarray. "I'd like to change first."

"It isn't necessary."

Unwilling to antagonize him by caviling over trifles, when she in fact had a matter of great import to negotiate with him, Alexandra acquiesced with a coolly polite inclination of her head. In tense silence she accompanied him downstairs to his study, mentally rehearsing for the last time what she intended to say.

Closing the double doors behind them, Jordan waited for Alexandra to be seated in one of the chairs arranged in a semicircle in front of his massive, intricately carved oaken desk. Instead of sitting behind it, he perched a hip on the edge of it, crossed his arms over his chest and studied her impassively, his leg swinging lazily to and fro, so close to her own leg that the fabric of his trousers whispered against hers.

It seemed like an eternity before he finally spoke. When he did, his voice was calm and authoritative: "We have had two 'beginnings,' you and I—that first one at my grand-mother's house a year ago, and the one here in this house yesterday. Because of the circumstances, neither of them has been particularly auspicious. Today is the third—and last—beginning for us. In a few minutes, I will decide what the course of our future will be. In order to do that, I'd first like to hear what you have to say about this . . ." Reaching behind him, he picked up a sheet of paper from his desk and calmly handed it to her.

Curious, Alexandra took the sheet, glanced at it, then nearly shot out of her chair as fury boiled up inside her, exploding through her body with the force of a holocaust. On the sheet, Jordan had listed more than a dozen "questionable activities" including her dueling practice with Roddy, her race in Hyde Park, her brush with disgrace when Lord Marbly tried to lure her off to Wilton, and several other escapades that had been relatively harmless, but when catalogued in this fashion read like an indictment.

"Before I decide on the course of our future," Jordan continued dispassionately, immune to the wrathful expression on her beautiful face, "I thought it only fair to give you a chance to deny any item on the list that isn't true, as well as to offer any explanations you may wish to give."

Rage, full-bodied and fortifying, sent Alexandra slowly to her feet, her hands clenched into fists at her sides. Never in her wildest dreams had she expected he would have the gall to criticize *her* behavior. Why, next to the life *he* had led, *she* was as innocent as a babe.

"Of all the loathsome, hypocritical, arrogant—!" she burst out furiously, and then with a superhuman effort, she took control of her rampaging ire. Lifting her chin, she looked straight into his enigmatic eyes and took infuriated pleasure in baldly admitting to the entire—grossly exaggerated—list. "I'm guilty," she wrathfully declared. "Guilty of every single meaningless, harmless, innocuous incident on that list."

Jordan gazed at the tempestuous beauty standing before him, her eyes flashing like angry jewels, her breasts rising and falling with suppressed fury, and his anger gave way to a reluctant admiration for her honesty and courage in admitting her guilt.

Alexandra, however, was not finished. "How *dare* you confront me with a list of accusations and give me ultimatums about my future!" she raged, and before he could react, she moved sideways out of his reach, turned on her heel, and headed for the door.

"Come back here!" Jordan ordered.

Alexandra spun around so swiftly that her shining hair came spilling over her left shoulder in a riotous waterfall of gleaming waves and curls. "I'll be back!" she assured wrathfully. "Just give me ten minutes."

Jordan let her go, his brow furrowed in a thoughtful frown as he stared at the door she had slammed behind her. He hadn't expected her to react quite so violently to the items on the list. In fact, he wasn't entirely certain what he'd hoped to achieve by showing her the list, other than to somehow discover from her reaction if that was *all* she'd been up to while he was gone. The only thing he wanted, *needed* to know, was the one question he couldn't possibly ask her—and that was who had shared her bed and her body while he was gone.

Reaching over to the stack of papers on his desk, he picked up a shipping contract and began absently reading it while he waited for her to return.

The list, he admitted to himself, had not been a sterling idea.

That conclusion was emphatically borne out a few minutes later, when Alexandra rapped upon the door, stalked into his study without waiting for him to invite her to do so, and slapped a sheet of paper on the desk beside his hip. "Since you want to exchange accusations and offer opportunities for denial," she told him furiously, "I'll give you the same 'courtesy' before I hand *you* an ultimatum about our future."

Jordan's curious glance shifted from her flushed, beautiful face to the sheet of paper lying on his desk. Laying aside the contract he'd been reviewing, he nodded toward the chair where she had been seated earlier, and waited until she sat down, then he picked up the list.

It consisted of only sixteen words. Eight names. Of his

former paramours. Setting the list aside, he quirked a speculative brow at her and said nothing.

"Well?" she demanded finally. "Are there any inaccuracies on that list?"

"One inaccuracy," he stated with infuriating calm, "and several omissions."

"Inaccuracy?" Alexandra demanded, distracted by the glint of amusement in his eyes.

"Maryanne Winthrop spells her first name with a 'y' rather than an 'i.'"

"Thank you for that edifying piece of information," Alexandra retorted. "If I ever decide to give her a gaudy diamond bracelet to match the necklace everyone says *you* gave her, I shall be sure to spell her name correctly on the card."

This time there was no doubting the humor tugging at the corner of his mouth and she came to her feet—a proudly enraged goddess dwarfed by a dark, arrogant giant of a man. "Now that you've admitted *your* guilt, *I* will tell you what the course of our future will be." Pausing to draw an infuriated breath, Alexandra announced triumphantly, "I am going to get an annulment."

The harsh words rebounded through the room, ricocheting off the walls, reverberating in the deafening silence. But not a flicker of emotion registered on Jordan's impassive features. "An annulment," he finally repeated. With the patience of a teacher discussing an absurd rhetorical issue with an inferior student, he said mildly, "Would you care to tell me how you intend to accomplish that?"

His damnable calm made Alexandra long to kick him in the shin. "I'll do nothing of the sort. You can discover what my legal grounds are from—from whoever it is that handles these things."

"Solicitors," Jordan provided helpfully, "handle 'these things.'"

Her ire at his condescending superiority was almost more than Alexandra could contain as he smoothly added, "I can recommend several excellent solicitors for you to consult. I keep them on retainer."

That outrageous suggestion was such an insult to her intelligence that Alexandra felt tears sting her eyes. "Was I such a gullible fool over you two years ago?" she demanded in a pain-edged whisper. "Was I so gullible that you honestly think I'd ask *your* solicitor to give *me* advice?"

Jordan's brows pulled together as several astonishing realizations struck him at once: First, despite her magnificent show of courage and unconcern, Alexandra was apparently on the brink of tears; second, the brave, innocent, engaging girl he had married had become a gorgeous creature of exotic beauty and spirit, but along the way she had also acquired an undesirable streak of fiery rebellion; last— and most disconcerting—was the discovery that he was as physically attracted to her now as he had been a year ago. More so. Much more.

Calmly he said, "I was merely trying to spare you what will be a very embarrassing and completely futile ordeal in the office of some unknown—and possibly indiscreet— solicitor."

"It will not be futile!"

"It will," he stated with certainty. "The marriage was consummated, or have you forgotten?"

The bold reminder of the night she had lain naked and willing in his arms was more than Alexandra's taut nerves could withstand. "I'm not senile," she retorted, and the spark of laughter in his eyes made her so desperate to demolish his damnable calm that she informed him how she intended to get an annulment, after all. "Our marriage is invalid because I didn't choose to marry you of my own free will!"

Instead of reacting with alarm, Hawk looked more amused than ever. "Tell that to a solicitor and he may laugh himself into a seizure. If a marriage was invalid merely because the bride felt obliged to marry a groom not of her choosing, then most of Society's couples are—at this very moment—living in sin."

"I wasn't merely 'obliged,'" Alexandra flung back. "I was coerced, cajoled, connived, and *seduced* into doing it!"

"Then find a solicitor and tell him that, but bring your smelling salts because you're going to have to revive him."

Alex was horribly certain he was right, and her heart plummeted sickeningly. In the last fifteen minutes, she had already vented all her pent-up resentment and fury on Jordan—without seeing a single gratifying scrap of reaction from him—and now she suddenly felt devoid of everything including hope and hate. Empty. Raising her eyes to his, she looked at him as if he were a stranger; an unfamiliar specimen of humanity for whom she felt . . . nothing. "If I can't get an annulment, I'll get a divorce."

Jordan's jaw hardened as he suddenly realized Tony had apparently lied about their "familial" feelings for each other. "Not without my consent, you won't," he clipped. "So you can forget the idea of marrying Tony."

"I haven't any intention of marrying Tony!" She blazed with such feeling that Jordan relaxed slightly. "And I haven't any intention of living as *your* wife, either."

His mood vastly improved by her denial of any wish to marry Tony, Jordan studied her without anger. "Forgive me if I'm being dense, but I'm rather surprised you want an annulment."

"No doubt you're amazed to discover there's a female on earth who finds you resistible," she retorted bitterly.

"And that's why you want an annulment? Because you find me 'resistible.'"

"I want an annulment," Alex replied, looking him right in the eye and speaking in a polite voice that completely belied her words, "because I don't *like* you."

Unbelievably, he smiled at that. "You don't know me well enough to dislike me," he teased.

"Oh, yes, I do!" Alex replied darkly. "And I refuse to be your wife."

"You have no choice, sweetheart."

The casual, empty endearment made her cheeks flame with ire. It was exactly the sort of thing she would have expected from a notorious flirt; no doubt she was supposed to melt at his feet now. "Don't call me 'sweetheart'! Whatever it takes, I'll be free of you. And I do have a choice," she decided on the spur of the moment. "I—I can go home to Morsham and buy a cottage there."

"And just how," he asked dryly, "do you intend to pay for that cottage? You have no money."

"But—when we were married you said you'd settled a large sum of money on me."

"Which is yours to use," Jordan clarified, "so long as *I* approve of the way you spend it."

"How very convenient for you," Alex said with stinging scorn. "You gave yourself money."

Seen in that light, it was close enough to the truth that Jordan almost chuckled. He stared down into her stormy blue eyes and flushed face, wondering why, from the very first, she had always been able to make him laugh—wondering why he felt this consuming, unquenchable need now to possess and gentle her without breaking her spirit. She had changed tremendously during the past year, but she still suited him better than any other woman he could ever hope to find. "All this discussion of legalities has reminded me rather forcibly that I have several legal rights I haven't claimed in more than a year," he said, and caught her firmly by the arms, pulling her between his thighs.

"Have you no decency—" Alex burst out, squirming in mindless panic. "I'm still legally betrothed to your cousin!"

His chuckle was rich and deep. "Now *there's* a persuasive argument."

"I don't want you to kiss me!" Alexandra warned furiously, pushing hard against his chest with her flattened hands and straining backward.

"That's too bad," he softly replied, and hauled her up against the solid wall of his chest, wrapping his arm around her back and effectively trapping her hands and forearms between their bodies, "because I intend to see if I can still make you feel 'overheated.'"

"You're wasting your time!" Alexandra cried, turning her head aside, drowning in humiliation at the brutal reminder of how openly besotted with him she had been when she told him his kisses had warmed her heart and body. According to all she'd heard, Jordan Townsende's kisses were responsible for raising the temperatures of half the female population of England. "I was a naive child. I'm a grown woman now and I've been kissed by other men who do it every bit as well as you! Better in fact!"

Jordan retaliated by plunging the fingers of his free hand into the heavy hair at her nape and tugging sharply, forcing her head back. "How many have there been?" he asked, a muscle leaping in his taut jaw.

"Dozens! A hundred!" she choked.

"In that case," he drawled in a soft, savage voice, "you ought to have learned enough to be able to make *me* burn."

Before she could reply his mouth swooped down and captured hers with angry possessiveness, his lips moving back and forth in a ruthless, punishing kiss that was nothing like Tony's gentle ones or the few stolen by the occasional overamorous gentlemen eager to see whether or not she would permit him some liberties. This kiss was unlike any other because, beneath the ruthlessness of it, there was flowing a demanding persuasion, an insistence that she kiss him back that was almost beyond denial—a promise that if she yielded, the kiss might gentle and become something quite different.

Alexandra felt the silent promise, understood it without knowing how she did, and her whole body began to shake with terror and shock as his mouth gentled imperceptibly and began molding itself to the contours of hers, exploring her lips with slow, searching intensity, urging her to participate in the kiss.

A gasp behind them made Jordan loosen his grip and Alexandra whirl around, only to have his arm tighten, clamping her firmly to his side as they both looked at a horrified Higgins, who was in the act of escorting three men, including Lord Camden, into the library.

The butler and the three men all stopped short. "I—I *beg* your pardon, your grace!" Higgins burst out, losing his composure for the first time since Alexandra had known him. "I understood you to say that when the earl arrived—"

"I'll join you in a quarter of an hour," Jordan told his three friends.

They left, but not before Alexandra had noted the amused expressions on all the men's faces, and she turned on Jordan in humiliated outrage. "They're going to think we mean to continue kissing for another quarter of an hour!" she burst out. "I hope you're satisfied, you—"

"Satisfied?" he interrupted with amusement as he studied this tempestuous, unfamiliar, wildly desirable young woman who had once regarded him with childlike admiration in her glowing blue eyes. Gone were her unruly curls. Gone was the admiration in her eyes. Gone was the ingenuous hoyden he had married. In her place was this ravishing young beauty of uncertain temperament whom he felt an uncontrollable, irrational need to tame and to make respond to him as she once had. "Satisfied?" he asked again. "With that pitiful excuse for a kiss? Hardly."

"I didn't mean that!" Alexandra cried miserably. "Three days ago I was marrying another man. Have you no idea how odd those men must have thought it was when they saw you kissing me?"

"I doubt if anything we do will ever seem 'odd' to anyone," Jordan answered with equal parts of amusement and irony, "not when they've already witnessed the entertaining spectacle of me barging in on your wedding to put a stop to it."

For the first time, it occurred to her how comical that must have looked to Society—and how embarrassing it must have been to him—and Alexandra felt a tiny bubble of satisfied mirth.

"Go ahead and laugh," he invited dryly, watching her visibly struggling to remain coldly aloof. "It was funny as hell."

"Not," Alexandra corrected, keeping her face scrupulously straight, "at the time, however."

"No," he agreed, and a lazy, devastating smile suddenly swept across his tanned features. "You should have seen the look on your face when you turned around at that altar and saw me standing there. You looked as if you were seeing a ghost." For one brief moment, she had looked overjoyed— as if she were seeing someone infinitely dear to her, he remembered.

"*You* looked like the wrath of God," she said, uneasily aware of the magnetic charm he was suddenly exuding.

"I *felt* ridiculous."

Reluctant admiration for his ability to laugh at himself blossomed in Alexandra's heart, and for the moment she ignored the things she'd learned about him. Time rolled back and he was once again the smiling, compelling, achingly handsome man who had married her, teased her, and fought a mock duel in a glade with her. Unaware of the seconds ticking past, she stared up into his bold, mesmerizing grey eyes while her dazed mind finally accepted, fully and completely, that he was truly alive—that this was not a dream that would end as all her earlier ones had ended. He was alive. And he was, unbelievably, her husband. At least for the moment.

So lost was she in her own thoughts that it took a moment

before she realized that his gaze had dropped to her lips and his arms were encircling her, drawing her against his hard frame.

"No! I—"

He smothered her objection with a hungry, wildly exciting kiss. Temporarily robbed of the anger that had fortified her resistance, Alexandra's traitorous body lost its rigidity, and the scream of warning issued by her mind was stifled by her pounding heart and the shocking pleasure of being held again in the strong arms of the husband she had believed dead. A large masculine hand curved round her nape, long fingers stroking and soothing, while his other hand slid up and down her back, moving her closer and tighter to his full length.

His warm lips moving on hers, the sensation of his hardening body pressing against hers—it was all so achingly, poignantly, vibrantly familiar to her, because she had lived it in her dreams a thousand times. Knowing she was playing with fire, she let him kiss her, permitting herself—just this once—the forbidden, fleeting joy of his mouth and hands and body. But she did not respond, dared not respond.

Pulling his mouth from hers, Jordan brushed a warm kiss against her temple. "Kiss me," he whispered, his breath sending vibrant warmth spilling through her veins. "Kiss me," he coaxed hotly, trailing his mouth across her cheek, brushing insistent kisses along the sensitive curve of her neck and ear. His hands slid into her heavy hair, tilting her face up to his and his eyes held hers, teasing, challenging. "Forgotten how to do it?"

Alex would have died rather than let him believe he'd been the only man to kiss her on the lips in the last fifteen months, and she could see he'd already sensed that was true.

"No," she said shakily. His parted lips came down on hers again, in another long, searching kiss. "Kiss me, princess," he urged hoarsely, kissing her temple, her ear, her cheek. "I want to see if it's as good as I remembered it."

The achingly poignant discovery that he, too, had dwelt on their few kisses was more than Alexandra could withstand. With a silent moan of despair, she turned her head and met his lips with her own while her hands crept up his chest. Jordan's mouth slanted fiercely over hers, and this time her lips yielded to his rough, tender kiss, parting beneath the sensual pressure and, at that moment, his tongue slid between them, invading her mouth and taking possession of her.

Lost in a stormy sea of desire, confusion, and yearning, Alexandra felt his hand splay across her lower spine, forcing her closer to him, but instead of resisting she slid her hands up over his shoulders, unwittingly molding her melting body to the hardening contours of his. A shudder racked his muscular body as she fitted herself to him and Jordan's arms tightened, crushing her to him, while his hand lifted, cupping her breast, his thumb brushing back and forth across her sensitized nipple while his tongue plunged into her mouth and withdrew, then plunged again and again in a wildly exciting, ever-increasing rhythm that drove her half mad with forbidden yearnings. The endless, drugging kiss, the provocative warmth of his hands moving ceaselessly over her back, then possessively cupping her breasts, the taut strength of his legs and thighs pressing intimately against hers worked their pagan magic on Alexandra; she kissed him back with all the helpless ardor she had felt so long ago, only this time her shy uncertainty was overwhelmed by the desire to clasp him to her, to pretend for a little while that he was all the things she had wanted him to be.

Jordan knew only that the woman in his arms was responding to his kiss with more ardor than ever before, and the effect was devastating on his starved body. When her tongue darted out to touch his lips, he crushed her to him, drawing her tongue into his mouth, while desire surged through his bloodstream like wildfire, pounding in his loins. Fighting back the wild urge to lay her down on the carpet and take her then and there, he dragged his lips from hers and drew a long, unsteady breath, slowly expelling it. Evidently, his wife had learned a great deal about kissing while he was rotting in prison, he realized grimly.

Surfacing slowly from the mists of desire, Alexandra stared into his hypnotic eyes, dazedly watching their color and mood change from the smoky darkness of passion to their usual enigmatic light silver, while she felt reality slowly return. Her hand still lay curved around his neck and it finally dawned on her that, beneath her fingers, his skin was fiery hot. *Make me burn,* he had coaxed . . .

Pride and satisfaction drifted through her as she realized she apparently had done exactly that, and her soft lips curved into an unconsciously provocative smile. Jordan's eyes narrowed on that satisfied smile, then lifted to her knowing blue eyes. His jaw tightened and he dropped his arms, stepping back from her.

"My compliments," he said curtly, and Alexandra watched his mercurial mood take an obvious, abrupt, bewildering turn for the worse. "You've learned a great deal in the past year."

A year ago, her sluggish mind reminded her, he had thought her a naive, pitiful nuisance. Fixing a bright, artificial smile on her face, she said lightly, "A year ago you found me excruciatingly naive. Now you're complaining because I'm not. There's simply no pleasing you."

To Alex's mortification, Jordan didn't deny he'd found her naive. "We can discuss how you can 'please' me when we're in bed tonight, after I return from White's. In the meantime," he continued in the implacable, authoritative tone of one issuing an edict, "I want a few things understood: First of all, an annulment is out of the question. So is divorce. Secondly, there will be no more mock duels, no more parading around in those trousers you are wearing, no racing in the parks, and no public appearances made by you with any man but me. Is that clear? You will not go out in company with any man but me."

Outrage exploded in Alexandra's brain. "Who do you think you are!" she demanded, her color rising with indignation. He hadn't changed one bit in two years. He still wanted to lock her away out of sight. No doubt he still had every intention of packing her off to Devon as well.

"I *know* who I am, Alexandra," he snapped cryptically. "I do not know who *you* are, however. Not anymore."

"I'm certain you do not," she bit out, wisely controlling the urge to warn him in advance that she intended to defy him. "You thought you married a complaisant, adoring female who would rush to do your tiniest bidding, didn't you?"

"Something like that," he admitted tightly.

"You didn't get one."

"I will."

Alexandra tossed her head and turned, pointedly refusing to curtsy to him. "You are wrong, your grace," she said, and started for the door.

"My name," he informed her bitingly, "is Jordan."

Alexandra stopped and half turned, her delicate brows arched in feigned surprise, her color gloriously high. Once, she had longed to have him ask her to use his given name, now she took greater pleasure in refusing. "I'm aware of that," she said and with calm defiance she added, *"your grace."* Having thus clearly informed him that she did not wish for the intimacy of using his given name, she turned and walked across the room, feeling his eyes boring holes through her shoulder blades, praying that her shaking knees would not buckle with the nervousness she was struggling to hide.

Not until she put her hand on the handle of the door did his low, ominous voice slash through the silence. "Alexandra!"

Despite herself she jumped. "Yes?" she said, looking at him over her shoulder.

"Think carefully before you make the mistake of defying my orders. You'll regret it, I promise you."

Despite the icy tingle of alarm his silken voice caused in her, Alexandra lifted her chin. "Are you finished?"

"Yes. Send Higgins in here when you leave."

The mention of the butler reminded Alex of her own servants' plight and she swung around, prepared to launch a final skirmish. "The next time you want to retaliate against me for some imagined slight against you, kindly leave my servants out of it. Those two gentle old men whom you banished to the kitchens this morning are the closest thing to a father I ever had. Penrose taught me to fish and swim. Filbert made a dolls' house for me with his own hands and later he built a raft for me and taught me how to sail it. I won't allow you to abuse them or humiliate—"

"Tell Higgins," he interrupted coolly, "to put them to work wherever it suits you—so long as it isn't in the front hall."

When the door closed behind her, Jordan sat down in his chair, dark brows pulled together in a black frown. He had accomplished what he had sent out to do, which was to make her understand the rules she would have to live by from now on, and he was certain she would obey those rules. The idea of being defied by a woman, particularly a young one who had once openly idolized him, was unthinkable. Moreover, his body's almost uncontrollable desire for her a few minutes ago had amazed, unnerved, and thoroughly displeased him—even though he realized his year of enforced abstinence was partially the cause.

Alexandra would never be the complaisant wife of his dreams, he realized, but in her fiery spirit he would find ample compensation. She would never bore him and she was not a liar or a coward. In the last half hour alone she had presented him with a list of his mistresses and openly admitted her behavior during the past two years; she had also angered, amused, and sexually aroused him. No, he would not be bored with her.

Picking up the quill from his desk, he rolled it absently between his fingers, a reluctant smile replacing his frown. God, she was lovely, with those stormy eyes flashing like angry green flames and her alabaster cheeks tinted with angry pink.

So long as she behaved herself, he was willing to let her enjoy the full benefits of her position as the Duchess of Hawthorne. So long as she behaved . . .

Higgins appeared in the doorway with John Camden in tow. "I gather," John said, grinning, "that you're making satisfactory progress with your wife?"

"She'll behave herself," Jordan replied with supreme confidence.

"In that case, perhaps you'll be in a mood to join us at White's tonight?"

"Fine," Jordan agreed, and the men began to discuss their joint venture with a mining company.

Chapter Twenty-Two

ALEXANDRA WENT DIRECTLY from Jordan's study to the front hall, where she informed the butler that Penrose and Filbert were not to be restricted to the kitchens, then she asked Higgins to send both men to her in the morning room, and, with a fixed smile on her face, headed down the hall.

Normally the morning room with its sunny yellow appointments and view of the garden brightened her spirits, but today as she walked inside and closed the doors behind her, the smile she had pasted on her face for the sake of the servants abruptly deserted her. The energy she had forced into her steps vanished as she walked slowly over to the windows and stood, staring blindly into the garden. She felt as if she had just done physical battle with an army of giants. And lost.

Shame and terror surged through her as she covered her face with her hands and bitterly faced the awful truth: Physically, she was no more immune to Jordan Townsende now than she had been a year ago. Oh, she could withstand his anger, but not his smile, not his kiss. The sweet violence of his kiss had wreaked havoc on her body, her soul, and her heart. Despite the experience and sophistication she had acquired during the last few months, despite everything she knew of him, Jordan Townsende could still twist her insides into hot, tight knots of yearning, exactly as he had done when she was a green girl of seventeen.

After all this time, his smile could still make her melt and his kisses could make her burn with longing to surrender her will to his. A dismal sigh escaped her as she leaned her forehead against the smooth, cool glass of the windowpane. From the moment they left the church yesterday, she'd been completely confident that he could never make her feel anything for him again. And all it had taken to prove her wrong was one of his lazy smiles, a kiss, a touch. Where he was concerned, she was still as susceptible as she had ever been.

"Dear God," she breathed aloud, what sort of diabolical sorcery did the man employ that he could have this effect on women? On *her,* when she harbored no illusions about any tender feelings he might have for her.

What was it about the man that made her feel that she had accomplished something rare whenever she made him smile or laugh. And why did she still have to struggle against this stupid, naive feeling that if she tried very hard, she might mean something special to him someday—she might be the one to soften and gentle him, to melt the core of cynicism in his eyes? No doubt he made all women feel that way—that if they tried very hard, *they* might mean something to him that no other woman had; no doubt that was why even experienced, sophisticated flirts turned themselves inside out to please him. They, however, were not in the same danger she was, for they were not married to him. And tonight Jordan had more in mind for his wife than kisses. *"We can discuss how you can please me in bed tonight."*

In bed tonight . . . in bed . . . Her traitorous mind began replaying tantalizing memories of their night at the inn, and Alexandra angrily shook her head, trying to deny the warmth already seeping through her. She could not, *would* not, let him take her to bed this night or any other. How dare he presume to walk back into her life and climb into her bed, and without even *pretending* to court her, as she now knew gentlemen of the *ton* were expected to do. Jordan had never bothered to court her, she thought wrathfully and inconsequentially.

As far as she was concerned, tonight he could take his amorous self off to one of dozens of other beds right here in London, occupied by dozens of other women, all of whom —according to gossip—had always been eager for his "affections." No doubt he had done exactly that last night. He had probably gone to his mistress. Tonight, he would probably be engaged in another liaison before he came to her bed.

That thought made her so angry she felt physically sick. Pulling her hands from her face, she looked around the cheerful room as if she were searching for some way to escape. Somehow, some way, she decided desperately, for the sake of sanity and serenity, she had to get away from here. From him. She did not want to face yet another emotional holocaust. Peace was what she wanted. Peace and quiet and reality for the rest of her life.

At the thought of leaving London and her newfound friends, she felt a pang of loss, but it was offset by the thought of finding peace and tranquillity somewhere else. He'd only been home one day, and already jealousy was beginning to torment her. The idea of returning to Morsham, which she'd conceived on the spur of the moment yesterday when she was talking to Melanie, took on new and greater appeal now, looming on the horizon of her mind like a sweet haven waiting for her.

But if she was going to find her way back to her old life, she knew there was no point in waiting idly for fate to lend a hand. Fate, she decided, had never been a reliable ally of hers. Fate had forced her into marriage with a man who didn't want her and who was, moreover, a cad. Fate had brought him back and now she was expected to meekly submit to the whims of a man who still didn't want her and who was not only a cad, but an arrogant, unfeeling, dictatorial one, to boot!

Women, she had learned to her pain, were nothing but chattel, particularly in the upper classes, where they were selected like mares for their bloodlines by men who mated with them for the sake of obtaining a suitably aristocratic heir, and then they were turned out to pasture. She, however, was not a helpless, highborn female, Alexandra reminded herself bracingly. She had taken care of herself, her mother, her house, and two elderly servants quite satisfactorily from the time she was fourteen.

Surely, as a grown woman now, she could return to her former life and continue to manage even better than she had. She would do what her grandfather had hoped she would—she would take up where he had left off, teaching children to read and write. She was a respectably married woman now, and Alexandra felt quite certain the villagers would not ostracize her for her single long-ago lapse in propriety. And even if they did, Alexandra rather thought she would prefer to live like an outcast until they forgave her than continue to be what she was now—a feather blown about by the whims of fate and of one rude, indomitable man.

It was now time, she decided staunchly, to take charge of her own life and to choose its direction. The latter was easy enough—she had only one direction open to her and that was back. She would go back home and be mistress of her own life. But in order to accomplish that, she had to dissuade her unwanted husband from his absurd decision to keep her as his wife. And she needed money.

The second part of that worried her the most. The only money she had was from the last quarterly allowance Tony had given her, but that wouldn't be enough to rent a cottage, buy wood for the winter, and purchase the things she and Filbert and Penrose would require until they could get a vegetable garden started. For that she would need ten times what she had. She couldn't sell the jewels that the duchess and Tony had given her; they were family heirlooms and not truly hers. The only thing of value she owned was her grandfather's watch. She would sell it, Alexandra decided with an awful, wrenching pain. She would have to sell it and quickly, without wasting precious time. Time, she had learned to her mortification, was Jordan's ally and her enemy. Given enough time and proximity, she was terrified that Jordan could and would have her melting in his arms.

Feeling slightly better, now that she had a plan, Alexandra walked over to the table where she always had tea after her fencing matches with Tony and sat down. She was pouring herself a cup from the tray that had been set out for her in advance, when her two faithful, elderly friends presented themselves.

"Lawd, Miss Alexandra, you've gotten yerself into the devil of a coil this time," Filbert exclaimed without tact, formality, or preamble, his nearsighted eyes searching her face through the spectacles she'd bought for him, which enabled him to see a great deal better than before. Almost wringing his hands with anxiety, he sat down across from her at the table—as he had always done when they were a "family" in Morsham. Penrose sat down across from him and leaned forward, straining to hear, as Filbert continued: "I heard what the duke said to you yesterday when the two of you were alone and I told Penrose. Yer husband's a hard man, and that's the simple truth, or he'd not've ripped up at you th' way he done. What," he demanded with anxious concern for her, "are we goin' to do?"

Alexandra looked at the two old men who had cared for her, cheered her, and borne her company for all of her life and smiled wanly. There was no point in lying to them, she knew; although they were slightly impaired physically, they were anything but mentally impaired. They were, in fact, nearly as sharp now as they were in the old days when she could never get by with a trick they didn't anticipate. "I want to take us back to Morsham," she declared, wearily raking her hair back off her forehead.

"Morsham!" Penrose whispered reverently, as if the name were "Heaven."

"But I need money to do it, and all I have is what's left of my last quarter's allowance."

"Money!" said Filbert grimly. "It's always been a lack of money for you, Miss Alexandra. Even when your papa was alive, curse his treacherous—"

"Don't," Alexandra said automatically. "It isn't fitting to speak ill of the dead."

"In my opinion," Penrose announced with lofty dislike, "it's a pity you saved Hawthorne's life. Instead of shooting his assailant, you should have shot *him.*"

"And afterward," Filbert spat, "you should've drove a stake through his heart, so the vampire couldn't come back from the dead like this and haunt yer life!"

That bloodthirsty speech made Alexandra shudder and laugh at the same time. Then she sobered, drew a long breath, and said to Penrose in a resolute voice that brooked no argument, "My grandfather's gold watch is in the drawer beside my bed. I want you to take it to Bond Street and sell it to whichever jeweler will pay the most for it."

Penrose opened his mouth to protest, saw the stubborn set of her small chin, and reluctantly nodded.

"Do it now, Penrose," she said in a pain-edged voice, "before I can change my mind."

When Penrose left, Filbert reached across the table and covered her hand with his blue-veined one. "Penrose and I got a tiny sum we've set aside over the last twenty years. It ain't much—seventeen pounds and two shillings atween us."

"No. Absolutely not," Alexandra said with great firmness. "You must keep your—"

The sound of Higgins' stately marching stride echoed in the hall, coming toward the breakfast room, and Filbert leapt with surprising agility to his feet. "Higgins goes purple every time he sees us talking friendlylike," Filbert explained unnecessarily as he snatched Alexandra's yellow linen napkin from beside her saucer and began energetically flicking it at nonexistent crumbs on the table. And that was the scene Higgins approvingly beheld when he entered the morning room to convey the news that Sir Roderick Carstairs wished to be announced to her grace.

A few minutes later, Roddy strode in, sat down at the table, beckoned to Filbert with a lofty nod of his head to pour him some tea, and then began cheerfully regaling her with the "delicious details" of his visit to Hawk last night.

Halfway through his astounding recitation, Alexandra half rose from her chair and cried in an accusing whisper, *"You* told him all those things about me? *You?"*

"Stop looking at me as if I just slithered out from beneath a rock, Alex," Roddy said with bored nonchalance, adding milk to his tea. "I told him all that to ensure he knows you've been the hit of the Season, so that when he discovers —which I assure you he will—that you made a complete cake of yourself over him when you first came to town, he will not be nearly so complacent. Melanie called last night to suggest I do exactly that, but I'd already come up with the idea on my own and gone to Hawk's."

Ignoring her stricken expression, he continued blithely: "I also did it because *I* wanted to see his face when he heard the news, although this was not my primary reason for going there, as I just explained. Actually," he added after taking a delicate sip of his tea and replacing the Sèvres cup in its saucer, "haring over to Mount Street to see him last night was the first truly noble gesture of my life—an indication, I fear, that I have developed a character weakness, for which I blame *you.*"

"Me?" Alexandra repeated, so distraught and distracted she was beginning to feel dazed. "What character weakness is that?"

"Nobility, my dear. When you look at me with those big, beautiful eyes of yours, I often have the terrifying feeling you see something better and finer in me than I see when I look in the mirror. Last night, I suddenly felt impelled to *do* something better and finer, so I hustled over to Hawk's filled with noble intent to save your pride. It was quite revolting of me, now that I repine on it." He looked so disgusted with himself that Alexandra hastily hid her smile behind her own teacup as he went on: "Unfortunately, my magnificent gesture may have been for naught. I couldn't be certain Hawk was paying me any heed, despite the fact that I rattled on quite abominably for the better part of an hour."

"He heard you, all right," Alexandra said wryly. "This morning he presented me with a written list of those very same transgressions and demanded I either confess or deny."

Roddy's eyes widened with delight. "Did he, indeed? I *thought* I was getting under his skin last night but, with Hawk, one can never tell. Did you admit to the list or deny it?"

Too tense and worried to remain seated another moment, Alexandra put her cup down and with an apologetic look, she stood up, restlessly walking over to the little settee by the windows and needlessly plumping its yellow flowered pillows. "I admitted it, of course."

Roddy swiveled in his chair, studying her profile with great interest. "I gather, then, that all is not honey and roses here between the reunited couple?" When Alexandra absently shook her head, he grinned with pleasure. "You realize, I suppose, that Society is already on tenterhooks, waiting to see if you succumb to Hawk's legendary charm again? The odds, at the moment, are four to one that you'll be his adoring wife by the day of the Queen's Race."

Alexandra whirled around, staring at him in angry horror. "What?" she breathed in disgust, unable to believe her ears. "What are you talking about?"

"Wagers," Roddy said succinctly. "The odds are four to one in favor of you putting your ribbon on Hawk's arm and cheering for him at the Queen's Race. Very domestic."

Alexandra didn't know it was possible to feel such revulsion for people she had begun to like. "People are *betting* on a thing like that?" she burst out.

"Naturally. On Queen's Race day, it's traditional for a lady to show her favor to a gentleman who is riding in the race by removing the ribbon from her bonnet and tying it on his arm herself, for good luck and encouragement. It is one of the few public displays of affection which we of the *ton* encourage—mostly, I believe, because the discussion of who ultimately wore whose colors provides us with titillating gossip and conjecture for the long winter months that follow. At this point, the odds are four to one in favor of *you* tying *your* ribbon on Hawk's arm."

Momentarily diverted from her major problems by a minor detail, Alexandra looked suspiciously at Roddy. "Who are *you* betting on?"

"I haven't placed my wager yet. I thought I'd stop here first—to test the atmosphere—before I dropped in at White's." Daintily wiping his mouth on a napkin, Roddy stood up, kissed her hand, and said in a challenging voice, "Well, my dear, what's it to be? Will you be showing your affection for your spouse by giving him your colors to wear on September seventh?"

"Of course not!" Alexandra said, inwardly shuddering at the thought of making such a public spectacle of herself over a man everyone knew didn't care a jot about her.

"You're quite certain? I'd hate to loose £1,000."

"Your money is very safe," Alexandra said bitterly, sinking down on the flowered settee and staring at her hands. He was halfway across the room when Alexandra jubilantly shouted his name and shot to her feet as if the cushions beneath her had burst into flames. Laughing with joy, she advanced upon the startled aristocrat. "Roddy, you're wonderful! You're brilliant! If I didn't already have a husband, I'd propose to *you!*"

Roddy said nothing to that flattering proclamation, but regarded her in wary amusement, one brow arched in inquiry.

"Please, please, say you'll do one little favor for me?" she pleaded prettily.

"What is it?"

Alexandra drew a steadying breath, unable to believe fate had just presented her with a perfect solution to what had seemed a hopeless dilemma. "Could you—possibly—place a wager for me?"

His look of comical shock was instantly replaced by one of dawning understanding, and then of irrepressible glee. "I suppose I could do that. Can you cover your bet if you lose?"

"I *can't* lose!" she said joyously. "If I understood what you said, in order to win, all I have to do is go to the Queen's Race and not tie my ribbon on Hawk's arm?"

"That's all you have to do."

Scarcely able to contain her excitement, Alexandra clasped his hand, her eyes eagerly searching his. "Do say you'll do it for me, Roddy—it's even more important to me than you realize."

A smile of sardonic delight crossed his features. "Naturally, I'll do it," he said, looking her over with new respect and approval. "There's never been any love lost between your husband and me, as you've undoubtedly guessed." He saw her puzzled smile and heaved an exaggerated sigh at her naiveté. "If your husband had done me the kindness to stay 'dead' and if Tony had cocked up his toes without a male heir, I—or my heirs—would be the next Hawthorne. You've seen Tony's brother, Bertie—he's a frail boy who's been hovering at the brink of eternity for all of his twenty years. Something went wrong at his birth, I'm told."

Alexandra, who had no idea Roddy was so high on the list of ascendant heirs, slowly shook her head. "I knew you were related to us—to the Townsendes, I mean—but I thought it was only a distant kinship, fourth or fifth cousins."

"It is. But with the exception of Jordan and Tony's fathers, the rest of the Townsendes have had the amazing bad luck to continually produce daughters, not sons, and not many of those either. The males in our family seem to die quite young, and we are not very prolific in the production of heirs, although," he added, deliberately attempting to shock her, "it is certainly not for want of trying."

"Too much inbreeding, I fear," Alexandra quipped, managing to keep her face from reflecting her acute embarrassment at Roddy's bald reference to lovemaking. "You see

275

it in collies, too. The entire *ton* is in need of new blood or they'll soon be scratching behind their ears and losing their hair."

Roddy threw back his head and laughed. "Irreverent chit!" he said, grinning. "You've learned to look quite bland when you're shocked, but you can't fool me yet. Keep practicing." Then briskly, "Back to business. How much do you wish to wager?"

Alexandra bit her lip, afraid to offend Dame Fortune, who was finally smiling upon her, by being too greedy. "Two thousand pounds," she began, but broke off as Filbert, who was at attention behind Roddy, suddenly coughed loudly, then cleared his throat with a meaningful "Ahem."

Her eyes dancing with merriment, Alexandra glanced at Filbert, then at Roddy, and quickly amended, "Two thousand and *seventeen* pound—"

"Ahem!" said Filbert again. "Ahem."

"Two thousand," Alexandra obediently amended again, "seventeen pounds, and *two* shillings."

Roddy, who was no fool, slowly turned around and cast his appraising eye over the footman, whom Alexandra had told him weeks ago had been with her since she was a child. "And your name is?" he drawled, regarding Filbert with lofty amusement.

"Filbert, my lord."

"You, I presume, are the owner of the seventeen pounds, two shillings?"

"Aye, my lord. Me 'n' Penrose."

"And Penrose is who?"

"The under-butler," Filbert replied, and then forgetting himself he added wrathfully, "or he *were,* 'til his noble highness strolled in here this morning and demoted him."

Roddy's expression took on a faraway look. "How utterly delicious," he murmured, then he recalled himself and bowed formally to Alexandra. "I don't suppose you'll be at the Lindworthy ball tonight?"

Alexandra hesitated a scant second before declaring with a mischievous little smile, "Since my husband is already engaged tonight, I can't see why not." Unbelievably, miraculously, she would soon have enough money to live cozily in Morsham for a decade. For the first time in her entire life, she was experiencing a taste of independence, of freedom, and freedom was bliss. It was sweet, it was divine. It tasted headier than wine. It made her daring. Her eyes positively shining with exuberant delight, she said, "And Roddy, if you still wish to test your skill with the rapier against me, I think tomorrow morning would be an excellent time. Invite anyone you'd like to watch. Invite the whole world!"

For the first time, Roddy looked uneasy. "Even our dear Tony, who let you have your own head, refused to let you fence with any of us. It's not quite the thing, my dear, and your husband is likely to turn nasty when he hears of it."

"I'm sorry, Roddy," she said, instantly contrite. "I wouldn't want to do anything which might cause you difficulty with—"

"I was concerned for *you*, my sweet child, not myself. I'm in no danger. Hawk won't call me out—He and I are much too civilized to stoop to a public display of unconstrained tempers, which is what dueling actually is. On the other hand," Roddy added bluntly, "I feel sure he will soon be looking for any opportunity to privately rearrange my face for me. Never fear," he added with supreme nonchalance, "I can handle myself with my fists. Contrary to what you may have thought, there's a man beneath these fine clothes I wear." Pressing a gallant kiss to the back of her hand, he said dryly, "I shall search you out at the Lindworthy ball tonight."

When Roddy left, Alexandra wrapped her arms around her middle, laughing as she looked heavenward. "Thank you, thank you, thank you!" she called to God, to fate, and to the ornate ceiling. Roddy had answered the first part of her problem by showing her a source of money, and now she had hit upon the solution to the second half: Jordan Townsende, she had observed during the last two days, was a man who was accustomed to, and demanded, unquestioning, instant obedience from everyone around him, including his wife. He was not a man who was accustomed to being defied by man, woman, or servant.

Therefore, Alexandra gleefully decided, defiance was obviously the key to her freedom. Several immediate and flagrant defiances were called for—ones that would cut up his peace, laugh at his dictatorship, and, most important, illustrate to him in the clearest possible way that he would be far more comfortable with Alexandra out of his way and out of his life.

"His majesty," Filbert disrespectfully declared, "ain't goin' to like yer betting against him or goin' out tonight." With a worried little frown, he said, "I was eavesdroppin' and I heard him say you couldn't."

Alexandra burst out laughing and hugged the concerned old man. "He'll never know about the bet," she cheerfully declared. "And if he doesn't like my going out, I suppose he can"—heading for the door she announced jubilantly—"send me back to Morsham! Or give me a divorce!" Humming a gay, lilting tune, she strolled jauntily down the hall and up the long staircase. In two months' time, when she collected her winnings, she would be able to simply walk away from Jordan Townsende as a wealthy woman by Morsham standards. Equally delightful was the knowledge that she had made the money using her own wit—and that Jordan would never know how she got the funds. In the doorway of his study, where he was about to bid his visitors goodbye, Jordan paused and turned, watching her as she walked jauntily up the stairs, a faint smile touching his lips. Alexandra, he realized, had a very pretty voice. A beautiful voice. Also an inviting sway to her hips. Very inviting.

The confidence that had buoyed her up all afternoon was higher than ever as Alexandra stood before her dressing table, her head turned toward the clock on the mantel. An hour and a half ago, when Jordan had entered the master bedchamber which adjoined hers, she had heard him tell his valet he was going to White's tonight. Twenty-five minutes ago, he had left.

White's was only a short distance from the Lindworthy mansion, and rather than risk the slightest possibility that Jordan might have lingered downstairs, or that she might encounter him en route, she thought it best to give him plenty of time to arrive at his destination before she left for hers.

By now, he surely ought to be there, she decided, and turned to the middle-aged French maid whom the duchess had hired for her. "Will I do, Marie?" she asked brightly, but Alexandra knew she had never looked better.

"You will leave them speechless, your grace," Marie declared with smiling certainty.

"That's what I'm afraid of," Alexandra chuckled ruefully as she glanced in the mirror at the breathtakingly gorgeous lemon chiffon gown that was gathered at the shoulders into tiny pleats that crossed her bodice on a diagonal and emphasized the enticing swell of her breasts and plunged at the neckline into a daringly low V. A wide band of horizontal pleats hugged her narrow waist, then fell into an airy drift of swirling chiffon skirts.

Long matching gloves encased her arms to well above the elbows, and diamonds flashed at her throat and peeped from beneath the soft tendrils at her ears. Her shining hair was twisted into an elegant chignon at her crown, with a rope of diamonds artfully woven into the wide coil.

The stark simplicity of her coiffure set off her finely sculpted features, giving her a more sophisticated appearance to offset her youth and complement her dramatic gown to perfection.

Picking up her little beaded reticule, Alexandra said gaily, "Don't wait up for me, Marie. I'm spending the night at the home of a friend." It was not quite the truth, but Alexandra had no intention of letting Jordan Townsende make love to her again, and for tonight at least she had a plan to prevent it.

White's, the most exclusive private gentlemen's club in England, looked exactly as it had when Jordan had last walked past its wide bow windows more than a year ago. And yet, the moment he walked into its hallowed confines, he was aware that something was subtly different tonight.

It was different, yet everything was the same: Comfortable chairs were still grouped around low tables so a man could lean back and relax while casually losing or acquiring a fortune on the turn of a card. The large book where bets were recorded—a book as sacrosanct to the gamblers of White's as the Bible to a Methodist—was still in its usual place. Except tonight there was a much larger crowd than normal gathered around it, Jordan noted as he strode forward.

"Hawthorne!" a hearty voice exclaimed—too heartily, and the group of men at the betting book lurched erect, then hastily started forward in a group. "Good to have you back, Hawk," Lord Hurly said, shaking Jordan's hand. "Wonderful to see you, Hawk," someone else said as his friends and acquaintances pressed around him, all eager to welcome him back. A little too desperately eager, Jordan thought . . .

"Have a drink, Jordan," John Camden said grimly and unceremoniously snatched a glass of Madeira from the tray of a passing footman, thrusting it into Jordan's hand.

With a faint, puzzled smile at Camden's odd behavior, Jordan handed the Madeira back to the footman. "Whisky," he said succinctly and, excusing himself, he started toward the betting book. "What sort of nonsense are the young bucks betting on these days?" he asked. "No more pig races, I hope." Six men abruptly blocked his path, fanning around the betting book in a semicircle and all six simultaneously burst into agitated conversation. "Odd weather we're . . . Devil of a time you had . . . Tell us about . . . How's Lord Anthony? . . . Is your grandmother well?"

Unseen by Jordan, John Camden shook his head, indicating the futility of their human blockade of the betting book, and the loyal band of sympathetic husbands trying to block Jordan's path all stepped awkwardly aside.

"My grandmother is fine, Hurly," Jordan said as he strolled through their midst to the book. "And so is Tony." Bracing his hand on the back of the chair, Jordan leaned slightly forward, flipping backward through the pages as he had flipped backward through old copies of the newspapers earlier today, bringing himself up to date with the world. There were bets on everything, from the anticipated date of the next snowstorm to the weight of old Bascombe's firstborn child.

Eight months ago, Jordan noted derisively, young Lord Thornton had bet £1,000 that his young friend Earl Stanley would take to his bed with a stomach ailment two months later, on December 20. On December 19, Thornton had bet Stanley £100 that he couldn't eat two dozen apples at one sitting. Stanley won that bet. But he lost £1,000 the next day. Jordan chuckled, glancing up at his friends, and remarked dryly: "I see Stanley is still as gullible as ever."

It was traditional, this remarking upon the betting follies of the younger set by the older, wiser, more worldly set. The fathers of the six men gathered around the betting book—and their fathers before them—had all stood there, doing exactly that.

In the past, Jordan's remark would have caused his friends to reply with amusing stories about other bets, or with good-natured reminders about some of *his* reckless foibles. Today all six men gave him uneasy smiles and said nothing.

With a puzzled, encompassing glance at them, Jordan returned his attention to the book. Stillness descended on the entire club as the gentlemen at the gaming tables ceased their play, waiting. A moment later, Jordan felt certain he knew the reason for the peculiar atmosphere all around him—throughout all of May and June, page after page of the betting book was suddenly covered with wagers on which suitor—and there had been dozens of them—Alexandra would ultimately choose to wed.

Annoyed but not surprised, Jordan turned the page and saw bets cropping up about the race on Queen's Day and whether Alexandra would tie her ribbon on his sleeve.

He was, he saw as he glanced idly down the names in the book, a vast favorite to succeed . . . although, near the bottom of the page, there were a few names betting against him: Carstairs, Jordan noted wryly, had bet £1,000 against him earlier that day. Typical!

The next wager was also against him—a large one in a very odd amount—£2,017.3—guaranteed by Carstairs but placed on behalf of . . .

Rage exploded in Jordan's brain as he straightened and turned to his friends. "Excuse me, gentlemen," he bit out in a soft, murderous voice, "I have just remembered that I have another engagement tonight." Without a glance at anyone else, he stalked out.

The six men surrounding the betting book gazed at one another in helpless consternation. "He's going after Carstairs," John Camden said grimly, and they all nodded agreement.

They were wrong. "Home!" Jordan snapped at his driver as he flung himself into his carriage. Idly slapping his gloves against his thigh, Jordan endured the ride to No. 3 Upper Brook Street in a state of deadly calm as he contemplated a variety of highly gratifying methods of teaching his outrageously willful, errant wife a badly needed, unforgettable lesson.

He had never been tempted to strike a woman in his life, yet now he could think of nothing more satisfying than the impending prospect of walking into Alexandra's bedchamber, jerking her over his lap, and paddling her until she could bear no more. It was, he decided, an eminently suitable punishment for what had been an eminently *childish* act of public defiance!

And after that, he decided, he would toss her onto the bed and put her to the use God intended her for!

In the mood he was in, he might well have done exactly that. But—as Higgins informed him when he stalked past the butler and headed up the staircase—Alexandra was "not at home."

A moment ago, Jordan would have sworn he could not have been angrier than he already was. The news that Alexandra had openly defied him by going out, when he had specifically *ordered* her to stay home, sent his blood to the boiling point. "Get her maid down here," Jordan demanded in a voice that made Higgins press backward against the door before scurrying off to do as he was bade.

Five minutes later, at ten-thirty, Jordan was en route to the Lindworthys'.

At that same moment, the Lindworthy butler was loudly proclaiming the arrival of: "Her grace, the Duchess of Hawthorne!"

Airily ignoring the swiveling heads and searching stares, Alexandra walked gracefully down the grand staircase in the most daring ensemble she had ever appeared in. It suited her perfectly—she felt wonderfully, independently daring tonight.

Partway down the staircase, she glanced casually over the packed ballroom, looking either for Roddy, Melanie, or the dowager duchess. She saw the duchess first, standing with a group of her elderly friends, and Alexandra headed toward her—a shimmering, glowing vision of youth and poise, her eyes shining as brightly as the jewels she wore, as she occasionally paused to nod regally at an acquaintance.

"Good evening, dear ma'am," Alexandra said gaily, pressing a kiss to the duchess' parchment cheek.

"I see you're in high spirits, child," her grace said, beaming at her and clasping Alexandra's gloved hands in her own. "I'm equally happy to see," she added, "that Hawthorne took my excellent advice this morning and removed his foolish restriction against your going out into company."

With a mischievous smile, Alexandra dropped into a deep, respectful curtsy that was a miracle of grace, then she raised her head and jauntily declared, "No, ma'am, he did not."

"You mean—"

"Exactly."

"Oh!"

Since Alexandra already knew where the duchess stood on the matter of her marital obligations, that unenthusiastic reaction to her rebellious behavior didn't dampen Alexandra's spirits in the least. In fact, in the mood she was in, she didn't think anything could dampen her spirits. Until a scant minute later, when Melanie rushed over to her, looking positively panicked. "Oh, Alex, how could you do such a thing!" she burst out, too overwrought to care that the dowager was standing right there. "There isn't a husband here who wouldn't like to wring your neck—including mine when he hears of it! You went too far, it's beyond what is pleasing! You can't *do*—"

"Whatever are you talking about?" Alexandra interrupted, but her heart was beginning to pound in automatic reaction to her usually imperturbable friend's wild anxiety.

"I'm talking about the wager you had Roddy place in your name in the betting book at White's, Alexandra!"

"In *my* name—" Alexandra exclaimed in panic-stricken disbelief. "Oh dear God! He *wouldn't* have!"

"What wager?" the dowager gruffly demanded.

"He would and he did! And everyone in this ballroom knows about it."

"Dear God!" Alexandra repeated faintly.

"What wager?" the dowager demanded in a low, thunderous voice.

Too shaken and angry to answer the dowager, Alexandra

left that to Melanie. Plucking up her skirts, she whirled around, searching for Roddy. What she saw was dozens of inimical male faces watching her.

She finally saw Roddy and bore down on him with murder in her eye and pain in her heart.

"Alexandra, my love," he said, grinning, "you look more smashing than—" He reached out to take her hand, but she snatched it away, glaring at him with angry, accusing eyes.

"How could you do this to me!" she burst out bitterly. "How could you write that wager down in some book and put *my* name on it!"

For the second time since she had met him, Roderick Carstairs lost momentary control of his bland expression. "What do you mean?" he demanded in a low, indignant voice. "I did what *you* wanted me to do. You wanted to demonstrate to Society that you are not going to fall at Hawk's feet, and I placed the wager for you at the best place to make your feelings public. And it was no easy task," he continued irritably. "Only members of White's are allowed to record wagers there, which is why I had to put my name over yours and guarantee your—"

"I wanted you to place a wager for me in *your* name, not mine, which is why I asked *you* to do it!" Alexandra cried in a voice raw with anxiety. "A quiet, *confidential, unwritten* gentlemen's wager!"

Roddy's brows snapped together as anger replaced his righteous indignation. "Don't be a nitwit! What could you possibly hope to gain from a 'quiet, confidential' wager?"

"Money!" Alexandra exclaimed miserably.

Roddy's mouth dropped open. "Money?" he repeated uncomprehendingly. "You made that wager because you want *money?"*

"Of course!" she naively replied. "Why else would anyone wager?"

Looking at her as if she were some curious specimen of humanity completely beyond his ken, Roddy informed her, "One wagers because one enjoys winning. You are married to one of the richest men in Europe. Why should you need money?"

That question, although logical, would have required Alexandra to discuss intentions that were entirely private.

"I can't explain," she said miserably, "but I'm sorry for blaming you."

Accepting her apology with a nod, Roddy stopped a passing footman and took two glasses of champagne from his tray, handing one of them to Alexandra. "Do you suppose," she said eagerly, after a moment, oblivious to the pregnant hush suddenly creeping over the huge room, "there's a chance Hawk may not discover my bet?"

Roddy, who was rarely oblivious to anything, glanced curiously about him and then upward, following the direction of everyone's gazes.

"Not much," he said wryly and, with a blasé motion of his hand, he directed her attention to the upper balcony at the same moment the Lindworthy butler announced in a booming voice . . .

"His grace, the *Duke of Hawthorne!*"

Jolts of shock and anticipation roared through the crowd and Alexandra's head snapped up, her eyes riveted in alarmed horror on the tall, daunting figure clad in stark black, who was stalking purposefully down the stairs. The staircase was less than fifteen yards from Alexandra, but when Jordan neared the bottom step, the giant sea of people in the ballroom seemed to press forward in a huge wave and an explosion of greetings erupted into a deafening cacophony of sound.

He was taller by half a head than nearly everyone, and from her corner, Alexandra saw him smile slightly as he seemed to listen to what people were saying to him, but his eyes were casually scanning the crowd—searching, Alexandra feared, for her. Panicked, she downed her champagne and handed the empty glass to Roddy, who then gave her his own. "Drink mine," he said dryly. "You're going to need it."

Alexandra looked around like a fox searching for a bolt-hole, her glance skidding to a stop in every direction that might inadvertently put her in Hawk's line of vision. Helpless to move, she pressed back against the wall and unthinkingly lifted Roddy's glass to her lips, just as her eyes encountered the dowager duchess off to her right. The duchess sent her an odd, quelling look, then turned and spoke rapidly to Melanie. A moment later, Melanie was wending her way around the crowd surrounding Jordan, moving toward Alexandra and Roddy.

"Your grandmother says," Melanie said in an urgent voice as soon as she reached Alexandra, "to pray *not* choose tonight of all nights to overindulge for the first time in your life, and *not* to worry because she says Hawthorne will know exactly how to act when he realizes you're here."

"Did she say anything else?" Alexandra begged, desperately needing reassurance.

"Yes," Melanie said with a vigorous nod. "She said I am to stick to your side like *glue* and not leave you, *no matter what happens tonight.*"

"Dear God!" Alexandra burst out. "I thought she said there was nothing to worry about!"

Roddy shrugged mildly. "Hawk may not know of your wager yet, so don't look so overwrought."

"I'm not worried solely about the wager," Alexandra informed him darkly, watching Jordan, trying to anticipate in which direction he would ultimately move when he disentangled himself from the large crowd around him, so that she could slide in the opposite one. "I'm worried he'll discover I'm—"

Someone on Jordan's right said something to him and he turned his head; his gaze sliding swiftly, searchingly along the wall where Alexandra stood . . . past Melanie, past Roddy, past Alexandra . . . and then slashed back, leveling on her like a pair of deadly black pistols. "—here," Alexandra finished weakly, while Jordan looked straight at her, impaling her on his gaze, leaving her in no doubt that he intended to seek her out at the first possible moment.

"I think he's just discovered it," Roddy teased.

Jerking her eyes from Hawk's, Alexandra looked around for a safe place to conceal herself until he moved out of her only path of escape—somewhere where it would not *seem* to anyone she was hiding. The safest thing to do, she decided quickly, was simply to stroll into the midst of the seven hundred guests and try to melt into the crowd until Jordan lost sight of her.

"Shall we 'mingle,' my dear?" Roddy suggested, obviously arriving at the same conclusion.

Slightly relieved, Alexandra nodded, but the idea of "mingling" lost its appeal a few minutes later when she passed by Lord and Lady Moseby and Lord North, who were all standing on the sidelines near the mirrored wall that ran the width of the ballroom. Lady Moseby held out her hand, detaining Alexandra as she said in a laughing voice tinged with admiration, "I heard about your wager, Alexandra."

Alexandra's polite smile froze on her face.

"It—it was merely a jest," Melanie Camden put in, materializing at Alexandra's side, in accordance with the duchess' earlier instruction.

Regarding Alexandra with a disapproving look, Lord North said stiffly, "I wonder if Hawk will find it amusing."

"*I* wouldn't, I assure you," Lord Moseby darkly informed Alexandra, then he took his wife's arm and, with a curt nod, firmly guided his lady away from Alexandra, with Lord North right beside him.

"I'll be damned!" Roddy said softly, glowering at the men's rigid backs. After a long, thoughtful moment, he slowly transferred his gaze to Alexandra's stricken face, regarding her with a combination of contrition, annoyance, and irony. "I fear I've done you a grave wrong by placing that wager at White's," he said. "I naturally expected a *few* of the more prudish of my sex to frown on our little wager. Regrettably, I failed to consider that in openly defying your husband with that wager, you would outrage every other husband in the *ton*."

Alexandra scarcely heard him. "Roddy," she said hastily, "you're very sweet to stay by my side, but you're quite tall and—"

"And you'd be less easily spotted without me at your side?" Roddy guessed, and Alexandra nodded. "In that case," he said contritely, "I shall take myself off."

"Thank you."

"Inasmuch as I feel inadvertently responsible for part of your dilemma, the least I can do is make myself scarce so you can escape it for now." With a brief bow, he strode into the crowd, heading in the opposite direction from Alexandra and Melanie.

Five minutes later, standing with her back angled toward the ballroom, Alexandra looked anxiously at Melanie. "Do you see him?"

"No," Melanie said, after casting a surreptitious look

over the crowded room. "He's no longer by the stairs, nor in your path."

"In that case, I'm going to leave now," Alexandra said quickly, pressing a brief kiss to Melanie's cheek. "I'll be fine—don't worry. I'll see you tomorrow if I can—"

"You can't," Melanie said unhappily. "My husband does not think the London air suitable for my condition. He's bent on taking me back to the country, and staying there until the baby comes."

The thought of having to face the near future without Melanie to confide in made Alexandra feel positively miserable. "I'll write to you," she promised, wondering dismally if she would ever see Melanie again. Unable to say more, Alexandra plucked up her skirts and began making her way toward the staircase. Behind her, Melanie called out her name, but the roar of laughing conversation in the crowded ballroom swallowed the warning as Alexandra walked quickly, staying close to the wall.

Without stopping, she bent to put her champagne glass on a table, then stifled a scream as a hand clamped cruelly onto her forearm and spun her around. At the same instant, Jordan stepped in front of her, neatly isolating them both from view of the ballroom guests. Bracing his hand high on the wall behind her, he managed to imprison her with his body and yet look to all appearances like a relaxed gentleman engaging in somewhat intimate conversation with a lady.

"Alexandra," he said in an ominously calm tone that belied the leaping fury in his eyes, "there are approximately four hundred men in this room, most of whom believe it's my *duty* to set an example for their wives by dragging you out of here in front of everyone, and then to take you home and beat some sense into you—which I am perfectly willing, no—*anxious*—to do."

To her terrified disbelief, he paused in that horrible announcement to reach out and take a glass of champagne from the tray on the pedestal beside them and then to blandly hand it to her—a gesture designed to keep up the charade of two people engaged in ordinary conversation. Continuing in that same deadly voice, he said, "Despite the fact that your public wager—and your flagrant disobedience in coming here tonight—more than deserve public retaliation, I am going to offer you two choices." Silkily he said, "I want you to listen to them very carefully."

To her angry shame, Alexandra was so terrified her chest was rising and falling like a frightened bird and she could only nod her head.

Unmoved by her obvious fright, he gave her the first choice: "You can either leave with me right now—quietly and ostensibly willingly, or kicking and screaming—it doesn't matter to me. Either way, if we do leave now, everyone in this ballroom is going to know why I'm taking you out of here."

When he paused, Alexandra swallowed convulsively, her voice a parched whisper. "What is the second choice?"

"To salvage your pride," he replied, giving her the second choice, "I am willing to walk onto that dance floor with you and try to make it appear that we both regard your wager as nothing more than a harmless little jest. But whichever choice you make," he finished ominously, "I am still going to deal with you when we get home, do you understand that?"

His last sentence and the unmistakable threat of physical retribution it carried were dire enough to make Alexandra agree to anything—anything that would delay their leavetaking.

Somewhere in the tumult of her mind, it dimly occurred to her that, in offering her a chance to salvage her pride this way, he was treating her with more consideration than she had done when she placed a public bet against him. On the other hand, she could hardly find it in her heart to be very grateful to him for sparing her public humiliation—not when he was promising private, physical retribution later. With a supreme effort of will, she managed to steady her voice and arrange her features into a reasonably calm mask. "I would prefer to dance."

Jordan stared down into her lovely pale face and had to stifle a spurt of admiration for her courage. Instead, he politely offered her his arm and she placed her trembling hand on it.

The moment Jordan stepped out of her way, Alexandra glimpsed the swift, guilty movements of heads turning away, and she realized that a great many people had been watching their little tête-à-tête. With an outward appearance of unhurried dignity, she strolled with Jordan through the fascinated crowd, which parted like the Red Sea to let them pass, then turned to watch their progress.

Alexandra's control slipped a notch, however, when the couple in their path turned to let them pass and she found herself face to face with Elizabeth Grangerfield, whose elderly husband had recently died. The shock of encountering Jordan's former paramour nearly sent Alexandra to her knees, though Jordan and Elizabeth seemed perfectly at ease as they greeted at each other.

"Welcome home, your grace," Elizabeth said in her husky voice as she held out her hand.

"Thank you," Jordan said with a polite smile and pressed a gallant kiss to the back of it.

Watching them, Alexandra felt as if someone had punched her in the stomach. Somehow, she managed to keep her expression politely neutral as they walked away, but when they reached the dance floor and Jordan tried to put his hand on her waist, she jerked back, glaring at him.

"Would you prefer to leave now?" he asked silkily, while all around them dancers began to whirl and dip.

Too infuriated to notice that they'd become the object of six hundred pairs of fascinated eyes the instant they stepped onto the floor, Alexandra reluctantly put her hand on the sleeve of his black jacket—but her expression made it eloquently obvious that she found the contact with him quite revolting.

Jordan jerked her into his arms and they moved into the colorful whirl of waltzing couples. "If you have a shred of sense—or if you've learned anything about manners and behavior," he said in an explosive underbreath, "you'll wipe that martyred expression off your face and try to look congenial!"

That remark, with all its attendant arrogant superiority, made Alexandra long to slap his aristocratic face. "How *dare* you lecture me on manners and propriety, when you have just fawned over your precious paramour with your own wife standing there!"

"What the hell did you expect me to do?" Jordan demanded shortly. "Mow her down? She was standing right in our path!"

"You might have included me in your conversation,"

Alexandra flung back, too overwrought to consider that such a thing would have been a worse embarrassment to her.

This hostile exchange between the Duke of Hawthorne and his errant wife did not go unnoticed by the occupants of the ballroom. Dancers were colliding with one another in their efforts to eavesdrop; the musicians were leaning from side to side, trying for a better view; and quizzing glasses were focused in unison upon the pair.

"*Include* you," Jordan blazed in disbelief. "Include you with a woman who—" At the last instant he cut off the words he'd been about to use, but Alexandra provided them for him—"who shared your *bed*?" she hissed.

"You're scarcely in a position to lecture *me* on manners, madam. From all accounts, *your* behavior in the last weeks has been anything but that which befits my wife!"

"*My* behavior!" Alexandra exploded. "For your information," she informed him with blazing sarcasm, "if *I* behaved in a way that befits *your* wife, I would have to try to seduce every member of the opposite sex who crosses my path!"

That outburst so stunned Jordan that for a split second he felt like shaking her for her insolence and, at the same time, he was suddenly struck with the realization that she was jealous. His temper slightly mollified, he glanced up and realized that half the dancers had moved off the floor to better observe the unprecedented altercation between him and his infuriating wife, and the rest were openly staring at them.

Jerking his gaze from their audience, he clenched his teeth in an artificial smile aimed at Alexandra's head and snapped, "Smile at me, dammit! The whole ballroom is watching us."

"I most certainly will not," she blazed irrationally, but she managed to smooth her features into a semblance of calm. "I'm still engaged to your cousin!"

That excuse was so inane, so unexpected, that Jordan swallowed a stunned laugh. "What a peculiar code of ethics you have, my love. You happen to be *married* to me at the moment."

"Don't you *dare* call me your love, and the least you could do is consider Anthony's position in all this," Alexandra cried. "Think how humbling it will be to him if everyone thinks I've fallen straight into your arms. Have you no loyalty at all to your cousin?"

"A difficult moral dilemma for me," Jordan agreed mendaciously, "but in this case, I find my loyalties are entirely with myself."

"Damn you!"

Jordan stared down at the tempestuous young beauty in the provocative lemon-yellow gown, her face both delicate and vivid with her stormy Aegean-blue eyes and rose-petal lips, and he suddenly saw her as she'd looked the last time she'd worn light yellow—standing in his grandmother's garden, her enchanting face turned up to the sky, while she explained to him in her soft, sweet voice: *"Every season of the year comes with a promise that something wonderful is going to happen to me someday. In winter, the promise comes with the smell of snow. . . . In summer, I hear it in the boom of thunder and the lightning that streaks across the sky. . . . Most of all, I feel it now, in springtime, when everything is green and black—"*

She'd been hoping for something wonderful, and all she'd gotten was a four-day marriage followed by fifteen months of widowhood, along with what appeared to be a great deal of disillusioning information about the life he had led before he married her.

The fury within him died abruptly and, as he looked down into her glorious eyes, his stomach clenched at the thought of taking her home and making her cry.

"Tell me something," he asked softly. "Do you still think dirt smells like perfume?"

"Do I what?" she said, warily studying his slightly softened features, a bewildered frown creasing her smooth forehead. "Oh—now I remember, and no I don't," she hastily added, reminded that he had found her pitiful. "I've grown up now."

"So I see." Jordan said with a mixture of tenderness and budding desire.

Alexandra saw his expression gentle and hastily looked away, but her own anger had begun to drain. Her conscience reminded her that her public wager and her hostile conduct on this dance floor—where he had taken her to salvage her pride—had been inexcusable. No longer feeling entirely the innocent and injured party, she bit her lip and raised her eyes to his.

"Truce?" he offered with a lazy smile.

"Until we're out of here," Alexandra instantly agreed, and when she gave him a tentative smile, she could have sworn she glimpsed approval in those inscrutable grey eyes.

"What happened to the puppy I bought you?" he asked, his smile deepening.

"Henry is at Hawthorne. Oh, and you were wrong," she added mischievously. "The boy who sold him to you didn't lie—he's a purebred."

"Huge?" Jordan asked. "With paws the size of saucers?"

She shook her head. "Dinner plates."

Jordan laughed and she smiled. The couples on the dance floor renewed their interest in the music, quizzing glasses were lowered, and conversations resumed. When the dance ended, Jordan put his hand under her elbow and guided her forward into the crowd, but their departure was immediately delayed by groups of Jordan's friends who pressed around them, anxious to welcome him home.

Alexandra, who already had a reasonably viable plan to ensure he would not find her in her rooms tonight, expected him to rush her off, but instead he spent the next half hour talking to the people who sought his attention, his hand covering her fingers where they rested on his arm.

Left with no other choice, Alexandra stood reluctantly by his side, trying to appear calm and to look as if standing by Jordan were no different than standing by Tony had been.

But if she tried to treat Jordan as she had treated Tony, she noticed at once that the *ton* certainly didn't. They had treated Tony cordially, and with the respect due his rank, but never with the near-reverence they were showing to Hawk tonight. As she watched bejeweled ladies curtsy to him and elegant gentlemen bow respectfully and shake his hand, Alexandra realized that, to them, Tony had been merely the custodian of a title, but Jordan *was* the title.

He *was* Hawthorne, as he had been born to be.

Standing at his side, she began to fear she might have overestimated her ability to manipulate him into letting her go back to Morsham once she had money. After being amongst the *ton* for all these weeks, she'd erroneously equated Jordan with the other aristocrats she'd come to know—polished, fastidious, and urbane. But also soft. Placid.

Now, as she watched Jordan interact with the other men, she was miserably aware that beneath his civilized, urbane facade, he was *nothing* like them.

Beside her, Jordan bent his head to her and spoke in a polite, but forceful voice. "If you'll give me your word to go straight home, you can leave now. That way, it will appear that you're going on with your evening and I with mine. I'll follow you in a quarter hour."

Amazed by his thoughtful gesture and relieved beyond words because it made her plan even easier to execute, Alexandra nodded and started to step away, but his hand clamped down on her arm. "Your word, Alexandra," he demanded shortly.

"I give you my word to go straight home," she said with a dazzling smile born of relief, and hastily left.

Jordan watched her, his eyes slightly narrowed as he contemplated the reason for that suspiciously bright smile of hers, as well as the wisdom of trusting her. It was not so much his faith in her word that had led him to make his offer, but rather that he could not honestly believe she would defy him again, now that she understood the lengths to which he would go to ensure her obedience to his will. Besides, he decided philosophically, turning his attention back to his friends and acquaintances, where else could she possibly go but home? No one, not even his grandmother, would shelter her from her husband.

Jordan was not the only one who watched Alexandra leave; a great many other guests did so as well, and they were not at all fooled by her apparently harmonious departure from her husband.

"Hawk means to deal with her when he gets home," Lord Ogilvie assured the large group of people around him. "You can be sure he won't let her behavior go unpunished a single night. What's more, he'll wear her ribbon on Queen's Race day."

"To be sure!" agreed young Sir Billowby.

"Indubitably!" seconded the Earl of Thurston.

"No doubt about it," declared Lord Carleton stoutly.

Lady Carleton looked at the Duchess of Hawthorne, who

was ascending the staircase, and bravely declared, "I hope all of you are wrong. Hawthorne has broken hearts from all over England. It's time a woman broke his!"

Sir Billowby's shy young wife put up her chin and seconded that opinion. "I hope she gives her ribbon to someone *else* to wear!"

"Don't be ridiculous, Honor," said her husband. "I'm going to wager £100 that she'll give it to Hawk."

The two ladies looked at each other and then at the gentlemen. "My lord," Lady Honor informed her scandalized husband as she withdrew £100 from her reticule, "I'll take that wager."

"So will I!" Lady Carleton declared.

By the time Alexandra climbed into her carriage, enough money had already been wagered in that ballroom to fatten Prinny's coffers for years, and the odds had soared to 25 to 1 in Jordan's favor. Only the younger ladies held out any hope that Alexandra would be the first female to resist the "irresistible" Duke of Hawthorne.

Chapter Twenty-Three

MOONLIGHT SPILLED ACROSS the mansions that marched along Upper Brook Street as Alexandra waved her coachman off and stealthily slid her key into the lock of No. 3. Pushing the door open a scant inch, she peered into the front hall. As she'd hoped, Higgins and the rest of the servants had retired for the night.

She slipped inside, silently closed the door behind her, and tiptoed up the long staircase. At the doorway to her bedchamber, she hesitated, wondering if her devoted maid had decided to await her return despite Alexandra's instructions. Deciding she dare not risk opening the door to find out, Alexandra hurried down the long hall, which was bordered on both sides with guest bedrooms. At the end of the hall a staircase led up to the next story, and she tiptoed up the steps and along the hall, stopping at the last door on the right. Silently, she turned the handle and peered into the dark, empty room that had been used long ago by the family governess, then slipped inside.

Smiling with delight at her own ingenuity, she pulled off her gloves and tossed them onto a shadowy object she identified as a small chest of drawers. She had not broken her word; she had come directly home.

Except when her husband marched into her bedchamber tonight, intending to mete out whatever punishment he had in mind, she would not be there.

A chill crept up her spine as she imagined how angry he was going to be, but the alternative of presenting herself to suffer God-knew-what fate tonight was too repugnant to consider.

Tomorrow, she decided, she would take whatever money Penrose had obtained for her grandfather's watch, and as soon as Jordan left the house, she and her two faithful old friends would leave London.

Stripping off her gown, Alexandra stretched out on the narrow bed, which had no linen on it, and closed her eyes. Weariness and confusion closed over her as she went over Jordan's behavior tonight. How could he be so murderously angry with her, and at the same time try to spare her public embarrassment, she wondered. She would never understand him. All she was sure of at that moment was that she was reduced to hiding from him in his own house—hiding in fear and anger from the same man whose disappearance had once made her want to die in order to be with him.

Lord Camden had arrived at the ball just as Jordan was leaving, only to discover that Melanie had already left. Politely refraining from showing the slightest surprise when Jordan suddenly recalled that he'd sent his own carriage home an hour earlier because he'd intended to ride home with Alexandra, Lord Camden obligingly offered him a ride home. The Camden carriage drew up before the house at No. 3, and Jordan bounded down. His mind on Alexandra, who would by now be awaiting him in her room, Jordan paid scant attention to the lone horseman who waited in the shadow of a house across the street, hat pulled low over his face, but his presence registered somewhere on the perimeter of Jordan's preoccupied mind. As if he scented danger, he turned on the second step to say goodbye to John Camden, but his gaze flicked to the slender horseman just as the shadowy figure raised his arm.

Jordan dove down and to the left just as the pistol fired, then came up in a running crouch, charging across the street in a futile attempt to give chase to the assassin who was already galloping away, wending deftly between the bulky carriages making their decorous way along Brook Street— the same crowd of carriages that prevented John Camden from giving chase in his own.

* * *

Edward Fawkes, a ruggedly built gentleman who specialized in handling delicate matters for a group of very select clients who did not want the authorities involved, glanced at his watch. It was nearly one o'clock in the morning as he sat across from the Duke of Hawthorne, who had employed him yesterday to investigate the two attempts on the duke's life and to learn who was behind them.

"My wife and I will depart for Hawthorne in the morning after we arise," the duke was saying. "An assassin can melt into the streets and alleys of London far easier than he can conceal himself in the country. If it were only my own life that is in jeopardy, I'd stay in the city. But if my cousin is behind this, he won't be able to risk my producing an heir, therefore my wife is now also endangered."

Fawkes nodded his agreement. "In the country, my men will be able to spot an unfamiliar person on the grounds of Hawthorne or loitering about the village. We can watch him."

"Your primary job is to protect my wife," the duke said curtly. "Once we're all at Hawthorne, I'll think of some plan to draw whoever is doing this out of hiding. Arrange for four of your men to ride guard around my coach tomorrow. With my own people, that will give us a total of twelve outriders."

"Is it possible the person who shot at you tonight could have been your cousin?" Edward Fawkes asked. "You said he wasn't at White's or the Lindworthy ball tonight."

Jordan wearily kneaded the knotted muscles at his nape. "It wasn't him. The horseman was much smaller than my cousin. Moreover, as I told you, I'm not completely convinced my cousin is behind this." Until today, when he learned old Grangerfield was dead, Jordan had hoped *he* was the one. After all, the first attempt had been made the night Jordan met Alexandra—only two days after he wounded Grangerfield in a duel. After tonight's episode, however, Jordan could no longer hold on to that hope.

"The two most common motives for murder are revenge and personal gain," Fawkes said carefully. "Your cousin has a great deal to gain from your death. More now even than before."

Jordan didn't ask what he meant; he already knew it was

Alexandra. Alexandra—? His face paled as he recalled the vaguely familiar, slender figure who'd shot at him tonight. It could have been a woman . . .

"You've thought of something important?" the investigator said quickly, correctly assessing Jordan's expression.

"No," Jordan snapped and surged to his feet, abruptly concluding the meeting. The idea of Alexandra trying to kill him was ludicrous. Absurd. But the words she'd hurled at him this morning came back to haunt him: *Whatever it takes, I'll be free of this marriage.*

"Just one more thing, your grace," Fawkes said as he also arose. "Could the person who shot at you tonight have been the same one you thought you'd killed on the road near Morsham last spring—the one you left for dead? You described him as being of small stature."

Jordan felt dizzy with relief. "It could have been. As I said, I couldn't see his face tonight."

When Fawkes left, Jordan climbed the stairs to his own chamber. Tired, angry, and frustrated at being the target of some unknown lunatic who wanted him dead, he sent his sleepy valet off to bed and slowly removed his shirt. Alexandra was in the next room, he thought, and his weariness began to dissipate as he visualized awakening her from sleep with a kiss.

Walking over to the connecting door, he strode through her dressing room and into the dark bedchamber. Moonlight sifted through the windows, casting a silvery beam across the perfectly smooth satin coverlet atop her bed.

Alexandra had not come home.

Striding swiftly into his own room, he jerked the bellrope. Thirty minutes later, the entire sleepy-eyed household staff was lined up before him in the drawing room answering his questions—with the single notable exception of Penrose, Alexandra's elderly servant. He, too, was mysteriously missing.

After intensive questioning, all Jordan had learned for certain was that his coachman had watched Alexandra walk up the front steps of the house and safely reach the door. Then she had waved him off—an action which the coachman confirmed was unprecedented.

"You may go back to bed," he told all thirty-one servants

but one old man with spectacles, whom Jordan identified as Alexandra's footman, hung back looking worried and angry.

Jordan went over to the side table, poured the last of his port into a glass, and with a cursory glance at Filbert, instructed him to bring up another bottle. Negligently tossing down the liquid, he sank into a chair and stretched his legs out, trying to calm his rampaging fear. Somehow, he didn't quite believe Alexandra had come to any harm, and he would not let himself consider that her absence incriminated her in the attempt on his life tonight.

The more he concentrated on that inexplicably bright smile she had given him when she promised to come directly home after the ball, the more convinced he became she'd simply gone somewhere else after tricking the coachman into believing she'd come inside. Before she actually left the ball, she'd undoubtedly asked some cicisbeo of hers to follow her home and then take her up. Since Jordan had threatened to beat some sense into her tonight, that wasn't at all surprising, he thought. She had probably gone to his grandmother, Jordan decided as the port began to soothe his raw nerves.

"Bring the bottle over here," he ordered, eyeing the sour-faced, elderly footman, with ill-concealed belligerence. "Tell me something," he said shortly, addressing a servant on a personal matter for the first time in his life, "was she always like this—your mistress?"

The old footman stiffened resentfully, in the act of pouring port in the duke's glass. "Miss Alex—" Filbert began, but Jordan interrupted him in a glacial voice: "You will refer to my wife properly," he snapped. "She is the Duchess of Hawthorne!"

"And a lotta good it's done her!" the servant flung back furiously.

"Just exactly what is that supposed to mean?" Jordan demanded, so taken aback by this unprecedented display of temper from a mere servant that he failed to react with the outrage one might have reasonably expected from a man of his temperament and rank.

"It means what it says," Filbert snapped, slamming the bottle down on the table. "Bein' the Duchess of Hawthorne ain't never brought her nothing but heartbreak! Yer as bad

300

as her pa was—no, yer worse! He only broke her heart, you broke her heart and now yer tryin' to break her spirit!"

He was halfway across the room when Jordan's voice boomed like a thunderclap. "Get back here!"

Filbert obeyed, but his gnarled hands were clenched into fists at his sides, and he glared resentfully at the man who had made Miss Alexandra's life a misery from the day she met him.

"What the hell are you talking about?"

Filbert's jaw jutted belligerently. "If you think I'm gonna tell you things so's you can use them agin' *Miss Alex,* then yer in fer a shock, yer high holiness!"

Jordan opened his mouth to tell the incredibly insolent man to pack his bag and get out, but more than satisfaction, he wanted an explanation for the servant's startling revelations. Reining in his temper with a supreme effort, Jordan said icily, "If you have anything to say that might soften my attitude toward your beloved mistress, then you'd be wise to speak out now." The servant still looked balky. "In the mood I'm in," Jordan warned him honestly, "when I get my hands on her, she'll wish to God she'd stayed out of my sight."

The old man paled and swallowed, but he remained mutinously silent. Sensing that Filbert was wavering but that intimidation alone would never get him to talk freely, Jordan poured some port into a glass and in an action that would have knocked Society onto its collective face, the Duke of Hawthorne held the glass toward a lowly footman and invited in a man-to-man voice, "Now then, since I apparently hurt your mistress—unintentionally—suppose you have a drink and tell me how I'm like her father. What did he do?"

Filbert's suspicious gaze shifted from the duke's face to the glass of port in his outstretched hand, then he slowly reached for it. "D'you mind if I sit whilst I drink?"

"By all means," Jordan replied, straightfaced.

"Her father was the lowest scoundrel what ever lived," Filbert began, oblivious to the way the duke's brows shot up at this added insult. He paused to take a long, fortifying swallow of his drink, then he shuddered, glaring at the stuff in the glass with unhidden revulsion. "Gawd!" he uttered. "What *is* this?"

"Port—a special kind that is made exclusively for me."

"Probably ain't no call fer it from no one else," Filbert replied, wholly unimpressed. "Vile stuff."

"That opinion is shared by most people. I seem to be the only one who likes it. Now, what did her father do to her?"

"Do yer happen to have any ale about?"

"I'm afraid not."

"Whisky?" Filbert asked hopefully.

"Certainly. In the cabinet over there. Help yourself."

It took six glasses of whisky and two hours to drag the story out of the reluctant footman. By the time Filbert was nearly finished, Jordan—who had felt challenged to switch to whisky and match him drink for drink—was slouched in his chair, his shirt unbuttoned halfway down his chest, trying to keep his head clear.

"And one day, about six, seven weeks after her pa dies," Filbert was finishing, "this fine carriage pulls up and in it is this beauteous lady and her pretty yellow-haired daughter. I was there when Miss Alex opened the door and the lady—who weren't no *real* lady—announces bald as you please that *she's* Lawrence's wife and the gel with her is his daughter!"

Jordan's head jerked around. "He was a bigamist?"

"Yep. And you shoulda seen the helter-pelter argument atween the two Mrs. Lawrences. But Miss Alex, she doesn't get mad. She jest looks at the yellow-haired girl and says in that sweet way o' hers: 'You're very pretty.'

"The blond chit don't say nothin', she sticks her nose up in the air. Then the chit notices this tin locket, shaped like a heart, that Miss Alex was wearin' round her neck. It was gived to Miss Alex by her pa on her birthday, and she treasured that locket like you wouldn't believe—always touchin' it whilst she wore it and worryin' it'd get lost. The blond chit asks Miss Alex if her pa gived her that, and when Miss Alex said he had, the gel pulls out this gold chain hangin' round her neck, and on the end o' it is this beautiful gold locket in the shape o' a heart.

"'He gave *me* a valuable *gold* one,' the chit says in a way that made my hand itch to slap her. 'Yours is jest old tin.'"

Filbert paused to have another swallow of his whisky and smack his lips. "Miss Alex didn't say a word, she jest lifts her chin—like she does when she's tryin' to be brave—but there's so much pain in her eyes it would have made a grown man cry. I cried," Filbert admitted hoarsely. "I went to my room, an' I cried like a babe."

Jordan swallowed against the unfamiliar aching lump in his throat. "Then what happened?"

"The next mornin' Miss Alex comes down to breakfast, jest like always, and she smiles at me, jest like always. But for the first time since her pa gave it to her, she weren't wearin' that locket. She never wore it again."

"And you think *I'm* like her father?" Jordan bit out furiously.

"Ain't you?" Filbert said contemptuously. "Ye break her heart every time yer around, and then it's left to me 'n' Penrose to try to pick up the pieces."

"What are you talking about?" Jordan insisted, clumsily splashing more whisky into his glass. Filbert stuck his empty glass forward and Jordan obediently filled it, too.

"I'm talkin' about the way she cried when she thought you was dead. One day I come upon her standin' in front o' yer portrait at yer big country house. She used to spend hours jest lookin' at you, and I think to myself she's so thin you can see clean through her. She points to you and she says to me in that shaky little voice that means she's tryin not to cry, 'Look, Filbert. Wasn't he *beautiful?*'" Filbert paused to sniff distasefully—an eloquent expression of his private opinion of Jordan's looks.

Slightly pacified by the astounding news that Alexandra had apparently cared enough to grieve for him after all, Jordan overlooked the servant's unflattering opinion of his face. "Go on," he said.

Filbert's eyes suddenly narrowed with anger as he warmed to his story: "You made her fall in love with you, then she comes to London an' finds out you never meant to treat her like a proper wife. You only married her for pity! You meant to send her off to Devon, just like her papa done to her mama."

"She knows about Devon?" Jordan said, stunned.

"She knows about *all* o' it. Lord Anthony finally had t' tell her the truth 'cause all your fancy London friends were laughin' at her behind their hands for lovin' you. They all knew how you felt about her, because you talked 'bout her to yer ladybird, and she talked to everyone else. You called it a marriage of *in*convenience. Ye shamed Miss Alex and made her cry all over again. But you'll not be able to hurt her again—she knows you for the lyin' cad you be!"

Having said his piece, Filbert shoved to his feet, put down his glass, drew himself up to his full height, and said with great dignity, "I told her, an' I'll tell you: She shoulda let you die the night she found you!"

Jordan watched the old man march off without displaying any effects from the astonishing quantity of liquor he'd consumed.

He stared blindly at his empty glass, while the reasons for Alexandra's complete change in attitude since his disappearance slowly began to crystallize. Filbert's brief but eloquent description of a painfully thin Alexandra staring at his portrait at Hawthorne made his heart wrench. Across his mind paraded a vivid image of Alexandra coming to London wearing her heart on her sleeve—and then facing the cold disdain Elise had apparently instigated by repeating Jordan's thoughtless, joking remark.

Leaning his head against the back of his chair, Jordan closed his eyes while regret and relief flooded through him. Alexandra *had* cared for him. The image he had cherished of the enchanting, artless girl who had loved him had not been false, and for that he was suddenly, profoundly overjoyed. The fact that he had wounded her in countless ways made him wince, but not for one moment was he willing to believe the damage was irreparable. Neither was he fool enough to think she'd believe any explanation he could make. Actions, not words, would be the only way to make her lower her guard and love him again.

A faint, preoccupied smile played about his lips as he contemplated his strategy.

Jordan was not smiling at nine o'clock the following morning, however, when a footman returned with the information that Alexandra had most assuredly not gone to his grandmother's house; nor was he smiling a half hour later when the dowager duchess herself marched into his study to tell him that *he* was entirely to blame for Alex's flight, and to deliver a stinging diatribe on Jordan's lack of sensitivity, his high-handedness, and his lack of good sense.

Clad in her gown from the night before, Alexandra

combed her fingers through her tousled hair, peeked into the upper hall, and then walked swiftly along the corridor and down the staircase to her own rooms.

If Jordan followed the same morning schedule as the previous two days, he would be locked away in his study with the men who came to discuss business with him in the mornings. Carefully considering ways to get herself, Filbert, and Penrose out of the house without being noticed, she walked over to the wardrobe and opened the door. The wardrobe was empty, save for a single traveling costume. Turning, Alexandra surveyed the room and noticed that all her perfumes had been cleared from the dressing table. The queer sensation that she was in the wrong room made her turn slowly round just as the door opened and a maid let out a stifled scream.

Before Alexandra could stop her, the servant turned on her heel and fled along the balcony. "Her grace is back!" she called over the balcony to Higgins.

So much for escaping without first encountering Jordan, Alexandra thought with a tremor of fear. She had not completely expected to avoid a confrontation with her husband—but she had rather hoped to do it. "Marie," she called after the maid who was already rushing down the staircase to spread the glad tidings. "Where is the duke? I'll announce my presence to him myself."

"In the study, your grace."

Raking his hands through his dark hair, Jordan paced the length of his huge, book-lined study like a caged tiger, waiting for Alexandra to appear from wherever she had spent the night, refusing to consider that she had come to harm, and unable to banish the gnawing fear that she had.

Anticipating that Hawk was going to unleash his wrath on her the moment he clapped eyes on her, Alexandra stepped quietly into the study and carefully closed the door behind her before she said, "You want to see me, I gather?"

Jordan jerked around, his emotions veering crazily from joy to relief to fury as he beheld her standing before him, her face fresh from a night's sleep that *he* hadn't had.

"Where in the hell have you been?" he demanded, striding to her. "Remind me never to take your 'word' again," he added with blazing sarcasm.

Alexandra restrained the cowardly impulse to back away.

"I kept my word, my lord. I came directly home and went to bed."

A muscle jerked ominously in his taut cheek. "Don't lie to me."

"I slept in the governess' room," she clarified politely. "You did not, after all, order me to go to my own room."

The desire to murder exploded in Jordan's brain, followed instantaneously by the opposing urge to wrap his arms around her and shout with laughter at her incredibly ingenious defiance. She had been upstairs, blissfully asleep, the entire time he'd been prowling and drinking down here in an agony of uncertainty. "Tell me something," he said irritably, "have you always been like this?"

"Like what?" Alexandra said warily, not certain of his mood.

"A blight on peace."

"Wh-what do you mean?"

"I'll tell you what I mean," he drawled, and as he advanced upon her, Alexandra began cautiously retreating step for step. "In the last twelve hours, I have rudely walked out on my friends at White's. I've been involved in a public quarrel on a dance floor, and I've been chastised by a footman, who incidentally can drink me under the table. I've had to listen to a lecture from my grandmother, who for the first time in her life so forgot herself as to raise her voice to what can only be described as a *shout!* Do you know," he finished darkly while Alexandra fought to hide a wayward grin, "that I used to lead a reasonably well-ordered life before I laid eyes on you? But from that moment on, every time I turn around, something else—"

He broke off his diatribe as Higgins raced into the study, without stopping to knock, his coattails flapping behind him. "Your grace!" he panted, "there's a constable here who insists on seeing you, or her grace, personally."

With a quelling glance at Alexandra that warned her to remain where she was until he returned to finish with her, Jordan strode swiftly from the study. Two minutes later he returned, an indescribable expression of amusement and annoyance on his tanned face.

"Is—is something wrong?" she dared to venture when he seemed not to *know* what to say.

"Not much," he drawled dryly. "I'd say it's just another ordinary little event in what seems to be a typical day with you."

"What event?" Alexandra persisted, aware that he seemed to be holding her accountable for whatever had just happened.

"Your faithful old butler has just appeared on my doorstep in the custody of a constable."

"Penrose?" Alexandra gasped.

"The very same."

"But—what did he do?"

"Do, my dear? He went to Bond Street and was caught red-handed yesterday trying to sell my watch." So saying, Jordan lifted his hand, from which hung Alexandra's grandfather's gold watch and chain.

"Attempted bigamy, larceny, and gambling," Jordan summarized with a twitch of ironic humor at his lips. "Do you have any plans for the immediate future? Extortion, perhaps?"

"It isn't *your* watch." Alexandra's eyes were riveted on the watch, her only hope for purchasing her freedom. "Please give it to me. It belongs to me."

Jordan's brows drew together in surprise, but he slowly held his hand out. "I was under the impression you had given it to me as a gift."

"You accepted it under false pretenses," Alexandra insisted with angry obstinacy, reaching for the watch. "My grandfather was a man of . . . of noble virtue . . . a warm, caring, *gentle* man. His watch ought to go to a man like him, not like you."

"I see," Jordan replied quietly, his face suddenly wiped clean of expression as he put the watch into her outstretched palm.

"Thank you," Alexandra said, feeling somehow as if she had actually hurt him by taking the watch back. Since he had no heart, perhaps she had hurt his ego, she decided. "Where is Penrose? I must go to the authorities and explain."

"If he followed my instructions, he's in his room," Jordan dryly replied, "meditating on the Eighth Commandment."

Alexandra, who had leapt to the understandable conclu-

307

sion that her cold-hearted, autocratic husband would have let the authorities haul poor Penrose off to be hanged, stared at him in confusion. "That's all you did? Send him to his room?"

"I could hardly have the closest thing I have to a father-*in-law* carted off to a dungeon, now could I?" Jordan replied.

Utterly dumbfounded by his odd mood this morning, Alexandra stared searchingly at him. "Actually, I thought you could and would."

"Only because you don't really know me, Alexandra," he said in a tone Alexandra could have sworn was conciliatory. Briskly, he continued, "However, I intend to remedy that, beginning"—he glanced up as footmen came trooping downstairs bearing several trunks, including hers—"in one hour, when we leave for Hawthorne."

Alexandra swung around, saw her trunks and turned back to him, her eyes blazing with rebellion. "I won't go."

"I think you'll agree to go when I set forth the terms for your consideration, but first, I would like to know why Penrose was trying to sell my . . . your *grandfather's* . . . watch."

Alexandra hesitated, then decided silence was best.

"The obvious answer to that is that you wanted money," Jordan continued in a matter-of-fact voice. "And I can think of only two reasons why you should need funds. The first reason would be that you've been placing more scandalous wagers against me, which I forbade you to do. Frankly, I doubt you've done that." He held up his hand when Alexandra looked angry at his supposition that she would meekly accede to his orders. "My reason for discounting the possibility you've placed additional wagers against me since yesterday has nothing to do with the fact that I forbade it. I simply don't think you've had the *time* to defy me again."

His lazy grin was so unexpected and so contagious that Alexandra had to fight the urge to smile back at him.

"Therefore," he concluded, "I would assume the reason you suddenly want money is the same reason you gave me two days ago—you want to leave me and live on your own. Is that it?"

He sounded so understanding that Alexandra reversed her former decision and nodded in the affirmative.

"Just as I thought. In that case, let me offer a solution to your predicament which should also appeal to your penchant for gambling. May I?" he politely asked, motioning her to a chair in front of his desk.

"Yes," Alexandra agreed, sitting down while he leaned against his desk.

When she was settled, Jordan said, "I will give you enough money to live out the rest of your life in regal splendor, if after three months you still wish to leave me."

"I—I don't entirely understand," Alexandra said, scrutinizing his tanned face.

"It's quite simple. For three full months, you must agree to be my most obedient, loving, biddable wife. During that time, I will endeavor to make myself so—shall we say— 'agreeable' to you that you no longer wish to leave me. If I fail, you may leave at the end of three months. It's as simple as that."

"No!" Alexandra burst out before she could stop herself. The thought of Jordan deliberately trying to charm and entice her was more than she could bear to contemplate, and the intimate implications of being his "loving" wife made her face burn.

"Afraid you'll fall under my 'spell'?"

"Certainly not," she lied primly.

"Then why should you not agree to the wager? I'm betting a fortune that I can make you wish to stay. Evidently, you're afraid you'll lose, or you wouldn't hesitate."

He slid the challenge in so smoothly that Alexandra scarcely saw it coming before he'd hit home.

"I—there are other things to consider—" She stalled lamely, too shaken to think of any.

"Ah, yes—there's the possibility that in the ardent performance of my husbandly duties, I might get you with child, is that it?"

Speechless with dismay and horror at that heretofore unthought-of possibility, Alexandra simply stared at him, pink-cheeked, as he idly picked up a paperweight from his desk. "I intend to do my utmost to bring that about, my sweet," he baldly promised. "Moreover," he continued, balancing the weight in his palm, exactly as he was balancing her future, "our wager is contingent upon your granting me your favors in bed without resentment. In other words," he finished with smiling bluntness, "if you shirk or protest or fail to cooperate—you lose."

"You're mad!" Alexandra burst out, leaping from her chair, but her frantic mind could come up with no better means of ending this unwanted marriage.

"I must be," he agreed without rancor. "Three months doesn't give me much time. Six months would be more fair, now that I think on it."

"Three is more than fair!" Alexandra exclaimed.

"Agreed," he smoothly said. "Three months it is. Three months of wedded bliss for me, in return for—shall we say—a half million pounds?"

Alexandra clenched her trembling hands and hid them behind her back, her mind whirling with a dizzying combination of jubilation and resentment. A half million pounds. . . . A half *million* pounds. . . . A fortune!

In payment for services to be rendered in his bed.

By offering her the money, he was reducing her to the status of one of his mistresses; offering to "pay her off" when they were finished.

"Don't think of it in that way," Jordan quietly suggested, watching the reactions play across her expressive face and correctly interpreting them. "If I lose the wager, then consider the money as a belated 'reward' for saving my life."

With her pride somewhat soothed by that, Alexandra hesitated and then nodded slightly, noncommittally. "It's a highly irregular proposition in most regards—"

"Our marriage has been 'highly irregular' in *every* regard," Jordan said dryly. "Now then, do I need to put our wager in writing, or shall we trust one another to keep to the terms?"

"Trust!" Alexandra repeated scornfully. "You told me yourself you don't trust anyone." He had told her that in bed, and she had asked him to trust her. She had told him that love could not survive without trust. Watching him, she knew he was recalling the conversation.

He hesitated as if coming to an important decision. Then he said with gentle solemnity, "I trust *you.*"

The three quietly spoken words carried a wealth of underlying meaning that Alexandra adamantly refused to believe he intended. She tried to ignore the warmth in his steady gaze, but she could not sustain her animosity when he was behaving in this odd, almost tender fashion. Deciding that the best way to deal with her enigmatic spouse was to remain calm and reserved at all times, she politely said, "I'll consider your wager."

"You do that," he urged, a gleam of amusement in his eyes as more footmen came trooping downstairs with their trunks. "Will two minutes give you enough time?" He nodded toward the crowded hallway outside his study.

"What!"

"We're leaving for Hawthorne within the hour."

"But—"

"Alexandra," he said quietly, "you have no choice." Reaching out, Jordan ran his hands up her arms while he silently fought the urge to pull her to him and seal the victory he already knew was his.

Inwardly, Alexandra bridled, but she knew he was right. Roddy's words came back to reassure her. *We are not a very prolific family* . . . "Very well," she agreed ungraciously. And the rest of Roddy's sentence hit her. *Although it is not for want of trying* . . .

"You're blushing," Jordan remarked, his eyes smiling into hers.

"Any female would blush when baldly presented with the prospect of spending three months of . . . of . . ."

"Naked splendor in my arms?" Jordan provided helpfully.

She gave him a look that could have pulverized rock.

Chuckling, he said, "Consider the risk *I* am taking. Suppose I lose my head entirely and become enslaved by your bod—beauty?" he corrected belatedly, positively oozing good humor. "And then you go off, taking my money and all hope of a legal heir with you."

"You don't for a moment believe I *could* do that, do you?" Alexandra snapped irritably.

"No."

It was his insufferable grin, as much as his arrogant confidence, that made her turn on her heel. Jordan caught her arm and pulled her firmly back around, his voice calm but authoritative. "Not until we reach an agreement. Do we have a bet, or do I take you to Hawthorne—under guard if

311

necessary—and without promise of remuneration if you decide to leave me in three months?"

Put in that context, Alexandra had absolutely no choice. Lifting her head, she looked him in the eye and declared with unconcealed dislike, "We have a wager."

"You agree to all the terms?"

"With great reluctance, your grace," she said stonily and, jerking her arm free, started to leave.

"Jordan," he said to her back.

Alexandra turned. "Pardon?"

"My name is Jordan. In future, please call me that."

"I prefer not to."

Raising his hand in an exaggerated, mock warning, he said, "Sweetheart, be cautious lest you lose your bet in less than five minutes. You agreed to be my most 'obedient, loving, and *biddable* wife.' And I *bid* you call me by my given name."

Her eyes shot daggers into his, but she inclined her pretty head. "As you wish."

She had already walked out of the study before Jordan realized she had simply managed not to call him anything at all. A smile swept across his features as he absently rolled the paperweight between his palms, contemplating the impending, highly satisfactory sojourn in the country with his enticingly pretty—albeit reluctant—wife.

Chapter Twenty-Four

*E*IGHT UNIFORMED OUTRIDERS, mounted upon prancing steeds and carrying maroon pennants bearing the Duke of Hawthorne's insignia, rode ahead of a procession that included Jordan's splendid coach and three others containing luggage and various personal servants, and eight additional armed outriders followed behind it. All day, as they traveled regally through villages and lush countryside, peasants flocked to the roads to enjoy the spectacle of fluttering pennants, jangling silver harnesses, outriders in maroon and gold livery, and the shiny, black-lacquered coach with the gold crest of the Duke of Hawthorne emblazoned upon its doors.

They passed the drive leading up to Tony's house, and Alexandra began to look forward to seeing Tony's mother and younger brother again. They were such a kind family, and their house so cozy and inviting in comparison to the daunting magnificence of Hawthorne.

A tiny, whimsical smile played at the corners of Alexandra's lips as they neared the village of Winslow, near Hawthorne. Whenever their procession passed through a village, they created a sensation, but nothing like the one they were about to cause, she realized, as she saw the entire population of Winslow lined up in the streets and roads, already waving colorful scarves and kerchiefs to welcome their Duke home. Obviously, servants had been sent ahead to alert the staff at Hawthorne that the duke was coming home, and word had spread swiftly to the village.

How different this festive, excited greeting was from the half-hearted greeting Anthony received a year ago, when these same villagers stood along the roads to salute him dutifully as their new duke.

"You're pleased about something?" Jordan remarked, watching her.

Alexandra unconsciously turned the full force of her dazzling smile on him. "I love parades," she admitted, laughing a little ruefully. "It's the child in me, I suppose."

Jordan, who only moments ago had been dwelling on the stirring prospect of putting his own child inside her, perhaps this very night, tried to ignore the surge of hot lust her words ignited in him.

After her ungracious acceptance of his wager this morning, he had fully expected her to sulk throughout their journey, but to his increasing confusion, from the moment they left London, Alexandra had treated him with polite cordiality, albeit with a trace of shyness. After trying to find a reason for her pleasant but unexplainable mood change, he decided to take a more direct approach and bluntly remarked upon it.

Startled, Alexandra tore her attention from the coach window and self-consciously looked at her hands before slowly raising her magnificent aqua eyes to his. "After taking time to reflect upon the matter, my lord," she said candidly, "I decided your wager was more than fair. It is no more your fault that we had to marry than it was mine, and neither you nor I can be blamed because we cannot possibly suit. You have offered me a way out of an impossible situation, which is more than most men in your position would probably do. Therefore, I decided it would be altogether churlish in me to behave badly to you during the next three months."

Before Jordan could recover from the shock that she honestly and truly believed she would *win* the wager, she had stretched her graceful, gloved hand out toward his. "Friends?" she offered.

Jordan took her hand, his thumb lightly caressing her sensitive palm. "Friends," he agreed, and not by a flicker of an eye did he betray either his pique or his admiration for her spirit of fair play.

"We're home," Alexandra said, smiling when their pro-

314

cession drew up before the ornate black-iron gates with the Hawthorne crest upon them.

"So we are," he said indifferently, as the gatekeeper saluted his coach, then rushed forward to open wide the gates.

His cavalcade swept down the smooth road and he glanced at the magnificence of his "home," feeling no pride in its palatial splendor, nor any warm sensation of home-coming. Hawthorne represented the bleakness of his parents' marriage and his own boyhood.

"After all I've seen in the last year, I still think this is the most splendid estate in England." Alexandra sighed happily, her gaze roving lovingly over the immense, elegant house, then lifting to the flag already flying high above the hall, indicating the duke was now in residence.

"My ancestors would be pleased to hear it," Jordan remarked dryly as he glanced at his estate in the waning light of dusk. "They intended Hawthorne to rival the king's residence. It was designed to impress and intimidate."

"You—you don't like it?" Alexandra gasped.

"Not particularly. I find it oppressive. I have other houses which I think are infinitely more pleasing, although not so convenient to town."

She gaped at him in amazement. "They're more beautiful than Hawthorne?"

"Cozier."

"Hawthorne does rather overawe one," Alex admitted. "The house is so—so silent."

The entire staff of two hundred servants, including maids, gamekeepers, grooms, and footmen, were lined up on the terraced steps in formal uniforms, their faces wreathed in smiles as the coach drew to a stop before the house.

Footmen rushed forward to let down the steps, but Jordan insisted on lifting Alexandra down from the coach himself, his hands lingering at her waist after he set her down. "Welcome home," he said, his smile intimate. "Our rooms have been prepared, and an excellent supper awaits us."

"I'm much too exhausted to eat," Alexandra said hastily, in hopes of deterring him from trying to make love to her until tomorrow night. "I'd like to bathe and retire immediately."

The ploy was both obvious and futile. "In that case, we'll

both skip supper and go straight to bed," Jordan countered patiently, but implacably.

"I assumed you would at least grant me a night's rest after our journey!"

"No welshing on your bet, sweetheart."

"Don't call me that, my lord," she warned.

"Jordan," he corrected.

"Here they come," Gibbons chortled to Smarth, peering excitedly around the shoulder of the gamekeeper who was blocking their view. "I can't wait to see Miss Alexandra's face, now the master is back," he said, echoing the thoughts of most of Hawthorne's staff, who were aware of her heartwrenching devotion to Jordan when she believed him dead.

"She'll be happy as a songbird," agreed Mrs. Brimley, the housekeeper, craning her neck.

"She'll be glowin' with happiness, shinin' like a—" Gibbons broke off, stunned, as Alexandra swept past them with an expression on her face that could best be described as thoroughly irate. "Well, I'll be . . ." he breathed, turning his bewildered face first to Smarth and then to Mrs. Brimley.

Alexandra ate in uneasy silence across the candlelit table from Jordan. "The wine doesn't suit you?" he asked.

Alexandra startled at the sound of his deep voice and her spoon clattered against the fragile Sèvres china bowl. "I—I don't care for port, your grace."

"Jordan," he reminded her.

Alexandra swallowed, unable to force his name past her lips. She glanced at the plump red strawberries in her bowl and set her spoon down, her stomach churning with tension over what she knew would be happening to her an hour from now.

"You've scarcely eaten a bite," Jordan observed, his deep voice husky.

Suffocated by what she regarded as his deliberate, unprecedented efforts to charm and disarm her, Alexandra shook her head. "I'm not very hungry."

"In that case," he said, laying his napkin aside, "shall we retire, my dear?" A footman stepped forward to pull his chair back, and Alexandra snatched up her fork. "I believe I could eat some of the pheasant," she said hastily.

Jordan politely placed his napkin back in his lap, but she could have sworn his eyes gleamed with laughter.

Stalling for time, Alexandra made a positive production of dissecting the succulent slice of pheasant she was given into precise, bite-sized rectangles and of chewing each small rectangle until it was nearly liquefied. When the last geometric shape disappeared from her plate and she put down her fork, Jordan quirked a questioning brow at her, asking if she was finished.

Alexandra's panicked gaze flew to the nearest footman. "I—I would enjoy some of cook's delicious asparagus now," she desperately announced, and this time there was no denying the smile that quirked Jordan's lips. She followed the asparagus with a small helping of peas in cream sauce, pork stuffed with apples, lobster in a pastry shell, and then blueberries.

When she asked for the blueberries, Jordan didn't bother trying to hide his amusement. Lounging back in his chair, he watched her valiant struggle to swallow every last blueberry, a smile playing about his sensual mouth.

Carefully avoiding his eyes, Alexandra managed to finish the blueberries, but when she was done, her stomach was churning in protest against so much food.

"Something more to fortify you, my sweet?" Jordan suggested helpfully. "Some chocolate cake?"

The mention of dessert made her shudder and she hastily shook her head.

"Beef in wine sauce?"

Alexandra swallowed and whispered, "No, thank you."

"A litter, perhaps?" he offered, grinning wickedly, "to carry you upstairs?"

Before she could answer, he purposefully laid his napkin aside and rose, coming around the table to help her up. "If you continue to eat like that," he remarked teasingly as they walked up the long, curving staircase, "you'll soon be too fat to climb these stairs. I shall have to install a winch and cargo net to lift you up and over the balcony."

Under different circumstances, Alexandra would have laughed at his joke, but tonight tension and acute self-consciousness had strangled her sense of humor. She realized he was trying to put her at ease but she could hardly be grateful when it was his fault she was so uneasy in the first place. Moreover, she couldn't understand how he could be so *un*embarrassed about what they were about to do. Then she recollected his reputation as a womanizer and realized that he could hardly be embarrassed or uneasy about something he'd done hundreds of times with dozens of women!

An hour later, Jordan opened the connecting door between their suites of rooms and walked into hers, then stopped short, staring in angry disbelief at the bed. The curtains were pulled back and the pale blue satin coverlet was turned back invitingly, displaying cream silk sheets, but Alexandra was not between them.

He swung around, fully prepared to have every nook and cranny of Hawthorne searched tonight, and then he saw her—standing at the opposite side of the immense room, staring out the mullioned windows into the darkness, her arms wrapped around her as if she were cold. Or afraid. Relief replaced his anger as he approached her, his footsteps muffled by the thick Aubusson carpet, his eyes roving appreciatively over the enticing vision she created. Her hair tumbled over her shoulders in molten waves, and her skin above the low bodice of her white satin gown gleamed in the candlelight.

She swung around when he came up behind her and she saw his reflection in the window glass. Jordan stretched his hand out, gently running it down her shining hair, and anger flashed in her eyes but she did not pull away. Her hair felt like satin in his hand. "So," he said, voicing his thoughts aloud and smiling into her angry eyes, "my little sparrow turned into a beautiful swan."

"Empty compliments from—"

"With teeth," Jordan amended, grinning.

Before she could react, he leaned down and swept her up into his arms.

"Where are you taking me?" she demanded as he strode past her bed.

"To my bed," he whispered, nuzzling her neck. "It's bigger." A bank of candles burned on the mantel at the far end of the room, casting a mellow glow into the shadows. Jordan stepped up onto the huge dais that supported his bed and slowly lowered Alexandra to the floor, enjoying the exquisite sensation of her legs sliding down his. But when he lifted his head and looked into her eyes, something in those huge blue orbs—or perhaps it was the rapid shallow breaths she was taking—finally made him realize that Alexandra was not angry. She was frightened.

"Alexandra?" he asked gently, feeling her tremble when he ran his hands up her arms beneath the satin-and-lace sleeves of her dressing gown. "You're trembling. Are you afraid?"

Unable to force a word out, Alexandra gazed up at the tall, daunting, virile man who was about to do all manner of intimate things to her naked body. She nodded.

With a tender smile, Jordan gently smoothed her hair back off her pale cheek. "It won't hurt you this time, I promise."

"It isn't that!" Alexandra burst out as his hands slid down to the ribbon at her breasts. She clamped her hands over his fingers, her voice strained and rushed as she tried to plead for time. "You don't understand! I don't even *know* you."

"You 'know' me in the most biblical sense of the word, my sweet," Jordan teased huskily.

"But—but it's been so long . . ."

Lifting his head, Jordan looked searchingly into her eyes. "Has it?" he asked softly, while an amazing tide of relief swept through him. Based on the accounts of her behavior during the last three months and on his own knowledge of the relaxed morals of the married women in his set, he had been afraid to let himself hope she had known no other men and adamantly unwilling to face the fact that she might well have done so. But there was no mistaking the embarrassed innocence in her eyes as she nodded, and his heart warmed with the certainty that his intoxicatingly lovely wife was still entirely and exclusively his.

"It's been much too long for both of us," he whispered, tenderly kissing her ear.

"Please, stop!" she burst out, and Jordan lifted his head at the sound of genuine panic in her voice. "I—I'm afraid," she admitted, and he knew instinctively how much that admission had cost the courageous girl who'd pitted her will against his for the last three days.

Too wise to laugh at her fears, he tried to make *her* laugh at them. "I'm a little afraid too," he admitted with a tender smile at her upturned face.

"You—you are? Why?"

His voice was light, reassuring as he untied the ribbon at her bodice, exposing the satin globes of her breasts. "As you said, it's been a very long time." Dragging his gaze from them, he smiled into her eyes and slid her dressing gown off her shoulders. "Suppose I've forgotten exactly how it's done," he said with mock horror. "Once we're in bed, it's too late to ask someone how to go on, isn't it? I mean, I could summon your friend Penrose and ask him for advice, but I'd have to shout the problem at him in order to be heard, which would then wake all the servants and bring them running in here to see what the furor was about . . ."

Despite her misery, Alexandra couldn't suppress the giggle that rose in her chest, and she scarcely noticed as Jordan's fingers sent her dressing gown sliding down her body, landing in a pool of satin at her feet. "That's better," he said huskily, deliberately keeping his eyes on hers and not her gleaming, naked body as he drew her into his arms. "I like it when you laugh, do you know that?" he continued, trying to ease her shyness as he untied his maroon brocade robe. "Your eyes glow when you smile," he said, and tenderly but inexorably eased her back onto the bed, following her down.

Alexandra looked up into his mesmerizing grey eyes as he leaned up on an elbow, his free hand sliding gently up her midriff, then encompassing her breast while he slowly bent his head and took her mouth in an endless, drugging kiss that made her senses reel.

He kissed her again and again and again, his hands shifting, tormenting, seducing until Alexandra lost all control. Moaning helplessly, she turned into him and kissed him back with all the suppressed longing of the last year. Her parted lips crushed his, her tongue darting into his mouth, her fingers tangling in the crisp, thick hair at his nape as she held his mouth to hers. And in her surrender she gained the victory, for this time it was Jordan who groaned and lost himself in the kiss.

Wrapping his arms around her, he rolled onto his back, taking her with him, his hands eloquent of his urgency as they raced over her satiny skin, his legs tangling with hers, his body slowly thrusting against her hips, telling her what he wanted.

Somewhere in the fiery tumult of his mind, Jordan warned himself to slow down, but his body, starved for more than a year for her, would not listen to the commands of his will—particularly not when Alexandra was kissing his ear as he had kissed hers, sliding her tongue along the sensitive lobe . . . Shuddering with a need that refused to be denied any longer, Jordan rolled her onto her back, his hand sliding down between her thighs to the warm wetness that assured him she was ready for him.

"I'm sorry, love," he whispered hoarsely, cupping her bottom in his hands and lifting her hips to receive him. "I . . . can't . . . wait." His breath caught as he eased himself slowly into her incredibly welcoming warmth, careful lest he hurt her, then he stopped in agonized surprise when she suddenly turned her face away from him and two bright tears slid from beneath her long, curly lashes.

"Alexandra?" he whispered, his arms and shoulders taut with the effort he was exerting to control the pounding need of his body to be fully sheathed within her. Bracing himself on one forearm, he took her chin between his thumb and forefinger and firmly turned her face on the pillow. "Open your eyes and look at me," he commanded quietly.

Her tear-drenched lashes fluttered, and he stared into aqua eyes swimming with tears.

"Am I hurting you?" he asked in disbelief.

Alexandra swallowed and shook her head, fighting down the wanton urge to plead with him to take her, to beg him to love her with his heart and his body, as she had been longing to do almost from the moment he stretched out beside her and took her in his arms. And that was why she was crying. In a few short minutes, his lovemaking had broken down every barrier she had erected against him, battered down her defenses and left her as weak and eager for him as she'd been as a naive girl.

"Darling, what is it?" he asked, leaning down and kissing the tear from her cheek. "Don't you want me?"

It was the humble, boyish innocence of the question, combined with the tender endearment, that was her undoing. "Yes," she whispered, gazing up into his eyes, seeing the passion he was fighting to restrain.

"Then why the tears?" he whispered.

"Because," she admitted in a fierce, suffocated little voice, "I don't *want* to want you."

A sound that was part groan, part laughter escaped him as he shoved his fingers into her luxuriant hair, imprisoning her face between his hands at the same moment he thrust himself full-length into her, plunging deep. Her hips arched spasmodically beneath him and Jordan lost all control. "I want *you*," he groaned hoarsely, withdrawing and then plunging again, deeper and deeper with each stroke, his heart swelling with joy as he felt his wife wrap her arms around his shoulders and surrender completely to his stormy desire. "I want you so much," he gasped, "that I can't wait—"

Her nails dug into the bunched muscles at his back and her hips lifted and Jordan climaxed within her with a force that tore her name from his chest in an agonized gasp.

When he moved onto his side, he wrapped his arms around her, cradling her against him while he waited for his labored breathing to even out. Staring into the candlelit darkness beyond the dais, he felt sanity finally return and with it came two stunning realizations: The first was that he had actually asked his own wife if she wanted him—like a small boy pleading for favors.

Never in his entire life had he asked a woman to want him. For that matter, never had he rushed one into bed so quickly as he'd rushed Alexandra tonight, nor had he ever spent himself so fast either. His pride rebelled at his performance in bed tonight and his general lack of control.

Beneath him, Alexandra stirred and lifted her head, tilting it back on the pillow so that she could see his face in the candlelight, studying his taut jaw as he stared straight ahead, lost in thought. "You're angry?" she whispered, filled with disbelief and dismay.

Jordan tipped his chin down and smiled without humor. "At myself, not you."

"Why?" she asked, all lovely innocence and naked woman, her eyes searching his.

"Because I—" He shook his head and clamped his mouth shut. *Because I want you too much,* he admitted angrily to himself. *Because I lost control tonight. Because the simple touch of your hands on me makes me insane with wanting.*

Because you can make me angrier than anyone alive and because, in the throes of my fury, you can make me laugh. Because where you are concerned, I'm vulnerable. Soft . . .

His father's voice shouted scathingly in Jordan's head: "You can't be soft and be a man, Jordan. . . . A man is hard, tough, invulnerable. . . . A man doesn't need to trust anyone but himself. . . . We use women for pleasure but we don't need them. . . . A man doesn't *need* anyone."

Jordan shoved the memories from his head and forcibly reminded himself what a mockery his father's marriage had been. Still, he wished to God he'd taken Alexandra somewhere else; Hawthorne and the memories that dwelled here made him edgy.

Alexandra's soft, timid words drew him from his thoughts. "May I go to my own room now? I can see that I've somehow displeased you."

Unexpectedly, his heart wrenched at the thought of her believing that. "On the contrary," he said, grinning to hide the truth of his words. "You please me *too* much."

She looked so skeptical that he chuckled. "In bed, you please me," he clarified teasingly, smiling into her eyes. "Out of it, you infuriate me. I suppose the only solution," he huskily added as desire surged through him with renewed force, "is to keep you in bed with me." Bending his head, he took her sweet lips in a deep kiss that soothed his raw emotions. He had made too much of everything associated with their lovemaking tonight, he decided. After all, this was the first time in his life since he turned fourteen that he'd been without a woman for more than a month, let alone an entire year. Naturally, he'd been overeager, overemotional . . .

And this time, when he made love to her, Jordan lingered over her for hours, holding himself back while he guided Alexandra to peak after peak of trembling ecstasy, and then joining her there.

Dawn was already streaking the purple sky with wide pink slices when Jordan made love to her for the last time and finally fell into a deep slumber.

Cautiously lifting his imprisoning arm from around her waist, Alexandra inched forward and slid out from beneath the sheets. Her body, unused to such vigorous lovemaking, felt weak, limp, and deliciously weary as she walked silently around to his side of the bed and picked up her satin dressing gown.

Sliding her arms into the sleeves, she wrapped the gown around her, then hesitated, looking down at her husband. His dark hair was inky against the gleaming whiteness of the pillow, and sleep softened the rugged contours of his tanned face, making him look almost boyish. The sheet had slid down to his hips, exposing to her view the full expanse of his broad, muscled chest and arms. He was tanned there too, she realized with a start. She hadn't noticed that in the night, but evidently he must have left his shirt off while he was sailing home to England. He was thinner, too, from his imprisonment. Much too thin.

Her gaze moved over him, reveling in the freedom to look at him to her heart's content. He was splendid, truly splendid, she decided with wistful impartiality. In fact, she had not been entirely naive and foolish a year ago when she had likened him to Michelangelo's David.

Unaware of the tenderness of the gesture, Alexandra leaned down and carefully drew the sheet up over his shoulder, then she straightened, but she did not leave. She absently rubbed her arms as the memory of when he had said, *Don't you want me?* sent a thrill of pure tenderness through her.

She thought about the way he'd made love to her the first time tonight, with an urgency and need he couldn't hide, despite all his experience in lovemaking. That first time had been better for her than all the others, because it was the only time he seemed to lose control. A fresh surge of delight washed over her as she recalled his helpless apology . . . *"I'm sorry, love. I can't wait."* How joyously, gloriously good she had felt—to know that while he was able to make her body feel as if it was on fire for him, *she* had been able to make him burn as well.

He had made love to her repeatedly after that, throughout the night, but each time thereafterwards, he had exercised rigid control, touching and kissing her with the skill and expertise of a virtuoso playing a violin. He had enjoyed her, she knew that, but never again with the sweet abandon of the first time.

And yet, conversely, he had done his utmost to make *her* lose her control. But Alexandra was no longer the child who

324

blurted out her undying love after one kiss—or one entire night of stormy lovemaking. She was no longer a reckless, naive, starry-eyed girl. She was cautious now, wiser.

She was also dangerously fascinated by this unexpected, vulnerable side of her enigmatic husband, she realized, and turned away from his sleeping profile. Returning to her own bedchamber, she softly closed the door behind her.

Chapter Twenty-Five

$\mathcal{S}$HE AWOKE LATE in the morning and chafed under the ministrations of Marie, who insisted on brushing her hair until it gleamed before she was ready to discuss whether Alexandra ought to wear her lavender sprigged muslin or the flounced rose frock.

Alexandra, who could not completely suppress her eager curiosity to see how Jordan might treat her this morning, had to force herself to walk slowly and decorously down the steps. With feigned casualness, she walked by Jordan's study. Through the open door, she saw him at his desk talking to one of his bailiffs. He glanced up as she passed and their eyes met; he nodded a brief greeting at her, but there was something in his expression that hinted of displeasure.

Confused by this unexpected attitude, Alexandra politely returned his nod and continued past his study to the morning room, where she ate in thoughtful, somewhat dismal silence, while Penrose and Filbert hovered about, casting anxious, worried looks back and forth between them.

Wisely deciding that the next three months would pass much more quickly if she kept herself busy, she decided to begin paying duty calls on the cottagers, as well as resuming the reading and writing lessons she'd started before the family had gone to London.

She stopped at the stable to play with Henry, whose

sociable nature made him prefer the atmosphere of the busy stable to the hushed emptiness of the house. It was late in the afternoon when she finally returned. Exhilarated from the blissful freedom of driving her own carriage through the picturesque winding lanes that meandered through Jordan's vast estate, Alexandra drove her horse at a smart trot past the house and straight to the stables.

Smarth came rushing forward to take the reins from her, his face wreathed in an overbright smile. Apparently eager to foster matrimonial harmony between Alexandra and her husband, he said, while beaming at her, "His grace has been here more'n an hour awaitin' for you—prowling back and forth, fair champin' at the bit with impatience to see you—"

Surprised and shamefully pleased, Alexandra smiled at Jordan as he strode out of the stables, but her smile abruptly faded when she saw that his face was as dark as a thundercloud.

"Don't ever leave the house without telling someone *exactly* where you're going, and *exactly* when you expect to return," he snapped, catching her none too gently at the waist and hauling her down from the carriage. "Furthermore, you are not to leave the grounds of this estate without a groom accompanying you. Olsen there"—he nodded toward a huge, muscular bear of a man who was standing in the doorway of the stable—"is your personal groom."

His anger seemed so unjustified, his orders so seemingly unreasonable, and his attitude so different from his compelling tenderness last night, that for a moment Alexandra just stared at him in wide-eyed astonishment, then she felt her temper begin to boil as Smarth hastily and wisely removed himself from earshot.

"Are you quite finished?" Alexandra snapped, intending to leave him there and start for the house.

"No," Jordan bit out, looking angrier than ever. "There's one more thing—don't ever crawl out of my bed in the middle of the night when I'm asleep again, like a doxy returning to the wharves!"

"How dare you!" Alexandra exploded, so enraged she swung her hand to strike him before she realized what she was doing.

Jordan caught her wrist in midswing, his hand clamping around the slender bones like a vise, his eyes like shards of ice . . . and for one moment Alexandra actually thought he was going to strike her. Then without warning he dropped her arm, turned on his heel, and strode off toward the house.

"Now, my lady," Smarth soothed, coming to her side, "the master must be havin' a bad day, for I've not seen him in a temper like that in all his life." Despite his reassuring tone, Smarth's kindly old face was twisted with bewildered concern as he stared at Jordan's broad, retreating back.

In silence, Alexandra turned her head and stared at her old confidant, her eyes alive with anger and painful confusion as he continued. "Why, afore today, I never knew he *had* a temper—not one like that. I put him on his first pony, and I've known him since he was a boy, and there be no braver, finer—"

"Please!" Alexandra burst out, unable to endure another of the glowing stories she used to enjoy so much. "No more lies! You cannot make him gallant and fine to me, when he's alive and I can see perfectly well he's—he's an evil-tempered, heartless monster!"

"No, my lady, he's not. I knowed him since he was a boy, just as I knowed his father before him—"

"I'm sure his father was a monster, too!" Alexandra said, too hurt and angry to heed what she was saying. "I've no doubt they're exactly alike!"

"No, my lady! No. You're wrong. Wronger than anybody's ever been if you think a thing like that! Why would you say such a thing?"

Stunned by the intensity of that denial, Alexandra brought her temper under control and managed a weak smile and a shrug, "My grandfather always said that if you want to know what a man will become, look to his father."

"Your grandsire was wrong when it comes to Master Jordan and his father," Smarth said vehemently.

It occurred to Alexandra that Smarth could be a veritable treasure trove of information about Jordan, if she could only get him to tell her the unembellished truth. Stoically, she told herself she didn't care to know anything about her temporary husband, but even while she thought it, she was already saying, albeit a little irritably, "Since I'm not allowed to go anywhere without a guard, would you care to walk over to the fence with me so I may watch the colts frolic?"

Smarth nodded, and when they were standing at the fence, he said abruptly: "You shouldn'ta placed that wager against him, my lady, if you'll forgive me for sayin' it."

"How did you know about the wager?"

"Everybody knows 'bout it. John Coachman had it from Lord Hackson's groom the same afternoon it was writ in the book at White's."

"I see."

"It was a bad mistake, announcin' to everyone you don't care nothin' for his grace, and don't never intend to do it. It's a sign o' how much he cares for you that he didn't let it bother him much. Why, even the master's mama wouldn'ta dared do such a—" Smarth stopped abruptly, flushed, and stared miserably at his feet.

"I never meant for it to be a public wager," Alexandra said, then with an appearance of mild interest, she casually inquired, "Speaking of my husband's mother, what was she like?"

Smarth shifted uneasily from one foot to the other. "Beautiful, o' course. Liked parties—had all sorts of 'em here, all the time."

"She sounds quite gay and lovely."

"She weren't *nothin'* like you!" Smarth exploded, and Alexandra gaped at him, taken aback both by his vehemence and the realization that he regarded her in such flattering terms. "She never noticed nobody beneath her rank, nor cared for nobody but herself."

"What an odd thing to say! What do you mean?"

"I got to get to work, my lady," Smarth said miserably. "Anytime you want to hear *good* things 'bout his grace, you come back and I'll think o' some."

Seeing that it would be futile to press him further, Alexandra let him go. Yet she couldn't banish the feeling, nor her curiosity over its source.

On the pretext of needing a door hinge oiled, she summoned Gibbons, the footman who was as devoted to Jordan as Smarth, and who had also been her confidante while she stayed at Hawthorne. Like Smarth, the old footman was delighted to see her, and more than eager to launch into tales of Jordan as a boy, but the moment she asked about his parents, Gibbons hemmed and hedged and suddenly recalled he had urgent work to do belowstairs.

Dressed in a peach silk gown, with her hair falling loose over her shoulders, Alexandra left her room at nine, the appointed hour for supper, and walked slowly downstairs. Now that she was about to face Jordan for the first time since their angry confrontation at the stable, her curiosity over him gave way to a return of her earlier indignation and not a small amount of dread.

Higgins stepped forward as she turned toward the dining room and swiftly opened the doors to the drawing room instead. Confused, Alexandra glanced at him and hesitated. "His grace," the butler informed her, "always partakes of a glass of sherry in the drawing room before supper."

Jordan glanced up when Alexandra walked into the drawing room, and he went over to the sideboard where he poured sherry into a glass for her. Alexandra watched his deft movements as he filled her glass, her gaze running over his tall, lithe frame while she tried to ignore how incredibly handsome he looked in a wine-colored coat that clung to his broad shoulders and grey trousers that emphasized his long, muscular legs. A single red ruby winked in the folds of the snowy neckcloth that contrasted sharply with his sun-bronzed face. Wordlessly he held the glass of sherry toward her.

Uncertain of his mood, Alexandra walked forward and took the glass from his outstretched hand. His first words made her long to pour the sherry over his head. "It is my custom," he informed her, like a teacher reprimanding a tardy student, "to have sherry in the drawing room at eight-thirty and supper at nine. In future, please join me here promptly at eight-thirty, Alexandra."

Fire ignited in Alexandra's eyes, but she managed to keep her voice level. "You've already told me where I may sleep, where I may go, who must accompany me, and when I must eat. Would you care to instruct me as to when I may breathe?"

Jordan's brows snapped together, then he leaned his head

330

back and sighed heavily. Reaching up in a gesture of frustration and uncertainty, he massaged the muscles at the back of his neck as if they were tense, then he dropped his hand. "Alexandra," he said, sounding both rueful and exasperated, "I meant to begin by apologizing for the way I treated you at the stable today. You were an hour late returning, and I was worried about you. I didn't intend to start our evening off now by reprimanding you or suffocating you with more rules. I'm not an ogre—" He broke off as Higgins tapped discreetly at the door, before carrying in a note on a silver tray.

Very slightly mollified by his apology, Alexandra sat on a velvet upholstered chair and idly glanced around the immense drawing room, noting the heavy baroque furniture upholstered in wine velvet that actually conveyed an almost oppressive splendor. *Oppressive splendor,* she thought, mentally chiding herself. Jordan's moody attitude about his home must be rubbing off on her.

Taking the note from the tray, Jordan sat down across from her and broke the seal, his eyes scanning the brief missive, his expression going from curiosity to disbelief to fury. "This is from Tony," he informed her, his grey eyes suddenly flinty, his jaw clenched so tight the bones of his face stood out. "It seems that he has decided to leave London in the midst of the Season and is even now in residence at his house not three miles from here."

The realization that her friend was now so close filled Alexandra with delight. Her face glowing with pleasure, Alexandra said, "I meant to call upon his mama and brother tomorrow—"

"I forbid you to go there," Jordan interrupted coolly. "I'll send Tony a note and explain that we wish to have the next few weeks entirely to ourselves." When she looked thoroughly mutinous, Jordan's voice became clipped: "Do you understand me, Alexandra? I *forbid* you to go there."

Slowly, Alexandra arose and Jordan stood too, towering over her. "Do you know," she breathed, staring up at him in dazed, quiet anger, as if he belonged in Bedlam, "I think you are quite mad."

Unexplainably, he smiled a little at that. "I don't doubt it," he said, unable to tell her Tony's return to the district now practically confirmed Fawkes' suspicions, and that her life was also likely to be in danger from him since she could, at this moment, be carrying the next Hawthorne heir. With quiet firmness, he added, "But I expect you to obey me, nonetheless."

Alexandra opened her mouth to tell him she didn't care a snap for his silly rules, but he pressed his finger to her lips, his smile widening. "The wager, Alexandra—you promised to be my *obedient* wife. You wouldn't want to forfeit this early in the game, would you?"

Alexandra gave him a look of well-bred disdain. "I'm in no danger of losing the bet, my lord. You've already lost it." Holding her glass, she walked over to the fireplace and pretended to inspect a fragile fourteenth-century vase.

"What's that supposed to mean?" Jordan asked, coming up silently behind her.

Alexandra ran a finger over the base of the priceless treasure. "Your part of the wager was to try to make yourself so agreeable to me that I would want to stay with you."

"And?"

"And," she replied with an arch glance at him over her shoulder, "you're failing."

She expected him to dismiss that with arrogant unconcern. Instead, he put his hands on her shoulders and turned her around to face him. "In that case," he said, gazing down at her with a solemn smile, "I shall have to try harder, shan't I?"

Caught unawares by the combination of gravity and tenderness in his expression, Alexandra let him kiss her, clinging to her sanity while his strong arms encircled her, drawing her against him, as he bent his head and his mouth captured hers. He kissed her long and lingeringly, tasting her lips as if truly savoring each moment.

When he finally dropped his arms many minutes later, Alexandra stared at him in speechless amazement. How could he be so impossibly tender one moment and so cold, withdrawn, and arbitrary the next, she wondered, staring up into his heavy-lidded, mesmerizing grey eyes. Her voice was quiet as she voiced the thought running through her mind. "I truly wish I understood you."

"What is it you don't understand?" Jordan asked, but he already knew.

"I'd like to know the real reason you ripped up at me at the stables today."

She expected him to dismiss the matter with a teasing remark or try to shrug it off, but he surprised her by doing neither. With quiet honesty he said, "Actually I gave you the real reason, but I left it for last."

"What?"

"My pride was hurt that you left me in the middle of the night," he admitted.

"*Your* pride was hurt," Alexandra repeated, gaping at him, "so you called *me* a dox—a bad name?"

Alexandra missed the glint of amusement in his eyes, and so it took a moment before she realized he was ridiculing himself, not her. "Naturally I did that," he admitted gravely. "Surely, you don't expect an intelligent grown man, who has fought bloody battles in two countries, to have the courage to look a woman in the eye and simply *ask* her in a calm, reasonable voice why she didn't want to spend the night with him?"

"Why not?" she uttered, perplexed, and then she laughed aloud as she realized what he was saying.

"Male ego," he admitted with a lopsided grin. "We'll go to any lengths to protect our egos, I fear."

"Thank you," Alexandra said gently, "for telling me the truth."

"That's the main reason why I tore into you. But I must admit there is something about this house that always puts me in a grim mood."

"But you grew up here!"

"And that," he said lightly as he took her arm and guided her into the drawing room, "is probably why I don't like it."

"What do you mean?" she blurted.

Jordan smiled down at her, but he shook his head. "A long time ago, in my grandmother's garden, you asked me to say what I feel and think, and I'm trying to do that. However, I'm not accustomed to baring my soul yet. We'll have to ease into it," he teased. "I'll answer your question someday."

Jordan had set out to "try harder to make himself agreeable" and during their meal he accomplished that goal with a resounding success that was devastating to Alexandra's peace of mind.

When they first married, she thought that he had tried to be pleasing to her, but his efforts were nothing compared to this. For two hours as they dined, he turned the full force of his devastating charm on her, teasing her with his flashing white smile and amusing her with scandalous, hilarious *on dits* about people she knew in London.

And afterward, he took her to his bed and made love to her with a passionate intensity so hot it should have forged them into one body and one soul. Then he held her in his arms against his heart throughout the night.

Accepting the basket of sweets she'd asked cook to prepare, Alexandra climbed into her carriage the next morning, determined to call upon Tony in blatant defiance of Jordan's orders. She tried to convince herself she wasn't falling in love with Jordan, that she was simply *curious* about Jordan's parents, but in her heart she knew that wasn't entirely true. She was dangerously close to losing her heart to him and desperately anxious to understand the enigmatic, compelling man she'd married. Tony was the only one she could turn to now who might be able to give her the answers she sought.

After informing Olsen, her appointed "personal groom," that she would not require his attendance to call upon the Wilkinsons, Alexandra set out on her way to the Wilkinsons' little cottage. When she finished her brief visit, she left and turned her horse toward Tony's house. Blissfully unaware of Olsen, who followed alertly behind her, keeping to the cover of the woods whenever possible, she sent her horse trotting down the country lane.

"Alexandra!" Tony exclaimed, grinning and holding out his hands to her as he strode from the house and down the short flight of steps to the narrow, tree-lined drive. "I gathered, from the note Jordan sent me this morning, that he meant to keep you exclusively to himself for the next few weeks."

"He doesn't know I've come," Alexandra said, hugging him warmly. "Will you swear to keep it a secret?"

"Of course. I give you my word," Tony promised with a solemn smile. "Come in and see my mother and Bertie—they'll be delighted to see you. They won't breathe a word of your visit," he reiterated when Alexandra hesitated.

"After we visit with them," Alexandra said quickly, "could we walk outside? I have something to ask you."

"Of course we can," Tony readily agreed.

Tucking her hand in the crook of his proffered arm, Alexandra walked to the open front door of the house. "I assume you left London because of the gossip about all of us," she said in a tone of apology.

"Partly, and also because I was dying to know how you're getting on. There's one more reason," he admitted with an odd grin. "Sally Farnsworth sent a note asking to see me yesterday in London."

The name of the girl he had admitted loving registered instantly on Alexandra. "And did she come to see you?" Alexandra asked eagerly, studying his handsome face.

"Yes."

"What did you say?—What did she do?" she burst out.

"She proposed," Tony admitted wryly.

Alexandra laughed with amazed delight. "And?"

"And I'm considering it," he teased. "No, really, she's coming for a visit next week. I want her to see firsthand what I have to offer her by way of a home and family. I'm no longer a duke, you know. When I was, I couldn't believe she wanted me for any other reason. Now I know she does, and I haven't much to offer. Don't mention it to my mother, though. I want to break the news of Sally's visit to her gently. My mother doesn't hold her in high regard because of what happened—before."

Alexandra agreed instantly and they went inside.

"My dear, it is so very good to see you!" Lady Townsende exclaimed in her soft, smiling voice as Tony escorted Alexandra into the cheerful little salon where Lady Townsende was sitting with Bertie, Tony's younger brother. "What a jolt we've received from our dear Jordan—returning from the dead as it were."

Alexandra acknowledged her greeting, worriedly noting how pale and thin Tony's white-haired mother looked. The shock of Jordan's return had obviously affected her fragile health.

Peering around Alex, Lady Townsende glanced hopefully toward the doorway. "Jordan didn't come with you?" she asked, her disappointment obvious.

"No, I—I'm sorry, he didn't. He—"

"He's working like a demon as usual, I've no doubt," Bertie said with a grin as he came awkwardly to his feet, leaning on the cane which he used to take the weight off his crippled left leg. "And determined to keep you all to himself so that you can renew your acquaintance after his long absence."

"He is working very hard," Alexandra said, grateful that Bertie had provided her with an excuse. At one inch over six feet, Bertie was slightly taller than Tony, with sandy hair and hazel eyes. Although he possessed the Townsende charm in full measure, the constant pain from the twisted leg he'd been born with had taken its toll on Bertie's face. Lines of strain were permanently etched beside his mouth, creating a permanent grimness in his features, a grimness that was not reflected in his cheerful personality.

"He wanted Alexandra to wait before calling on us, so that he could accompany her here," Tony improvised helpfully, addressing his mother and brother. "I've promised her we won't spoil Jordan's future visit by telling him that she's already come here to see us, and to tell us how he's faring."

"How *is* he faring?" Lady Townsende implored.

Uneasy with the fabrications she was being forced to participate in, Alexandra gladly spent the next ten minutes reciting every detail of Jordan's capture and imprisonment. When she had finally finished answering all of Lady Townsende's worried questions about his health, Tony stood up and invited Alexandra to accompany him for a stroll about the lawns.

"I can see from those tiny lines on your pretty forehead that something's amiss with you. What is it?" he asked as they walked across the small, neatly kept front lawn toward the gardens off to the right.

"I'm not certain," Alexandra admitted ruefully. "From the moment Hawthorne came into view, Jordan has been different somehow. Last night he told me he grew up at Hawthorne and because of that, the place always makes him feel 'grim.' But when I asked him why, he wouldn't tell me. And then yesterday, Smarth said the oddest things about Jordan's parents . . ." she continued, using her husband's given name for the first time since he returned. Turning to

336

Tony, she said abruptly, "What were his parents like? His boyhood?"

Tony's smile remained but he looked uneasy. "What difference does all that make?"

"It wouldn't make a *difference*," Alexandra burst out desperately, "if everyone didn't become so edgy when I asked those questions."

"Who have you been asking?"

"Well, Gibbons and Smarth."

"Good God!" Tony said, stopping short and staring at her in laughing dismay. "Don't let Jordan catch you. He disapproves of familiarity with servants. It's a family taboo," he added, "—although not in *my* branch of the family. We only have six servants, and it's impossible not to regard them rather as dependents."

Tony paused to bend down and pluck a rose growing in the small garden. "You should ask Jordan these questions."

"He won't tell me. A long time ago I told him I preferred truth to platitudes. Last night when I asked why he didn't like Hawthorne, he told me he's *trying* to learn to say what he thinks and feels, but that he isn't accustomed to baring his soul yet. He said we'd have to ease into that," she added with a faint smile as she remembered his teasing tone. "He promised to answer my question someday."

"My God," Tony uttered in amazement, staring at her. "Jordan said all that? He said he was willing to 'bare' his soul to you someday? He must care more for you than I ever imagined." Tucking the rose behind her ear, he chucked her under the chin.

"It's become a mystery I have to solve," Alexandra prodded, when Tony seemed disinclined to say more.

"Because you're falling in love with him?"

"Because I'm frightfully, inexcusably curious," Alexandra prevaricated, and when Tony appeared to refuse her request, she sighed miserably. "Very well. I'm afraid to fall in love with a stranger and he's in no hurry to let me know him."

Tony hesitated and then took pity on her. "Very well, since it isn't idle curiosity, I'll try to answer your questions. What do you want to know?"

Pulling the rose from behind her ear, Alexandra twirled

337

the stem absently between her fingers. "First of all, was there something wrong at Hawthorne when he was growing up? What was his boyhood like?"

"Amongst noble families," Tony began slowly, "'the heir' is generally singled out for special attention from his parents. In Jordan's case it was more pronounced because he also happened to be an only child. While I was allowed to climb trees and roll in the dirt, Jordan was required to remember his station at all times; to be clean, neat, punctual, solemn, and aware of his importance at every moment.

"His father and mother were in complete agreement on one thing, and that was the superiority of their rank. Unlike the sons of other nobles, who are allowed the company of children their own age who live on the estate—even if the children happen to be sons of the grooms—my aunt and uncle found it entirely unseemly for Jordan to associate with any but his own rank. Since fledgling dukes and earls are rather scarce, particularly in this part of the country, he grew up here in complete isolation."

Pausing for a moment, Tony gazed up at the treetops and sighed. "I used to wonder how he could bear the loneliness."

"But surely Jordan's parents didn't consider your company unacceptable?"

"No, they didn't, but I rarely visited him at Hawthorne unless my aunt and uncle were away. When they were in residence, I couldn't stand the stifling atmosphere of the place—it gave me the creeps. Besides, my uncle made it clear to me and to my parents that my presence at Hawthorne was not desired. They said I disrupted Jordan's studies and took his mind from serious matters. On those occasions when he was allowed time off, he preferred to come here, rather than have me come to Hawthorne because he adored my mother and he liked being with us." With a sad, whimsical smile, Tony finished, "When he was eight years old, he tried to trade me his inheritance for my family. He volunteered to let me be the marquess, if I'd live at Hawthorne."

"That's not at all as I imagined his life," Alexandra remarked when Tony fell silent. "When I was young, I thought it must be heavenly to be rich." She recalled her own childhood; the games she'd played with her friends, the lighthearted, carefree times, the warmth of her friendship with Mary Ellen and her family. She felt incredibly sad to know Jordan had evidently missed out on his own childhood.

"Not all children of noble families are raised with such rigidity."

"What about his parents—what were they like exactly?"

She was watching him with such earnest concern that Tony put his arm around her shoulders in a gesture of comfort and capitulation. "To sum it up as succinctly as possible, Jordan's mother was a notorious flirt whose amatory exploits were famous. My uncle didn't appear to care. He seemed to regard women as weak, amoral creatures who couldn't control their passions—or so he said. On the other hand, *he* was as promiscuous as she was. When it came to Jordan, however, he was positively rigid. He never let Jordan forget he was a Townsende and the next Duke of Hawthorne. He never let up on him. He insisted Jordan be smarter, braver, more dignified, and more worthy of the Townsende name than any Townsende before him, and the harder Jordan tried to please him, the more demanding his father became.

"If Jordan did poorly in a lesson, his tutor was instructed to cane him; if he didn't appear for supper on the dot of nine—not a minute before or a minute after—he was not allowed to eat until the following night. When he was eight or nine, he was already a better horseman than most men are, but on one particular hunt Jordan's horse refused a jump, either because Jordan was too little to force him to take it—or because Jordan was a little scared to try it. I'll never forget that day. Not one of the riders had dared that hedge with the creek on the other side of it, but my uncle rode up and called the entire hunt to a halt. With all of us looking on, he taunted Jordan with cowardice. Then he made him take the hedge."

"To think," Alexandra said in a suffocated voice, "I used to believe all children whose fathers lived with them were luckier than I. Did he . . . did he clear the hedge?"

"Three times," Tony said dryly. "On the fourth, his horse stumbled and when it fell, it rolled on Jordan and broke his arm."

Alexandra paled, but Tony was lost in his story now and

didn't notice. "Jordan didn't cry of course. Jordan wasn't permitted to cry, not even as a little boy. According to my uncle, tears were unmanly. He had very rigid ideas about things like that."

Alexandra turned her face up to the sun, blinking back the tears at the back of her eyes. "What sort of ideas?"

"He believed a man had to be hard and completely self-sufficient to truly be a man, and that was the way he raised Jordan to think. Any emotion that was 'soft' was unmanly, and therefore abhorrent. Sentimentality was soft —unmanly; so was love and genuine affection. Anything at all that showed a male to be 'vulnerable' was unmanly. My uncle disapproved of all forms of frivolity, too, with the exception of dalliances with the opposite sex, which my uncle viewed as the epitome of manliness. I don't think I ever saw the man laugh—not a real, genuine laugh that sprang from mirth, rather than sarcasm. For that matter, I've rarely seen Jordan laugh. To work and to excel at whatever one did was all that mattered to my uncle—a very peculiar attitude for a nobleman as you've undoubtedly gathered."

"I make him laugh," Alexandra said with a mixture of pride and sadness.

Tony grinned. "That smile of yours would lighten any man's heart."

"No wonder he didn't want to talk about his boyhood."

"Some good things came of my uncle's determination to make Jordan excel at whatever he did."

"What sort of things?" Alexandra asked with disbelief.

"Well, for example, Jordan was forced to excel at his studies, and by the time we went to university, he was so far ahead of everyone that he was given private courses in subjects the rest of us couldn't fathom. Moreover, he obviously found ways to put all his learning to excellent use, because when Jordan's father died, Jordan was only twenty. He inherited eleven estates along with his title, but the Townsende coffers had never been very full, and Hawthorne was the only one of his estates that was well kept-up. Within three years, every one of Jordan's estates were prospering, and he was well on his way to becoming one of the richest men in Europe. Not a mean accomplishment for a young man of twenty-three. Beyond that, there's little else I could tell you about him."

Overwhelmed with gratitude, Alexandra reached up and hugged Tony tightly. Leaning back in his arms, she smiled a little shakily. "Thank you," she said simply, her eyes glowing with fondness, then she glanced apprehensively at the sun. "I can't stay any longer. I said I'd only be gone an hour and it's more than that already."

"What will happen if you're gone longer?" Tony teased, but he looked puzzled.

"I'll be found out."

"So?"

"So I'll lose the wager I made with Jordan."

"What wager?"

Alexandra started to explain, but tenderness and loyalty to her proud, dominating husband were already stirring to vibrant life within her, and she couldn't bear to shame Jordan by telling his cousin that the only reason she had agreed to come to Hawthorne was because Jordan had virtually bribed her to do it. "Just a . . . a foolish bet we have between us," she hedged as Tony handed her up into her carriage.

Lost in thought, Alexandra drove right past the footman who ran out of the great house to take the reins, and continued down to the stables which were situated behind and off to the side of the mansion. Tony's disclosures about Jordan's boyhood at Hawthorne whirled through her mind, stabbing at her heart and filling her with compassion. Now she understood so many things about Jordan that had puzzled and angered and hurt her, including the subtle change in him since their arrival at Hawthorne. To think she had actually believed, when she was a girl, that happiness was simply a matter of having both parents at home with one. Her grandfather had been right again, she realized, for he had repeatedly said that no one is ever quite what they seem.

So absorbed was she in her thoughts that she said nothing to Smarth when she drew up at the stables and he rushed out to assist her down from the carriage. Instead, she simply looked at him as if he didn't exist, then she turned and started toward the house.

Smarth incorrectly assumed his mistress was looking right through him because he had forfeited her trust and affection by refusing to discuss his master with her. "My lady!" Smarth said, looking both wounded by her unintentional snub, and extremely apprehensive as well.

Alexandra turned and glanced at him, but in her mind she was seeing a little boy who had never been permitted to be one.

"Please, my lady," Smarth said wretchedly, "don't look at me like I hurt ye beyond fixin'." Dropping his voice, he nodded toward the fence where two colts were frisking about, kicking up their heels. "If ye'd walk over t' the fence wit me, I've somethin' to tell ye that ye'll want to know."

With an effort, Alexandra made herself concentrate on the unhappy footman, and she did as he asked.

Staring fixedly at the horses, Smarth lowered his voice and said, "Me 'n' Gibbons talked it over, and we decided that ye've a right to know why the master is the way he is. He's not a harsh man, my lady, but from what I hear is a-goin' on atween the two o' you since the master came back, yer bound to get the idea he's hard as a rock."

Alexandra opened her mouth to tell the apprehensive servant that he need not betray his knowledge, but his next words floored her: "Th' other reason we decided to tell you is 'cause the way we heerd it, you ain't here at Hawthorne to stay and be his wife—except fer three months, that is."

"How on earth—?" Alexandra burst out.

"Servants' grapevine, my lady," Smarth averred with a touch of pride. "Hawthorne has the best in England, I'll vow. Why, the staff knows what's happenin' within twenty minutes of it takin' place—unless o' course Mr. Higgins or Mrs. Brimley the housekeeper are the only ones to hear of it. Their mouths are tight as virg—They don't tell nobody nothin'," he amended, turning scarlet.

"That must be extremely vexatious for you," Alexandra said dryly, when Smarth flushed deeper.

He shifted from one foot to the other, shoved his hands in his pockets, took them out again and looked at her in helpless dismay, his weathered face creased with unhappiness. "You wanted me ter tell you 'bout his grace's parents, and me 'n' Gibbons agreed we cain't deny yer command. Besides, ye've a right t' know." And in a voice low and uneasy, Smarth related very nearly the same general history that Tony had told her.

"And now you know what it's been like around here fer all these years," Smarth finished, "me 'n' Gibbons is hopin' you'll stay here and bring laughter to th' place, th' way you did when you was here afore."

"*Real* laughter," Smarth clarified. "Not the kind what comes from the mouth—the kind what comes from the heart like you gived us afore. The master ain't never heard the sound o' it at Hawthorne, and it would do him a world a good, specially if you could git him ter join in wit it."

Everything Alexandra had learned today revolved in her head like a dizzying kaleidoscope, turning and changing shape, taking on new dimensions throughout the rest of the day and long after Jordan had pulled her to him and fallen asleep.

The sky was already lightening, and still she lay awake, staring at the ceiling, hesitating to take a course of action that could—and undoubtedly would—make her vulnerable to Jordan once again. Until now, she'd made leaving here her goal; and, in line with that, she'd kept her every emotion and every action in careful check.

She turned onto her side and Jordan's arm encircled her, drawing her back against his chest and the backs of her legs against his own while he buried his face in her hair. His hand lifted, cupping her breast in a sleepy caress and sending a tremor of delight through her entire body.

She wanted him, Alexandra realized with a despondent inner sigh. Despite everything he had been—a libertine, a heartless flirt, and an unwilling husband—she wanted him. In the safe silence of her heart, she was finally willing to admit that to herself now . . . because *now* she realized that he was more than just a spoiled, shallow aristocrat.

She wanted his love, his trust, and his children. She wanted to make this house ring with laughter for him, and to make Hawthorne seem beautiful to him. She wanted to make the entire world beautiful for him.

Tony, the dowager duchess, and even Melanie had all believed she could make Jordan fall in love with her. She couldn't give up without trying, she knew that now.

But she didn't know how she was going to endure it if she failed.

Chapter Twenty-Six

M Y LORD?" she whispered at dawn the next morning.

Jordan opened one sleepy eye and beheld his wife looking bright and alert as she sat down on his bed beside his hip. "Good morning," he murmured, his appreciative gaze shifting to the V of tantalizing flesh exposed by the bodice of her belted silk dressing gown. "What time is it?" he asked, his voice husky with sleep. He glanced toward the windows and realized the sky was not blue, but a weak shade of grey streaked with pale pink.

Unlike Jordan, Alexandra had been awake all night and was therefore not suffering from any foggy remnants of drowsiness. "Six o'clock," she answered brightly.

"You're joking!" he uttered. Appalled by the early hour, he promptly closed his eyes and required an explanation for being awakened at dawn: "Is someone ill?"

"No."

"Dead?"

"No."

A faint smile tugged at his firm lips and creased the sides of his closed eyes as he mumbled, "Illness or death are the only acceptable reasons for a rational human to be awake this early in the morning. Come back to bed."

Alexandra chuckled at his lighthearted, sleepy banter, but she shook her head. "No."

Despite his closed eyes and apparent sleepiness, Jordan had already registered the unusually bright smile on his wife's face, as well as the fact that her hip was pressing against his thigh. Normally, Alexandra's smiles were reserved, not relaxed, and she scrupulously avoided touching him whenever possible, unless he was making love to her.

Curiosity over the reason for her very pleasant, but very unusual behavior this morning made him open his eyes and look at her. With her hair tumbling over her shoulders and her skin glowing with health, she looked delicious. She also looked like she had something on her mind. "Well?" he said lightly, restraining the urge to pull her down on top of him. "I am, as you can see, awake."

"Good," she said, hiding her uncertainty behind a vivacious smile, "because there's something special I'd like to do this morning."

"At this hour?" Jordan teased. "What *is* there to do, save to sneak out to the road, pounce on an unwary traveler, and steal his purse. Only thieves and servants are about now."

"We don't have to leave for a while yet." Alexandra hedged as her courage began to ebb, and she braced for his refusal. "And if you'll recall, you *did* say you wanted to make yourself agreeable to me—"

"What is it you'd like to do?" Jordan asked with a sigh, mentally considering the usual things women tried to get men to do with them.

"Guess."

"You want me to take you shopping for a new bonnet in the village?" he ventured unenthusiastically.

She shook her head, sending her hair tumbling over her left shoulder and breast.

"You want to ride out early to see the sun rise over the hills so you can sketch the view?"

"I can't draw a straight line," Alexandra confessed. Drawing a shaky breath, she summoned all her courage and announced, "I want to go fishing!"

"Fishing?" Jordan repeated, gaping at her as if she'd taken leave of her senses. "You want me to to go fishing at this hour of the morning?" Before she could answer, he shoved his head deeper into the pillows and firmly closed his eyes, apparently rejecting the idea—but there was a smile in his voice as he said, "Not unless there wasn't a scrap of food to eat and we were both prostrate from starvation."

346

Encouraged by his tone, if not his words, she cajoled, "You wouldn't have to spend your time teaching me the proper technique—I already know how to fish."

He opened one eye, his voice amused. "What makes you think *I* do?"

"If you don't know how, I'll show you."

"Thank you, but I can manage on my own," he said with asperity, studying her intently.

"Good," Alexandra said, so relieved she was almost babbling. "So can I. I can do everything for myself, including put my own worm on my own hook—"

His lips quirked in a smile. "Excellent, then *you* can bait *my* hook. I refuse to awaken helpless worms at this ungodly hour and then compound the crime by torturing them."

His humor was so contagious that a gurgle of laughter escaped Alexandra as she stood up and tightened the belt on her rosesilk dressing robe. "I'll take care of all the arrangements," she said happily and headed for her bedchamber.

Leaning back against the pillows, Jordan admired the unconsciously seductive sway of her hips as she walked away, while he fought down the urge to summon her back to his bed and spend the next hour in the delightful—and laudable—occupation of siring his heir. He did not want to go fishing. Nor did he understand why *she* did, but he was certain there was a reason for it, and he was curious to discover what it was.

Alexandra had indeed taken "care of all the arrangements," he realized when they wended their way on horseback down the opposite side of the high ridge that blocked the house from view of a wide, rushing stream.

Tying their horses to a pair of trees at the base of the ridge, he walked beside her down to the grassy banks of the stream, where a bright blue blanket had been spread out beneath a giant oak tree. "What's all that?" he asked, indicating the two large baskets and one small one beside the blanket.

"Breakfast," Alexandra replied, shooting him a laughing glance. "And dinner, too, from the looks of it. Evidently, cook doesn't have much faith in your ability to catch our meal."

"In any case, I haven't more than an hour to spend trying."

Alexandra paused in the act of picking up a fishing pole, her face confused and disappointed. "An hour?"

"I have a dozen things to do today," Jordan replied. Crouching down, he selected a pole from the ones brought out earlier by the servants and tested its flexibility by bending it between his hands. "I'm a very busy man, Alexandra," he added absently, by way of explanation.

"You're also a very wealthy man," she answered, affecting an offhand attitude as she tested her own pole. "So why must you work so hard all the time?"

He thought for a moment and chuckled. "So I can remain a very wealthy man."

"If being wealthy costs you the right to relax and enjoy life, then the price of wealth is altogether too high," she said, pivoting on her heels and looking at him.

His brow furrowed in thought, Jordan tried to recall the philosopher who authored that quotation, and couldn't. "Who said that?"

She gave him a plucky smile. *"I* did."

Jordan shook his head in silent amazement at her quick mind as he put a worm on his hook, then walked over to the bank. Sitting down beside a huge fallen tree with its branches stretching out over the water, he cast his line in.

"That's not the best place to catch the big ones," his wife advised him with an air of vast superiority as she came up behind him. "Would you hold my pole for me, please?"

"I thought you said you could do everything for yourself," he teased, noticing she'd taken off her riding boots and stockings. Before he could guess what she was about, Alexandra hitched up her skirts, displaying a pair of slim calves, trim ankles, and small bare feet, then she scampered up onto the wide trunk of the fallen tree with the agile grace of a gazelle. "Thank you," she said, reaching for her pole.

He handed it to her, expecting her to sit down where she stood, but to his alarmed surprise, she walked out along a thick branch hanging above the rushing water, balancing like an acrobat. "Come back here!" Jordan said sharply, raising his voice in alarm. "You could fall in."

"I swim like a fish," she informed him, grinning over her shoulder, and then she sat down—a barefoot duchess with her shapely legs dangling over the water and sunlight shining in her hair. "I've been fishing since I was a girl," she said conversationally as she cast her line into the stream.

Jordan nodded. "Penrose taught you." He had taught her well, Jordan thought with an inward smile, for true to her boast, she'd reached into the basket of worms the servants had brought out to the stream and had deftly put a worm on the end of her hook.

Evidently their thoughts were running in the same direction, because a moment later she smiled down at him from her high perch and remarked, "I'm happy to see you aren't truly squeamish about worms."

"I was never squeamish," he protested with an expression of earnest gravity on his upturned face. "It's only that I hate to hear the sound worms make when you stick them the first time. Normally we kill things before we use them for bait. That's more humane, don't you agree?"

"There is no sound!" Alexandra denied heatedly, but he looked so certain that her own conviction wavered a bit.

"Only people with extraordinary hearing can detect it, but it's there," Jordan argued, straightfaced.

"Penrose told me it doesn't hurt them," she said uneasily.

"Penrose is deaf as a post. He can't hear them scream."

An indescribable expression of queasy apprehension crossed Alexandra's face as she looked at the pole in her hand. Swiftly turning his face away to hide his laughter, Jordan gazed off to his right, but he couldn't stop his shoulders from shaking with mirth, and Alexandra finally spotted the telltale movement. A moment later, a fistful of twigs and leaves hit him on the left shoulder. "Beast!" she said cheerfully from above.

"My dear, foolish wife," he replied, grinning impenitently as he reached up and calmly brushed leaves and twigs off his sleeve, "were I perched precariously over the water on the limb of a tree, as you are, I'd take great care to treat me with more respect." To illustrate, he reached up with his free hand and gently nudged the stout limb she was perched upon.

His disrespectful wife lifted her graceful brows. "My dear, foolish husband," she softly replied, sending a momentary shaft of unexpected pleasure through Jordan, "if you unseat me, you'll be making a terrible mistake *and* setting yourself up for a wetting in the process."

"Me?" he said, enjoying their banter. "Why?"

"Because," she quietly and earnestly replied, "I can't swim."

Jordan paled and surged to his feet. "Don't, for God's sake," he ordered sharply, "move *one inch*. I don't know how deep the water is below you, but it's deep enough to drown in and it's murky enough to prevent me from seeing you below the surface. Stay where you are until I get there."

With the lithe agility of an athlete, he bounded onto the tree trunk and began walking toward her, moving out along the branch until she was within arm's reach. "Alexandra," he said, speaking in a calm, reassuring voice, "if I come any closer, my weight may break this branch or bend it enough to throw you into the water."

He edged another few inches closer to her and bent at the waist, extending his hand toward her. "Don't be afraid. Just reach out and clasp my hand."

For once she didn't argue, Jordan noted with relief. Instead she reached up with her left hand and tightly grasped the limb above her head for balance, then she extended her right hand to his, catching his wrist in a strong grasp, at the same time Jordan's fingers closed tightly around her wrist. "Now get your legs beneath you and stand up. Use my wrist for leverage."

"I'd rather not," she replied. His amazed gaze narrowed sharply on her laughing face, while she tightened her grasp on his wrist and threateningly said, "I'd rather swim, wouldn't you?"

"Don't try it," Jordan warned darkly, unable to free his wrist. In his awkward position, bent at the waist and his arm imprisoned, he was completely at the mercy of her whim and they both knew it.

"If you can't swim, I'll rescue you," she sweetly volunteered.

"Alexandra," he threatened in a soft, ominous tone, "if you toss me into that freezing water, you'd better swim for your life in the opposite direction."

He meant it and she knew it. "Yes, my lord," she meekly replied and obediently released his wrist.

Jordan straightened slowly and stood looking down at her with an expression of exasperation and amusement. "You are the most outrageous—" He broke off, unable to control his grin.

"Thank you," she replied brightly. "Predictability is so very dull, don't you agree?" she called after him as he turned and walked along the branch, then jumped down to the grass.

"How would I know?" he replied with grim amusement as he stretched out on the grassy bank and picked up his pole. "I haven't had a predictable hour since I set eyes on you."

The next three hours passed as if they were but a few minutes, and by the end of it, Jordan had confirmed she was not only an excellent fisherman, but a thoroughly delightful, witty, and intelligent companion as well.

"Look!" she called suddenly and unnecessarily as Jordan's pole bent nearly in half, almost jerking him to his feet as he fought to hold it. "You have a bite—!"

After five minutes of the most deft maneuvering and skillful fighting on Jordan's part, his line abruptly went slack. His disrespectful young wife, standing upon her tree limb, from whence she had observed his unsuccessful struggle for supremacy while calling out advice and encouragement, groaned and threw up her hands in disgust. "You lost the fish!"

"That was not a fish," Jordan retorted, looking up at her. "That was a whale with large teeth."

"Only because it got away," she retorted, laughing.

Her laughter was as infectious as her enthusiasm, and Jordan couldn't stop himself from grinning even though he tried to sound stern. "Kindly stop belittling my whale and let's open those baskets. I'm starved."

Standing back, he watched in admiration as she scampered down from the fallen limb. When she tried to hand him her pole and climb down herself, he caught her by the waist and lowered her to the ground, but she stiffened when her body brushed against his, and he abruptly let her go.

The pleasure he had taken in their morning faded somewhat at her reaction to his touch. Sitting down across from her on the blanket, he leaned his back against a tree and studied her in impassive silence, watching her unpack the baskets of food while he tried to guess her motive for instigating this outing. Obviously, she'd not wanted it to be a "romantic interlude."

"It's been a lovely morning," Alexandra said, pausing to watch the sunlight dance on the water's surface in front of them.

Drawing one knee up against his chest, Jordan draped his arm across it and said flatly, "Now that we've finished, suppose you tell me what this is all about."

Alexandra tore her gaze from the water and looked at him. "What do you mean?"

"I mean, why did you want to spend the morning like this?"

She'd expected him to wonder, she had *not* expected him to flatly demand an answer, and she wasn't at all prepared with one. With a shrug, she said uneasily, "I thought I'd show you the sort of life I truly like to lead."

Cynicism twisted his lips. "And now that you've shown me that you're not completely the refined, elegant young woman you've appeared to be, I'm supposed to develop a disgust for you and let you go back to Morsham, is that it?"

That was so far from the truth that Alexandra burst out laughing. "I'd never have conceived such a convoluted plan in a hundred years," she said, looking nonetheless impressed at the ingenuity of it. "I'm afraid I'm not quite that inventive." For a split second, Alexandra could have sworn she saw relief flicker in his hooded grey eyes, and she was suddenly determined to recover the companionable, easy mood they'd enjoyed while fishing together. "You don't believe me, do you?"

"I'm not certain."

"Have I ever done anything to make you think I'm devious?"

"Your sex is not noted for being either forthright or frank," he replied dryly.

"The fault for that must be laid at the door of men," she teased, flopping down on her back and resting her head on her arm as she stared up at the fluffy white clouds drifting across the powder-blue sky. Men couldn't endure it if we were forthright and frank."

"Is that right?" he retorted, stretching out beside her, propped up on his elbow.

Nodding, she turned her head and looked at him. "If

352

women were forthright and blunt, we wouldn't have been able to convince men that they are smarter, wiser, and braver than we are, when in truth you are superior to us only in the brute strength occasionally required to lift extremely heavy objects."

"Alexandra," he whispered, as his lips slowly descended to hers, "beware of shattering a man's ego. It forces him to show his supremacy in the time-honored way."

The huskiness of his voice, combined with the seductive languor in his grey eyes, was already making Alexandra's heart hammer. Longing to put her arms around his broad shoulders and bring him down to her, she asked shakily, "Have I shattered your ego?"

"Yes."

"Be-because I said women are smarter, wiser, and braver than men?"

"No," he whispered, his smiling lips almost touching hers now, "because you caught a bigger *fish* than I did."

Her startled giggle was abruptly smothered by his lips.

Feeling utterly languid and thoroughly content, Jordan decided to forestall their lovemaking for a few minutes, and after allowing himself a long, hungry kiss, he lay back beside her.

She looked a little surprised and a little disappointed that he hadn't continued.

"Later," he promised with a lazy grin that made her blush and smile and then hastily avert her gaze. After a minute she seemed to become fascinated with something in the sky.

"What are you looking at?" Jordan demanded finally, watching her.

"A dragon." When he looked bewildered she lifted her arm and pointed to the sky in the southeast. "Right there—that cloud—what do *you* see when you look at it?"

"A fat cloud."

Alexandra rolled her eyes at him. "What *else* do you see?"

He was quiet for a moment studying the sky. "Five more fat clouds and three thin ones." To Jordan's surprised pleasure, she burst out laughing, rolled onto her side, and kissed him full on the mouth, but when he tried to hold her tighter and begin to make love to her, Alexandra drew back and insisted on resuming her study of the sky.

"Have you no imagination at all?" she chided softly.

"Look at those clouds—surely you must see *one* that reminds you of something. It can be something whimsical or real."

Goaded by her insinuation that he possessed no imagination, Jordan narrowed his eyes and stared hard—and then he finally discerned a shape he recognized. Off in the sky, on the right, there was a cloud that looked remarkably like, exactly like—breasts! No sooner did he recognize the shape than Alexandra excitedly asked, "What do you see?" and Jordan's whole body shook with silent laughter.

"I'm thinking," he said quickly. In his haste to come up with some acceptable shape to tell her, he suddenly found one. "A swan," he said, and then almost in awe, "I see a swan."

The study of cloud formations, Jordan soon realized, was an unexpectedly pleasurable pastime—particularly with Alexandra's hand clasped in his, and her body pressed against his side. A few minutes later, however, the combined distraction of her nearness and the scent of her delicate perfume became too potent to ignore. Leaning upon his forearm, Jordan braced his other arm on the opposite side of her, then he slowly lowered his mouth to hers. Her response to his first kiss was so warm and eager that Jordan felt as if his heart was melting. Pulling his lips from hers, he gazed down at her lovely face, feeling humbled by her gentleness and warmth. "Have I ever told you," he whispered solemnly, "how sweet I think you are?"

Before she could answer, he kissed her with all the hungry urgency he felt.

It was midafternoon when they rode back to the stables. Unaware of the surreptitious glances of Smarth and the two dozen stablekeeps and grooms, who were all avidly curious about the outcome of the morning's jaunt, Alexandra put her hands on Jordan's broad shoulders, smiling into his eyes as he reached up to lift her down from her sidesaddle.

"Thank you for a lovely day," she said as he slowly lowered her to the ground.

"You're welcome," he replied, his hands lingering unnecessarily at her waist, keeping her body only inches from his.

"Would you like to do it again?" she offered, thinking of their fishing.

Jordan's chuckle was rich and deep. "Again," he promised huskily, thinking of their lovemaking. "And again . . . and again . . ."

Alexandra's smooth cheeks turned as pink as roses, but an answering sparkle lit her eyes. "I meant would you like to go *fishing* again?"

"Will you let me catch the biggest fish next time?"

"Certainly not," she said, her face glowing with merriment, "but I suppose I'd be willing to vouch for you if you want to tell everyone about the whale *you* caught that got away."

Jordan threw back his head and shouted with laughter.

The sound of his mirth echoed through the stables where Smarth was standing at a window beside one of the grooms, watching the duke and his young duchess. "Told ye she could do it!" Smarth said, nudging the groom and winking. "Told ye she'd make him happier 'n he's ever been afore!" Humming cheerfully, he picked up a brush and began to groom a chestnut stallion.

John Coachman paused in the act of polishing the silver-trimmed harness to study the pair of lovers, then he bent his head to his task again, but now he began to whistle a happy little melody between his teeth.

A stablekeep laid down his pitchfork and watched the duke and duchess, then he, too, began to whistle as he reached for another bundle of hay.

Putting his hand beneath Alexandra's elbow, Jordan started to escort her back to the house, then he stopped abruptly and turned as the stableyard seemed to fill with tuneless, discordant melodies being hummed and whistled by servants going about their tasks with jaunty vigor.

"Is something wrong?" Alexandra asked, following his glance.

A slight, puzzled frown creased his forehead, then he shrugged, unable to discern exactly what had caught his attention. "No," he said, guiding her back to the house. "But I've lazed away most of the day, and I'll have to work twice as hard today and tomorrow to make up for it."

Disappointed, but still determined, Alexandra said brightly, "In that case, I won't try to corrupt you with amusing distractions—until the day after that."

"What sort of distraction do you have in mind?" Jordan asked, grinning.

"A picnic."

"I suppose I could find time for that."

"Sit down, Fawkes, I'll be with you in a few minutes," Jordan said later that afternoon without bothering to look up from the letter he was reading from his London business agent.

Undaunted by his client's discourtesy—which he correctly attributed to the duke's understandable annoyance at needing his services—the investigator, who was masquerading as an assistant bailiff while at Hawthorne, sat down across from Jordan's massive desk.

Several minutes later, the duke tossed down his quill, leaned back in his chair, and abruptly demanded, "Well, what is it?"

"Your grace," Fawkes began briskly, "when you gave me Lord Anthony's note last evening, did you not tell me that you'd instructed your wife not to visit him?"

"I did."

"And you're certain she heard and understood your wishes?"

"Perfectly certain."

"You made them very clear?"

Expelling his breath in an irritated rush, Jordan clipped, "Impeccably clear."

The first sign of uneasiness and concern tightened Fawkes' face into a mild frown, then he quickly recovered and said in a brisk, impersonal voice, "Late yesterday afternoon, your wife went down to the stables and asked for a carriage. She told my man, Olsen, that she was merely going to visit a cottage on the estate, and would therefore not require his services. As we agreed last night, after learning Lord Anthony had mysteriously decided to return to Winslow, Olsen followed your wife, staying well out of sight, so as to be able to protect her without alarming her."

Fawkes paused and then said meaningfully, "After paying a brief visit to one of your cottagers, your wife went directly to Lord Anthony's house. In light of what transpired while she was there, I find this incident disturbing and possibly even suspect."

Jordan's dark brows snapped together over frigid grey eyes. "I fail to see why *you* should be 'disturbed' by it," Jordan said in a cutting voice. "She ignored my orders, which is *my* problem, not yours. It is not, however, cause to suspect her of any . . ." He trailed off, unable to voice the word.

"Complicity?" Fawkes provided quietly. "Perhaps not—at least not yet. My men, who have been watching Lord Anthony's house to spot any suspicious strangers who might call there, tell me that Lord Anthony's brother and mother were both inside the house. However, I must inform you that your wife spent little time in the house visiting with them. After approximately a quarter of an hour, Lord Anthony and your wife left the house together and went into the garden at the side of the house, out of sight of the occupants of the house. They then carried on a private conversation which Olsen could not hear, but which appeared to him to be of an extremely intense nature—judging from their expressions and mannerisms."

The investigator's gaze shifted from Jordan's unreadable face to a point upon the far wall. "While they were in the garden they embraced and kissed one another. Twice."

Pain, suspicion, and doubt blazed through Jordan's brain like hot axes as he envisioned Alexandra wrapped in Tony's arms . . . his mouth on hers . . . his hands . . .

"But not for a prolonged period of time," Fawkes said in the taut silence.

Drawing a long, steadying breath, Jordan briefly closed his eyes. When he spoke, his voice was calm, cold, and hardened with implacable conviction. "My wife and my cousin are related by marriage. They are, moreover, friends. Since she does not know my cousin is suspected of trying to assassinate me—or that her life may also be in danger from the same assassin—she undoubtedly felt my restriction against her visiting my cousin was unjust and unreasonable and she chose to disregard my orders."

"Your wife flagrantly ignores your wishes, yet you don't find that, er . . . suspicious? Or at least odd, your grace?"

"I find it infuriating, not 'suspicious,'" he replied with biting sarcasm, "and it is anything but 'odd.' My wife has been doing as she damned well pleases since she was a child.

It's an unpleasant habit of which I intend to break her, but it does not make her a willing accomplice to an assassin."

Realizing that it was pointless to argue the issue any further, Fawkes nodded politely and reluctantly stood up. He turned to leave, but his employer's icy voice made him halt and turn back.

"In the future, Fawkes," Jordan ordered tightly, "instruct your men to keep their backs to my wife and me when we are out of the house. They're supposed to be looking for a possible assassin, not spying on us."

"S-spying on you," Fawkes stuttered in dismay.

Jordan nodded curtly. "On the way back today, I saw two of your men in the woods. They were watching my wife, not watching for an assassin among the trees. Get rid of them."

"There must be some mistake, your grace. My men are highly trained, professional—"

"Get rid of them!"

"As you wish," he agreed, bowing.

"Also, when I am with my wife, you can tell your people to keep their distance. If they're doing their jobs, we should be able to wander about the grounds without fear of danger. I will not sacrifice our privacy, nor will I be forced to hide inside my house day and night. When I'm with my wife, I'll look out for her myself."

"Your grace," Fawkes said, holding out his hands in a gesture of conciliation, "I know from years of experience that situations like this are trying, to put it mildly, particularly to men of your station. But I would be remiss in my duty if I didn't tell you that Lord Townsende's unprecedented decision to return to his home at this time of the year makes him a prime suspect. Furthermore, my men and I are only trying to protect your wife—"

"For which I am paying you a fortune!" Jordan interrupted acidly. "Therefore, you can damn well do it my way."

. Fawkes, who was no stranger to the unfair demands the nobility were accustomed to making upon all those around them, nodded resignedly. "We shall try, your grace."

"And I'll countenance no more of your groundless suspicions about my wife."

Fawkes bowed again and left. But when the study doors

closed behind him, the resolve, the absolute certainty slowly drained from Jordan's hard face. Shoving his hands in his pockets, he leaned his head back against his chair and closed his eyes, trying to block out the words Fawkes had spoken, but they pounded in his brain like a thousand vicious hammers. *Lord Townsende's unprecedented return makes him a prime suspect. . . . Your wife and Lord Townsende went for a stroll and carried on an intense conversation. . . . They embraced and kissed one another. . . . I find their actions suspect . . .*

A silent shout of denial in Jordan's brain drowned out the investigator's words, and he lurched forward in his chair, shaking his head as if to clear it. This was madness! It was hard enough to face the fact that Tony, whom he loved like a brother, was probably trying to kill him. But he would not allow himself to think for another moment that Alexandra was also betraying him. The artless, enchanting young beauty who had teased and laughed with him today and then clasped him to her while he made love to her, was not secretly lusting after Tony, he told himself furiously. Such an idea was insane! Obscene!

He refused to believe it.

Because he couldn't bear to believe it.

A ragged sigh escaped Jordan as he faced the truth. From the moment she had hurtled into his life, Alexandra had stolen his heart. As a girl, she had enchanted and amused him. As a woman, she delighted, infuriated, enticed, and intrigued him. But no matter what she did, her smile warmed him, her touch heated his blood, and her musical laughter made his spirits soar.

Even now, beset by jealousy and plagued by doubt, he smiled when he thought of the way she had looked this morning, seated upon a tree limb with the sunlight glinting in her hair and her long, bare legs exposed to his view.

In a ball gown, she was elegant and serene as a goddess; in his bed, she was as unconsciously provocative as the most exotic temptress; and seated on a blanket with her bare legs curled beneath her and her gorgeous hair blowing in the wind, she was still every inch a duchess.

A barefoot duchess. *His* barefoot duchess, Jordan thought possessively. She was his by the law of God and man.

Picking up his quill, Jordan determinedly threw himself into his work, blocking out everything else on his mind. But for the first time in his life, he could not completely lose himself in it.

Nor could he entirely forget that Alexandra had lied to him about her whereabouts yesterday.

Chapter Twenty-Seven

SUNLIGHT STREAMED THROUGH the single high window of the austere room where Jordan had once learned his lessons under the harsh threat of a cane. Smoothing a wisp of hair back into her neat chignon, Alexandra studied the titles of the books which filled the low bookcases that ran the full length of one long wall, searching for primers she could use to teach elementary reading skills to the children who would soon be assembling in the gamekeeper's cottage.

Awe and admiration filled her as she gazed at the titles and began fully to realize the scope and depth of the knowledge Jordan must possess. There were thick leatherbound volumes containing the words of Plato, Socrates, Plutarch, as well as dozens of lesser-known philosophers, whose names Alexandra scarcely recognized. There were entire sections on architecture, on every period of European history and the lives and accomplishments of every European ruler. Some were written in English; others in Latin, Greek, and French. Mathematics must have been a special interest of Jordan's, for there was a mind-boggling array of books on that specific subject, many of them with titles so complicated that Alexandra could only guess what they referred to. Geography books, books by explorers, books on ancient cultures; every subject her grandfather had ever mentioned seemed to be represented here and in great depth.

Smiling slightly, Alexandra came to the end of the last

case, and there on the bottom shelf were the reading primers she sought. Bending down, she selected two that would do for a start. With the books and a slate cradled in one arm, she walked slowly across the wooden floor, sensing the same peculiar combination of sentimentality and depression she'd felt the first time she entered this unwelcoming room more than a year ago.

How *could* he have spent years up here in this lonely place, she wondered. Her own lessons had been learned in a sunny room, or outdoors in the sunshine, she remembered fondly—taught by her grandfather who found peace and delight in knowledge—and who had instilled in her that same joy while he taught her.

Pausing at the desk that faced the tutor's larger one, Alexandra gazed down at the initials carved on the top and lovingly traced each one with a fingertip: J.A.M.T.

The first time she had seen those initials she had believed Jordan was dead, and she remembered the desolation she had felt that day and during the months that followed. But now, this very moment, he was downstairs, working in his study—alive and vital and handsome. Instead of lying in a watery grave, Jordan was seated at his desk, wearing a snowy-white shirt that set off his tanned face and clung to his broad shoulders and buff-colored riding breeches that emphasized his long, muscular legs and thighs.

He was alive and healthy and here with her, exactly as she had once prayed and dreamed he would be. God had truly answered her prayers, she realized, and the knowledge suddenly filled her with a piercing sweetness and profound gratitude. He had sent Jordan back to her and even helped her begin to understand the gentle, autocratic, tender, brilliant, sometimes cynical man she loved.

Her mind absorbed with her thoughts, Alexandra walked slowly to the door, but as she pulled it closed, there was a loud clatter and the sound of something rolling across the wooden floor. Realizing that she had dislodged something that had been leaning against the doorframe, Alexandra turned around. Her puzzled gaze scanned the floor, then riveted in horror and hatred upon the stout, polished wooden cane that some faceless tutor had been instructed to use on Jordan.

Her eyes blazed with blue fire as she stared at the evil

thing, while she actually longed to do bodily injury to the nameless tutor who had used it. Then she turned on her heel and slammed the door to the schoolroom behind her. As she passed a servant in the hall, she thrust the cane at him and said, "Burn this."

Standing at the study window, Jordan watched Alexandra walking toward the stables with what appeared to be several books cradled in her arm. An almost overpowering urge to call and offer to spend the day with her swept over him, surprising him with its intensity. He missed her already.

Two hours later, Jordan's bewildered secretary, Adams, who had been summoned for the usual afternoon of dictation, sat with his quill poised in readiness to take down the rest of a letter to Sir George Bently, which his employer had been in the process of dictating. In the midst of dictating, the Duke of Hawthorne's rapid-fire composition had slowed and he had fallen silent, gazing absently out the window.

Bewildered by the duke's unprecedented gaps in concentration—which had persisted all afternoon—Adams hesitantly cleared his throat, wondering if perhaps the duke's silence was a dismissal.

Jordan jerked his wandering attention from rapt contemplation of the fluffy cloud formations in the bright blue sky and straightened self-consciously, glancing at the secretary. "Where was I?"

"Sir George's letter," Adams said. "You had just begun to issue instructions for the investment of the profits from the last voyage of *The Citadel.*

"Yes, of course," Jordan said, his eyes wandering back to the windows. A cloud shaped like a chariot was rearranging itself and becoming a giant sea gull. "Tell him to outfit *The Sea Gull*—er—*The Valkyrie,"* Jordan amended, "for sailing at once."

"The Valkyrie, your grace?" Adams asked, bewildered.

The duke's gaze shifted reluctantly from the windows to Adams' confused face. "Isn't that what I just said?"

"Well, yes, it is. But a paragraph earlier, you'd desired Sir George to outfit *The Four Winds."*

Adams watched in amazement as an expression that could only be described as acute embarrassment crossed his employer's aristocratic face before the duke tossed the documents in his hand aside and curtly said, "That will be all for today, Adams. We'll continue tomorrow afternoon as usual."

While Adams was secretly wondering what momentous, dire event had caused his employer to cancel his afternoon work for the second time in eight years—the first time occurring on the day of the duke's uncle's interment—his employer added blandly, "No, not tomorrow afternoon, either."

Already partway across the room, Adams turned round and looked at his employer in startled inquiry, more amazed than ever by this additional postponement of a stack of rather urgent correspondence.

"I'm engaged for the afternoon," the duke explained blandly. "A picnic."

Struggling valiantly to maintain an impassive visage, Adams nodded and bowed. Then he turned and tripped over a chair.

Telling himself that he was merely restless and too long cooped up indoors, Jordan walked out of the house and headed for the stables. But when Smarth rushed out of the stables to ask if he wanted a mount, Jordan changed his mind and instead strolled along the path that led to one of the gamekeeper's cottages at the edge of the woods beyond the stables, where Alexandra had said she gave her lessons.

A few minutes later, the sound of singing reached him, and as he ascended the two wooden steps of the cottage, he smiled to himself as he realized that, instead of "wasting time" with song as he'd first supposed, Alexandra was teaching her pupils the alphabet, using a cheerful little song that named each letter. Shoving his hands into his pockets, he stood unseen in the doorway, listening to the sound of her lilting voice and looking about him with inner amazement.

Seated upon the floor, singing with rapt attention, were not only children of all ages, but several adults as well. After some thought, he was able to identify two of the women as wives of his tenants, and an elderly man as the grandfather of his head bailiff. Beyond that, he had no idea who the other adults were or to which families the children belonged.

They recognized him, however, and the singing began to grind down to an awkward unmelodious halt as older children stopped singing and silenced their younger siblings. A few yards to his right, Alexandra tipped her head to the side, smiling at her pupils. "Had enough for today?" she asked sympathetically, misunderstanding the reason for their sudden lack of attention. "In that case, here's your 'thought to remember' until we meet again on Friday: 'All men are equal,'" she quoted as she moved toward the doorway where Jordan was standing, obviously intending to bid her students goodbye as they left. "It is not birth that makes the difference, it is virtue." Her left shoulder collided with Jordan's and she whirled around.

"What a thing to tell them," Jordan said in a soft, teasing voice, ignoring the occupants of the cabin, who had hastily leapt to their feet and were gaping at him in awe. "You'll incite anarchy with quotations like that."

He stepped out of the doorway and the cottagers, correctly interpreting his movement as a dismissal, hastily lined up and filed awkwardly outdoors.

"They didn't say a word to you," Alexandra said, watching in bewilderment as the cheerful, friendly students she liked so well, scooted guiltily past and then fled into the woods beside the cottage.

"Because I didn't say a word to them," Jordan explained with utter unconcern.

"Why didn't you?" Alexandra asked uncertainly, her pleasure at his unexpected arrival almost blotting out her confusion.

"Unlike many landholders, my forebears have never been on personal terms with their cottagers," Jordan replied indifferently.

Unbidden, a vision of a lonely little boy, forbidden to fraternize with anyone on this vast, populated estate, came to mind, and Alexandra's eyes filled with tenderness as she gazed up at him. Longing to lavish him with all the love in her heart, she linked her arm through his and said, "I'm surprised to see you this afternoon. "What brought you out here?"

I missed you, he thought. "I finished my work early," he lied. Covering her hand with his, Jordan strolled with her across the front lawns to the pavilion at the far edge of the lake. "This is my favorite spot at Hawthorne," he explained, propping a shoulder against one of the white columns that supported the pavilion's roof. Shoving his hands into his pockets, he swept the woods and lake with an absent glance, oblivious to the flowers she'd added to the clearing beside them. "I imagine that, if you combined all the hours I spent in this pavilion as a boy and young man, they'd amount to years."

Thrilled that the handsome, enigmatic man she had married was finally beginning to open himself to her, Alexandra smiled at him. "It was my favorite place while I was at Hawthorne before. What did you do when you were here?" she asked, remembering the vivid, hopeless daydreams she'd invented about Jordan, while sitting upon the brightly colored cushions of the pavilion.

"Studied," he answered flatly. "I didn't like the schoolroom much. Or my tutor, for that matter."

Alexandra's smile wobbled as she envisioned a handsome, solitary boy, driven by his father to excel in everything.

Jordan saw tenderness glowing in her blue eyes and grinned at her, completely unaware of *why* her attitude had warmed. "What did you do, when you came here?" he teased.

Alexandra shrugged uneasily. "Daydreamed, mostly."

"About what?"

"The usual things." She was spared the need to answer that, because Jordan was suddenly staring at a clearing in the woods with a puzzled frown. "What is that?" he asked, straightening from his lounging position and walking into the circular clearing. Strolling directly over to the wedge-shaped marble marker, he read the simple words upon it with an indescribable expression of disbelief on his face:

JORDAN MATTHEW ADDISON TOWNSENDE
12TH DUKE OF HAWTHORNE
BORN JUNE 27, 1786
DIED APRIL 16, 1814

Turning to Alexandra with a look of almost comical disgust, he demanded, "Anthony stuck me *out here* in the woods? Didn't I merit the family cemetery in his estimation?"

Alexandra chuckled at his unexpectedly droll reaction to

366

seeing his own passing engraved in marble. "There's a monument to you there, too. But I—we—thought this was such a pretty spot for a, well, little marker in your memory." She waited for him to remark upon the fact that the clearing had been widened and flowers added, and when he didn't notice, she prompted lightly, "Do you notice anything different about this place?"

Jordan glanced around, oblivious to the serenity and beauty she'd created. "No. Is something different?"

She rolled her eyes in laughing disgust. "How can you possibly overlook a veritable garden of flowers?"

"Flowers," he repeated without interest. "Yes, I see them," he added, turning away from the clearing.

"Did you really?" Alexandra teased, but she was serious too. "Without turning back to look, tell me what colors they were."

Jordan shot her a quizzical look and took her arm, starting toward the house. "Yellow?" he ventured after a moment.

"Pink and white."

"I was close," he joked.

But on the way back to the house, he noticed for the first time that the roses blooming lavishly in the manicured beds beside the house were divided by color, rather than mixed together, and that the pink ones reminded him of her lips. Slightly embarrassed by the heretofore untapped sentimentality she was awakening in him, Jordan glanced at her bent head, but the next thought he had was even more shockingly sentimental than the last: His birthday was only five days away, and he wondered if she'd noted that when they'd looked at the dates carved into the marble marker.

A vision of Alexandra awakening him with a kiss and a wish for his happy birthday floated delightfully through his mind, and suddenly he very much wanted her to remember the date, to do some small thing to show him he was important to her. "I'm getting old," he remarked with careful nonchalance.

"Mmmm," Alexandra mused absently, toying with an idea so intriguing, so perfect, she was fairly bursting to think it through and begin to execute it.

Obviously, Jordan realized with disappointed chagrin, she neither knew nor cared that his birthday was near, and by hinting to her about it, he was behaving like a lovestruck boy who yearned for some special token of affection from his ladylove.

As soon as they entered the front hall, Jordan started to leave her and summon his bailiff, but Alexandra's voice stopped him. "My lord," she said.

"Jordan!" he said shortly.

"Jordan," she repeated, smiling into his eyes in a way that made him long to pull her into his arms, "are we still to have our picnic tomorrow at the stream?" When Jordan nodded, she explained, "I have some calls to make in the morning— Mrs. Little, the gamekeeper's wife, has just given birth to a baby boy, and I must bring her a gift. There are other calls, as well. May I meet you at the stream?"

"Fine."

Alarmed and annoyed by his ever-increasing desire to have her near him all the time, Jordan deliberately did not join her for supper nor did he take her to his bed that night. Instead, he lay awake in his huge bed atop its dais, his hands linked behind his head, staring at the ceiling and forcing himself not to go to her room. At dawn, he was still awake—mentally redesigning Alexandra's bedroom suite. She ought to have a spacious marble bathing room like his own, he had charitably concluded, and a much larger dressing area as well. Of course, if that were done, there would be no room in her own bedchamber for a bed. A faint, thoroughly satisfied smile touched his lips and he closed his eyes at last. He would let her sleep with him in his bed, he generously decided.

In the interest of modernization, no sacrifice was too great.

Chapter Twenty-Eight

*H*ER HEART SINGING with the plans she'd been putting into effect all morning, Alexandra rode to the clearing and dismounted. Jordan was standing on the bank of the stream, his broad back to her, gazing across the water, apparently lost in thought. She felt neither guilt nor concern about her secret visit to Tony today, for she was confident Jordan wouldn't object when he discovered the reason for it tomorrow.

With the lush grass muffling the sound of her approach, she walked toward him, her emotions wavering between joy at seeing him and uncertainty because he had neither dined with her last night nor made love to her. Aware that his attitude toward her had begun to cool when they walked back from the pavilion, she hesitated and then threw caution to the winds. She loved him, and she was determined to teach him to love and to laugh.

In line with that resolve, she walked silently up behind him, rose up on her toes, and covered his eyes with her hands. Obviously, he'd heard her approach because he didn't flinch or move a single muscle. "You're late," he said with a smile in his voice because she was still covering his eyes.

"Quick," Alexandra said, "tell me what color are the flowers on the hill you've been looking at."

"Yellow," he said promptly.

"White," she sighed, taking her hands away.

369

"If I keep saying yellow," he dryly replied, turning to face her, "sooner or later I'm bound to be right."

Alexandra shook her head in mock despair and headed toward the blanket he'd spread out on the bank. "You are the most coldly unsentimental man alive," she told him over her shoulder.

"Is that right?" he asked, catching her shoulders and drawing her back against the lean, hard strength of his legs and chest. His breath stirred the hair at her temple. "Do you really find me cold, Alexandra?"

Alexandra swallowed, vibrantly aware of the compelling sexual magnetism emanating from Jordan's powerful body. "Not cold, precisely," she said shakily, shamefully longing to turn in his arms and ask him why he hadn't wanted her with him last night. Forcibly trying to ignore her wanton longing for him, she knelt upon the blanket and quickly began removing food from the baskets.

"Are you so hungry?" he teased, sitting down beside her.

"I'm starved," she lied, sensing that he was going to kiss her at any moment and trying to get control of her senses before he did. It was one thing to banter with him and try to establish some sort of rapport; that was permissible. But it was *not* permissible to let him see that she was ready to fall into his arms whenever he decided to kiss her—particularly because he had ignored her completely last night. As if her life depended upon arranging their plates and crystal symmetrically, she remained kneeling, keeping her profile to him.

As she leaned forward to straighten their snowy linen napkins, Jordan's hand lifted, brushing away a lock of hair that had blown across her cheek. "You have gorgeous hair," he murmured in a velvety voice that sent an uncontrollable thrill shooting through her. "It sparkles in the sunlight like dark honey, and your skin is soft as a peach."

Alexandra sought safety in light humor. "Obviously, I am not the only one who's hungry."

He chuckled at her evasion, but his hand began trailing sensuously down her cheek and along her bare arm. "Didn't any of my cottagers offer you refreshment?"

"Mrs. Scottsworth did, but her sister Mrs. Tilberry was in the part of the house they use for a kitchen, so I didn't accept." Alexandra wrinkled her pert nose, thinking of the sharp-tongued Mrs. Tilberry, who mercilessly bullied her daughter-in-law, even in Alexandra's presence.

Jordan's hand tightened on Alexandra's arm, inexorably pulling her hand away from the napkin she was determinedly rearranging, until she had no choice except to turn her face up to his sultry gaze.

"What was Mrs. Tilberry doing in Mrs. Scottsworth's kitchen?" he murmured as his sensual mouth descended toward hers.

"Chanting incantations and waving a stick over a pot," Alexandra joked shakily.

"Chanting incant—" Jordan burst out laughing, caught her shoulders, and in one horrifyingly swift move, twisted her onto her back and leaned over her, his arm beneath her. "If there's a witch around here casting spells, it's *you*," he chuckled huskily.

Mesmerized by his silver gaze, Alexandra simultaneously wanted the kiss he was going to give her, and resented the easy conquest he made of her whenever he wished. When he bent his head, she turned her face slightly so that his lips could only graze her cheek. Undaunted by that, Jordan lazily trailed his lips across her cheek to her sensitive earlobe. Abruptly he plunged his tongue into her ear, and Alexandra's whole body jerked into rigid, automatic response. "I—I'm hungry," she gasped desperately.

"So am I," he whispered meaningfully in her ear, and her heart began to hammer like a maddened thing. Lifting his head, he gazed down into her languorous blue eyes. "Put your arms around me."

"How about after dinner—when I'm stronger?" Alexandra stalled.

She watched in absorbed fascination as his firm male lips formed a single word of implacable command: "Now."

Drawing a shattered breath, Alexandra reached up and curved her hands over his broad shoulders. Without any conscious order from her mind, her hands tightened, drawing him down toward her, then she stopped, panicked by the desire suddenly shooting through her.

"Now," Jordan repeated in a husky whisper, his lips a fraction of an inch from hers.

"W-wouldn't you like a—a glass of wine, first?"

"Now."

With a silent moan of despair and surrender, Alexandra curved her hand around his nape and eagerly brought his lips against her own. At first the kiss was a gentle, tentative greeting between two lovers, but the longer it continued the more pleasurable it became for both of them, and the tighter they clung to each other, seeking more. Jordan's tongue sensuously parted her lips, slipped between them for one sweet, arousing taste, and withdrew . . . then hungrily, urgently, plunged again, and desire exploded between them.

His hands opened her gown, tugging down her chemise, baring her breasts to his hot eyes. His hand cupped her breast, pushing it upward, his thumb circling her nipple, while he watched the pink tip harden into a tight bud. And then with deliberate, aching slowness, he bent his head and put his mouth where his thumb had been. His mouth closed around her aroused nipple, his lips and tongue toying with it until Alexandra gasped with pleasure, then he lavished the same reverent attention on her other breast.

Passion was raging through Alexandra's entire nerve stream by the time he finally removed their clothes and stretched out beside her, leaning up on his forearm. "I can't get enough of you," he whispered achingly, his eyes molten with desire as they gazed into hers while his hand sought and found the triangle between her legs. His eyes still holding hers, he parted her thighs, his fingers toying and teasing her, penetrating her moist warmth, until Alexandra was writhing in helpless need, arching her hips against his hand, but still he would not stop. Hot, convulsive waves were racing through her in a trembling fury, and finally she moaned aloud, her hands running up and down the bunched muscles of his arms, then she wrapped her arms around his shoulders and leaned into him. His skillful fingers became more insistent, and another moan tore from Alexandra's throat. "I know, darling," he told her achingly, "I want you, too."

He had unselfishly intended to give her a bursting climax this way, before he joined with her in yet another one—as he had done the other night—but his wife made him forget that idea. Tearing her mouth from his heated kiss, she slid her fingers into the sides of his hair and whispered brokenly, "It's lonely this way, without you deep inside of me—"

With a shattered groan, Jordan gave her what they both

wanted. Still lying on his side, he wrapped his arms around her, pulled her to him, and entered her with one sure, powerful thrust. Alexandra pressed her hips hard against his pulsing thighs, and with his hands cupping her bottom, Jordan joined with her in the most selfless act of lovemaking of his life. Driving slowly, rhythmically into her, he sought only to give her pleasure with each deep thrust, while she, in the same desperate need to please him, matched his movements.

I love you, he thought with each thrust of his body; *I love you,* his heart shouted with each thunderous beat; *I love you,* his soul cried out as Alexandra's spasms clenched him tightly. *I love you.* The words exploded in his being as he drove into her one last time and poured his life, his future, and all the disillusionment of his past into her tender keeping.

And when it was over, he held her in his arms, filled with a joy that was almost past bearing as he gazed at the white clouds floating in the powder blue sky. All of them had shapes and meaning to him now. All his life had shape and meaning to him now.

When Alexandra surfaced to reality an eternity later, she found herself lying on her side, stretched full length against his naked body. Jordan's hand was splayed across her bare back, his other hand still wrapped in her hair, holding her face pressed to his chest. With an effort, Alexandra lifted her head, opened her languorous blue eyes and gazed at him, then she flushed at the knowing look in those hooded grey eyes, and the faint, satisfied smile touching the corner of his lips. She had behaved like a shocking wanton and she had done it in broad daylight! Suddenly overwhelmed by his ability to overcome all of her defenses, she drew back and said lamely, "I'm hungry."

"When I'm stronger," he promised teasingly, deliberately misunderstanding what she was hungry for.

"For food!" she gasped.

"Oh, that," he said dismissively, but he obligingly rolled to his feet and politely turned his back, allowing her privacy while they both put on their clothes. "You have grass in your hair," he chuckled, brushing the few blades from her glorious tangle of mahogany tresses.

Instead of answering him with a smile or a quip, Alexan-

373

dra bit her lip, her gaze sliding away from his as she began to unpack the picnic dinner.

Finally understanding her unspoken need to be alone for a few minutes, Jordan strolled down to the bank of the stream where he remained for several minutes, his foot propped upon a boulder. The flowers on the hill, he suddenly noticed with dazzling clarity, were indeed white—a joyous, cheery carpet of white against dark green.

When he returned, Alexandra was holding a crystal decanter of wine. "Would you like a glass of wine?" she asked with the extreme courtesy that only very uneasy people employ. "It—it's the special kind you drink—I can tell from this decanter."

Crouching down, Jordan took the glass from her outstretched hand, but he put it aside and gazed directly into her eyes. "Alex," he said gently, "there is nothing immoral, nothing shameful, and nothing wrong about what just happened between us here."

Alexandra swallowed and glanced uneasily about them. "But it's broad daylight."

"I left instructions at the stables that we wished to be private here this afternoon."

Color flared in her cheeks. "No doubt everyone knew why."

Lowering himself into a sitting position, he put his arm reassuringly around her shoulders and grinned at her upturned face. "No doubt they did," he agreed without a trace of her own embarrassment. "It is, after all, how heirs are made."

To Jordan's astonishment, a stunned look crossed Alexandra's face and she suddenly buried her face against his chest, her slim shoulders rocking with mirth. "Did I say something funny?" he asked, tipping his chin down, trying to see her face.

Her laughing voice was muffled by his shirt. "No. I—I was thinking of something Mary Ellen told me long ago—about how babies are made. It was so outlandish, I couldn't believe her."

"What did she tell you?" Jordan asked.

She raised her laughing face to his and managed to gasp, "The truth!"

Their laughter rang out across the valley, startling birds in the trees overhead.

"Did you have enough port, or would you like more?" Alexandra asked when they had finished eating.

Jordan reached behind him and picked up the empty glass he'd inadvertently tipped over in the grass. "No," he said with a lazy, white smile, "but I like having you wait on me like this."

Alexandra managed to hold his gaze as she quietly and shyly admitted the truth: "I like doing it."

In the carriage on the way home, Alexandra could not tear her thoughts from the stormy passion of their lovemaking or the quiet tenderness that stayed with them afterward while they ate. "Touch me," he had told her. "I like it when you touch me." Did Jordan mean he wanted her to touch him when they weren't making love, the way a few wives amongst the *ton* often touched their husbands' sleeve when they spoke to them. The idea of voluntarily touching him was vibrantly appealing, and yet she cringed at the idea that such an action might be construed as clinging or childish.

She gave him a short, speculative sideways glance through her lashes, and wondered what he would do if she—very casually—rested her head against his shoulder. She could always pretend to be half-asleep, she decided. Having ventured that far in her imagination, she decided to try it and see what happened. With the well-sprung carriage swaying gently beneath her, and her heart beating a little faster within her, Alexandra partially closed her eyes and leaned her head lightly against his shoulder. It was the first time she had ever voluntarily touched him in affection, and she instantly knew from the way Jordan swiftly turned his head to look at her, that he was surprised by her gesture. She could not tell, however, what he thought of it.

"Sleepy?" he asked.

Alexandra opened her mouth, intending to save face by saying yes, at the precise moment Jordan lifted his arm and put it around her shoulders. "No," she said instead.

She felt the slight stiffening of his body as he registered that she had just indirectly told him she wanted to be close to him, and her heart pounded as she wondered what he would do next.

She did not have long to wait. Jordan's hand shifted from her shoulder and came to rest against the side of her face, his fingers gently caressing her cheek as he cuddled her closer to him and then began slowly stroking her hair.

When she awoke, they had driven up to the stables and Jordan was gently lifting her down from the carriage. Ignoring the avidly curious, surreptitious stares of the servants at the stable, Jordan lowered her to the ground and grinned at her. "Did I tire you out, sweet?" he asked, and chuckled huskily when she blushed.

With her hand linked through his arm, they began strolling toward the house, while behind them a groom began to hum off-key, another whistled, and Smarth began to sing an outrageously bawdy ditty whose tune Jordan recognized. Stopping in his tracks, Jordan turned and stared hard at his servants. Beneath his penetrating gaze, the whistles abruptly died down and the humming wavered to a tuneless stop. Smarth reached quickly for the reins of Jordan's restive horse and led him into the stable; a groom snatched up his pitchfork and energetically dug it into the hay.

"Is something wrong?" Alexandra asked.

"I must be paying them too much," Jordan joked, but his expression was puzzled. "They're entirely too cheerful."

"At least you're finally beginning to notice there's music in the air," his wife pointed out with an irreverent smile.

"Shrew," he teased with a chuckle that was rich and deep, but his grin faded as he looked down into her beautiful face and soberly thought, *I love you.*

The words crashed into his brain, almost bursting out of him in their need to be said. She wanted to hear those words, Jordan realized instinctively as her eyes held his, looking into his soul.

He would tell her tonight, he decided. When they were alone in his bed, he would say the words he'd never said before. He'd release her from their wager and solemnly ask her to stay with him. She wanted to stay, he knew that, as well as he knew this lovely, bewitching, joyous girl loved him.

"What are you thinking?" she softly asked.

"I'll tell you tonight," he promised huskily. Putting his arm around her waist, Jordan drew her tightly against his side and they strolled together back to the house—two

376

lovers returning from a halcyon day, sated, unhurried, content.

As they passed the wide, rose-covered arch that marked the entrance to the formal gardens, Jordan grinned ruefully to himself and shook his head as he realized, for the first time in his life, that the roses tumbling over the arch were red. Rich, vibrant red.

Chapter Twenty-Nine

UNWILLING TO RELINQUISH her company, Jordan walked upstairs with her and into her bedchamber. "Did you enjoy your afternoon, princess?" he asked.

The endearment made her eyes glow like twin aquamarines. "Very much."

He kissed her and then, because he wanted some reason to linger, he walked slowly toward the adjoining door. As he passed her dressing table, he saw upon it her grandfather's watch in a velvet case and paused to study the heavy gold timepiece. "Do you have a likeness of your grandfather?" he asked idly, picking up the watch and turning it over in his hand.

"No. I keep his watch there as sort of a reminder of him."

"It's an exceptionally fine piece," he remarked.

"He was an exceptionally fine man," she replied in a polite tone that completely belied the secret smile in her eyes as she watched his profile.

Unaware of her smile or her scrutiny, Jordan looked at the watch. A year ago, he remembered, he had accepted this watch as if it were merely his due. Now he wanted it more than he'd ever wanted anything in his life. He wanted Alexandra to give it to him again. He wanted her to look at him as she once had, with love and admiration shining in her eyes, and to give him the watch that she had intended for a man she deemed "worthy" of it.

"It was a gift from a Scottish earl who admired my grandfather's knowledge of philosophy," she said softly.

Putting the watch down, Jordan turned away. It would take a while longer to earn her trust, he decided, but someday she would surely find him worthy of it. On the other hand, she might give it to him for his birthday, he decided with an inward smile—allowing, of course, that she realized his birthday was only four days away. "It's a beautiful piece," he repeated, adding, "Time certainly has a way of passing. Before you know it, another year is gone. I'll join you in the drawing room before supper."

Jordan leaned nearer to the mirror, inspecting the closeness of his shave. In an exceptionally good humor because he was about to join Alexandra in the drawing room, he grinned at his valet in the mirror and said jokingly, "Well, Mathison, what do you think—will this face of mine spoil the lady's appetite?"

Behind him, Mathison, who was patiently holding up an impeccably tailored black evening coat for Jordan to put his arms into, was so startled to be addressed in this comradely fashion by his normally taciturn employer, that the poor valet had to clear his throat twice before answering in a stammering, blustering tone, "I daresay her grace, being of refined tastes herself, can only delight in your appearance this evening!"

Jordan's lips quirked with amusement at the memory of his "refined" young wife perched upon a tree limb with a fishing pole in her hand. "Tell me something, Mathison," Jordan asked as he shrugged into the black coat. "What color are the roses on the arch at the gardens?"

Startled by the abrupt change of topic and the question itself, Mathison replied blankly, "Roses, your grace? What roses?"

"You need a wife," Jordan replied, chuckling as he clapped the astonished manservant on the arm like a brother. "You're worse off than I was. At least *I* knew there were roses on—" He broke off abruptly as Higgins hammered on his door in an unprecedented frenzy, calling "Your grace—your grace!"

Waving Mathison aside, Jordan stalked to the door and yanked it open, angrily confronting the stately butler. "What the devil is the matter with you?" he demanded.

"It's Nordstrom—a footman, your grace," Higgins said,

so distraught that he actually tugged on Jordan's sleeve, pulling him into the hallway and closing the door before he began to babble disjointedly, "I told Mr. Fawkes at once, just as you said to do should anything unusual happen. Mr. Fawkes needs to see you at once in your study. At once. He told me not to tell anyone, so only Jean in the kitchen and I are aware of the dire event which—"

"Calm yourself!" Jordan snapped, already heading for the red-carpeted staircase.

"What's this all about, Fawkes?" Jordan demanded as he sat down behind his desk and waited for the investigator to be seated across from him.

"Before I explain," Fawkes began cautiously, "I need to ask you a question, your grace. From the time you drove away from the front of the house in your carriage with the picnic baskets today, who handled the decanter of port that was packed into the picnic basket this afternoon?"

"The port?" Jordan repeated, caught off guard by a discussion of wine rather than a footman. "My wife handled it when she poured a glassful for me."

An odd, almost sad expression darkened the investigator's hazel eyes, then it vanished as he said, "Did you drink any of it?"

"No," Jordan said. "The glass tipped over in the grass."

"I see. And your wife, of course, had none of it either?"

"No," Jordan said shortly. "I seem to be the only one who can stomach the stuff."

"Did you stop anywhere and leave the baskets unattended before you arrived at your destination? The stables, perhaps? A cottage?"

"Nowhere," Jordan clipped, eager to see Alexandra and angry because this interview was delaying that. "What the hell is this all about? I thought you wanted to discuss a footman named Nordstrom."

"Nordstrom is dead," Fawkes said flatly. "Poisoned. I suspected the cause of his death when Higgins came to fetch me, and the local physician, Dr. Danvers, has just confirmed it."

"Poisoned," Jordan repeated, unable to entirely absorb such a macabre event taking place in his own house. "How in God's name could such an accident happen here?"

"The only accidental thing about it was the victim. That

poison was intended for you. I blame myself for never having believed your assassin would actually try to accomplish your death from inside your own home. In a way," the investigator said in a harsh voice, "I'm to blame for your footman's death."

Oddly enough, Jordan's first fleeting thought was that he'd been wrong about Fawkes. In contrast to his earlier impression of the investigator, he was now inclined to believe that Fawkes was deeply committed to protecting the lives of those he served, rather than to turning a profit. Then it hit him that someone in his own house was apparently trying to poison him, and the thought was so repugnant that he could scarcely believe it. "What in God's name makes you think what could be an explainable accident was actually a miscarried attempt on my life?" he demanded angrily.

"To explain as succinctly as possible, the poison was placed in the decanter of your special port, which was included among the items provided for your picnic. The picnic baskets were unpacked here, after your return, by a kitchen servant by the name of Jean. Higgins was present at the time, and he noticed a few blades of grass clinging to the outside of the decanter. Higgins inspected the decanter, felt that some grass or other minute debris might have gotten into it, and accordingly judged it unfit for your consumption. I gather," Fawkes added, digressing slightly, "that at Hawthorne you adhere to the prevailing custom amongst Society which dictates that any untouched wine poured at meals goes to the butler for his own use, or to be given out as he chooses?"

"We do," Jordan confirmed, his expression composed, watchful, as he waited for the investigator to continue.

Fawkes nodded. "That is what I was told, but I wanted to confirm it with you. In accordance with that custom, the undrunk port was Higgins'. Since he doesn't care for your special port, he gave it to Nordstrom, the footman, to celebrate becoming a grandfather yesterday. Nordstrom took it to his room at four o'clock this afternoon. At seven o'clock he was found dead, the body still warm, the port beside him.

"The scullery maid told me that Nordstrom himself opened the bottle of port this morning, sampled it to be

381

certain it hadn't gone bad, then he filled the decanter and placed it in the basket. Nordstrom is the one who carried the basket with the port out to your coach this afternoon. Higgins tells me you were in a hurry to be off and followed Nordstrom out to the carriage a minute or two later. Is that right?"

"There was a groom holding my horses. I didn't see a footman."

"The groom didn't put the poison in the port," Fawkes said with absolute certainty. "He's *my* man. I considered Higgins as a possibility, but—"

"Higgins!" Jordan uttered, the idea so farfetched it almost made him laugh.

"Yes, but Higgins didn't do it," Fawkes reassured, mistaking Jordan's incredulity for suspicion. "Higgins has no motive. Besides, he hasn't the constitution to commit murder. The man was hysterical over Nordstrom—wringing his hands and carrying on worse than the scullery maid. We had to wave hartshorn under his nose."

Under other circumstances, Jordan would have been amused at the image of his stern, unflappable butler having hysterics, but there was no amusement in his chilly grey eyes at the moment. "Go on."

"It was also Nordstrom who unloaded your carriage and brought the baskets back down to the kitchens. Therefore Nordstrom was the only one to handle the decanter and the wine both before and after the picnic. Obviously, *he* didn't poison it. Jean, the scullery maid, assured me no one else touched the decanter.

"Then when was the poison put in the decanter?" Jordan demanded, without the slightest premonition that his entire world was about to be brought crashing down around his feet.

"Since we've ruled out the possibility that it was put into it before or after the picnic," Fawkes said quietly, "the obvious answer is that it was dropped into the port *during* the picnic."

"That's absurd!" Jordan clipped. "There were only two people there—my wife and myself."

Fawkes delicately shifted his gaze away from the duke's face as he said, "Exactly. And since *you* didn't do it, that only leaves . . . your wife."

Jordan's reaction was instaneous and volatile. His hand crashed down on his desk like a thunderclap, at the same instant he surged to his feet, his entire powerful body vibrating with rage. "Get out!" he warned in a low, savage breath, "and take along the fools who work for you. If you aren't off my property within fifteen minutes, I'll throw you off myself. And if I ever hear you've breathed a word of this groundless slander against my wife, I'll murder you with my own two hands, so help me God!"

Fawkes stood up slowly, but he wasn't finished. On the other hand, he wasn't fool enough to remain within arm's reach of his infuriated employer. Backing away a long step, he said sadly, "I regret to say it isn't 'groundless slander.'"

A feeling of inexpressible dread roared through Jordan's body, pounding in his brain, screaming in his heart as he recalled seeing Alexandra holding the decanter of port when he returned from the bank of the stream. *"Would you like some wine? It's the special kind you drink."*

"Your wife paid another secret visit to your cousin this morning."

Jordan shook his head as if to deny what his intellect was already beginning to suspect, while pain and shock and fury tore through every fiber of his being.

Correctly interpreting the signs of acceptance, Fawkes said quietly, "Your wife and your cousin were betrothed when you returned. Did it not seem odd to you that your cousin relinquished her to you so easily?"

The duke slowly turned his head and looked at Fawkes, his grey eyes iced with rage and pain. He said nothing. Wordlessly, he strode to the table where a decanter of brandy reposed on a silver tray, jerked the stopper from the decanter, and filled a glass to the brim. He tossed down two swallows.

Behind him, Fawkes said gently, "Will you permit me to tell you what I believe and why?"

Jordan inclined his head slightly, but did not turn.

"There is always a motive for premeditated murder, and in this instance personal gain is the most likely one. Since your cousin, Lord Townsende, has the most to gain by your death, he would naturally be the most likely suspect, even without the added evidence that points to him."

"What 'evidence'?"

"I'll get to that in a moment. But first, let me say that I believe the bandits who waylaid you near Morsham a year ago were not after your purse, nor did they pick you at random as a victim. That was the first attempt on your life. The second attempt was, of course, made shortly afterward when you were abducted from the docks. Until then, Lord Townsende's reason for trying to do away with you would have been to seize your title and holdings. Now, however, he has an additional reason."

Fawkes paused, waiting, but the duke remained silent, standing with his back to him, his broad shoulders rigid. "The additional reason is, of course, a desire to have your wife whom he tried to wed and whom he now continues to see in secret. Since she goes to him, I think it's safe to assume she also wishes to wed him, something she cannot do so long as you are alive. Which means Lord Townsende now has an accomplice—her."

Drawing a long breath, Fawkes said, "I must be blunt from now on, if I'm to have your cooperation and protect your life . . ."

When the tall man across the room said nothing, the investigator correctly interpreted his silence as reluctance and said briskly: "Very well. According to the gossip my men have overheard among your servants, on the night an attempt was made on your life in London, your wife gave everyone a fright by not returning home until the following morning. Do you know where she was?"

Jordan swallowed more of his brandy, his back still turned to the investigator. "She said she slept in a spare room on the servant's floor."

"Your grace, is it possible the horseman who shot at you that night might have been a woman, rather than a man?"

"My wife is an excellent shot," the duke clipped sarcastically. "If she'd tried to shoot me, she'd not have missed."

"It was dark and she was mounted," Fawkes murmured, more to himself than to Jordan. "Perhaps her horse moved slightly as she fired. Still, I'm inclined to doubt she actually tried to do it herself—it's too risky. In the past, outsiders have been hired to do you in, but now they're trying it on their own, which puts you in far greater peril and makes my job ten times as difficult. Which is why I'm going to ask you to pretend we haven't any idea Nordstrom the footman was poisoned. Let your wife and your cousin think you're ignorant of any scheme of theirs. I've instructed Dr. Danvers to say he thinks Nordstrom's heart simply stopped, and I was cautious when I questioned the kitchen servants about Nordstrom's activities that day, not to put any excessive emphasis on the decanter of wine. They've no reason to think we suspect foul play. If we can carry on that ruse and tighten the surveillance on your wife and Lord Townsende, we ought to have some forewarning of the next attempt on your life, and be able to catch them in the act," Fawkes concluded. "I think they'll try the poison again, since they think we're unaware of it, but perhaps not. If they do, they'll not risk poisoning anything which others might also ingest, because more than a single death would definitely awaken suspicion. For example, that brandy you're drinking is probably safe enough because it's served to guests, but I caution you against eating or drinking anything your wife gives you, which she could have touched without your seeing her. Beyond that, all we can do is watch and wait."

Finished, Fawkes fell silent, waiting for some reaction, but the duke remained as rigid as steel. He hesitated, then he bowed to the duke's stiff back. Softly, and with genuine regret, he said, "I'm very sorry, your grace."

Fawkes had just closed the study door when the deathly silence of the hallway was suddenly shattered by an explosive crash and the sound of breaking glass within the study. Thinking someone had fired through the windows, Fawkes flung the door open and then stopped short: A magnificent gold and crystal brandy decanter, which had once belonged to a French king, was now lying on the polished wood floor a few feet away from the wall against which the duke had hurled it. The duke, who had betrayed no trace of emotion throughout the interview, was standing with his hands braced wide against the mantel of the fireplace, gripping it for support; his broad shoulders were shaking with silent anguish.

Alexandra whirled around in a swirl of bright green silk as Jordan stalked into the drawing room, a dazzling smile on her face that faded slightly as she beheld the hardness of her husband's taut jaw and the cold glitter in his eyes. "Is—is something wrong, Jordan?"

At her gentle use of his name, the muscles of his face clenched so tight a nerve in his cheek began to pulse. "Wrong?" he repeated cynically while his gaze wandered over her body with insulting thoroughness, inspecting her breasts, her waist, then her hips, before lifting to her face. "Not that I can see," he replied with scathing indifference.

Alexandra's mouth went dry and her heart began to beat in heavy, terrifying dread as she sensed that Jordan had seemingly withdrawn from her, as if the closeness, the tenderness and laughter they'd shared had never existed. Panic drove her to try to recover what they had found by reaching for a decanter of sherry on the table. Jordan had said he liked having her do wifely things for him, and so she did the only thing she could think of. Filling a small stemmed glass with sherry, she turned and held it out to him, a wobbly smile on her face. "Would you like some sherry?"

His eyes turned to blazing daggers as they shifted to the glass she held, and the nerve in his cheek began to pulsate wildly. When he raised his gaze to her face, Alexandra stepped back in alarm from the unexplainable violence glittering in his eyes. With his gaze riveted to hers, he took the glass from her hand. "Thank you," he said a split second before the fragile stem snapped in his hand.

Alexandra uttered an alarmed little cry and whirled around, looking for something to use to blot the sherry from the magnificent Aubusson carpet before it stained.

"Don't bother," Jordan snapped, catching her elbow and jerking her roughly around. "It doesn't matter."

"Doesn't matter?" Alexandra uttered in confusion. "But—"

Softly, and without any emotion, he said, "Nothing matters."

"But—"

"Shall we dine, my sweet?"

Swallowing her rising panic, Alexandra nodded. He had made "my sweet" sound almost like an epithet. "No, wait!" she burst out nervously, and then shyly she added: "I have something I want to give you."

Poison? Jordan thought sarcastically, watching her.

"This," she said and held out her hand to him.

Lying across her open palm was her grandfather's treasured gold watch.

Raising her glowing eyes to his, Alexandra said unsteadily, "I—I want you to have it." For one horrible, incredible moment, she actually thought Jordan was going to refuse it. Instead, he took it from her and dropped it carelessly into his coat pocket. "Thank you," he said with curt indifference. "Assuming it keeps accurate time, it's a half hour past time to dine."

If he had slapped her, Alexandra could not have been more hurt or more bewildered. Like a puppet, she placed her hand upon his proffered arm and let him escort her to the dining room.

Throughout the meal, she tried vainly to convince herself she was merely imagining his complete change in attitude.

When he did not take her to his bed and make love to her that night, she lay awake, trying to understand what she had done to make him regard her with aversion.

When he ceased speaking to her altogether the next day, except when absolutely necessary at meals, she endured it for an entire day before she finally swallowed her pride and meekly *asked* him what she had done wrong.

He looked up from the work on his desk, furious at her interruption, his eyes raking over her as she stood before him like a nervous supplicant, her shaking hands clasped behind her back. "Wrong?" he repeated in the cool, voice of a complete stranger. "There is nothing wrong, Alexandra, except in your timing. Adams and I are working, as you can see."

Alexandra whirled around, embarrassed to the depths of her soul by the heretofore unnoticed presence of Adams, who was seated at a small desk near the windows. "I—I'm sorry, my lord."

"In that case," he nodded meaningfully toward the door, "if you don't mind—"

Alexandra took his rude hint to leave and did not attempt to speak to him until that night, when she heard him enter his bedchamber. Summoning all her courage, she put on a dressing robe, opened the adjoining door, and stepped inside.

Jordan was removing his shirt when he saw her reflection

387

in the mirror and his head jerked toward her. "Yes, what is it?" he snapped.

"Jordan, please," Alexandra burst out, walking toward him, an innocent temptress with her hair tumbling over her shoulders, sliding to and fro against the rich pink satin of her gown as she moved near him. "Tell me what I've done to anger you."

Jordan gazed down into her blue eyes and his hands clenched at his sides as he fought the simultaneous impulse to strangle her for her treachery and the stronger urge to take her to his bed and pretend for just one hour longer that she was still his enchanting, alluring, barefoot duchess. He wanted to hold her and kiss her, to wrap her around him like a blanket and lose himself in her, to blot out the last days of hell. Just for an hour. But he couldn't, because he couldn't blot out the tormenting picture of her and Tony embracing and planning his murder. Not even for an hour. Or a minute.

"I'm not angry, Alexandra," he said frigidly. "Now get out of here. When I want your company, I'll let you know."

"I see," Alexandra whispered, and turned away.

But all she "saw" was the tears that blinded her as she walked with painful dignity back to her own bed.

Chapter Thirty

ALEXANDRA STARED MINDLESSLY at the embroidery frame in her lap, her long fingers still, her heart as dark and bleak as the sky beyond the open curtains at the drawing-room windows. For three days and nights, Jordan had been a stranger to her; a cold, forbidding man who looked at her with icy blatant disinterest or contempt, on those rare occasions when he looked at her at all. It was as if someone else now inhabited his body—someone she did not know, someone she sometimes saw watching her with a expression in his eyes that was so malign it made her shiver.

Not even Uncle Monty's unexpected arrival and bluff presence had any effect on lightening the heavy atmosphere at Hawthorne. He had come to Alexandra's rescue—he explained to her privately after settling into his rooms yesterday and critically surveying the plump bottom of the upstairs maid who was turning down his bed—because he'd heard belatedly in London that "Hawthorne had looked like the wrath of God," when he discovered her wager in the book at White's.

But all of Uncle Monty's dogged, transparently obvious attempts to engage Jordan in friendly conversation yielded nothing but scrupulously courteous, extremely brief responses. And Alexandra's attempts to pretend that was normal and natural fooled no one, including the servants, into believing they were a happily married couple. The entire household, from Higgins the butler to Henry the dog, were vibrantly, nervously aware of the strained atmosphere.

In the oppressive silence of the drawing room, Uncle Monty's hearty voice boomed out like a thunderclap, making Alexandra jump: "I say, Hawthorne, capital weather we're having!" Lifting his white brows in an inquiring expression, hoping for an answer that might lead to further conversation, Uncle Monty waited.

Jordan raised his eyes from the book he was reading and replied, "Indeed."

"Not a bit wet," Uncle Monty persevered, his cheeks rosy from the wine he'd imbibed.

"Not wet at all," agreed Jordan, his face and voice devoid of expression.

Unnerved but undaunted, Uncle Monty said, "Warm, too. Good weather for crops."

"Is it?" Jordan replied in a tone that positively discouraged any additional attempt at conversation.

"Er . . . quite," Uncle Monty replied, retreating farther back in his chair and shooting Alexandra a desperate look.

"Do you have the time?" Alexandra asked, longing to retire.

Jordan looked up at her and said with deliberate cruelty, "No."

"Ought to have a watch, Hawthorne," Uncle Monty suggested, as if he thought the idea a wonderfully original one. "They're the very thing to keep abreast of the time!"

Alexandra quickly averted her face to hide her hurt that Jordan had for the second time accepted her grandfather's watch and then cast it aside.

"It's eleven o'clock," Uncle Monty provided helpfully, pointing to his own watch and chain. "*I* always wear a watch," he boasted. "Never need to wonder about the hour. Wondrous things, watches," he rhapsodized. "One can't help conjecturing about how they work, can one?"

Jordan slammed his book shut. "Yes," he said bluntly, "one *can.*"

Having failed utterly in his attempt to draw the duke into an animated discussion about watchmaking, Uncle Monty sent another pleading look to Alexandra, but it was Sir Henry who responded. The huge English sheepdog, while utterly nonchalant about his duty to protect people, was deeply cognizant of his duty to console them, lavish them with affection, and generally be underfoot in case they had need of his attention. Seeing the unhappy expression on Sir Montague's face, he roused himself from the hearth and trotted over to the distressed knight, whereupon he delivered two extremely wet licks to his hand. "Ye gods!" burst out Uncle Monty, leaping to his feet with more energy than he'd displayed in a quarter century and vigorously wiping the back of his hand against his trousers. "That animal has a tongue like a wet mop!"

Offended, Sir Henry cast a mournful look upon his disgruntled victim, then turned and flopped down on the hearth.

"If you don't mind, I think I'll retire," Alexandra said, unable to bear the atmosphere another moment.

"Is everything in readiness at the grove, Filbert?" Alexandra asked the next afternoon, when her faithful old footman answered her summons and appeared in her bedchamber.

"It is," the footman announced bitterly. "Not that yer husband deserves a birthday party. After the way 'e's been treatin' ye, 'e deserves a kick in the arse!"

Alexandra tucked a wayward curl beneath the brim of her sky-blue bonnet and did not argue the issue. She'd conceived the idea for a surprise party in honor of Jordan's birthday the day they'd strolled out to the pavilion—the happiest day of what was apparently a short-lived period of bliss.

After days of enduring Jordan's frigid, unexplainable disdain, her face was pale, and she was forever on the verge of tears. Her chest ached from holding them back, and her heart ached because she couldn't find a reason for Jordan's behavior. But as the hour for her surprise approached, she couldn't quell the burgeoning hope that perhaps when Jordan saw what she had planned with Tony and Melanie's help, he might either become the man he had been when they were together at the stream, or at least tell her what was bothering him.

"The whole staff's talkin' bout the way he's actin' t' ye," Filbert continued angrily. "Hardly speakin' t' ye and lockin' himself away in his study night and day, never doin' his husbandly—"

"Filbert, please!" Alexandra cried. "Don't spoil today for me with all that."

Contrite, but still determined to vent his spleen against the man who was causing the dark shadows beneath Alexandra's eyes, Filbert said, "Don't need to spoil it fer ye, he'll do that if'n he can. Surprised he even agreed to go wit ye to the grove when you tolt him you had somethin' to show 'im."

"So was I," Alexandra said with an attempt at a smile that immediately became a puzzled little frown. She had confronted Jordan in his study this morning when he was meeting with Fawkes, the new assistant bailiff, and she had fully expected to have to plead with him to accompany her for a carriage ride. At first, Jordan started to refuse her request, but then he hesitated, glanced at the bailiff, and then abruptly agreed.

"Everything is in readiness," Fawkes was assuring Jordan in the master bedchamber. "My men are stationed in the trees along the route to the grove and around the grove itself. They've been there for three hours—since twenty minutes after your wife suggested your little jaunt. I instructed my men to remain there, out of sight, until the assassin or assassins reveal themselves. Since they can't leave their positions without being seen, they can't report back to me, and I don't know what they're seeing. God knows why your cousin chose the grove instead of a cottage or somewhere more private."

"I do not believe this is happening," Jordan bit out, shrugging into a fresh shirt. He stopped, momentarily struck by the absurdity of putting on a fresh shirt so that he would look nice when his wife led him into a trap meant to kill him.

"It's happening," Fawkes said with the deadly calm of a seasoned soldier. "And it's a trap. I could tell it from the sound of your wife's voice and the look in her eyes when she asked you to ride out with her this afternoon. She was nervous and she was lying. I watched her eyes. Eyes don't lie."

Jordan regarded the investigator with bitter derision, remembering how deceptively, radiantly innocent Alexandra's eyes had once seemed to him. "That's a myth," he said contemptuously. "A myth I used to believe."

"The note we intercepted from Lord Townsende an hour

ago is no myth," Fawkes reminded Jordan with quiet conviction. "They're so confident we're ignorant of their plans that they're becoming careless."

At the mention of Tony's note, Jordan's face became as expressionless as a stone mask. As instructed, Higgins had brought Tony's note to Jordan before carrying it up to Alexandra, and the words seared into Jordan's brain:

Everything is ready at the grove. All you have to do is get him there.

An hour ago, the pain of reading that had nearly sent him to his knees, but now he felt—nothing. He was past the point of feeling anything, even a sense of betrayal or fear as he prepared to face his own beloved assassins. Now all he wanted was to have the thing over with, so he could somehow begin blotting Alexandra out of his heart and mind.

Last night he had lain awake in his bed, fighting the stupid urge to go to her and hold her, to give her money and warn her to flee—for whether or not she and Tony succeeded in killing him today, Fawkes already had enough evidence to ensure that she and Tony would spend the rest of their lives in a dungeon. The image of Alexandra clad in filthy rags, living out her life in a dark, rat-infested cell, was almost more than Jordan could bear, even now—when he was about to become her target in open country.

Alexandra was waiting for him in the hallway, looking as bright and innocent as spring in a blue muslin gown trimmed with wide cream ribbon at the full sleeves and hem. She turned and watched him walk down the staircase, her smile bright and eager. She was smiling, Jordan realized with a nearly uncontrollable surge of fury, because his beautiful young wife intended to rid herself of him for good.

"Ready to go?" she asked brightly.

Wordlessly he nodded, and they walked out to the carriage that was waiting for them in the drive.

Beneath the fringe of her lashes, Alexandra stole another sideways peek at Jordan's profile as their carriage swayed gently down the path through the trees that would soon open up into a wide, lush field that bordered the orchards. Despite Jordan's outwardly relaxed pose as he lounged back against the squabs, his hands light on the horses' reins, she saw his gaze move restlessly over the trees bordering the path—as if he were watching for something, waiting for it.

In fact, she had just started to wonder if he had somehow found out about her "surprise" and was expecting the revelers to burst out of the trees, when their carriage broke into the field, and Jordan's open shock at the spectacle that greeted him removed any possibility that he was fore-warned.

"What the—?" Jordan breathed in amazement as he gazed at the incredible sight before him: Colorful banners were waving in the breeze, and all his tenants and their children were gathered in the fields, dressed in their best clothing, grinning at him. Off to his left, he saw Tony, his mother, and his brother standing with Jordan's grandmoth-er. Melanie and John Camden had come with Roddy Carstairs and a half-dozen other Londoners of Jordan's acquaintance. On his right, at the far side of the clearing, a large raised platform had been set up, with two thronelike chairs and a half-dozen other, less elaborate chairs upon it. A canopy stretched above the platform, protecting it from the sun, and the Hawthorne pennants were flying from poles atop the canopy, displaying the Hawthorne crest—a hawk with its wings outspread.

Jordan's carriage moved toward the center of the field, and four enthusiastic trumpeters officially announced their duke's arrival—as arranged—with loud, emphatic blasts upon their horns, followed by a prolonged cheer that went up from the crowd.

Drawing the horses up short, Jordan turned sharply to Alexandra. "What is this all about?" he demanded.

The eyes she raised to his were full of love and uncertain-ty and hope. "Happy birthday," she said tenderly.

Jordan simply looked at her, his jaw tight, and said absolutely nothing. Smiling uncertainly, she explained, "It's a Morsham-style celebration, only more elaborate than the ones we used to have to celebrate birthdays." When he continued to stare at her, she laid her hand on his arm and explained eagerly, "It's a combination tournament and country fair—to celebrate the birthday of a duke. And to help you get to know your tenants a little, too."

Jordan looked around at the crowd in angry bewilderment. Could this whole elaborate setting actually be a backdrop for murder? he wondered. Was his wife an angel or a she-devil? Before the day was out, he would know. Turning, he helped her down from the carriage. "What am I supposed to do now?"

"Well let's see," she said brightly, trying not to let him see how foolish she felt or how hurt. "Do you see the livestock in the pens?"

Jordan glanced around at the half-dozen pens scattered about the field. "Yes."

"Well, the livestock belongs to your cottagers, and you're to select the best from each pen, and to give the owner a prize from the ones I've purchased in the village. Over there, where the ropes created lanes, there'll be a jousting contest, and over there—where the target is—an archery contest, and—"

"I think I have the gist of it," Jordan interrupted shortly.

"It would also be rather nice if you'd compete in some of the contests," Alexandra added a little hesitantly, not certain how willing her husband might be to mingle with his inferiors.

"Fine," he said, and without another word he escorted her to her chair on the platform and left her there.

After greeting his friends from London, he, Lord Camden, and Tony helped themselves to some of the ale the cottagers were already enjoying and began strolling around the fairgrounds, pausing to watch the squire's fourteen-year-old perform as an amateur juggler.

"So, my dear," Roddy Carstairs said, leaning toward her, "is he madly in love with you yet? Shall I win our wagers?"

"Behave yourself, Roddy," Melanie said from beside Alexandra.

"Do not dare to mention that dreadful wager in my presence!" snapped the dowager duchess.

Eager to watch Jordan from closer range, Alexandra stepped down from her chair and descended the steps from the platform, with Melanie right behind her. "It isn't that I'm not pleased to see him, but why is Roddy here? And the others?"

Melanie chuckled. "The others came with him for the

395

same reason. Roddy is here. Our proximity to Hawthorne is suddenly making us quite popular with people who would normally not set foot in the country for weeks yet—they arrived yesterday, determined to have a look at how things were going with you and the duke. You know Roddy—he prides himself on knowing the gossip before everyone else does. I've missed you so much," Melanie added, abruptly giving Alexandra a swift, affectionate hug, then she stood back, studying Alexandra's face. "Are you happy with him?"

"I—yes," Alexandra lied.

"I knew it!" Melanie said, squeezing Alexandra's hand, so delighted that her prophecy was coming true that Alexandra didn't have the heart to explain that she was married to a man whose moods were so unpredictable that she felt sometimes as if she were going quite mad. And so she held her silence and watched with bittersweet yearning as Jordan strolled around the livestock pens with his hands clasped behind his back, his expression suitably grave as he solemnly judged the plumpest poultry, the most promising pig, the best-trained dog, handing out prizes to their awed owners.

By the time the sun began to sink beneath the treetops, and the torches had been lit, the tenants and the nobles alike were all in rare high spirits, laughing and drinking ale together, while competing in every sort of contest from the serious to the silly. Jordan, Lord Camden, and even Roddy Carstairs, had joined in the archery contests, jousts, fencing and shooting matches. With quiet pride, Alexandra had stood on the sidelines, her heart swelling with tenderness while she watched Jordan deliberately miss his last shot in a shooting contest so that the thirteen-year-old son of one of his tenants would win. "The award goes to the best man," Jordan had declared untruthfully as he presented the awed youngster with a gold sovereign. Then he threw off all pretense of dignity by strolling over to the turtle races, choosing a turtle from the basket, and insisting that his friends do the same. But he never once turned to glance at Alexandra. It was as if he was exerting himself to participate solely for the sake of his guests. Side by side with the children, three of London's most illustrious nobles stood at the starting line, cheering their individual entrants, extolling them to run faster and then calling out in disgust when the turtles ignored their royal commands and retreated beneath their shells.

"I never liked turtles except in soup," Tony joked, nudging John Camden in the ribs, "but that turtle of mine showed some mettle there for a moment. I'll wager a pound yours stays under his shell longer than mine."

"Done!" John Camden agreed unhesitatingly and began extolling his laggard turtle to remove his head from his shell.

Jordan watched them, his expression closed, and then he turned and walked over to a table where mugs of ale were being served by some of his kitchen maids.

"What the devil's gotten into your illustrious cousin?" Roddy Carstairs inquired of Tony. "When the two of you were fencing, he looked like he was trying to draw your blood. Can it be he's still jealous because his wife nearly married you?"

Deliberately keeping his attention on his turtle, Tony shrugged lightly. "What gives you the idea Hawk was ever jealous?"

"My dear boy, don't forget I was at the Lindworthy ball the night he swooped down upon us like an avenging angel and ordered Alex home."

"Because of that outrageous wager which *you* coerced her into placing," Tony shot back, and pointedly turned all his attention to his turtle.

Helping himself to another glass of ale from the table, Jordan propped his shoulder against a tree, his expression thoughtful as he stood at the perimeter of the woods, watching Alexandra as her gaze searched the crowd, obviously looking for him. She'd been watching him all night, Jordan knew. So had Tony. And both of them were wearing the same baffled, uneasy expressions as if they expected him to be more overjoyed with his birthday celebration.

His gaze returned to Alexandra and he saw her laugh at something his grandmother said. He could almost hear the music of her laughter, and even in the encroaching dark he could almost see the way her eyes lit when she laughed. His wife. A murderess. Even as he thought it, his heart screamed a protest that his mind could no longer override. "I don't

397

believe it!" he bit out in a soft, furious whisper. The girl who had planned all this could not be planning his murder. The girl who had held him to her in the night, and teased him while they fished at the stream, and shyly presented him with her grandfather's treasured watch could not possibly be trying to murder him.

"Your grace?" Fawkes' urgent voice stopped Jordan as he straightened, intending to walk over to the shooting contests, which had become more humorous than intense as the contestants squinted through ale-blurred eyes at the target nailed to a tree. "I must insist you leave at once," Fawkes whispered, falling into step beside Jordan.

"Don't be a fool," Jordan snapped, completely out of patience with Fawkes and his theories. "The meaning behind my cousin's note is obvious—they'd planned this party for me together, and that is undoubtedly why they met in secret those two times."

"There isn't time to argue about all that," Fawkes said angrily. "It will be dark in a few more minutes and my men aren't owls. They can't see in the dark. I've sent them ahead to position themselves along your route home."

"Since it's already too late to reach the house in daylight, I fail to see what difference it makes if I stay here for a while."

"I cannot be responsible for what happens if you don't leave here at once," Fawkes warned before he turned on his heel and stalked off.

"Can you believe those grown men are actually cheering their turtles on to victory?" Melanie chuckled, watching Tony and her husband. "I suppose I ought to go and remind them of the decorum required of men in their exalted positions," she said, and carefully descended from the platform with no such intention in mind. "Actually, I want to be there to see the winner cross the line," she confessed with a wink.

Alexandra nodded absently, scanning the open, cheerful faces of the cottagers, her gaze stopping on one disturbingly familiar face that wasn't cheerful at all. Suddenly, for no reason at all, she found herself recalling the night she met Jordan—a balmy night just like this one—when two cutthroats held Jordan at gunpoint.

"Grandmama," she said, turning to the duchess. "Who is

that short man over there in the black shirt—the one with the red kerchief around his neck?"

The duchess followed her gaze and shrugged. "I'm sure I wouldn't have the vaguest idea *who* he is," she declared primly. "I've seen more of these cottagers today than I have in the entire thirty years I lived at Hawthorne. Not," she added a trifle reluctantly, "that I don't think your party was an excellent idea, my dear. Things have changed in England of late, and though I regret the necessity for pandering to those who serve us, it's wise for a landholder to be on good terms with his tenants these days. One hears talk of them demanding more and more and turning quite nasty . . ."

Alexandra's attention wandered, her mind returning to her dismal preoccupation with the night she met Jordan. Nervously, she glanced around the open field, looking for the man in the black shirt, who seemed to have vanished. A few minutes later, without realizing what she was doing, she began taking inventory of those she loved, watching to make certain they were safely within sight. She looked for Tony and could not see him, then she anxiously sought out Jordan and saw him standing at the perimeter of the woods, his shoulder propped casually against a tree, drinking ale and watching the festivities.

Jordan saw her looking at him, and he nodded slightly. The sweet tentative smile she sent him made him ache with uncertainty and regret. He raised his glass to her in a silent, sardonic toast, then froze at the sound of a vaguely familiar voice in the darkness beside him. "There's a gun pointing straight at yer head, milord, and another one pointing at yer wife over yonder. Make one sound and my partner will blow her head off. Now, move sideways toward the sound of my voice, right here in the woods."

Jordan tensed and slowly lowered the mug of ale. Relief, not fear, surged through his bloodstream as he turned toward the voice; he was ready for this long-awaited confrontation with his unknown enemy—*eager* for it. Not for an instant did he believe Alexandra was in any danger; that had merely been a ploy to make him obey.

Two paces brought him into the enfolding darkness of the dense woods, and another pace ahead he saw the deadly gleam of a pistol. "Where are we going?" he asked the shadow holding the gun.

"To a cozy little cottage down this path. Now get in front of me and start walkin'."

His body coiled like a tight spring now, Jordan moved another step forward onto the path, his right hand tightening on the heavy mug of ale. "What shall I do with this?" he inquired with feigned meekness, turning slightly and lifting his right hand.

The bandit glanced at the object in his hand for a split second, but that was all Jordan needed. He flung the contents of the mug in the startled bandit's eyes and simultaneously swung the heavy drinking vessel, bringing it crashing against his assailant's jaw and temple with a force that sent the surprised villain to his knees. Bending down, Jordan snatched the thug's gun from the ground, grabbed the stunned man's shoulders, and yanked him to his feet. "Start walking, you son of a bitch! We're going to take that little stroll you wanted."

The thug swayed slightly and Jordan gave him an impatient shove that sent him staggering down the path, with Jordan behind him. Reaching into his own pocket, Jordan felt for the small pistol he'd been carrying since he returned to England. Realizing that it must have fallen out of his coat when he bent over his captive, he tightened his grip on its replacement and followed his unfortunate prisoner down the path.

Five minutes later the dark shape of the old woodsman's cottage loomed up at the end of the path. "How many are inside?" Jordan demanded, even though there was no light showing through the slats of the closed shutters to indicate anyone was there, waiting.

"No one's there," the bandit grunted, then he gasped as he felt the cold kiss of the pistol's muzzle pressing against the back of his skull. "One or two. I don't know," he amended quickly.

Jordan's voice was as cold as death. "When we get to the door, tell them you've got me and to light a lamp. Say anything else, and I'll blow your head off." For emphasis, he shoved the pistol's muzzle harder against the frightened man's skull.

"Right!" he gasped, stumbling slightly as he rushed up the steps in his haste to escape the touch of the gun. "I've got him!" he called out in a low, frightened voice as he kicked at the door with his foot. It swung open on rusty, squeaking hinges. "Light a damn lamp, it's black as pitch in here," he added obediently, standing in the doorway.

There was the sound of tinder being struck, a shadow bent toward a lantern, light flickered— In one swift motion, Jordan struck his captive's skull with the butt of his pistol and sent him sprawling to the floor, unconscious, then he straightened his arm, leveling his pistol at the stunned figure bending over the flaring lantern.

The face staring back at him in the lantern's glow nearly sent him to his knees with shock and pain.

"Jordan!" his aunt said wildly. Her gaze flew toward the far corner and Jordan instinctively spun, crouching, and fired. Blood spurted from the chest of his aunt's other hired assassin, who clutched frantically at his wound and toppled to the floor, a gun dangling uselessly from his limp hand.

Jordan spared the man only a brief glance to ensure that he was dead, then he turned his head and looked at the woman he had loved better than his own mother until one minute ago. And he felt . . . nothing. A cold, hard core of empty nothingness was growing inside him, strangling every other emotion he'd ever felt, leaving him incapable of feeling anything—even anger. His voice devoid of all expression, he asked simply, "Why?"

His quiet, polite calm so unnerved his aunt that she stammered, "W-why are we going to k-kill you, you mean?"

The word "we" brought his head up sharply. Going swiftly to the dead man in the corner, he snatched the loaded gun from his hand and discarded the empty one he'd been holding. With the loaded gun ruthlessly trained on the woman he had once adored, Jordan walked to the doorway that opened off the room they were standing in and glanced into what appeared to be a small bedchamber. It was empty and yet his aunt still seemed to think he was going to be killed and, moreover, she had specifically said "we."

And then it dawned on him who she was probably waiting for, and he felt the first sparks of fury begin to ignite inside him: His cousin and possibly his wife were apparently expected here to see that he was properly finished off this time.

Walking back into the main room, he said in a cold, deadly voice, "Since you're obviously expecting reinforcements, why don't we both sit down and await their arrival."

Doubt and panic flickered in her eyes, and she sank slowly onto the crude wooden chair beside the table. With exaggerated courtesy, Jordan waited until she was seated before he casually perched his hip upon the table and waited, facing the closed door. "Now," he invited silkily, "suppose you answer some questions—quickly and briefly. The night I was waylaid outside Morsham was no random accident, was it?"

"I—I don't know what you mean."

Jordan glanced at the familiar face of the unconscious thug who had waylaid him that night and then at his aunt. Without a word, he lifted the gun he was holding in his crossed arms and pointed it at the terrified woman. "The truth, madam."

"It wasn't an accident!" she cried, her eyes riveted on the menacing pistol.

The gun lowered. "Go on."

"N-neither was your impressment, although you weren't supposed to be impressed, you were supposed to die, except you're—you're so very *hard* to *kill!*" she added in a tone of anguished accusation. "You always had the devil's own luck. You—with your money and your titles, and your strong, healthy legs, while poor Bertie is a cripple and my Tony a virtual pauper!"

Tears began spilling from her eyes and she whimpered furiously, *"You* had everything, including luck. You can't even be poisoned!" she cried, her shoulders shaking. "And we couldn't a-afford to hire more competent people to kill you, because *you* have all the money."

"How very thoughtless of me," Jordan drawled with bitter sarcasm. "Why didn't you simply *ask* me for money. I'd have given it to you, you know, had I dreamed you needed it. Not," he amended caustically, "to have me killed, however."

"Grandmama," Alexandra said a little desperately, "do you see Jordan anywhere? Or—or that man with the black shirt and red kerchief around his neck?"

"Alexandra, for goodness' sake," the duchess said in exasperation, "why are you constantly fidgeting and asking me to look about for people? Hawthorne is somewhere nearby, you may be sure of that. He was there by that tree, drinking a mug of that dreadful potion, but a moment ago."

Alexandra apologized, tried to sit still and remain calm, but a few minutes later she could no longer quell the unexplainable, rising panic she felt.

"Where are you going, dear?" the duchess asked when Alexandra abruptly arose and shook out her skirts.

"To look for my husband." With a rueful little laugh, Alexandra admitted, "I suppose I'm afraid he'll disappear again, the way he did a year ago. Silly of me, I know."

"Then you do care for him, don't you, child?" the duchess said fondly.

Alexandra nodded, too uneasy about Jordan's whereabouts to try to salvage her pride with a noncommittal answer. Her gaze shifted restlessly over the crowd as she picked up her skirts and began walking toward the place where she had last seen him. Tony was nowhere to be seen, but Melanie and John Camden were walking toward her, arm in arm.

"Wonderful party, Alexandra," John Camden admitted with an abashed grin. "I've never had as good a time at the fanciest affairs in the city."

"Thank you. H-have you seen my husband anywhere? Or Tony?"

"Not in the last fifteen minutes. Shall I look for them?"

"Yes please," Alexandra said, raking her hand through her hair. "I'm really in a sorry state tonight," she admitted, by way of an embarrassed apology. "I keep imagining things—earlier today I actually thought I saw a man up in one of the trees over there. And now Jordan seems to have vanished."

John Camden smiled and spoke in the soothing voice one might use with an overwrought child. "We were all together but a few minutes ago. I'll find them and send them to you."

Alexandra thanked him and hurried off toward the table where heavy pewter mugs of ale were being served. Passing it, she nodded at one of the scullery maids, and then walked over to the tree where Jordan had been standing. With a last glance at the milling partygoers in the clearing, she turned toward the woods and hesitantly began walking down the narrow path. Telling herself she was being fanciful and silly, she stopped after a few paces and looked about her, listening intently, but the sounds of laughter and fiddles from the clearing behind her drowned out the forest noises, and the thick branches overhead blotted out all the light, making her feel as if she were standing in an eerie void that contained only noise but no life.

"Jordan?" she called. When there was no answer, she bit her lip, her forehead furrowed into a worried frown. Intending to go back to the clearing, she started to turn, and it was then she saw the tankard lying in the path at her feet.

"Oh my God!" she whispered, snatching up the tankard and turning it over. A few drops of ale poured out of it. Wildly, she looked about her, expecting—*hoping*—to see Jordan lying in the path, perhaps passed out from too much drink, as Uncle Monty had occasionally done. Instead, she saw a small gleaming pistol on the side of the path.

Snatching it up, Alexandra whirled around and let out a stifled scream as she collided with a hard masculine body. "Tony! Thank God it's you," she cried.

"What the devil's wrong?" Tony said, gripping her shoulders hard in his anxiety as he steadied her. "Camden said Jordan's vanished and you saw a man hiding in the trees."

"I found Jordan's tankard of ale right here and a gun on the ground near it," Alexandra said, her voice and body trembling with terror. "And I saw a man I think was the same one who was trying to kill Jordan the night we met."

"Go back to the clearing and stay in the light!" Anthony said sharply. Snatching the gun from her hand, he turned and ran down the path, vanishing into the deep woods.

Stumbling over a thick root growing across the path, Alexandra raced back to the clearing, intending to get help rather than find safety. Wildly, she looked around for Roddy or John Camden, and seeing neither she ran straight toward one of the cottagers who had taken a brief respite from the shooting contest and was staggering toward the ale table in the same state of cheerful inebriation as the rest of his fellows. "Yer grace!" the man gasped, snatching off his cap and starting to execute a bow.

"Give me your gun!" Alexandra demanded breathlessly, and without waiting for him to hand it over, she snatched it out of the stunned man's hand. "Is it loaded?" she called over her shoulder, already racing toward the path.

"Shore is."

His breath labored from a long sprint down the path to the forester's cottage, Tony put his ear to the door, listening for sounds. Hearing none, he cautiously tried the latch, and when it stuck he reared back two paces and rammed his shoulder against the door with enough extra force to send it flying wide open. Off balance because the door had opened so easily, he staggered into the cabin, stumbled, and stopped short, his mouth falling open in shock. His mother was seated stiffly upon a chair in front of him. And beside her, sitting on the table, was Jordan. In his hand, Jordan was holding a gun.

It was pointing straight at Tony's heart.

"W-what the hell is going on?" Tony burst out, panting.

Tony's arrival demolished the last slender hope Jordan had clung to that Alexandra and his cousin had not conspired to end his life at this party. In a soft voice of deadly menace, he said to Tony, "Welcome to my party, cousin. I believe we're still expecting another guest this evening to make the party complete, aren't we, Tony? My wife?" Before Tony could answer, Jordan added, "Don't be impatient—she's bound to come looking for you, thinking I've been safely disposed of, won't she? I'm sure of it." His silken drawl suddenly became clipped. "There's a bulge in your pocket which is undoubtedly a gun. Take off your coat and throw it on the floor."

"Jordan—"

"Do it!" Jordan bit out savagely, and Tony slowly obeyed.

When Tony had dropped his coat on the floor, the point of Jordan's gun shifted slightly to the left, indicating the chair lying on its side by the shuttered window. "Sit down. And if you move an inch," he warned with frightening calm, "I'll kill you."

"You're mad!" Anthony whispered. "You must be. Jordan, for God's sake, tell me what the hell is going on."

"Shut up!" Jordan snapped, his head tipped toward the sound of footsteps on the cabin step. More than anyone, his

405

rage was directed at the girl he had been obsessed with for over a year—the scheming liar who had made him believe she loved him, the little bitch who had lain in his arms and surrendered her eager body to him; the beautiful, laughing, unforgettable barefoot girl who had made him believe that heaven was a stream with a picnic blanket beside it. And now, he thought, with a wrath he could barely contain, she was about to fall into his clutches.

The door creaked open, slowly, a few inches; a familiar lock of mahogany hair peeked through the opening, then a pair of blue eyes that widened like saucers as her gaze riveted on the gun in his hand.

"Don't be shy, darling," Jordan said in a voice so low it was a deadly whisper. "Come inside. We've been waiting for you."

Expelling her breath on a rush of relief, Alexandra pushed the door wide open, stared at the fallen thug, then rushed forward as Jordan stood up. Tears of fright streaming down her face, she wrapped her arms around him, the gun in her hand forgotten. "I knew it was him—I knew it! I—"

She cried out in surprised pain as Jordan wrapped his hand in her hair and viciously yanked her head back. His face only inches from hers, he bit out, "Of course you knew it was him, you murderous little bitch!" and with a cruel jerk of his wrist, he flung her sprawling onto the floor, her hip landing painfully on the gun in her hand.

For a moment, Alexandra simply sat there, staring at him through fear-widened eyes, unable to assimilate what was happening.

"Are you afraid, sweetheart?" he jeered smoothly. "You should be. Where you're going, there are no windows, no lovely gowns, no men—other than a few jailers who'll avail themselves of your delectable little body until it becomes too gaunt to interest them. Hopefully, it will hold their interest longer than it held mine," he added with deliberate cruelty.

"Don't look so surprised," he said, misinterpreting the reason for her shock. "I've bedded you because it was necessary to keep up the sham of the unsuspecting husband —not because I wanted you," he lied, feeling an almost uncontrollable urge to murder her for her treachery.

"Jordan, why are you doing this?" Alexandra cried, then

recoiled in terror from the blaze in his eyes when she called him by his given name.

"I want answers, not questions," Jordan snapped. Estimating that it might be another ten minutes before Fawkes realized he was missing and last seen heading in this direction, Jordan relaxed against the table again, his weight braced on one foot, the other swinging idly as he turned toward Tony. "While we're waiting," he invited smoothly, pointing the gun at him, "suppose you fill in some details for me. What else has been poisoned in my house?"

Tony's eyes lifted from the gun in Jordan's hand to his relentless features. "You're mad, Jordan."

"I wouldn't mind killing you," Jordan said thoughtfully, raising the gun higher as if he was about to do it.

"Wait!" his aunt screamed, casting desperate glances at the empty doorway and beginning to babble. "Don't hurt Tony! H-he can't answer because he d-doesn't know about the poison."

"And I suppose my wife knows nothing about it either," Jordan inserted sarcastically. "Do you, my dear?" he asked, the barrel of the gun shifting toward Alexandra.

Disbelief and fury drove Alexandra slowly to her feet, clutching her gun in the folds of her skirts. "You think we've been trying to *poison* you?" she breathed, staring at him as if he had kicked her in the stomach.

"I *know* you have," he countered, enjoying the anguish he saw in her eyes.

"Actually—" Bertie Townsende drawled from the doorway, his gun pointing straight at Jordan's head, "you're wrong. As my hysterical mother is undoubtedly about to confess, *I'm* the one who conceived these effective—admittedly, not successful—plots to rid us of you. Tony hasn't the stomach for murder, and since I have the brains of the family, if not the legs, I've handled the planning and the details. You look surprised, cousin. Like everyone else, you assume a cripple can't pose a significant threat to anyone, don't you? Drop your gun, Jordan. I have to kill you anyway, but if you don't drop it, I'll kill your charming wife first, while you watch."

His body coiled like a tight spring, Jordan tossed his gun down and slowly came to his feet, but Alexandra suddenly sidled up against him as if she mistakenly believed there was

407

safety there. "Move away!" he snapped under his breath, but she clasped his hand in an outward display of terror and simultaneously pressed a pistol into his palm.

"You'll have to kill me, too, Bertie," Tony said softly, standing up and starting forward.

"I suppose so," his brother agreed without hesitation. "I intended to eventually, anyway."

"Bertie!" his mother cried. "No! That's not what we planned—"

Alexandra's gaze riveted on the man on the floor; she saw him slide his arm toward Tony's coat and, behind him, another man stepping into the doorway, slowly raising a gun. "Jordan!" she screamed, and because there was no other way to protect him from three assailants, Alexandra threw herself in front of him at the exact moment two guns discharged.

Jordan's arms automatically clasped her to him as Bertie Townsende collapsed, shot by Fawkes from the doorway, and the bandit on the floor rolled over, clutching the wound in his arm inflicted by Jordan's gun. It happened so fast that it took a moment before Jordan realized that Alexandra was suddenly very heavy, a dead weight sliding down his body. Tightening his arms, he tipped his chin, intending to tease her about fainting *after* everything was over, but what he saw struck stark terror in his heart: Her head had fallen back, lolling limply on her shoulders, and blood was streaming from a wound at her temple. "Get a doctor!" he shouted at Tony, and lowered her to the floor.

His heart hammering with fear, he knelt beside her, ripped off his shirt, and tore it into strips, binding the ugly wound in her head. Before he'd half finished, blood had already soaked and spread around and through the white linen, and her color was rapidly turning an ashen grey.

"Oh my God!" he whispered. "Oh my God!" He had seen men die in battle countless times; he knew the signs of a hopelessly fatal wound, and even while his mind was recognizing that she would not live, Jordan was snatching her into his arms. Cradling her against his chest, he ran down the path, his heart hammering in frantic rhythm with the refrain pounding in his heart: *Don't die . . . don't die . . . Don't die . . .*

His chest heaving with exertion, Jordan burst into the

clearing, carrying his limp, beloved burden. Oblivious to the stricken faces of the cottagers, who stood in quiet, watchful groups, Jordan laid her gently in the carriage Tony had evidently told someone to pull up at the edge of the woods.

An old woman, a midwife, took one look at the bloody bandage around Alexandra's head and the deathly pallor of her skin and, as Jordan raced around to climb into the seat, she quickly felt for Alexandra's pluse. When she turned back to the cottagers gathered around the carriage, she sadly shook her head.

The women whom Alexandra had helped and befriended a year ago gazed lovingly at her still form in the carriage and, as Jordan drove off, the soft sounds of weeping began to fill the clearing. Only ten minutes before, it had rung with the gaiety she had brought to them.

Chapter Thirty-One

THE DEFEATED EXPRESSION on Dr. Danvers' face as he stepped into the hall outside Alexandra's bedchamber and closed the door made agony scream through Jordan's brain.

"I'm sorry," he said quietly to the distraught group waiting in the hall. "There was nothing I could do to save her. When I got here, she was already beyond hope and beyond reach."

The dowager pressed her handkerchief to her lips and turned into Tony's arms, weeping while Melanie sought her husband's embrace. John Camden's hand came to rest consolingly on Jordan's shoulder, then he took his sobbing wife downstairs to join Roddy Carstairs.

Turning to Jordan, Dr. Danvers continued, "You can go in now and say your goodbyes, but she won't hear you. She's in a deep coma. In a few minutes—a few hours, at most— she'll slip away quietly." At the expression of raw anguish on the duke's face, Dr. Danvers added gently, "She'll feel no pain, Jordan, I promise you."

A muscle worked spasmodically in Jordan's throat as, with a look of wordless, impotent rage directed at the innocent physician, he walked swiftly into Alexandra's bedchamber.

Candles burned beside her canopied bed, and she lay as still and white as death upon the satin pillows, her breathing so shallow it was almost imperceptible.

Swallowing past the lump in his throat, Jordan sat in the chair beside her bed and gazed down upon her beloved face, wanting to memorize every line of it. She had such smooth skin, he thought achingly, and such incredibly long eyelashes—they lay like lush, dark fans against her cheeks. . . . She wasn't breathing!

"No, don't die!" he cried hoarsely as he grabbed her limp hand, frantically feeling for a pulse. *"Don't die!"* He found a pulse—thready and faint but still there—and suddenly he couldn't stop talking to her. "Don't leave me, Alex," he pleaded, holding her tightly. "God, don't leave me! There are a thousand things I want to tell you, places I want to show you. But I can't if you go away. Alex, please, darling . . . please don't go away.

"Listen to me," Jordan begged urgently, somehow convinced that she would stay alive if she understood how much she meant to him. "Listen to what my life was like before you hurtled into it wearing that suit of armor— Life was empty. Colorless. And then you happened to me, and suddenly I felt feelings I never believed existed, and I *saw* things I'd never seen before. You don't believe that, do you, darling? But it's true, and I can prove it." His deep voice ragged with unshed tears, Jordan recited his proof: "The flowers in the meadow are blue," he told her brokenly. "The ones by the stream are white. And on the arch, by the arbor, the roses are red."

Lifting her hand to his face, he rubbed his cheek against it. "And that's not all I noticed. I noticed that the clearing by the pavilion—the one where my plaque is—looks like the very same one where we had our duel a year ago. Oh, and darling, there's something else I have to tell you: I love you, Alexandra."

Tears choked his voice and made it a tormented whisper. "I love you, and if you die I'll never be able to tell you that."

Driven by anger and desperation, Jordan clutched her hand tighter and abruptly switched from pleas to stern threats. "Alexandra, don't you dare leave me! If you do, I'll toss Penrose out on his deaf ear! I swear I will. And without a reference. Right on his ear, do you hear me? And then I'll kick Filbert out right behind him. I'll make Elizabeth Grangerfield my mistress again. She'd love to fill your shoes as the Duchess of Hawthorne . . ."

The minutes became an hour, and then another, and still Jordan kept on talking, switching mindlessly from pleas to threats and then, as hope finally began to die within him, to cajolery: "Think of my immortal soul, sweetheart. It's black and, without you here to make me mend my ways, I'll undoubtedly slip back into my old habits."

He waited, listening, watching, her lifeless hand gripped in his as he tried to infuse his own strength into her, and then, suddenly, the determination and hope that had driven him to talk ceaselessly to her crumbled. Despair wrapped around his heart, suffocating him, and tears stung his eyes. Gathering her limp body into his arms, Jordan laid his cheek against hers, his massive shoulders racked with sobs. "Oh, Alex," he wept, rocking her in his arms like a baby, "how will I go on living without you? Take me with you," he whispered. "I want to go with you . . ." And then he felt something—a whispered word against his cheek.

Jordan's breath stopped and he jerked his head back, his eyes frantically searching her face as he gently lowered her against the pillows. "Alex?" he implored achingly, bending over her, and just when he thought he'd imagined the faint flutter of her eyelids, her pale lips parted, trying to form a word.

"Tell me, darling," he said desperately, leaning close to her. "Say something, please, sweetheart."

Alexandra swallowed, and when she spoke, her words were so faint they were nearly inaudible. "What, darling?" he pleaded urgently, not certain what she was saying.

Again she whispered, and this time Jordan's eyes widened as he finally understood. He stared at her hands held tightly in his and then his shoulders shook as he began to laugh. It started as a low rumble in his chest, then exploded in great, gusty shouts of laughter that rang out along the balcony and brought the dowager, the doctor, and Tony running into the room in the obvious misapprehension that Jordan's grief had destroyed his mind.

"Tony," Jordan said with a wobbly grin, holding Alexandra's hand in his and beaming at her. "Alexandra thinks," he said, his shoulders beginning to rock with laughter again, "that Elizabeth Grangerfield has *big feet*."

Alexandra turned her head on the pillows as Jordan walked through the doorway that joined her suite with his.

412

It had been two days since she'd been injured, two days and nights of drifting in and out of wakefulness. Each time she had awakened, he was sitting beside her bed, keeping a silent vigil, his fear for her etched deeply into his drawn features.

Now that she was fully conscious, she would have liked to hear him talk to her in that same tender tone he'd used these past two days, or to look at her with love burning in his eyes. Unfortunately, however, Jordan's features were perfectly composed and completely unreadable this morning—so much that Alexandra wondered if she'd only dreamed the tender, tormenting sweetness of his words to her when he believed she was dying.

"How are you feeling?" he asked, his deep voice conveying only polite concern as he came to stand beside her bed.

"Very well, thank you," she returned with equal courtesy. "A little tired, that's all."

"I imagine you have some questions you'd like answered —about what happened two days ago."

What Alexandra wanted was for him to put his arms around her and tell her that he loved her. "Yes, of course," she replied, wary of his unfathomable mood.

"To be brief, a year and a half ago, Bertie caught one of their kitchen servants—a local peasant named Jean— stealing money from his purse. She admitted that she intended to give it to her brothers, who were waiting for her in the woods directly behind their house. Bertie and his mother had already hatched a scheme to have me killed, but until then neither of them had any idea where to find someone to do it. Rather than prosecute the maid for stealing the money, Bertie made her sign a confession, admitting to the theft. He paid her brothers to get rid of me the night I met you, and he kept the maid's confession to ensure her silence and her brothers' cooperation.

"You ruined their plans by riding to my rescue in that suit of armor, but one of the brothers—the one I shot— managed to crawl to his horse and escape while I took you to the inn.

"Bertie tried again four days after we were married, but this time the two men he hired took his money, and instead of killing me, they doubled their take by handing me over to

413

the press gang. As my aunt pointed out," Jordan added sardonically, "it's difficult to hire good people when one hasn't much money."

He shoved his hands into his pockets and then continued: "When I 'came back from the dead' a week ago, Bertie reminded the maid that he still had her incriminating confession and he used it to blackmail her brother into trying to kill me again. That time he shot at me in Brook Street—the same night you slept in the governess' room."

Alexandra gazed at him in astonishment. "You never told me that someone shot at you that night."

"I saw no reason to alarm you," Jordan said, then shook his head and gruffly added, "That's not the complete truth. I also had it in the back of my mind that *you* might have been the one who fired that pistol. From the standpoint of size, the gunman could have been you. And you had told me that very day that you'd do anything necessary to get out of our marriage."

Biting her lip, Alexandra turned her face away from him, but not before Jordan saw the pain and accusation in her eyes. He shoved his hands deeper into his pockets and went on: "Three days ago, a footman named Nordstrom died from drinking the port that was in the decanter at our picnic—the same port you repeatedly tried to make me drink."

Her gaze flew to his face, and he continued in a voice of harsh self-accusation, "Fawkes is not an assistant bailiff, he's an investigator whose men have been stationed all over Hawthorne since we came here. He investigated the incident with the port, and it looked as if you were the only one who could possibly have poisoned it."

"Me?" she cried softly. "How could you think such a thing!"

"Falkes' witness was a scullery maid who's worked here off and on when we need her for the last year and a half. Her name," Jordan finished, "is Jean. She poisoned the port, again at Bertie's instructions. I think you already know everything else that has happened since then."

Alexandra swallowed painfully. "In your mind, you accused and convicted me of trying to murder you, based on evidence as flimsy as that? Because I'm the same approximate height as someone who shot at you in Brook Street,

414

and because a scullery maid said *I* must have been the one who poisoned your wine?"

Inwardly, Jordan flinched at her words. "I did it based on those things and on the fact that Olsen, who is one of Falkes' men, followed you to Tony's house on two separate occasions. I knew you were meeting with him in secret, and that—combined with everything else—made the evidence against you seem very damning."

"I understand," she said bleakly.

But she didn't understand at all, and Jordan knew it. Or perhaps she understood too well, he thought grimly. No doubt she clearly understood that he had failed in his promise to trust her and that he had repeatedly rejected the love she offered. She also understood, he knew bitterly, that she had risked her life twice for his sake and in return he had rewarded her with callousness and mistrust.

Jordan gazed down at her beautiful pale face, knowing perfectly well that he deserved her hatred and contempt. Now that she was fully conscious of the true depth of his heartlessness and stupidity, he waited, half expecting her to banish him from her life.

When she didn't, he felt obliged to say the things *she* should be saying to him. "I realize my behavior to you has been unforgivable," he began tightly, and the sound of his voice filled Alex with dread. "Naturally, I don't expect you to want to remain married to me. As soon as you're well enough to leave here, I'll give you a bank draft for a half million pounds. If you ever need more . . ."

He stopped and cleared his throat as if it was clogged. "If you ever need more," he began again, his voice rough with emotion, "you have only to tell me. Anything I have will always be yours."

Alexandra listened to that speech with a mixture of tenderness, anger, and disbelief. She was about to reply when he cleared his throat again and added, "There's something else I want to tell you. . . . Before we left London, Filbert told me how you felt when you thought I was dead, and how you reacted when you came to London and had all your illusions shattered. Most of what you heard about me was true. However, I would like you to know that I did not sleep with Elise Grandeaux the night I saw her in London."

415

Pausing, Jordan gazed down at her, unconsciously memorizing every line of her face so that he would have it before him in the empty years that lay ahead of him. In silence, he looked at her, knowing she represented every hope and every dream he cherished in his heart. Alexandra was goodness and gentleness and trust. And love. She was flowers blooming on the hillsides and laughter floating through the halls.

Forcing himself to finish what he had come to say and then get out of her life, he drew a long breath and said unsteadily, "Filbert also told me about your father and what happened after he died. I can't wipe away the hurt he caused you, but I wanted to give you this . . ."

Jordan held out his hand and Alexandra saw within it a long, flat velvet case. She took it from him and with trembling fingers unfastened the latch.

Lying on a bed of white satin, suspended from a fine gold chain, was the largest ruby she had ever seen. It was cut in the shape of a heart. Beside it, in another shallow tray was an emerald surrounded by diamonds—in the shape of a heart. Beside the emerald was a magnificent, glittering diamond.

The diamond was cut in the shape of a tear.

Biting her lip to stop her chin from quivering, Alexandra raised her eyes to his. "I think," she whispered, trying to smile, "I shall wear the ruby on Queen's Race day, so that when I tie my ribbon on your sleeve—"

With a groan, Jordan pulled her into his arms.

"Now that you've said all those other things," she whispered when he finally lifted his lips from hers several minutes later, "do you think you could possibly say 'I love you'? I've been waiting to hear that since you began and—"

"I love you," he said fiercely. "I love you," he whispered softly, burying his face in her hair. "I love you," he groaned, kissing her lips. "I love you, I love you, I love you . . ."

Epilogue

WITH HIS BABY SON cradled in his arms, Jordan stared in fascination at the tiny face looking back at him. Not certain what to say, and absolutely unwilling to give up the pleasure of holding his baby, he decided to give some parental advice.

"Someday, little son, you will choose a wife, and it's important to know how that sort of thing should be done, so I will tell you a story:

"Once upon a time, there was an arrogant, cynical man. We'll call him—" Jordan hesitated a moment, thinking. "We'll call him the Duke of Hawthorne."

Standing in the doorway unobserved, Alexandra smothered a laugh as Jordan continued: "This duke was a wicked fellow, who did not see the good in anyone or anything—especially himself. Then, late one fateful night he was set upon by bandits, and, just when it seemed his life would come to an undignified end, a knight in rusty armor charged to his rescue on horseback. With the knight's help, the duke managed to subdue the bandits, but during the attack, the knight was injured.

"The wicked duke went to the aid of the unconscious knight, but, to his amazement he discovered the knight was not a man at all, but a lady. She was small and dainty with curly hair and the longest eyelashes the duke had ever seen. And when she opened her eyes, they were the color of aquamarines. The wicked duke with the empty heart looked into those eyes of hers, and what he saw took his breath away . . ."

The baby stared at him, enraptured.

"What did he see?" Alexandra asked in an aching whisper from the doorway.

Lifting his head, Jordan looked at her and his heart was in his eyes. With tender solemnity, he replied, "He saw something wonderful."

Dear Reader,

I hope the hours you've just spent with Jordan and Alexandra have been pleasurable ones for you.

As with all four of my other books, my goal for *Something Wonderful* has been to make you laugh and cry and then laugh again.

I hope I've succeeded.

Judith McNaught

P.S. I'm always delighted to hear from readers. If you have any comments or questions, my address is:

P.O. Box 795491
Dallas, TX 75379